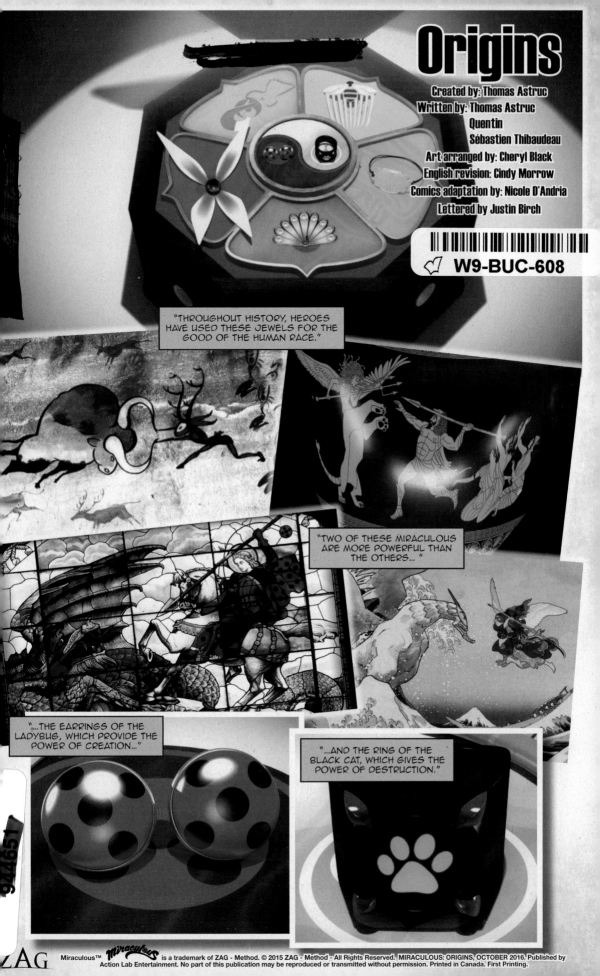

Origins

Created by: Thomas Astruc
Written by: Thomas Astruc
Quentin
Sébastien Thibaudeau
Art arranged by: Cheryl Black
English revision: Cindy Morrow
Comics adaptation by: Nicole D'Andria
Lettered by Justin Birch

W9-BUC-608

"THROUGHOUT HISTORY, HEROES HAVE USED THESE JEWELS FOR THE GOOD OF THE HUMAN RACE."

"TWO OF THESE MIRACULOUS ARE MORE POWERFUL THAN THE OTHERS..."

"...THE EARRINGS OF THE LADYBUG, WHICH PROVIDE THE POWER OF CREATION..."

"...AND THE RING OF THE BLACK CAT, WHICH GIVES THE POWER OF DESTRUCTION."

ZAG

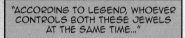

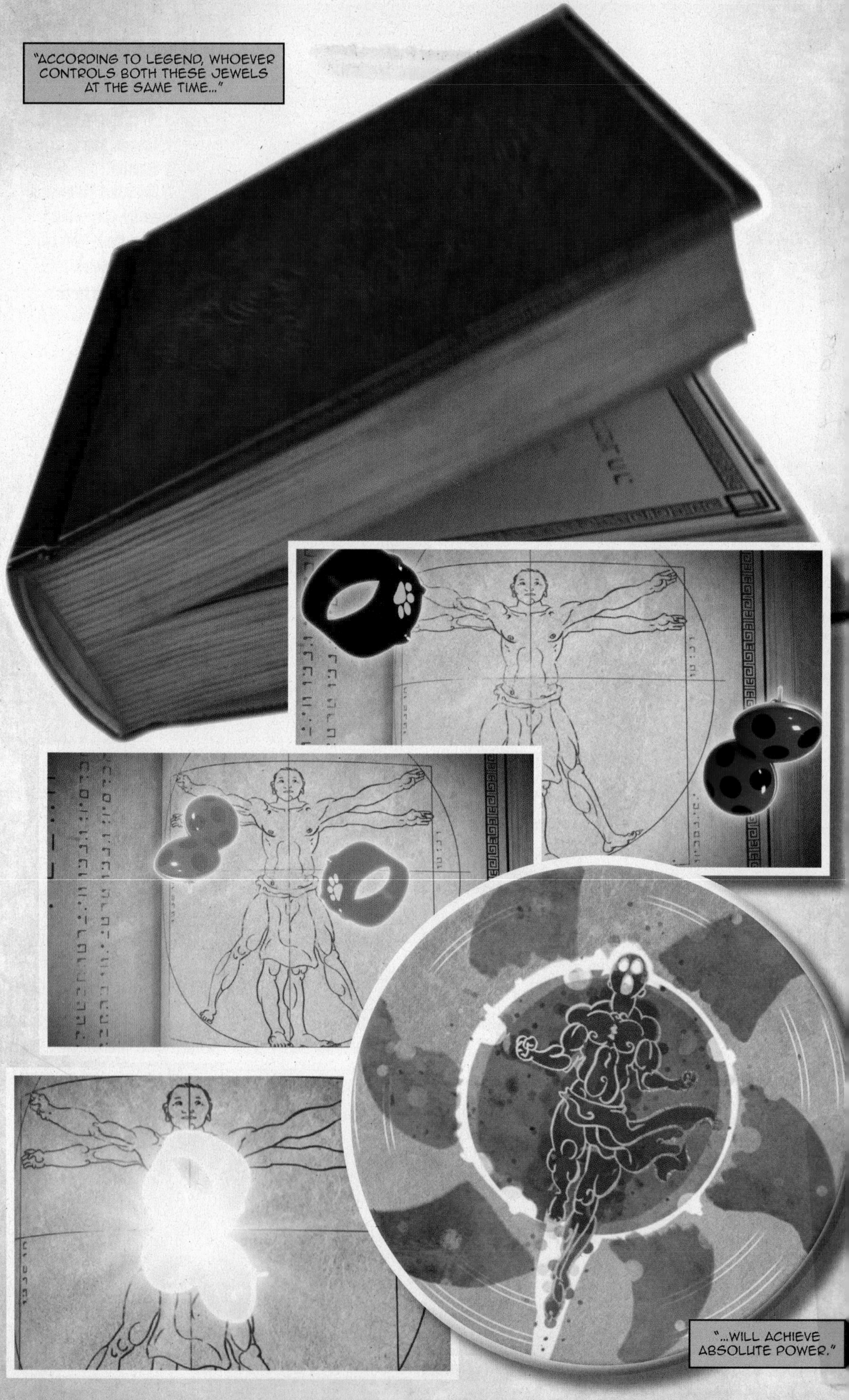

"ACCORDING TO LEGEND, WHOEVER CONTROLS BOTH THESE JEWELS AT THE SAME TIME..."

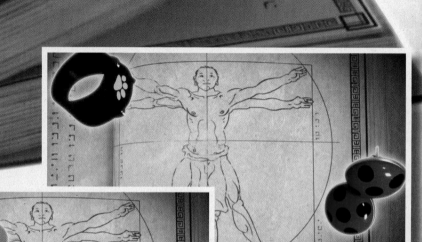

"...WILL ACHIEVE ABSOLUTE POWER."

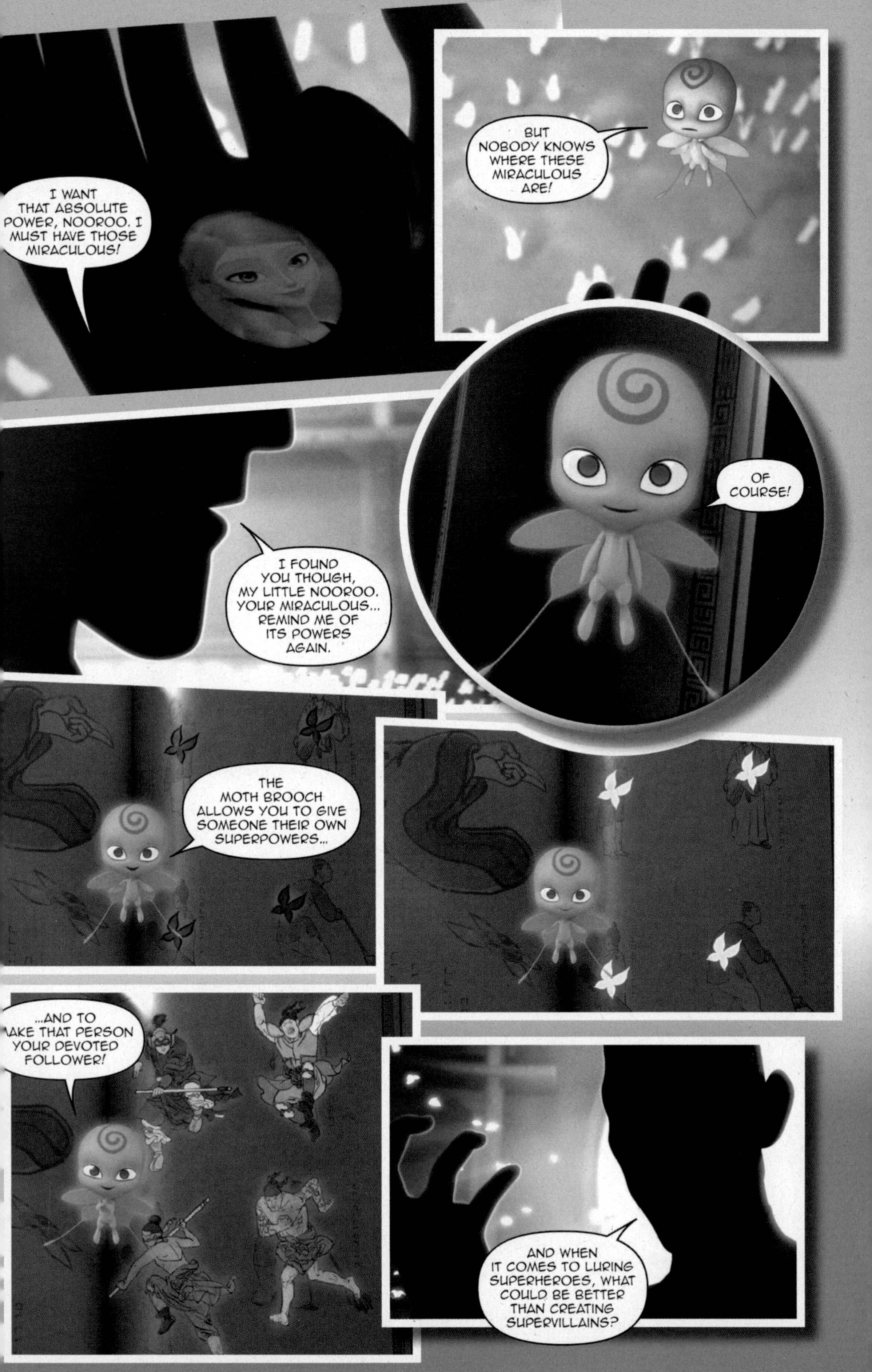
I WANT THAT ABSOLUTE POWER, NOOROO. I MUST HAVE THOSE MIRACULOUS!
BUT NOBODY KNOWS WHERE THESE MIRACULOUS ARE!
I FOUND YOU THOUGH, MY LITTLE NOOROO. YOUR MIRACULOUS... REMIND ME OF ITS POWERS AGAIN.
OF COURSE!
THE MOTH BROOCH ALLOWS YOU TO GIVE SOMEONE THEIR OWN SUPERPOWERS...
...AND TO MAKE THAT PERSON YOUR DEVOTED FOLLOWER!
AND WHEN IT COMES TO LURING SUPERHEROES, WHAT COULD BE BETTER THAN CREATING SUPERVILLAINS?

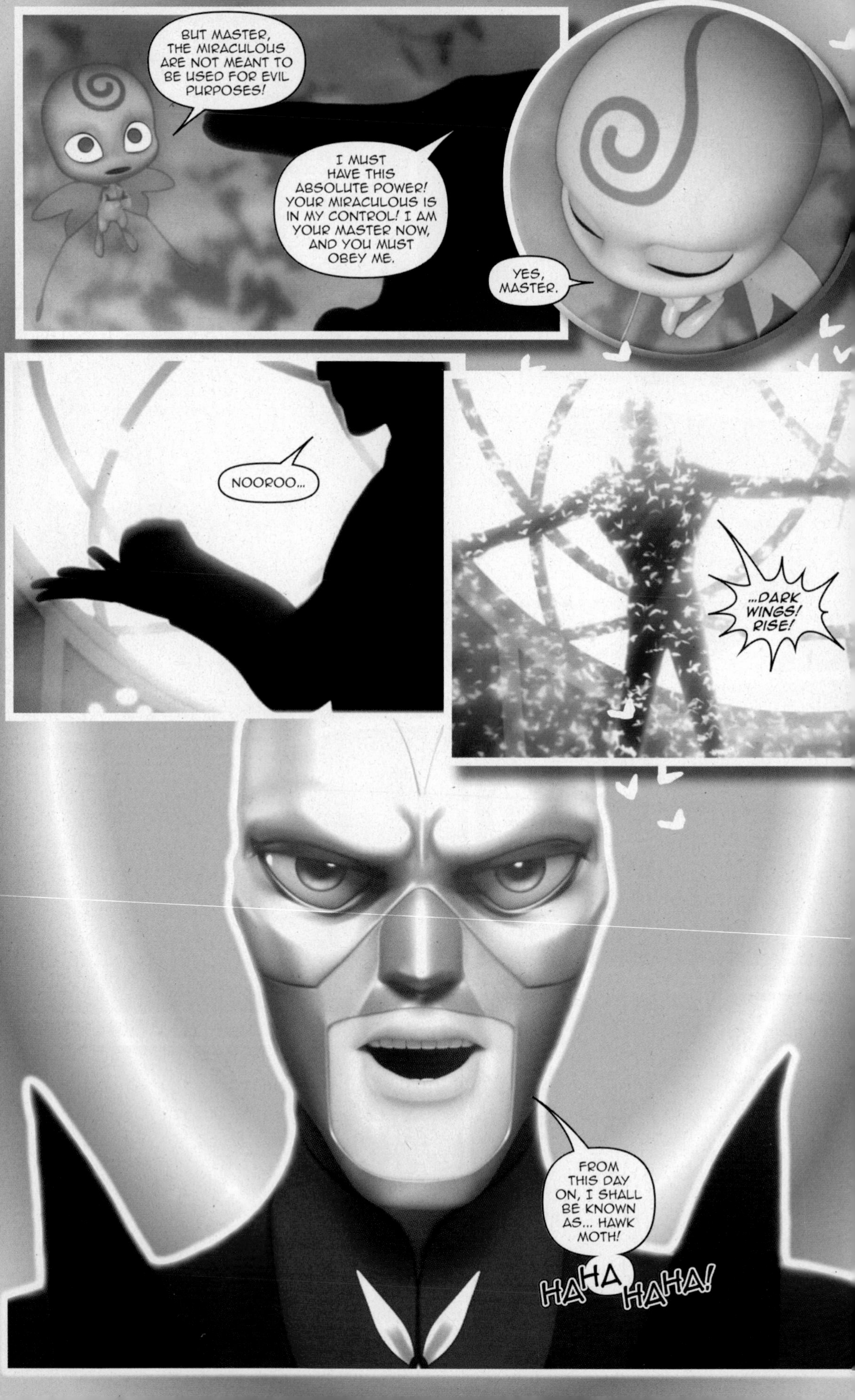
BUT MASTER, THE MIRACULOUS ARE NOT MEANT TO BE USED FOR EVIL PURPOSES!
I MUST HAVE THIS ABSOLUTE POWER! YOUR MIRACULOUS IS IN MY CONTROL! I AM YOUR MASTER NOW, AND YOU MUST OBEY ME.
YES, MASTER.
NOOROO...
...DARK WINGS! RISE!
FROM THIS DAY ON, I SHALL BE KNOWN AS... HAWK MOTH!
HAHA HAHA!

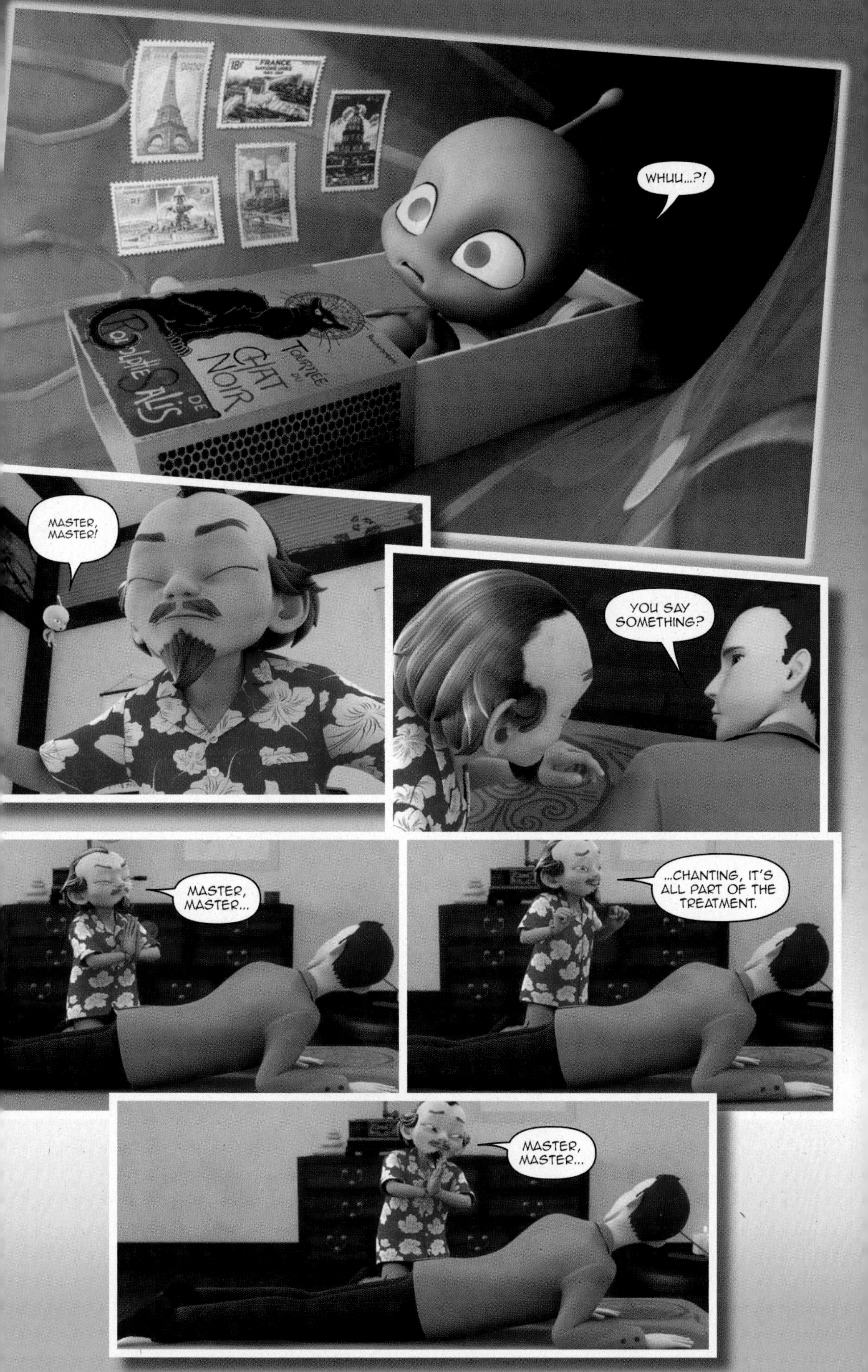
WHUU...?!
MASTER, MASTER!
YOU SAY SOMETHING?
MASTER, MASTER...
...CHANTING, IT'S ALL PART OF THE TREATMENT.
MASTER, MASTER...

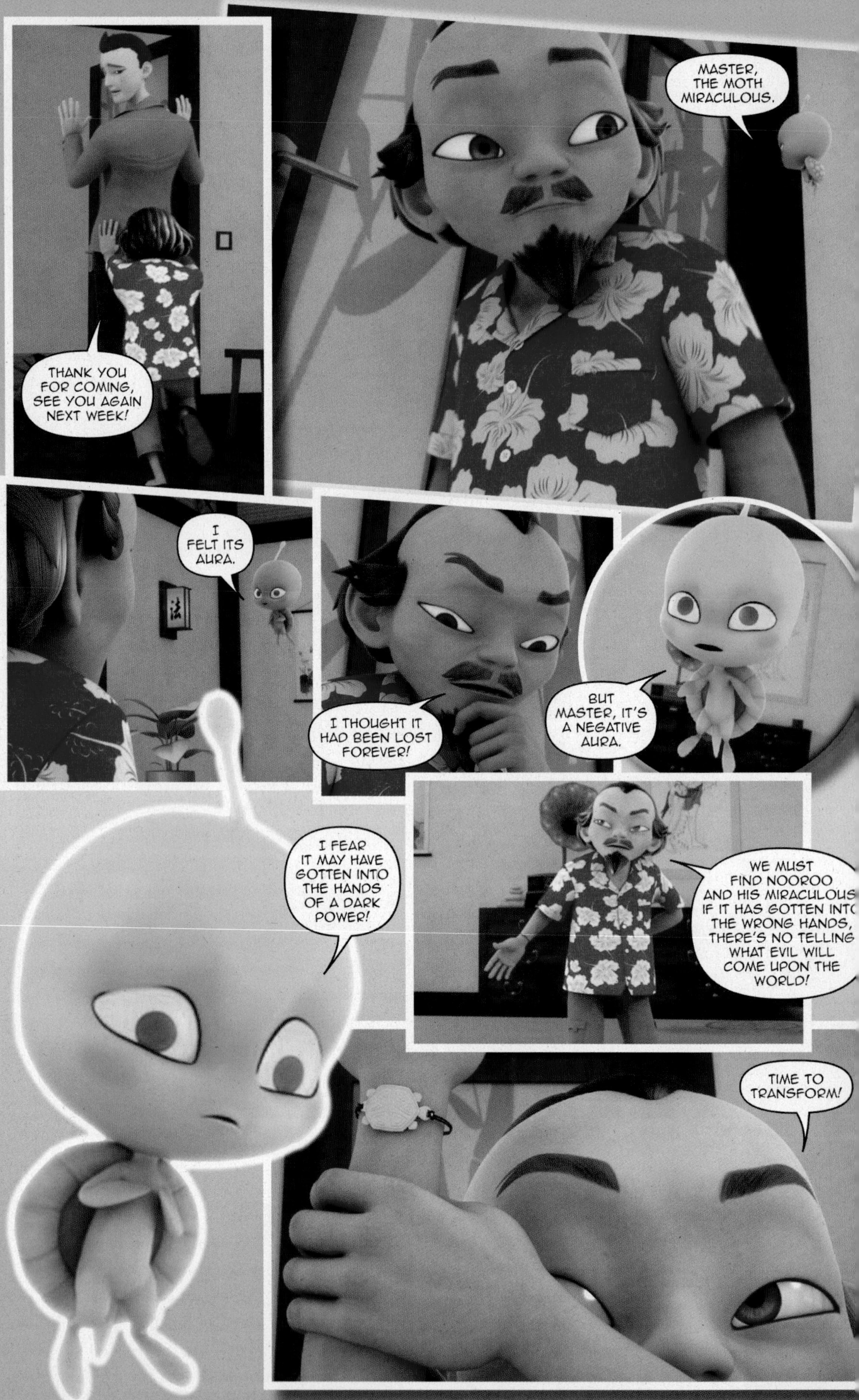
THANK YOU FOR COMING, SEE YOU AGAIN NEXT WEEK!
MASTER, THE MOTH MIRACULOUS.
I FELT ITS AURA.
I THOUGHT IT HAD BEEN LOST FOREVER!
BUT MASTER, IT'S A NEGATIVE AURA.
I FEAR IT MAY HAVE GOTTEN INTO THE HANDS OF A DARK POWER!
WE MUST FIND NOOROO AND HIS MIRACULOUS. IF IT HAS GOTTEN INTO THE WRONG HANDS, THERE'S NO TELLING WHAT EVIL WILL COME UPON THE WORLD!
TIME TO TRANSFORM!

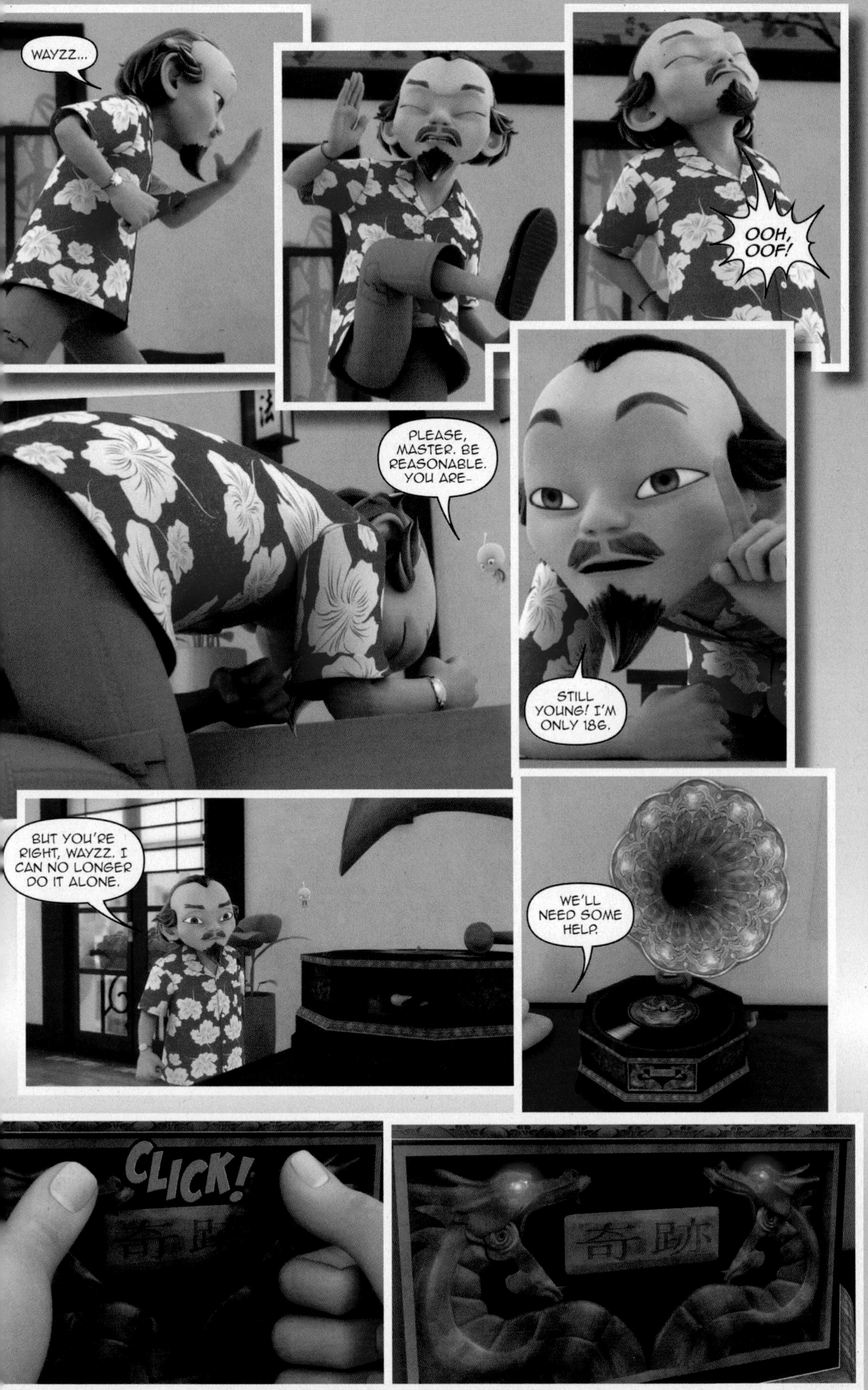
WAYZZ...
OOH, OOF!
PLEASE, MASTER. BE REASONABLE. YOU ARE-
STILL YOUNG! I'M ONLY 186.
BUT YOU'RE RIGHT, WAYZZ. I CAN NO LONGER DO IT ALONE.
WE'LL NEED SOME HELP.
CLICK!

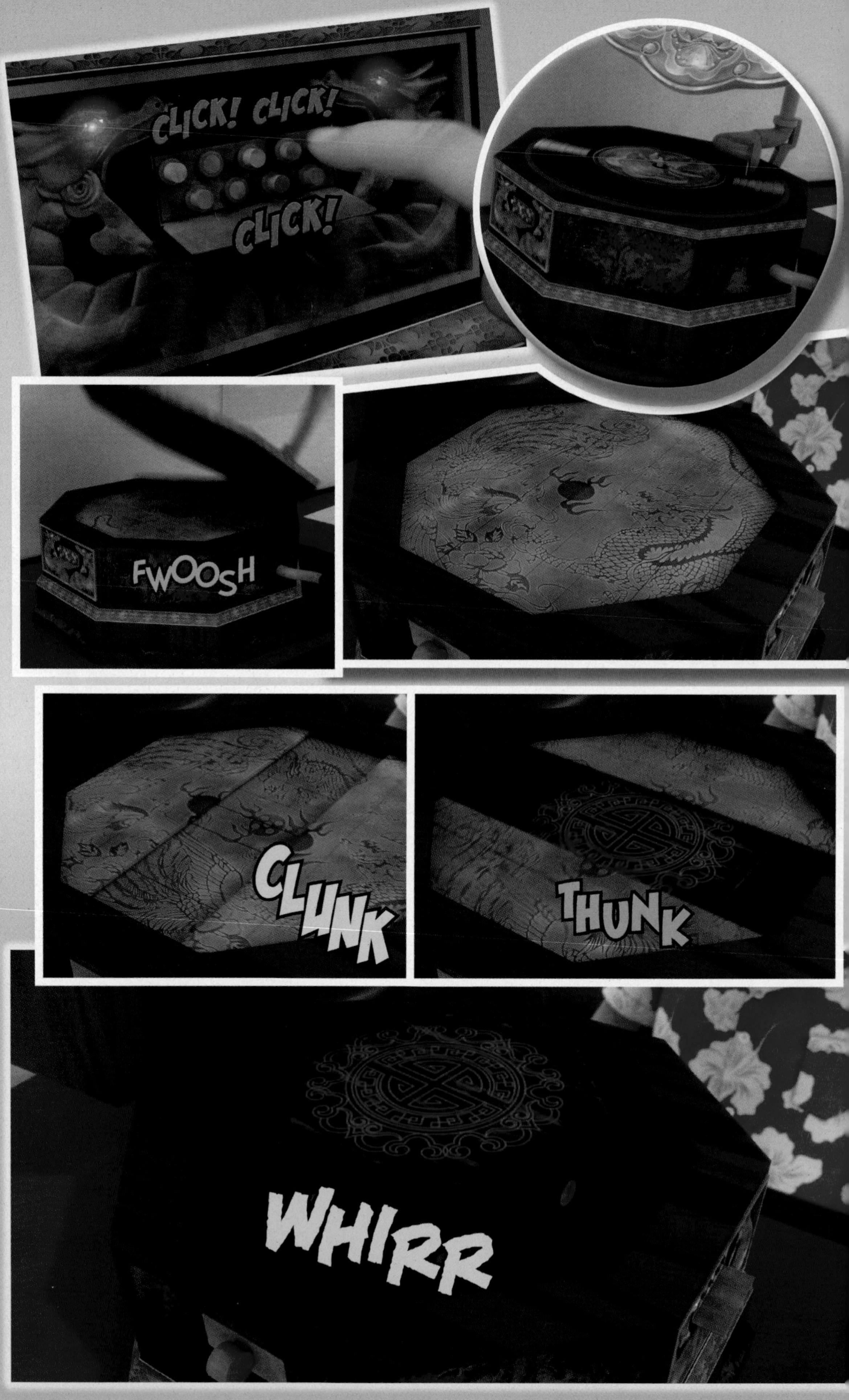
CLICK! CLICK!
CLICK!
FWOOSH
CLUNK
THUNK
WHIRR

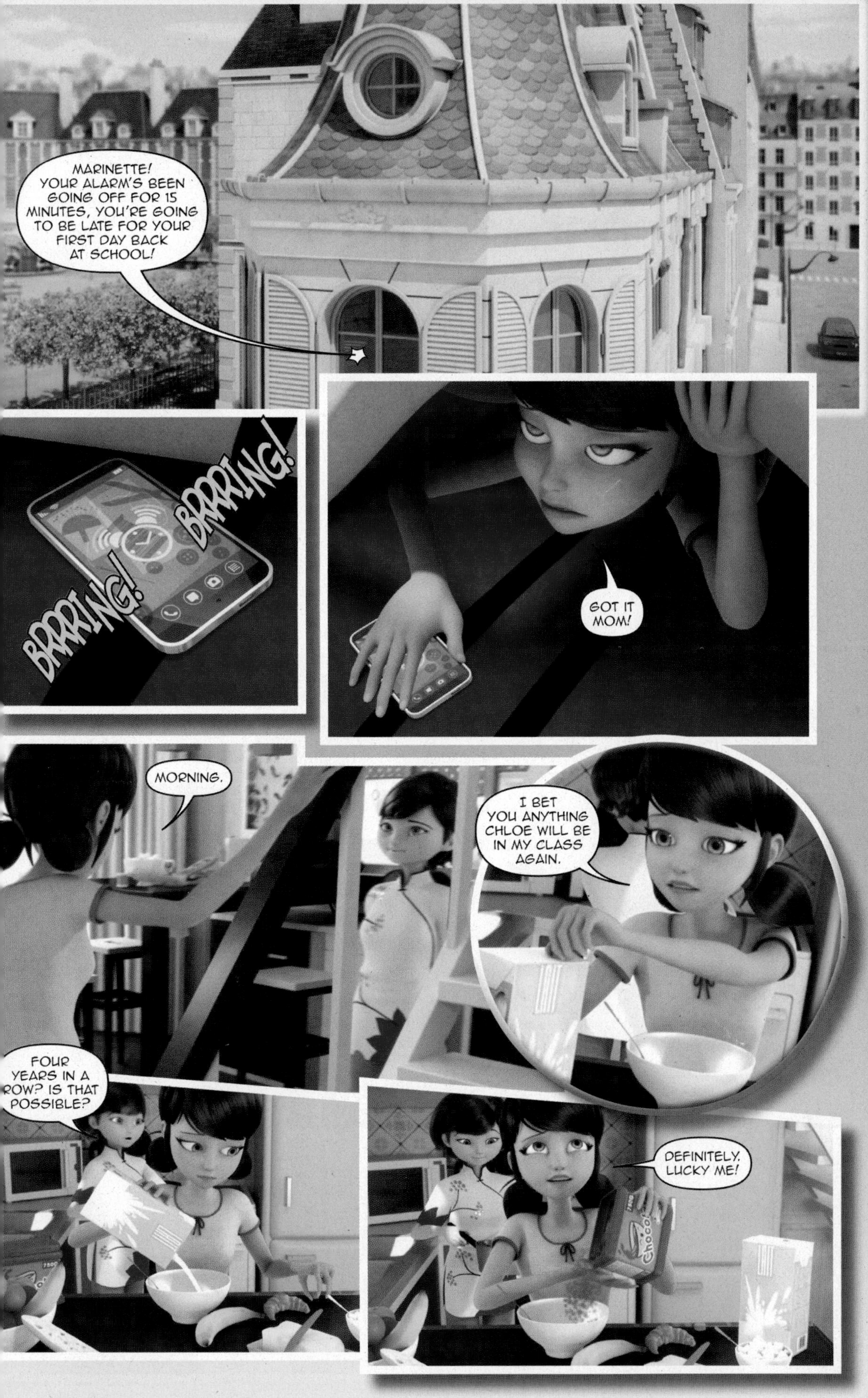
MARINETTE! YOUR ALARM'S BEEN GOING OFF FOR 15 MINUTES, YOU'RE GOING TO BE LATE FOR YOUR FIRST DAY BACK AT SCHOOL!
BRRRING! BRRRING!
GOT IT MOM!
MORNING.
I BET YOU ANYTHING CHLOE WILL BE IN MY CLASS AGAIN.
FOUR YEARS IN A ROW? IS THAT POSSIBLE?
DEFINITELY. LUCKY ME!

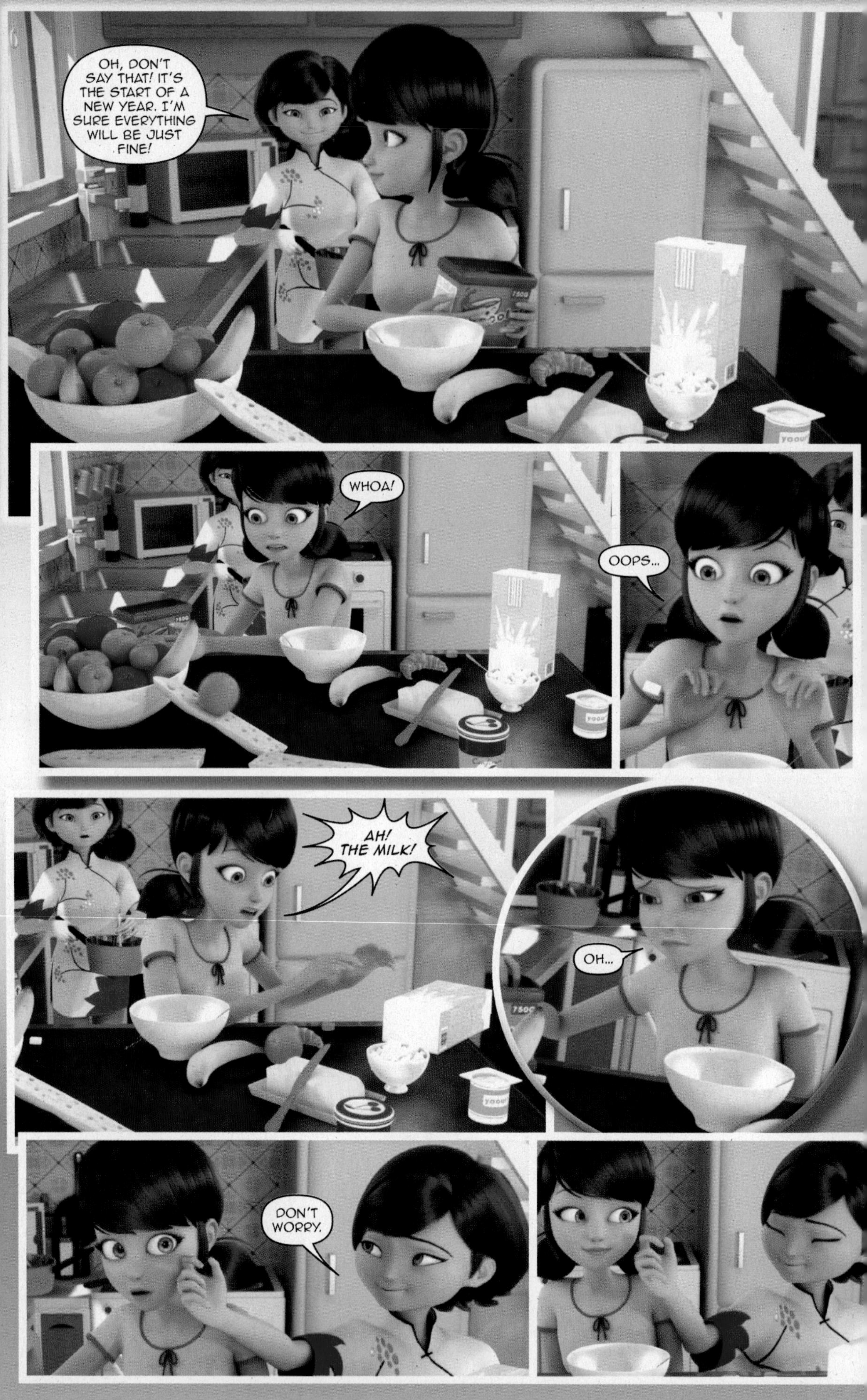
OH, DON'T SAY THAT! IT'S THE START OF A NEW YEAR. I'M SURE EVERYTHING WILL BE JUST FINE!
WHOA!
OOPS...
AH! THE MILK!
OH...
DON'T WORRY.

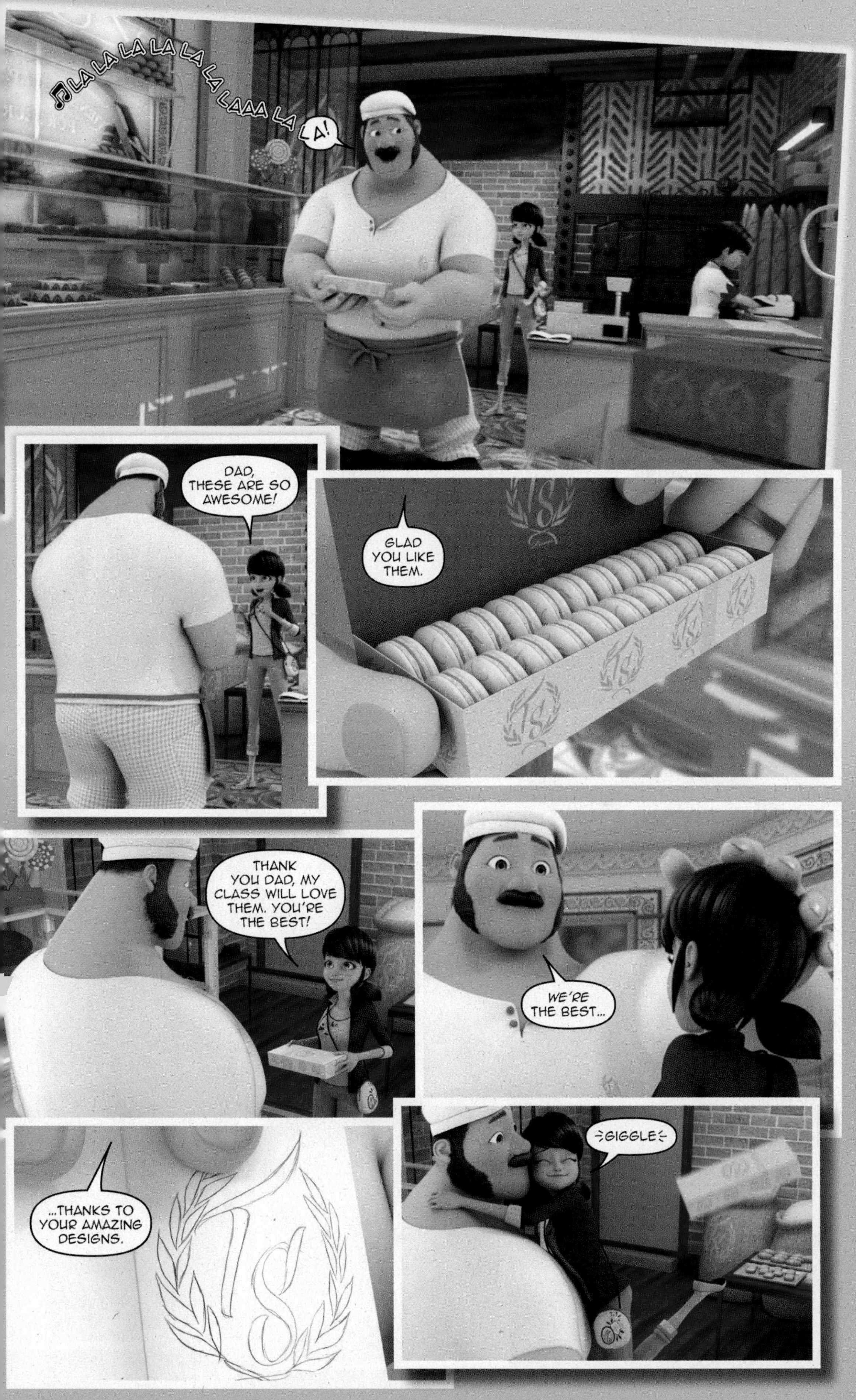
♫ LA LA LA LA LA LA LA LAAA LA LA!
DAD, THESE ARE SO AWESOME!
GLAD YOU LIKE THEM.
THANK YOU DAD, MY CLASS WILL LOVE THEM. YOU'RE THE BEST!
WE'RE THE BEST...
...THANKS TO YOUR AMAZING DESIGNS.
GIGGLE

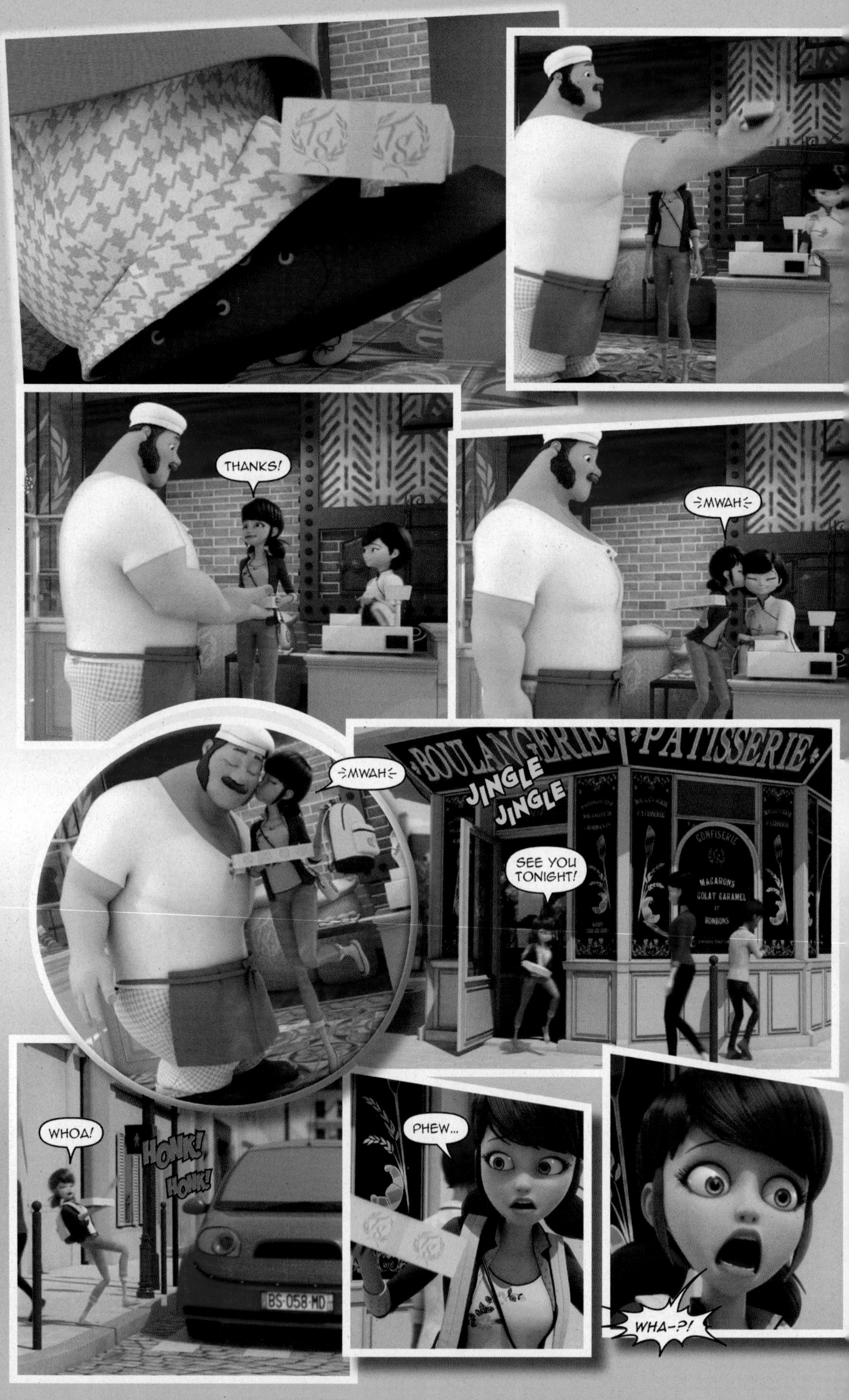
THANKS!
MWAH
MWAH
BOULANGERIE PATISSERIE
JINGLE JINGLE
SEE YOU TONIGHT!
CONFISERIE
MACARONS
CHOCOLAT CARAMEL
ET
BONBONS
WHOA!
HONK! HONK!
BS-058-MD
PHEW...
WHA-?!

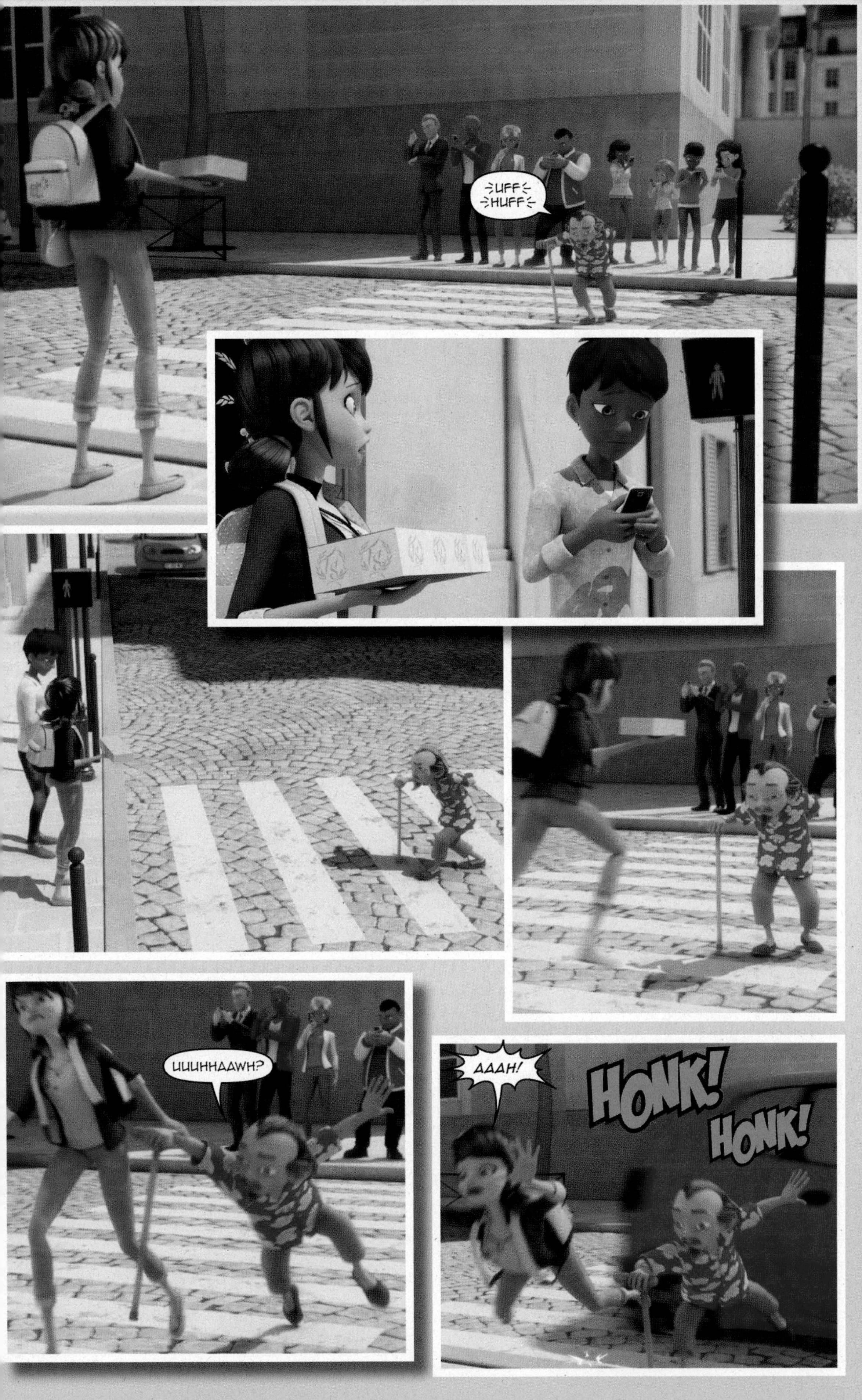
UFF
HUFF
UUUHHAAWH?
AAAH!
HONK!
HONK!

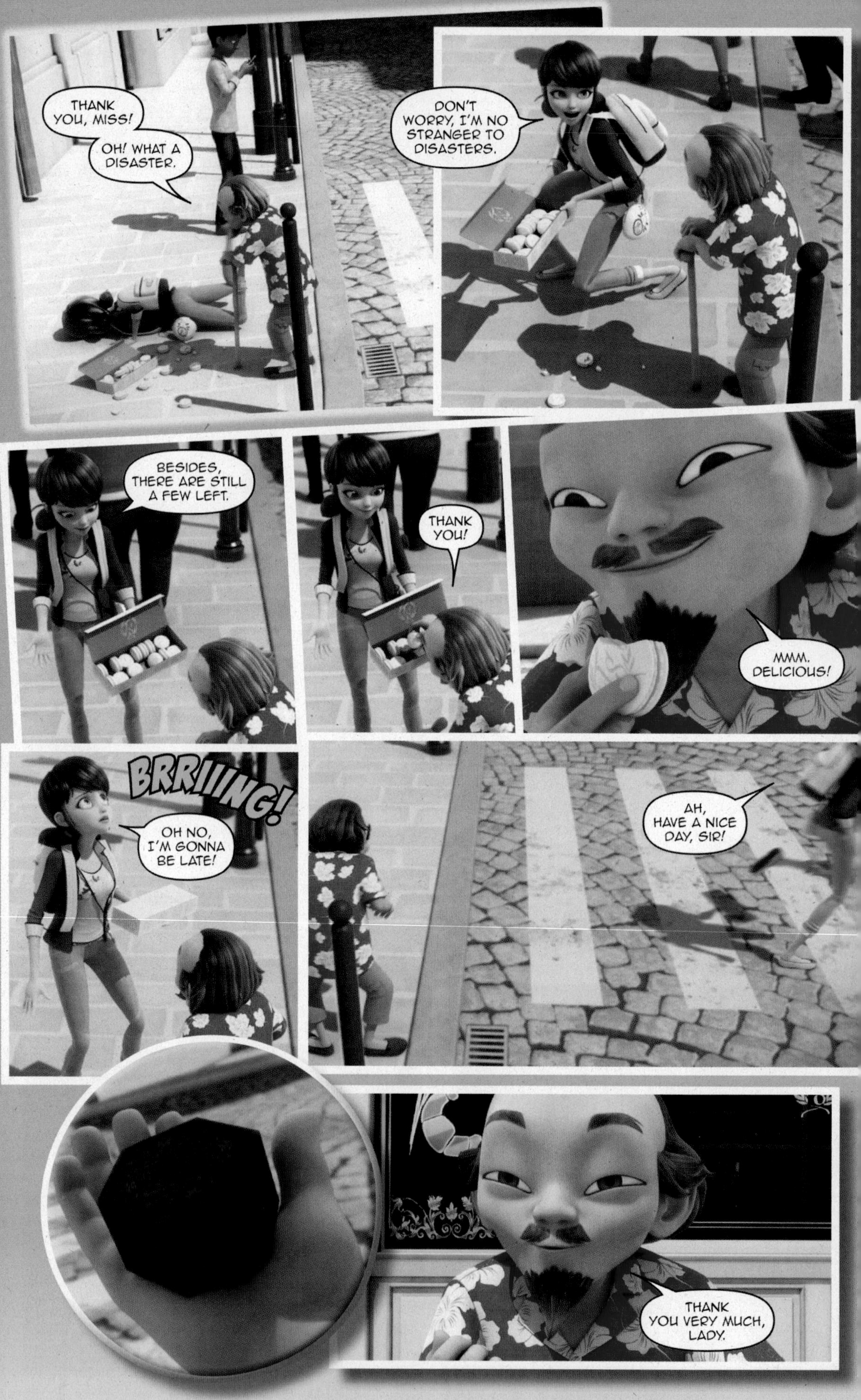
THANK YOU, MISS!
OH! WHAT A DISASTER.
DON'T WORRY, I'M NO STRANGER TO DISASTERS.
BESIDES, THERE ARE STILL A FEW LEFT.
THANK YOU!
MMM. DELICIOUS!
BRRIIING!
OH NO, I'M GONNA BE LATE!
AH, HAVE A NICE DAY, SIR!
THANK YOU VERY MUCH, LADY.

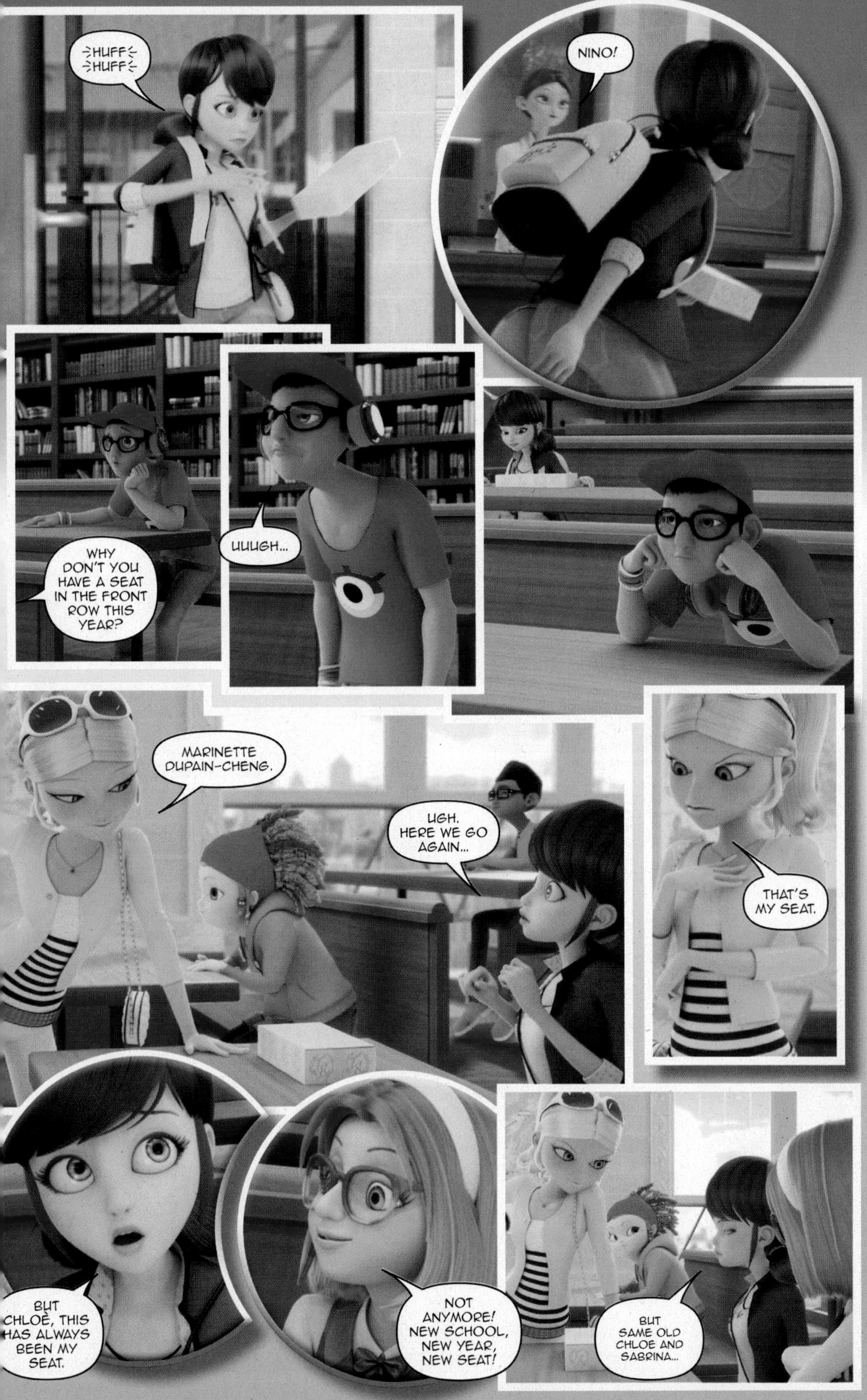

HUFF
HUFF
NINO!
WHY DON'T YOU HAVE A SEAT IN THE FRONT ROW THIS YEAR?
UUUGH...
MARINETTE DUPAIN-CHENG.
UGH. HERE WE GO AGAIN...
THAT'S MY SEAT.
BUT CHLOÈ, THIS HAS ALWAYS BEEN MY SEAT.
NOT ANYMORE! NEW SCHOOL, NEW YEAR, NEW SEAT!
BUT SAME OLD CHLOE AND SABRINA...

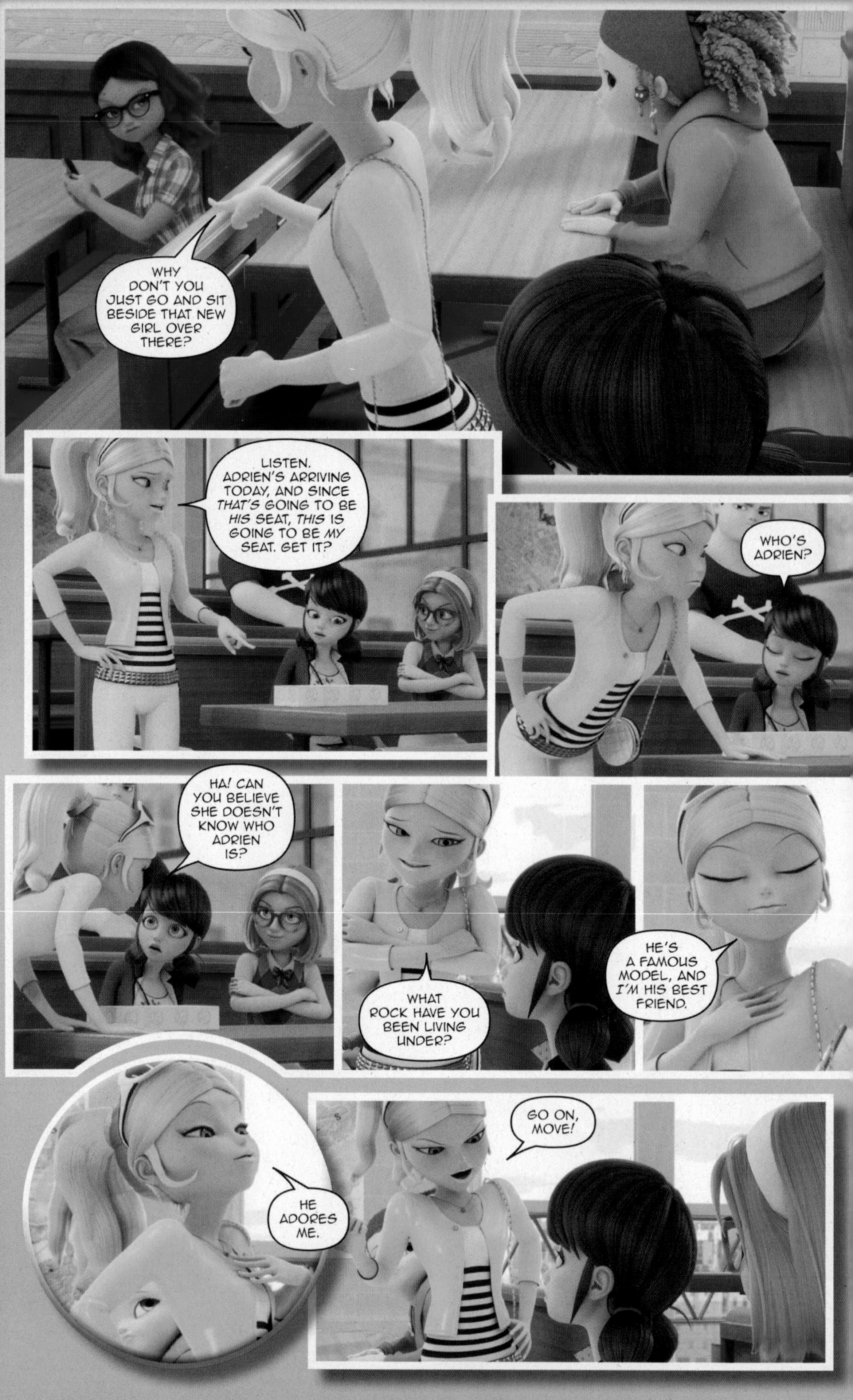
WHY DON'T YOU JUST GO AND SIT BESIDE THAT NEW GIRL OVER THERE?
LISTEN. ADRIEN'S ARRIVING TODAY, AND SINCE *THAT'S* GOING TO BE *HIS* SEAT, *THIS* IS GOING TO BE *MY* SEAT. GET IT?
WHO'S ADRIEN?
HA! CAN YOU BELIEVE SHE DOESN'T KNOW WHO ADRIEN IS?
WHAT ROCK HAVE YOU BEEN LIVING UNDER?
HE'S A FAMOUS MODEL, AND *I'M* HIS BEST FRIEND.
HE ADORES ME.
GO ON, MOVE!

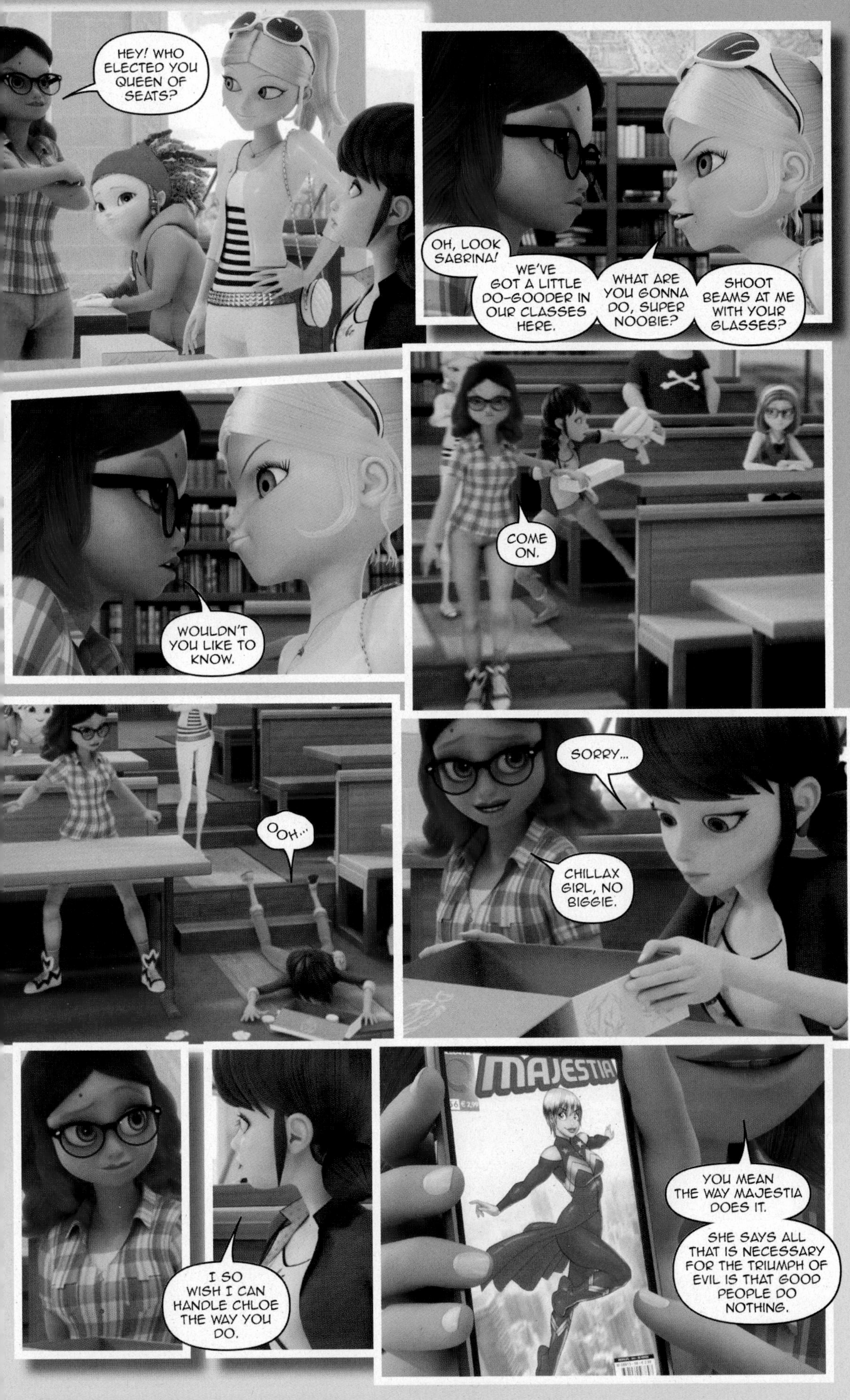
HEY! WHO ELECTED YOU QUEEN OF SEATS?
OH, LOOK SABRINA!
WE'VE GOT A LITTLE DO-GOODER IN OUR CLASSES HERE.
WHAT ARE YOU GONNA DO, SUPER NOOBIE?
SHOOT BEAMS AT ME WITH YOUR GLASSES?
WOULDN'T YOU LIKE TO KNOW.
COME ON.
OOH...
SORRY...
CHILLAX GIRL, NO BIGGIE.
I SO WISH I CAN HANDLE CHLOE THE WAY YOU DO.
MAJESTIA
YOU MEAN THE WAY MAJESTIA DOES IT.
SHE SAYS ALL THAT IS NECESSARY FOR THE TRIUMPH OF EVIL IS THAT GOOD PEOPLE DO NOTHING.

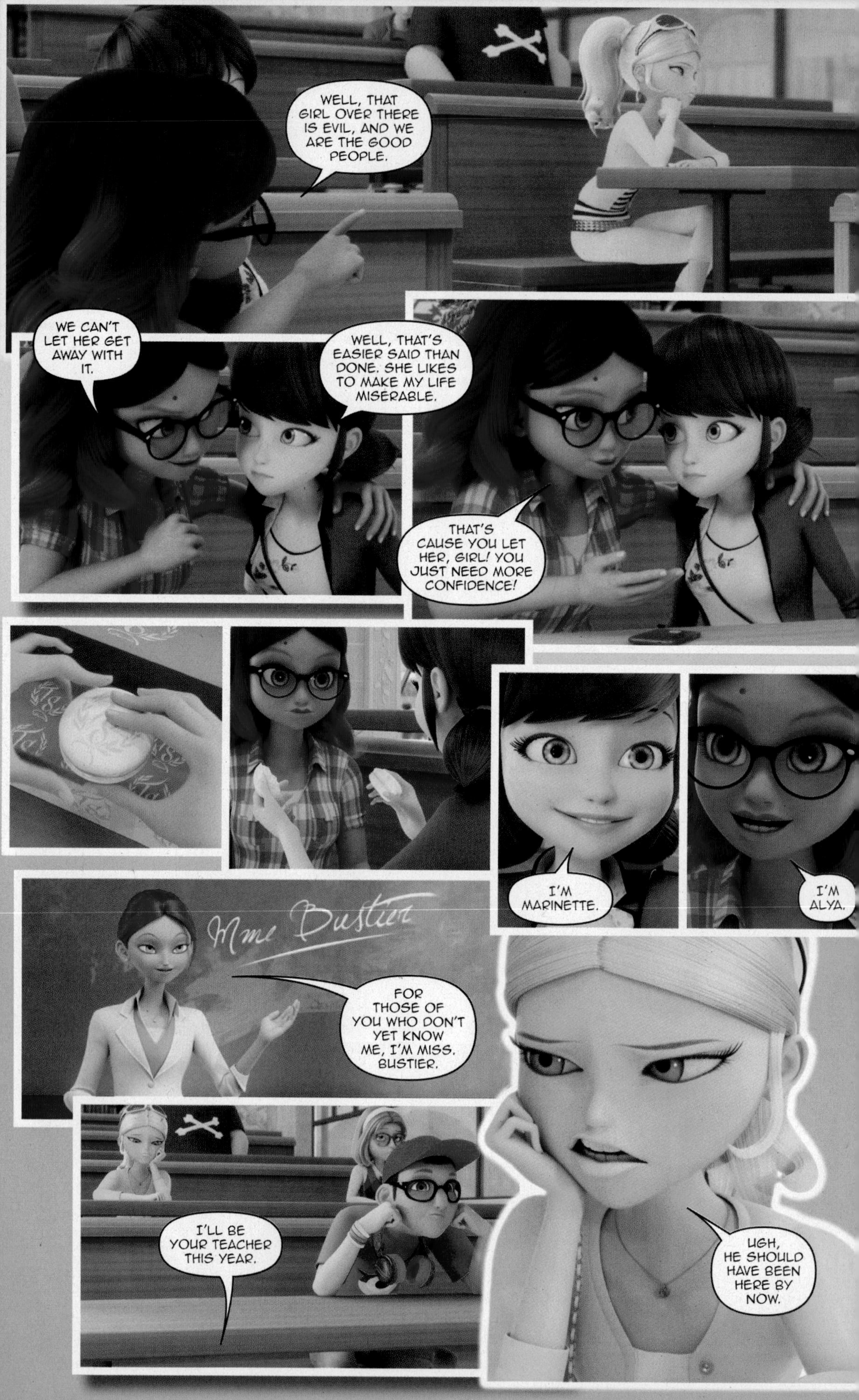
WELL, THAT GIRL OVER THERE IS EVIL, AND WE ARE THE GOOD PEOPLE.
WE CAN'T LET HER GET AWAY WITH IT.
WELL, THAT'S EASIER SAID THAN DONE. SHE LIKES TO MAKE MY LIFE MISERABLE.
THAT'S CAUSE YOU LET HER, GIRL! YOU JUST NEED MORE CONFIDENCE!
I'M MARINETTE.
I'M ALYA.
Mme Bustier
FOR THOSE OF YOU WHO DON'T YET KNOW ME, I'M MISS. BUSTIER.
I'LL BE YOUR TEACHER THIS YEAR.
UGH, HE SHOULD HAVE BEEN HERE BY NOW.

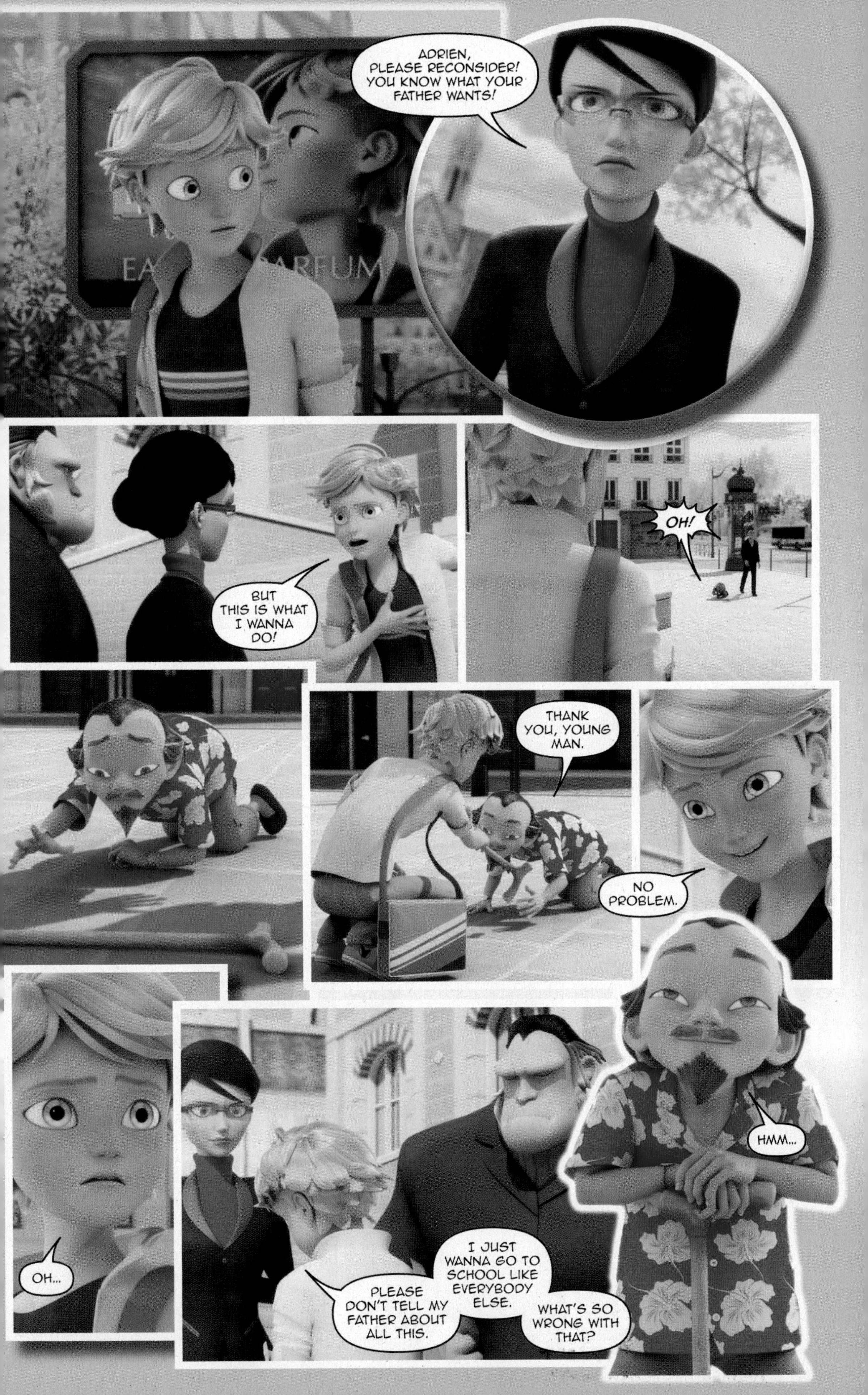
EA ARFUM
ADRIEN, PLEASE RECONSIDER! YOU KNOW WHAT YOUR FATHER WANTS!
BUT THIS IS WHAT I WANNA DO!
OH!
THANK YOU, YOUNG MAN.
NO PROBLEM.
OH...
PLEASE DON'T TELL MY FATHER ABOUT ALL THIS.
I JUST WANNA GO TO SCHOOL LIKE EVERYBODY ELSE.
WHAT'S SO WRONG WITH THAT?
HMM...

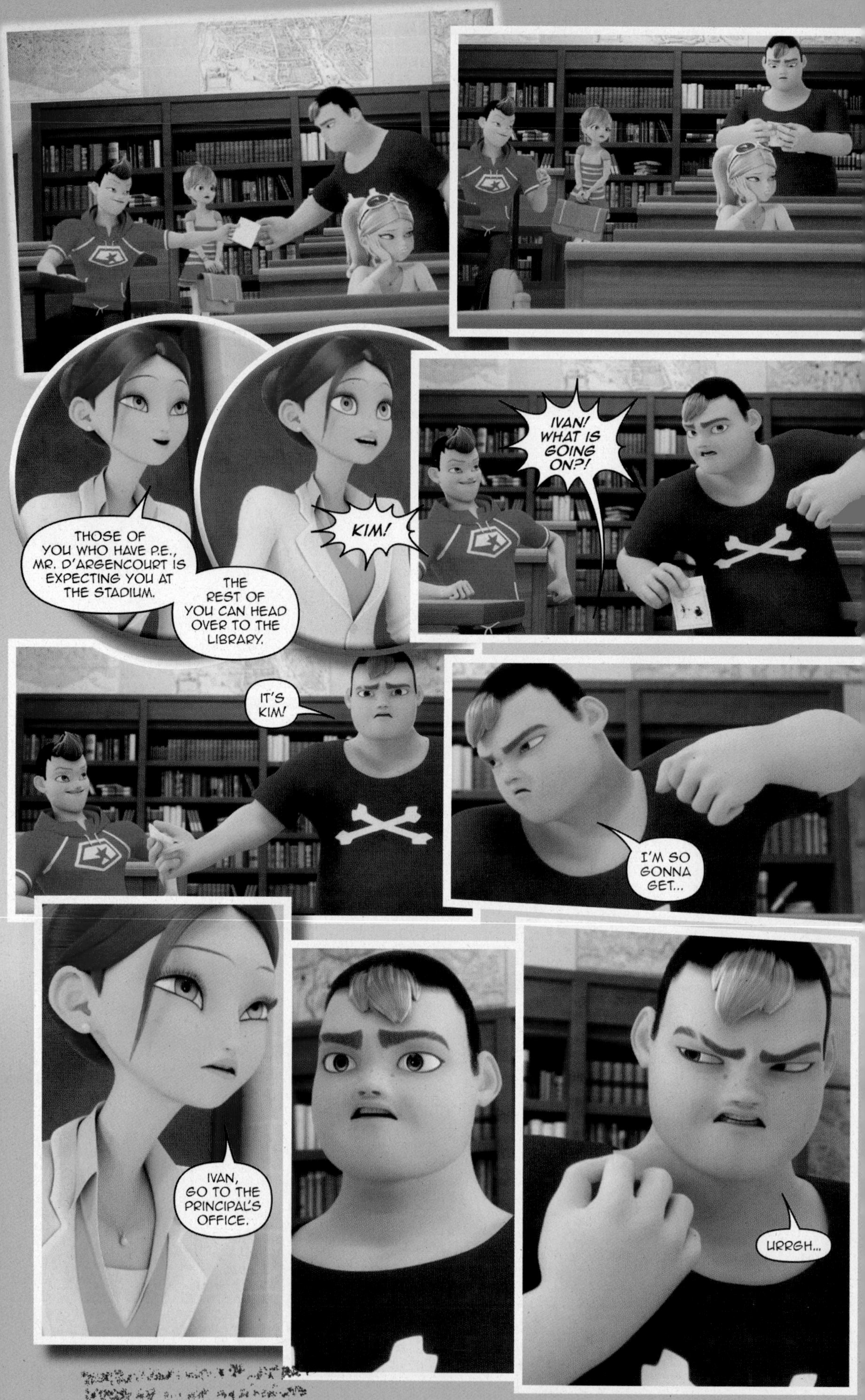
THOSE OF YOU WHO HAVE P.E., MR. D'ARGENCOURT IS EXPECTING YOU AT THE STADIUM.
THE REST OF YOU CAN HEAD OVER TO THE LIBRARY.
KIM!
IVAN! WHAT IS GOING ON?!
IT'S KIM!
I'M SO GONNA GET...
IVAN, GO TO THE PRINCIPAL'S OFFICE.
URRGH...

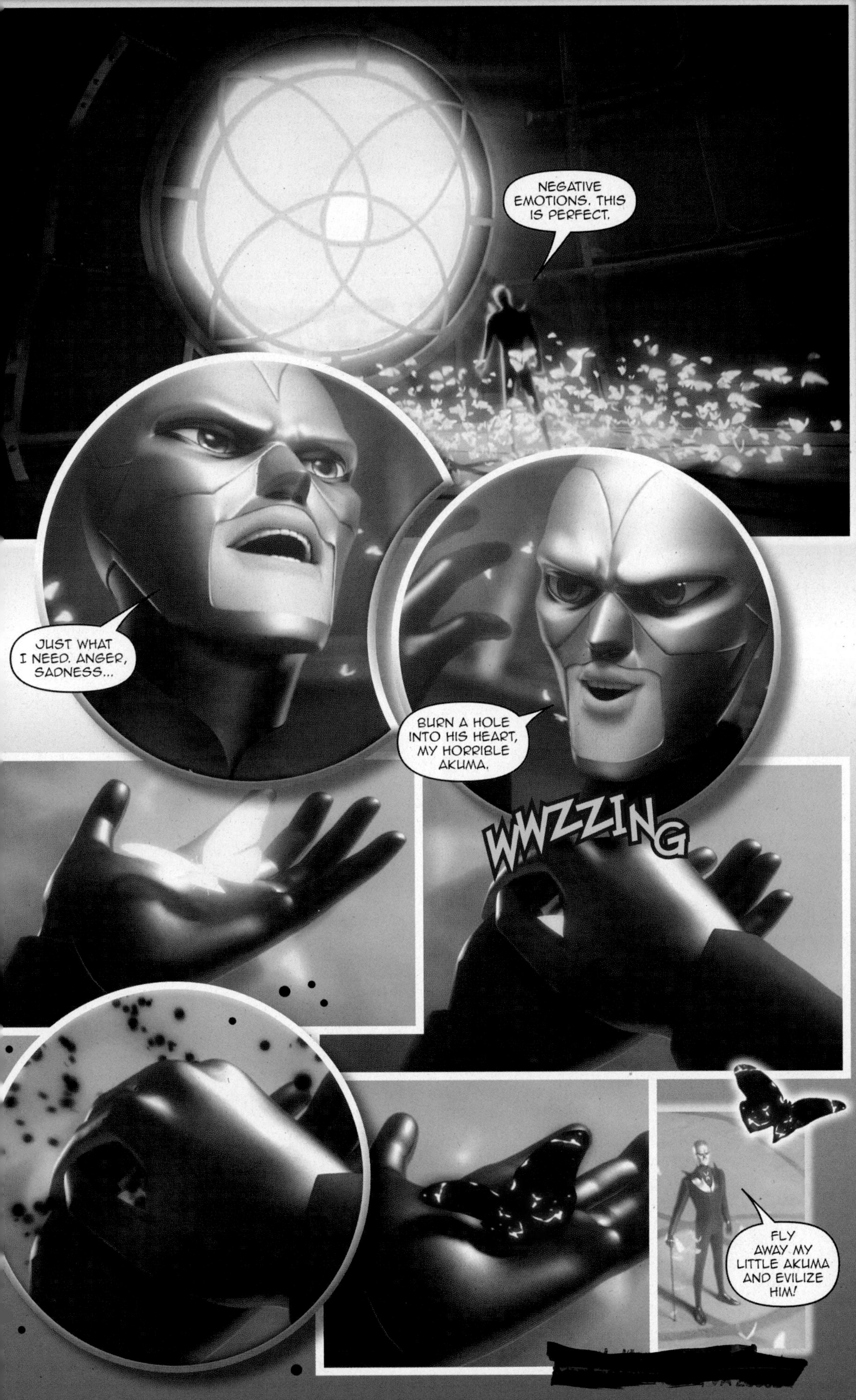
NEGATIVE EMOTIONS. THIS IS PERFECT.
JUST WHAT I NEED. ANGER, SADNESS...
BURN A HOLE INTO HIS HEART, MY HORRIBLE AKUMA.
WWZZING
FLY AWAY MY LITTLE AKUMA AND EVILIZE HIM!

[redacted]

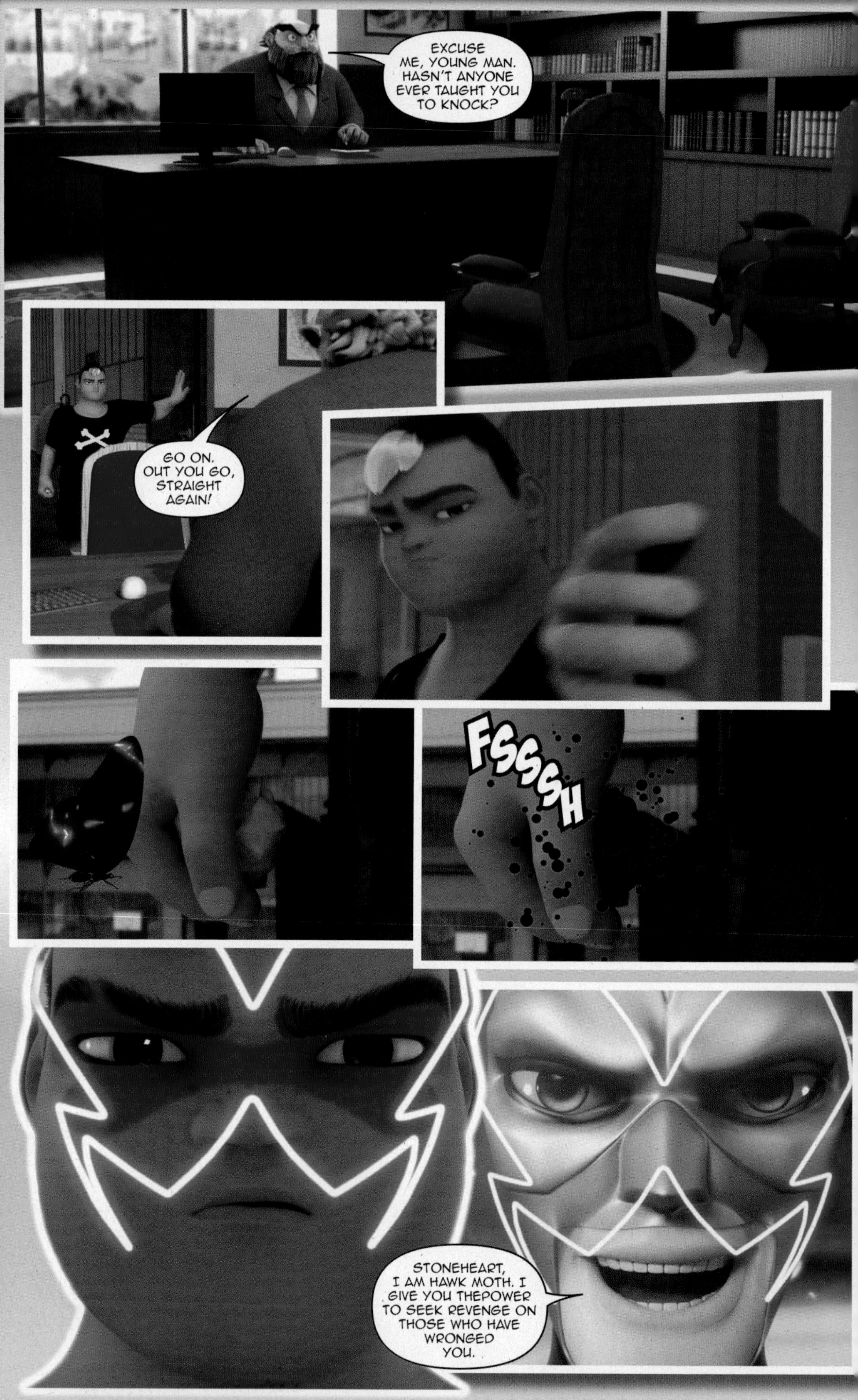
EXCUSE ME, YOUNG MAN. HASN'T ANYONE EVER TAUGHT YOU TO KNOCK?
GO ON. OUT YOU GO, STRAIGHT AGAIN!
FSSSH
STONEHEART, I AM HAWK MOTH. I GIVE YOU THEPOWER TO SEEK REVENGE ON THOSE WHO HAVE WRONGED YOU.

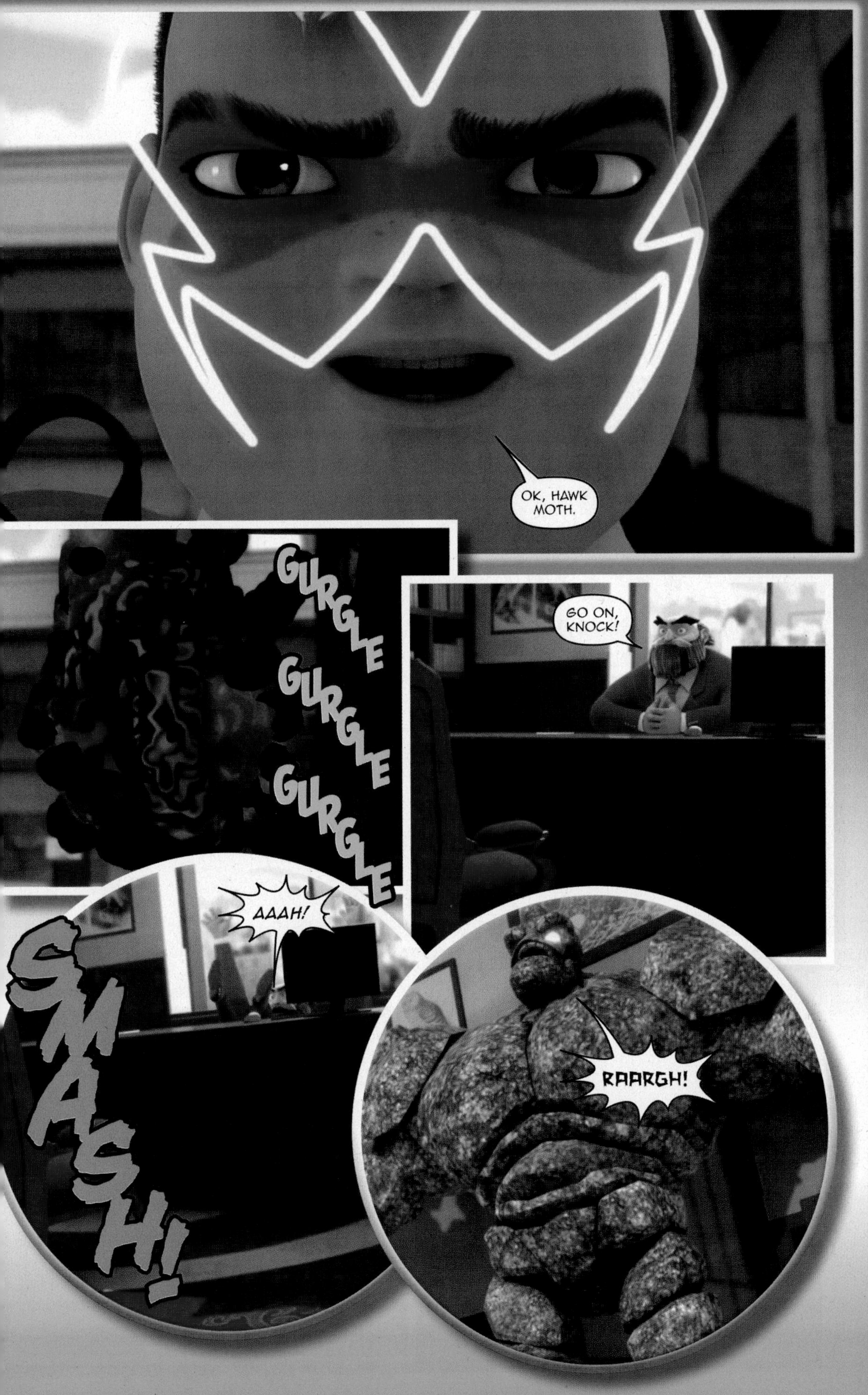
OK, HAWK MOTH.
GURGLE GURGLE GURGLE
GO ON, KNOCK!
AAAH!
SMASH!
RAARGH!

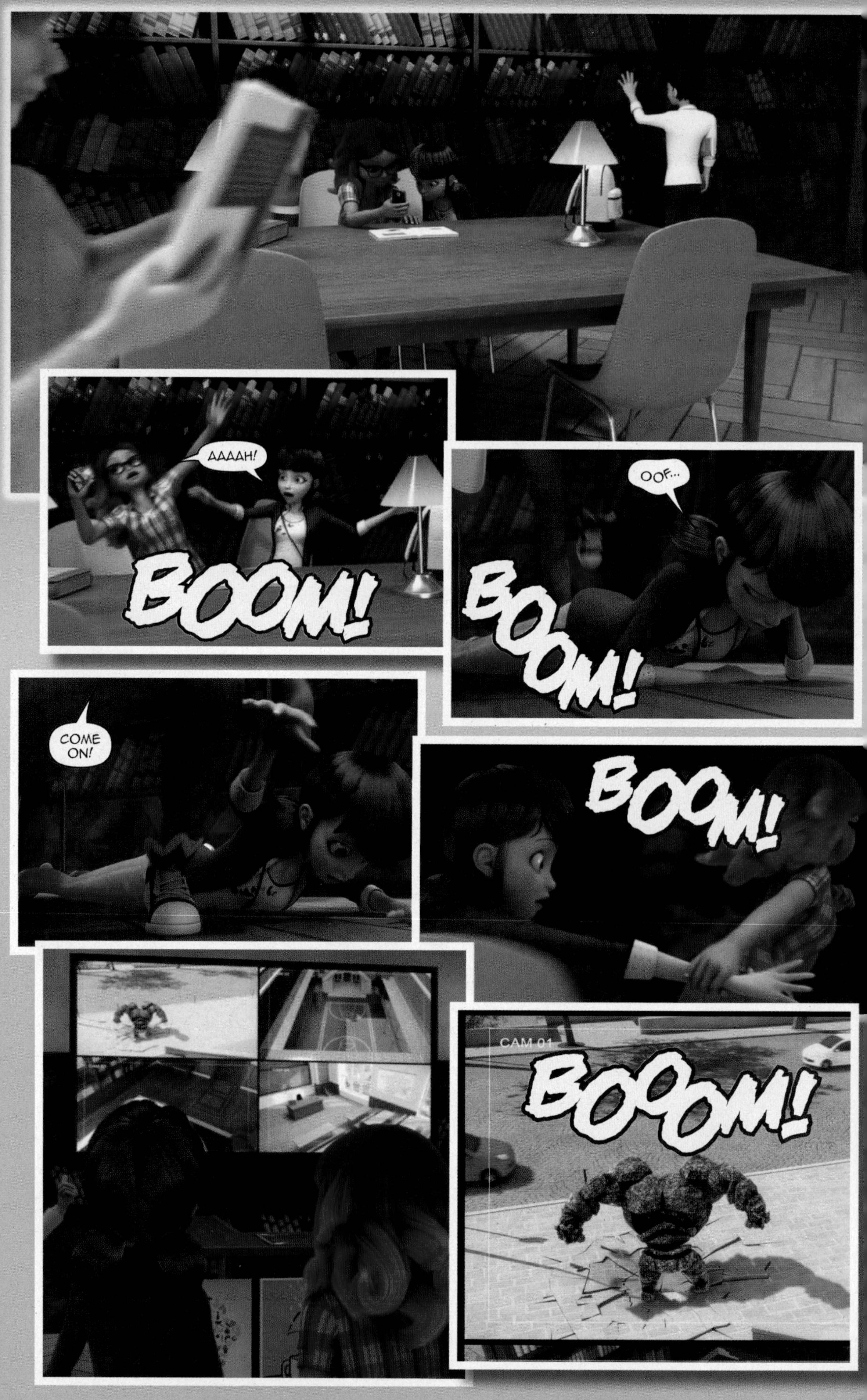
AAAAH!
BOOM!
OOF...
BOOM!
COME ON!
BOOM!
CAM 01
BOOOM!

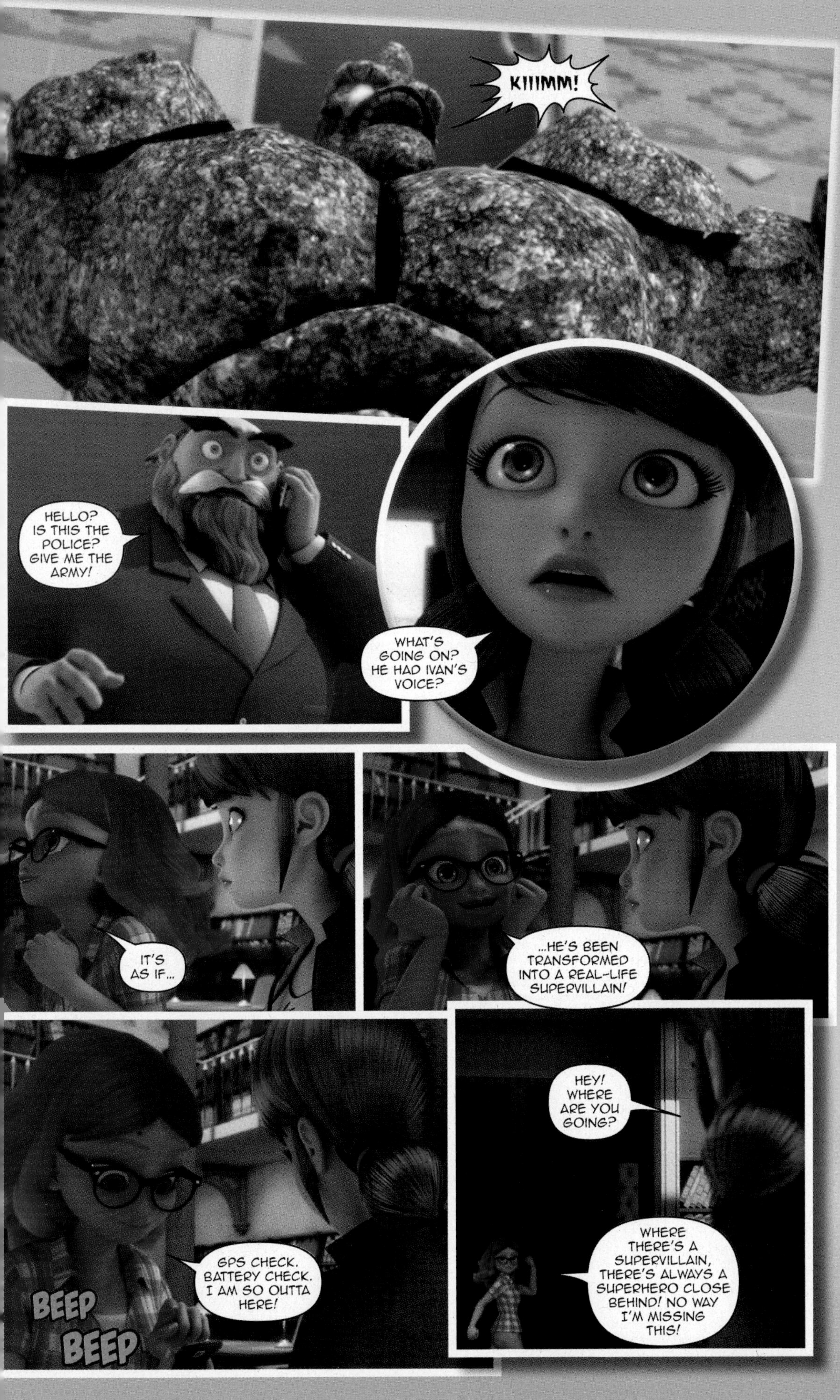
KIIIMM!
HELLO? IS THIS THE POLICE? GIVE ME THE ARMY!
WHAT'S GOING ON? HE HAD IVAN'S VOICE?
IT'S AS IF...
...HE'S BEEN TRANSFORMED INTO A REAL-LIFE SUPERVILLAIN!
GPS CHECK. BATTERY CHECK. I AM SO OUTTA HERE!
BEEP BEEP
HEY! WHERE ARE YOU GOING?
WHERE THERE'S A SUPERVILLAIN, THERE'S ALWAYS A SUPERHERO CLOSE BEHIND! NO WAY I'M MISSING THIS!

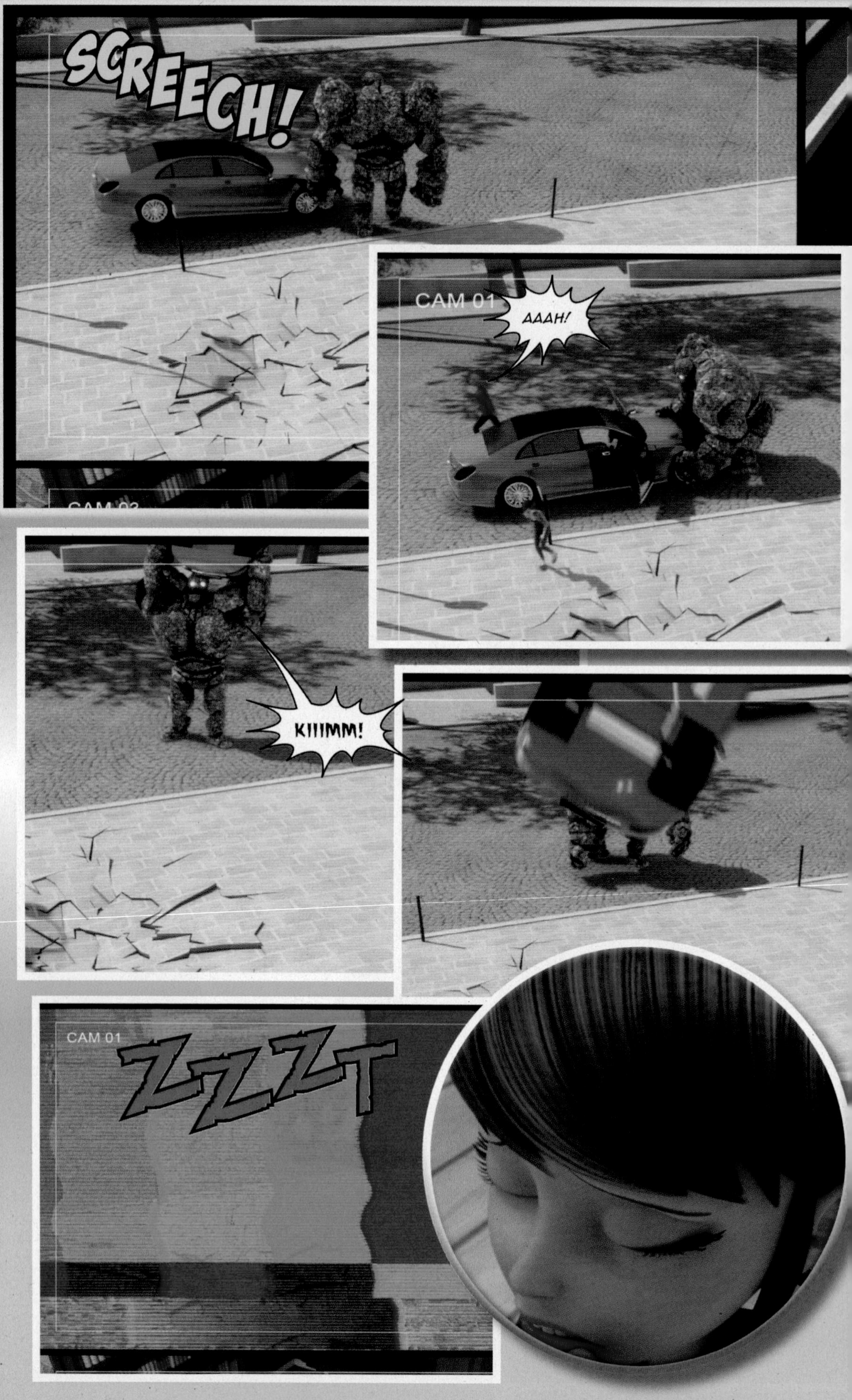
SCREECH!
CAM 01
AAAH!
KIIIMM!
CAM 01
ZZZT

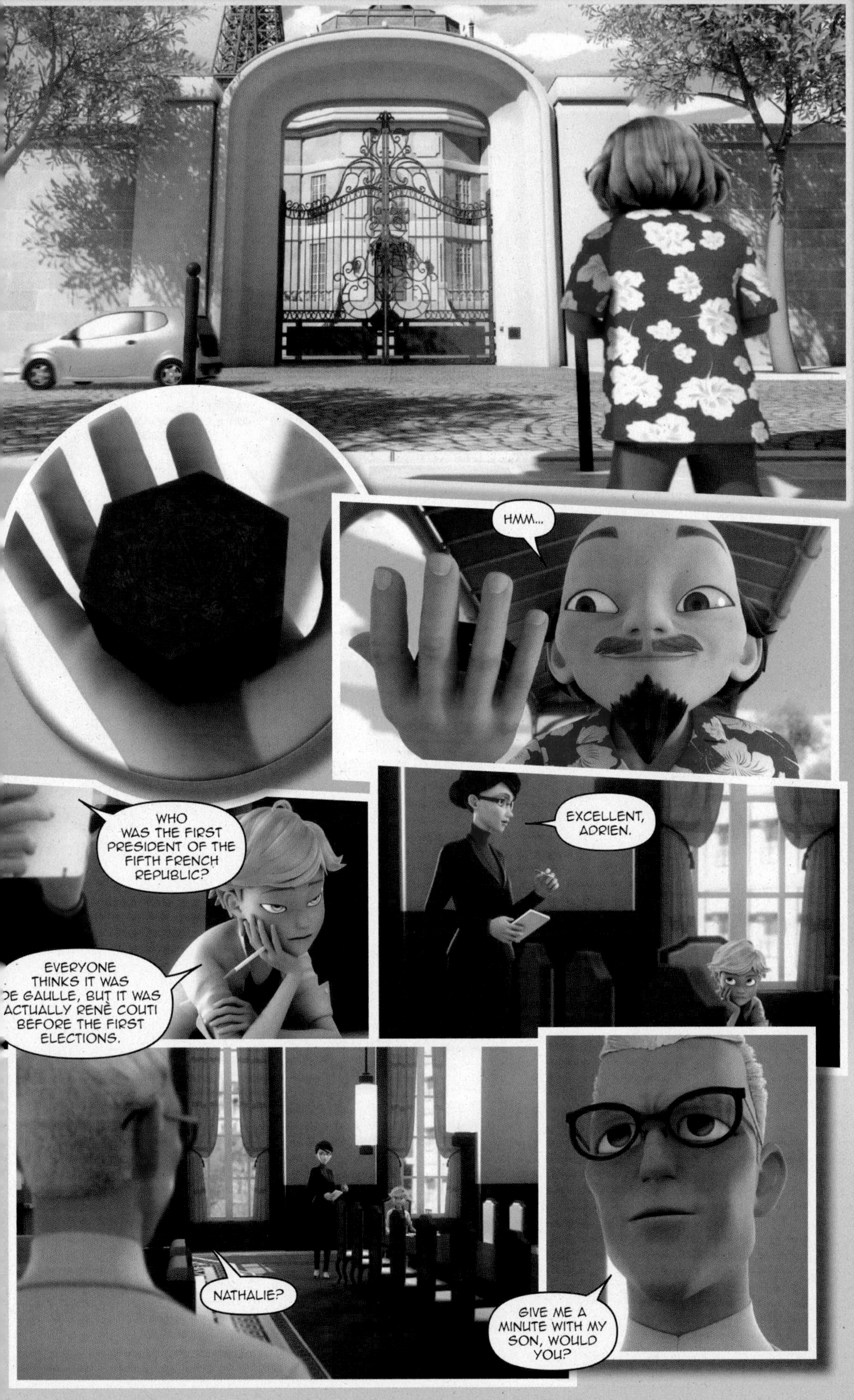
HMM...
WHO WAS THE FIRST PRESIDENT OF THE FIFTH FRENCH REPUBLIC?
EVERYONE THINKS IT WAS DE GAULLE, BUT IT WAS ACTUALLY RENÉ COUTI BEFORE THE FIRST ELECTIONS.
EXCELLENT, ADRIEN.
NATHALIE?
GIVE ME A MINUTE WITH MY SON, WOULD YOU?

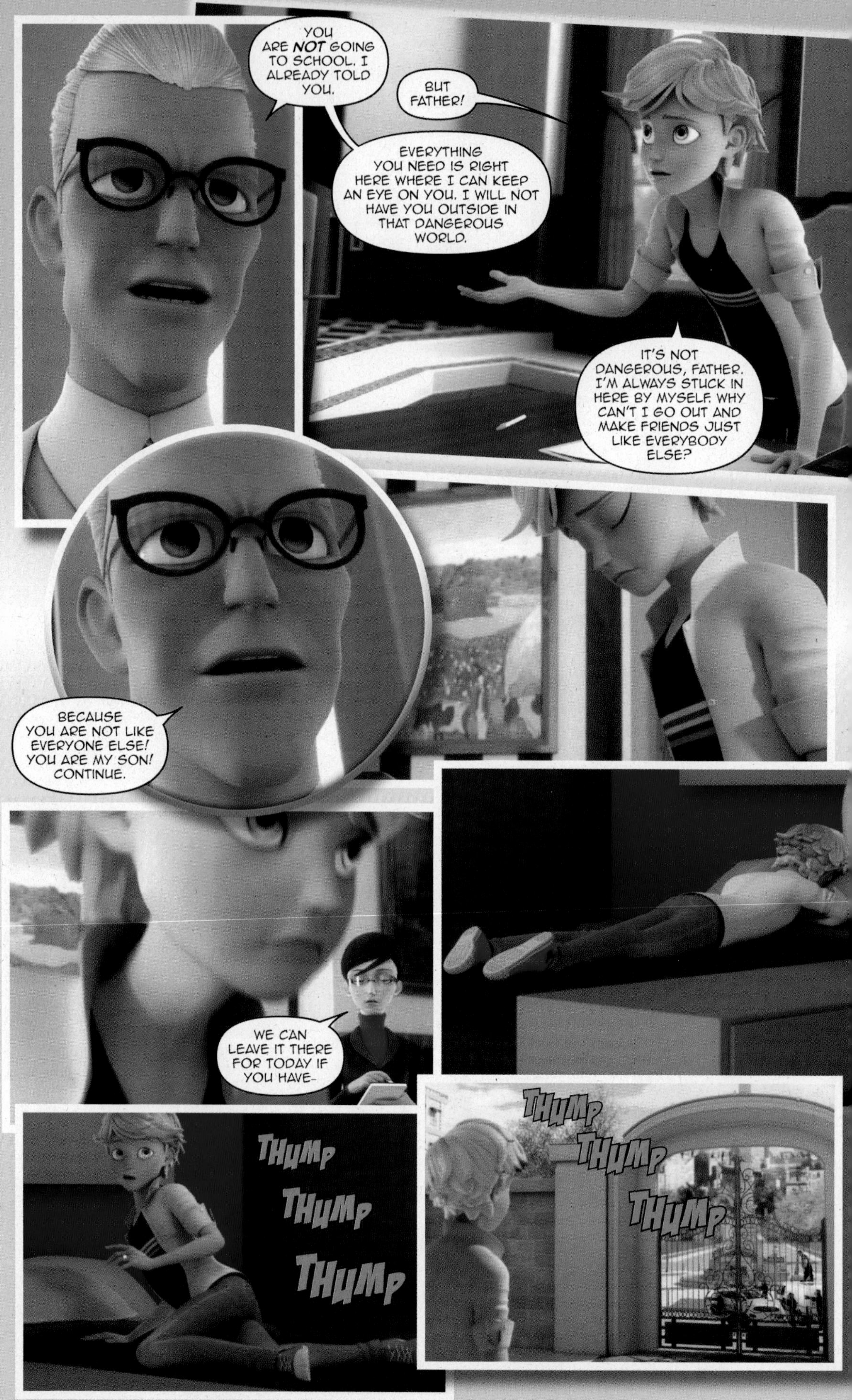

YOU ARE **NOT** GOING TO SCHOOL. I ALREADY TOLD YOU.
BUT FATHER!
EVERYTHING YOU NEED IS RIGHT HERE WHERE I CAN KEEP AN EYE ON YOU. I WILL NOT HAVE YOU OUTSIDE IN THAT DANGEROUS WORLD.
IT'S NOT DANGEROUS, FATHER. I'M ALWAYS STUCK IN HERE BY MYSELF. WHY CAN'T I GO OUT AND MAKE FRIENDS JUST LIKE EVERYBODY ELSE?
BECAUSE YOU ARE NOT LIKE EVERYONE ELSE! YOU ARE MY SON! CONTINUE.
WE CAN LEAVE IT THERE FOR TODAY IF YOU HAVE-
THUMP
THUMP
THUMP
THUMP
THUMP
THUMP

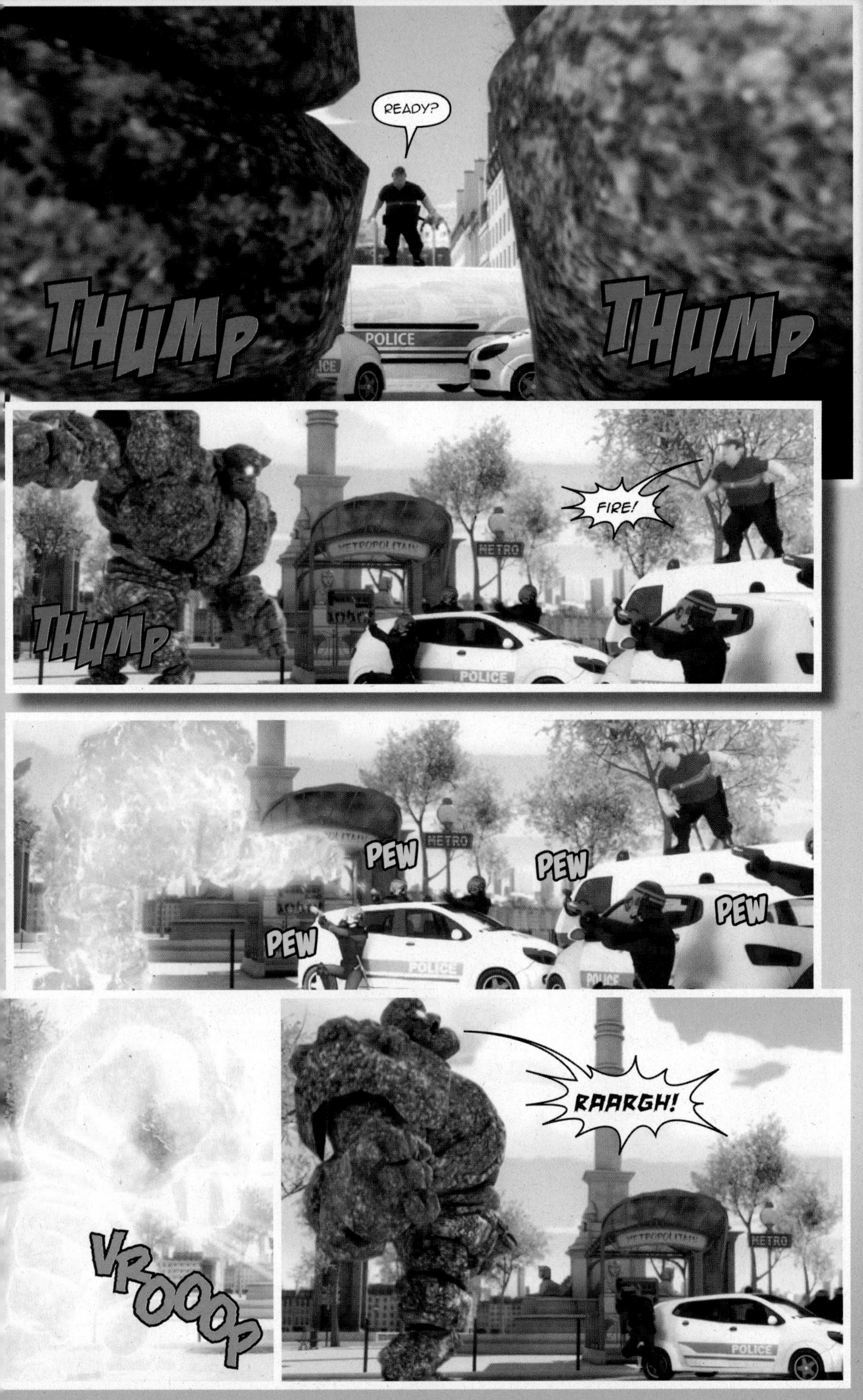
READY?
THUMP
THUMP
FIRE!
THUMP
POLICE
METROPOLITAIN
METRO
POLICE
PEW
PEW
PEW
PEW
VROOOP
RAAARGH!

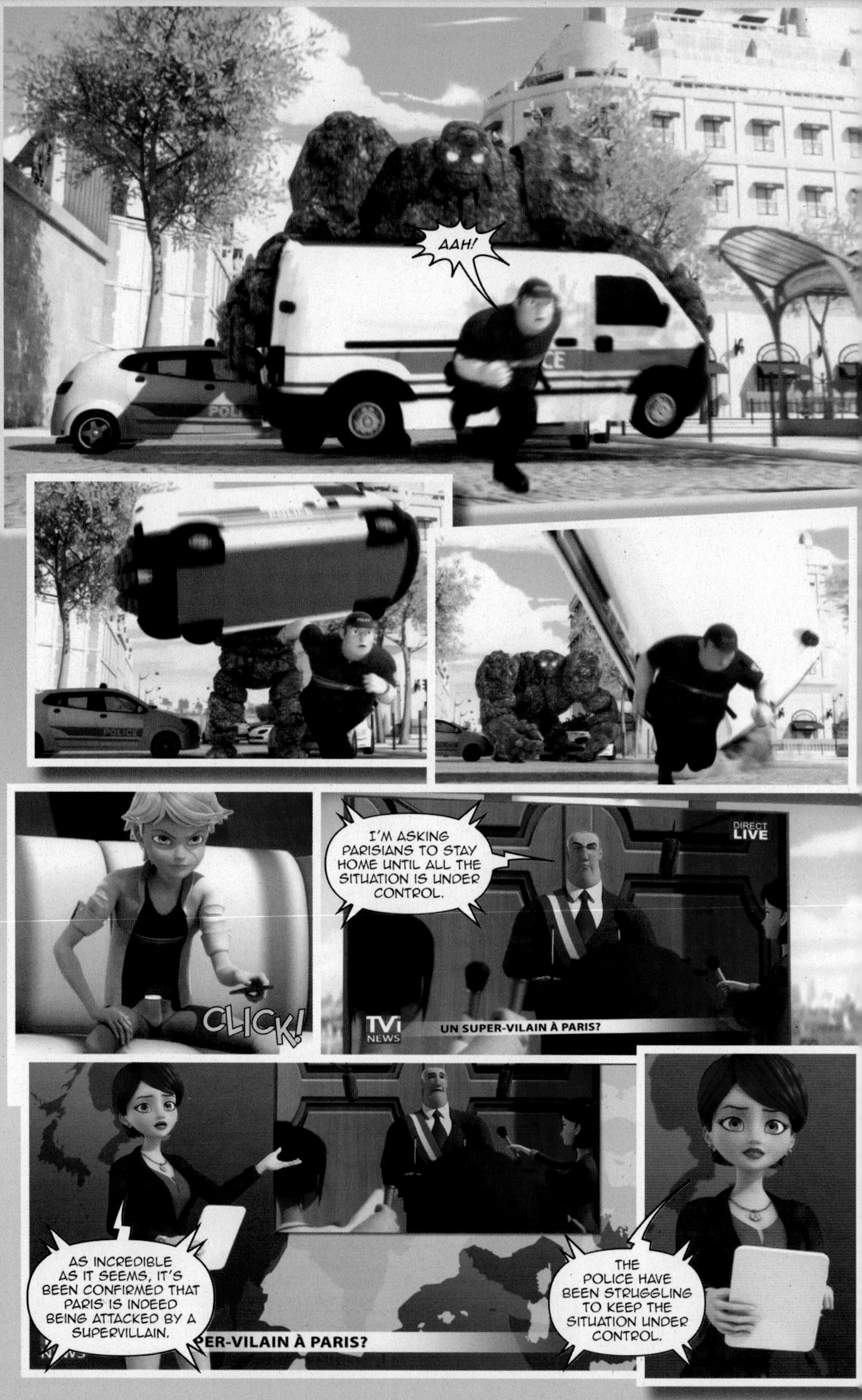
AAH!
CLICK!
DIRECT LIVE
I'M ASKING PARISIANS TO STAY HOME UNTIL ALL THE SITUATION IS UNDER CONTROL.
TVi NEWS
UN SUPER-VILAIN À PARIS?
AS INCREDIBLE AS IT SEEMS, IT'S BEEN CONFIRMED THAT PARIS IS INDEED BEING ATTACKED BY A SUPERVILLAIN.
PER-VILAIN À PARIS?
THE POLICE HAVE BEEN STRUGGLING TO KEEP THE SITUATION UNDER CONTROL.

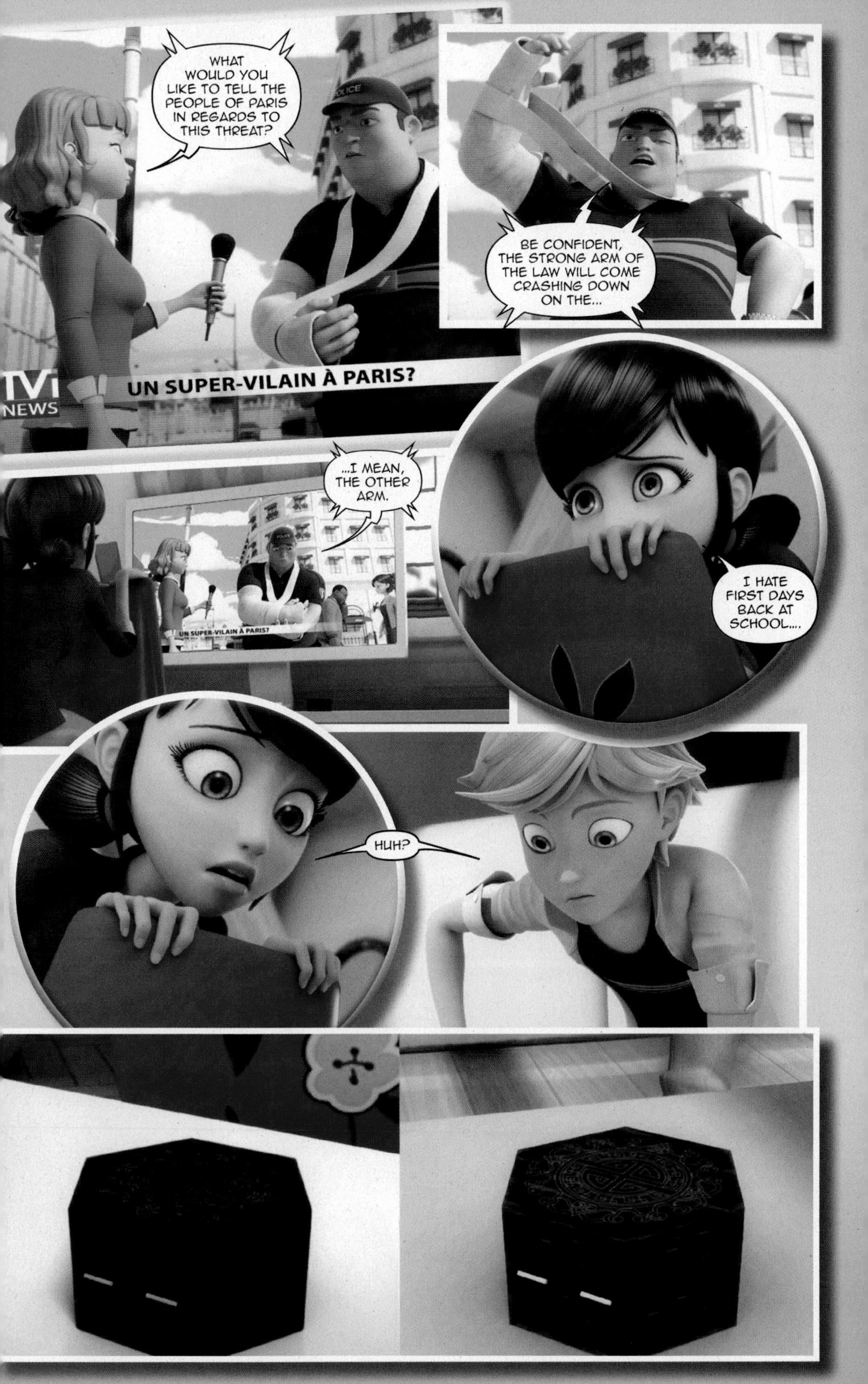
WHAT WOULD YOU LIKE TO TELL THE PEOPLE OF PARIS IN REGARDS TO THIS THREAT?
BE CONFIDENT, THE STRONG ARM OF THE LAW WILL COME CRASHING DOWN ON THE...
TVi NEWS
UN SUPER-VILAIN À PARIS?
...I MEAN, THE OTHER ARM.
UN SUPER-VILAIN À PARIS?
I HATE FIRST DAYS BACK AT SCHOOL....
HUH?

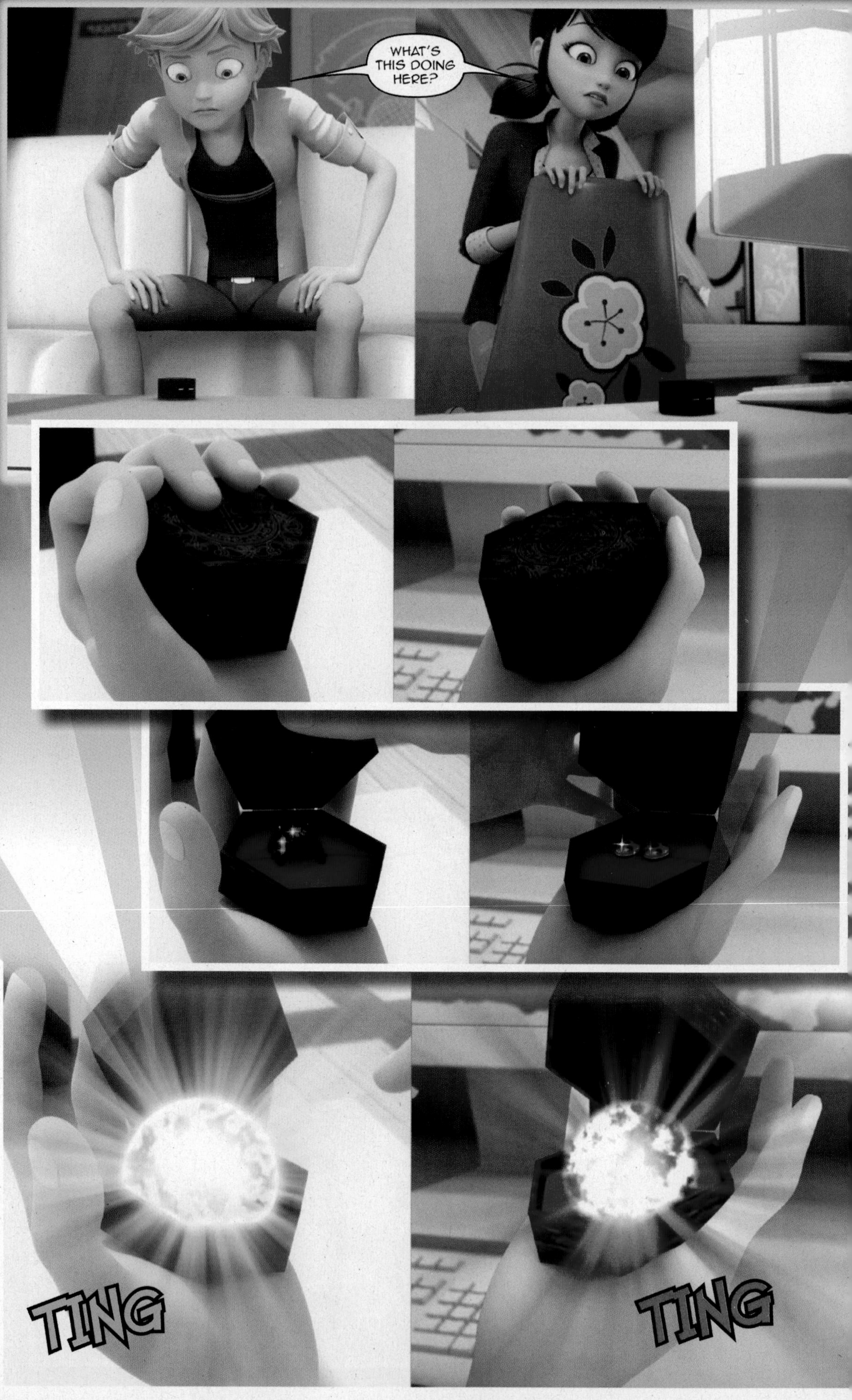
WHAT'S THIS DOING HERE?
TING
TING

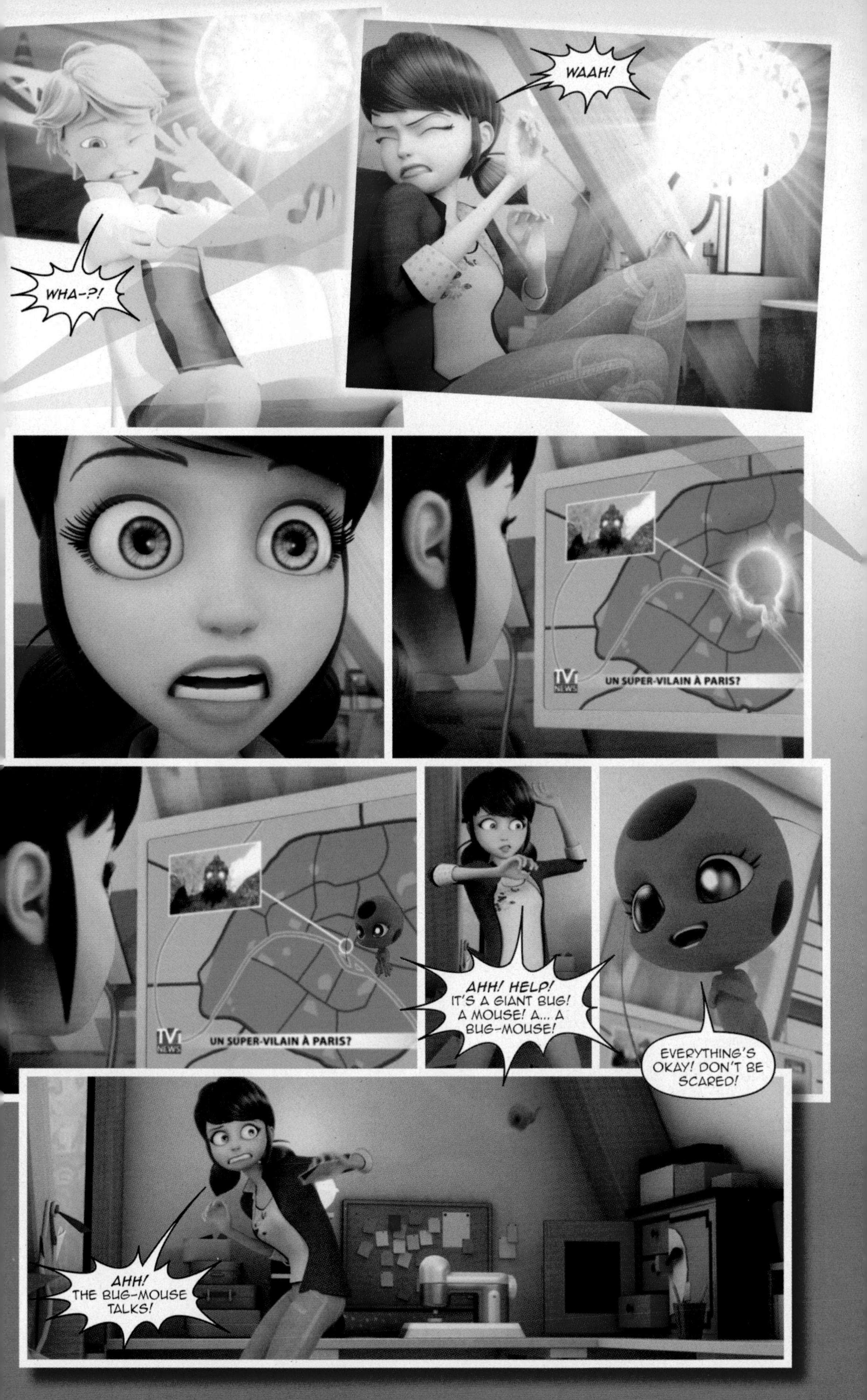
WHA-?!
WAAH!
UN SUPER-VILAIN À PARIS?
UN SUPER-VILAIN À PARIS?
AHH! HELP! IT'S A GIANT BUG! A MOUSE! A... A BUG-MOUSE!
EVERYTHING'S OKAY! DON'T BE SCARED!
AHH! THE BUG-MOUSE TALKS!

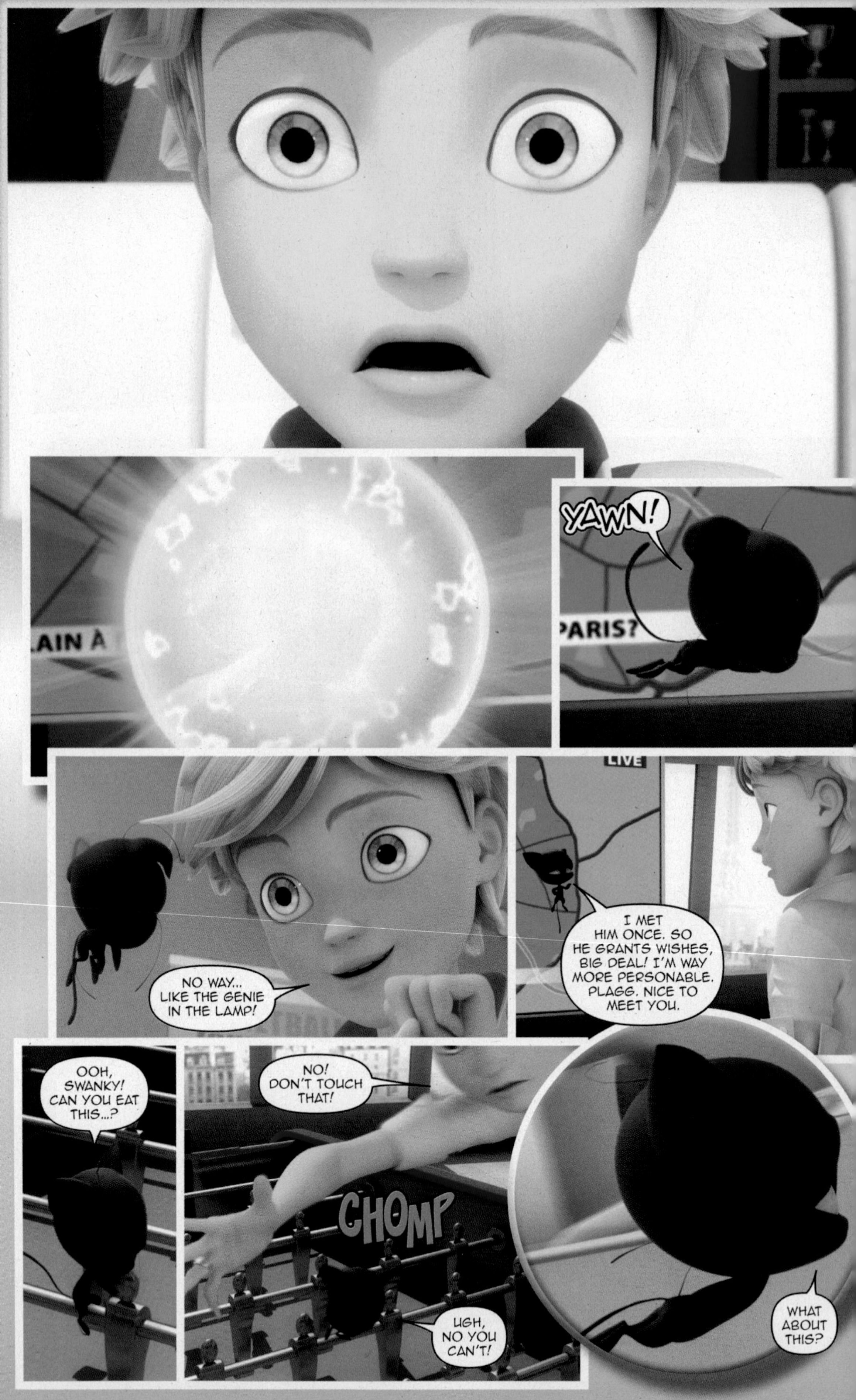

AIN À
YAWN!
PARIS?
NO WAY...
LIKE THE GENIE
IN THE LAMP!
LIVE
I MET
HIM ONCE. SO
HE GRANTS WISHES,
BIG DEAL! I'M WAY
MORE PERSONABLE.
PLAGG. NICE TO
MEET YOU.
OOH,
SWANKY!
CAN YOU EAT
THIS...?
NO!
DON'T TOUCH
THAT!
CHOMP
UGH,
NO YOU
CAN'T!
WHAT
ABOUT
THIS?

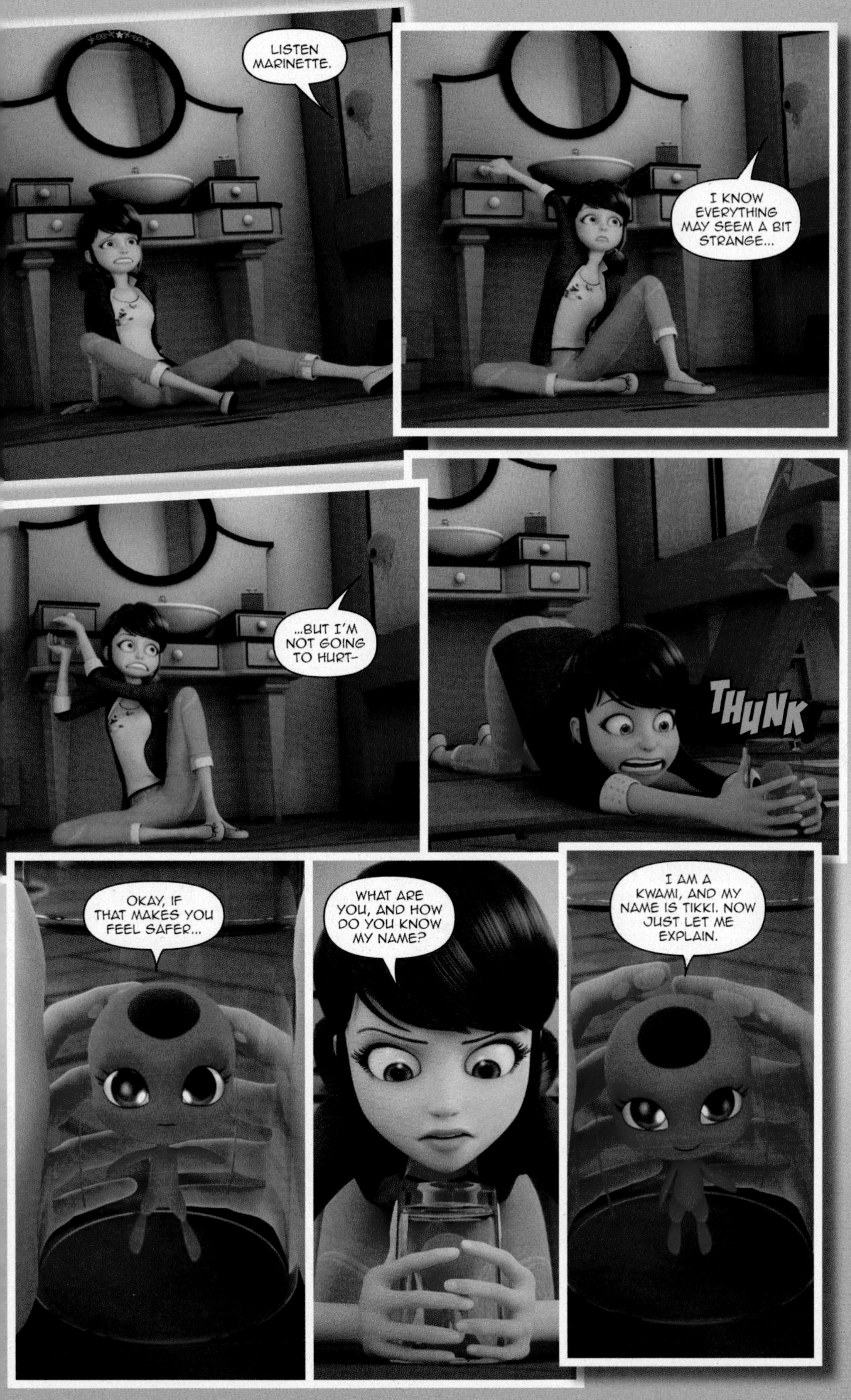
LISTEN MARINETTE.
I KNOW EVERYTHING MAY SEEM A BIT STRANGE...
...BUT I'M NOT GOING TO HURT-
THUNK
OKAY, IF THAT MAKES YOU FEEL SAFER...
WHAT ARE YOU, AND HOW DO YOU KNOW MY NAME?
I AM A KWAMI, AND MY NAME IS TIKKI. NOW JUST LET ME EXPLAIN.

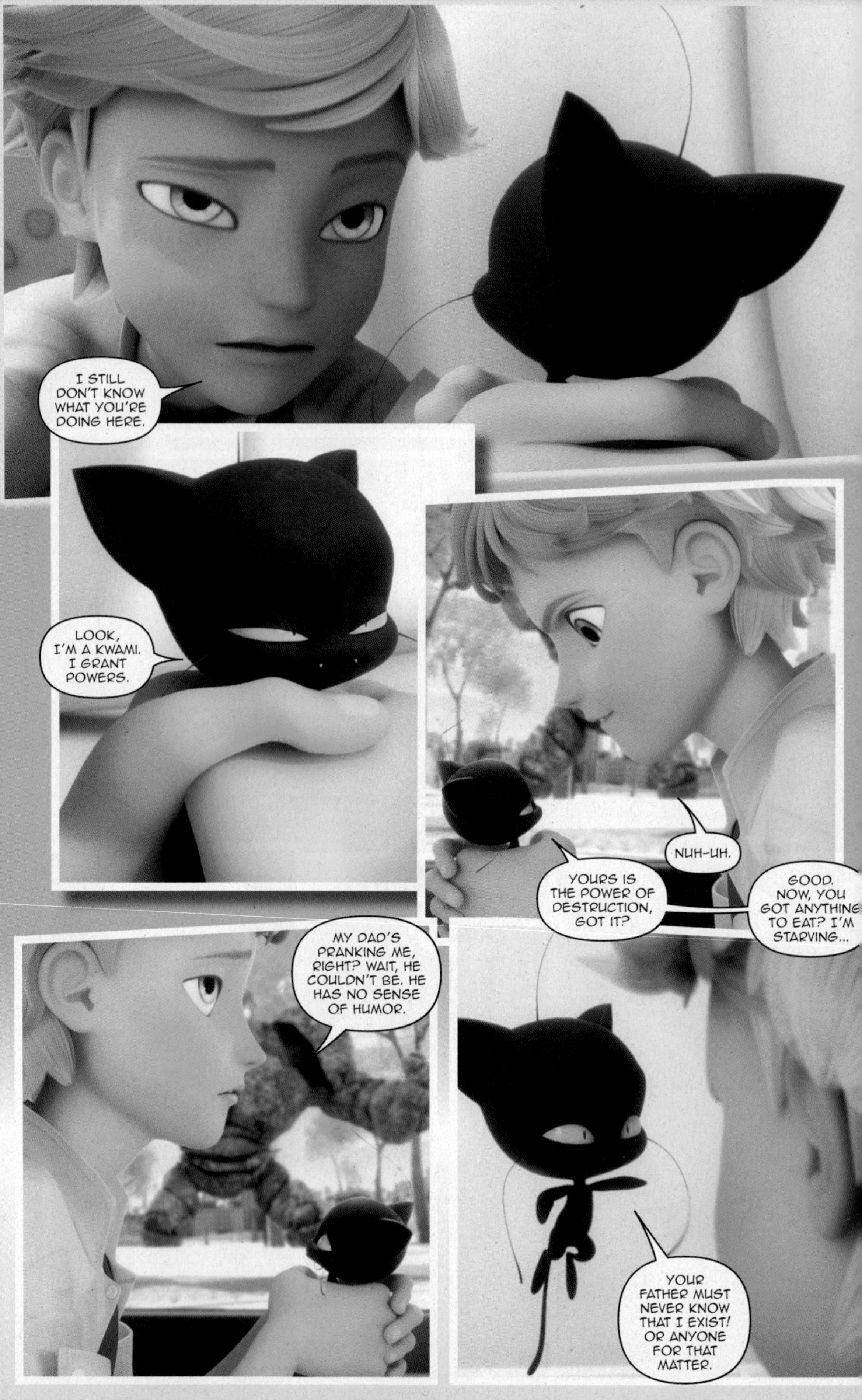
I STILL DON'T KNOW WHAT YOU'RE DOING HERE.
LOOK, I'M A KWAMI. I GRANT POWERS.
YOURS IS THE POWER OF DESTRUCTION, GOT IT?
NUH-UH.
GOOD. NOW, YOU GOT ANYTHING TO EAT? I'M STARVING...
MY DAD'S PRANKING ME, RIGHT? WAIT, HE COULDN'T BE. HE HAS NO SENSE OF HUMOR.
YOUR FATHER MUST NEVER KNOW THAT I EXIST! OR ANYONE FOR THAT MATTER.

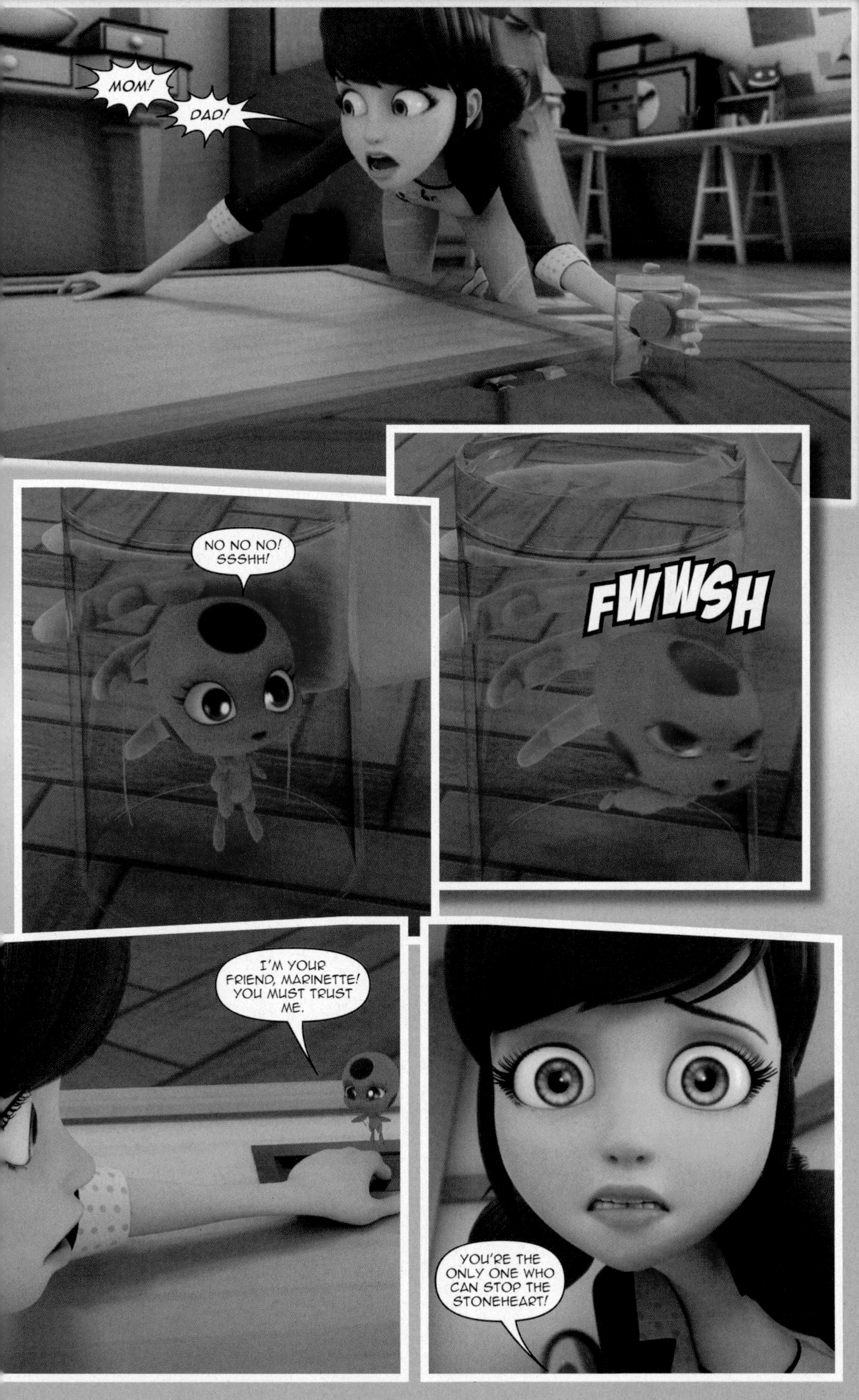
MOM!
DAD!
NO NO NO! SSSHH!
FWWSH
I'M YOUR FRIEND, MARINETTE! YOU MUST TRUST ME.
YOU'RE THE ONLY ONE WHO CAN STOP THE STONEHEART!

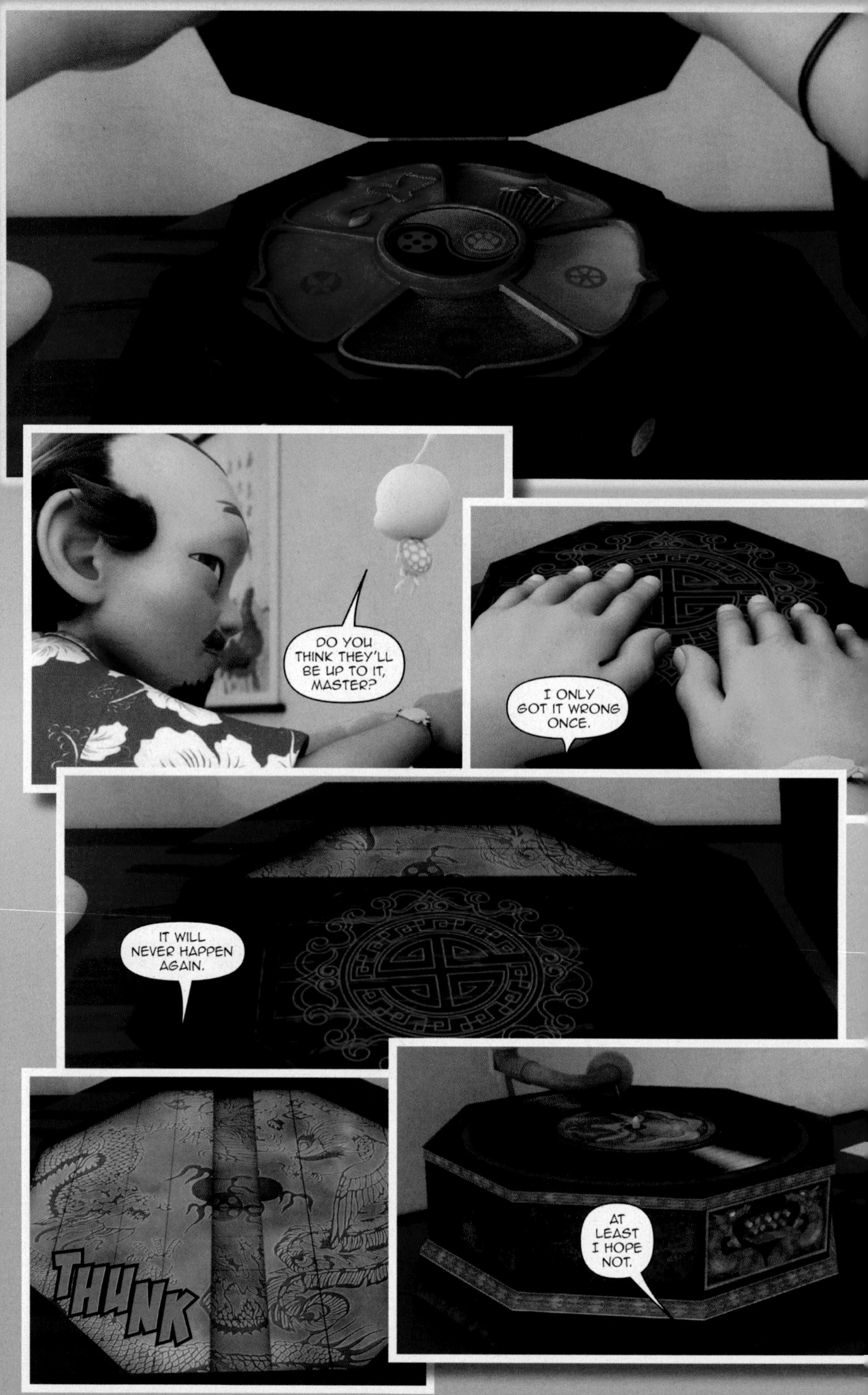
DO YOU THINK THEY'LL BE UP TO IT, MASTER?
I ONLY GOT IT WRONG ONCE.
IT WILL NEVER HAPPEN AGAIN.
THUNK
AT LEAST I HOPE NOT.

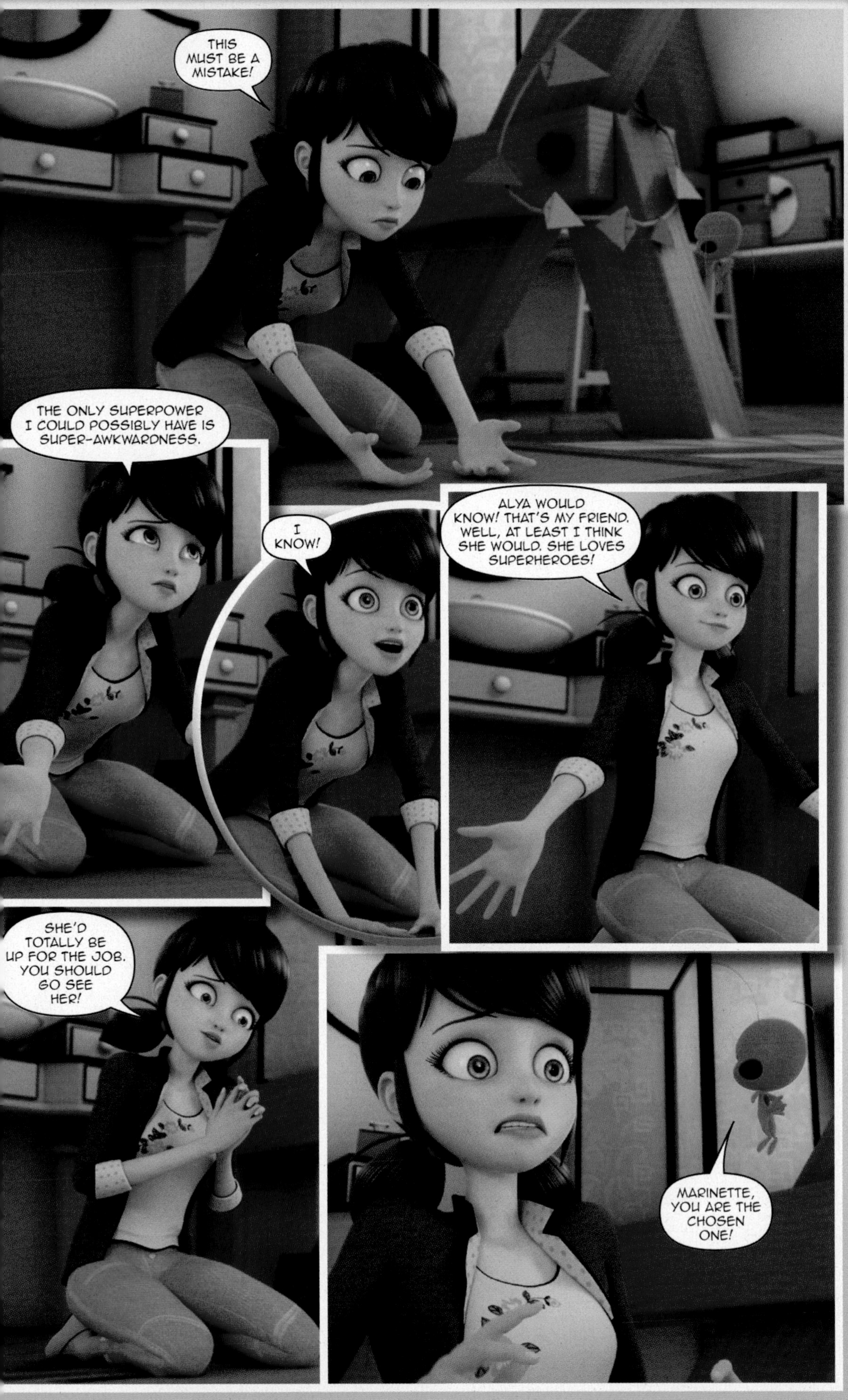
THIS MUST BE A MISTAKE!
THE ONLY SUPERPOWER I COULD POSSIBLY HAVE IS SUPER-AWKWARDNESS.
I KNOW!
ALYA WOULD KNOW! THAT'S MY FRIEND. WELL, AT LEAST I THINK SHE WOULD. SHE LOVES SUPERHEROES!
SHE'D TOTALLY BE UP FOR THE JOB. YOU SHOULD GO SEE HER!
MARINETTE, YOU ARE THE CHOSEN ONE!

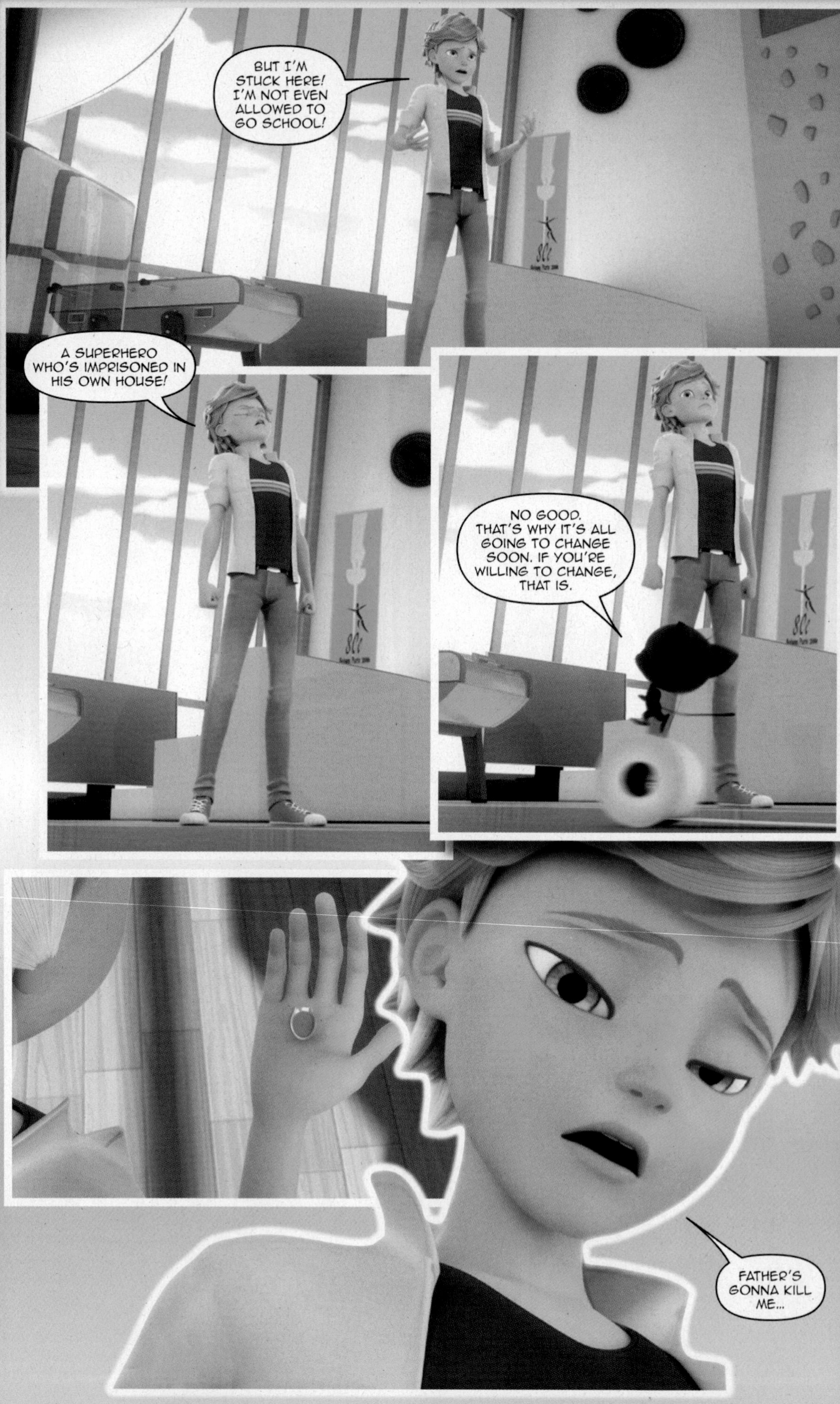
BUT I'M STUCK HERE! I'M NOT EVEN ALLOWED TO GO SCHOOL!
A SUPERHERO WHO'S IMPRISONED IN HIS OWN HOUSE!
NO GOOD. THAT'S WHY IT'S ALL GOING TO CHANGE SOON. IF YOU'RE WILLING TO CHANGE, THAT IS.
FATHER'S GONNA KILL ME...

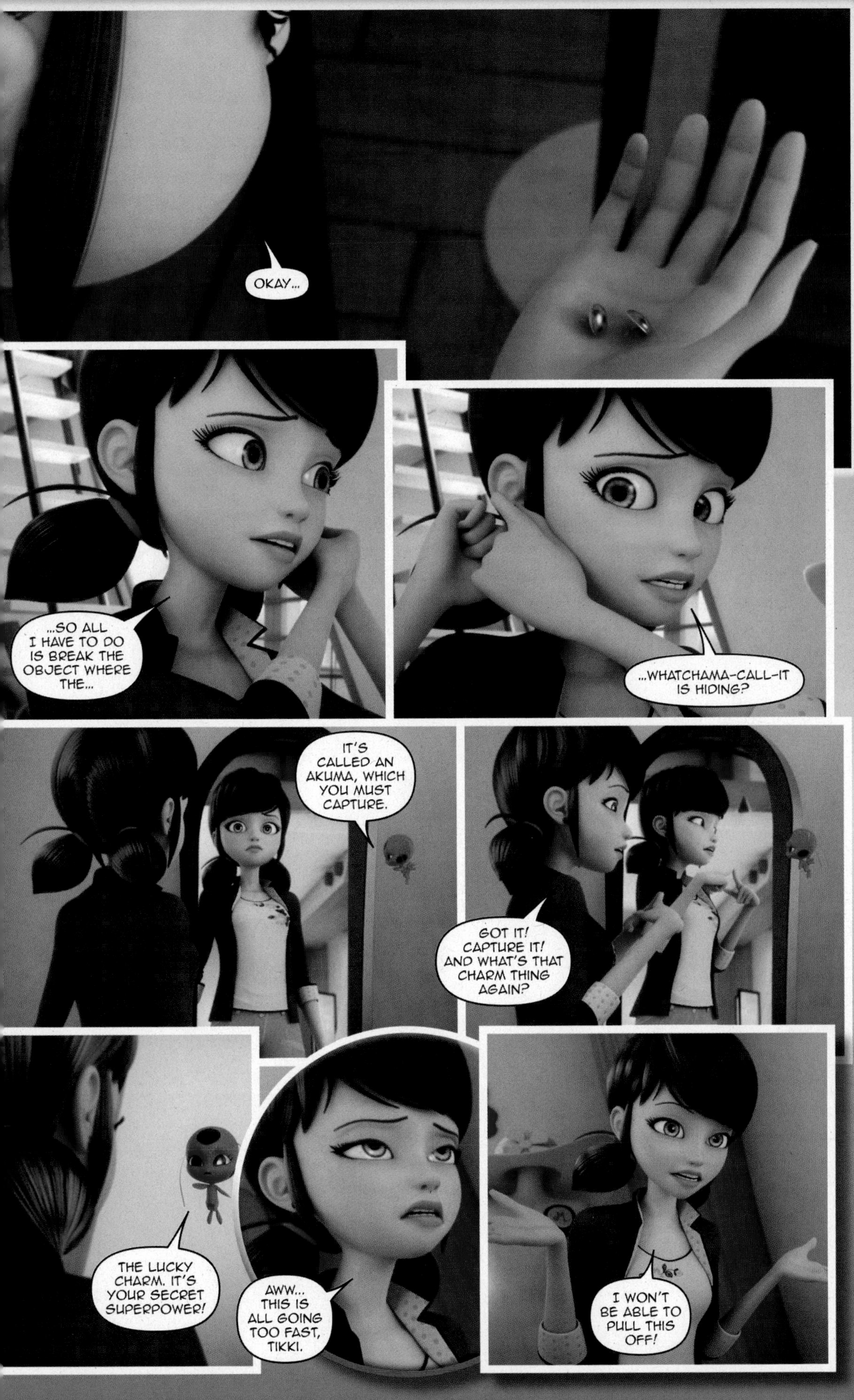
OKAY...
...SO ALL I HAVE TO DO IS BREAK THE OBJECT WHERE THE...
...WHATCHAMA-CALL-IT IS HIDING?
IT'S CALLED AN AKUMA, WHICH YOU MUST CAPTURE.
GOT IT! CAPTURE IT! AND WHAT'S THAT CHARM THING AGAIN?
THE LUCKY CHARM. IT'S YOUR SECRET SUPERPOWER!
AWW... THIS IS ALL GOING TOO FAST, TIKKI.
I WON'T BE ABLE TO PULL THIS OFF!

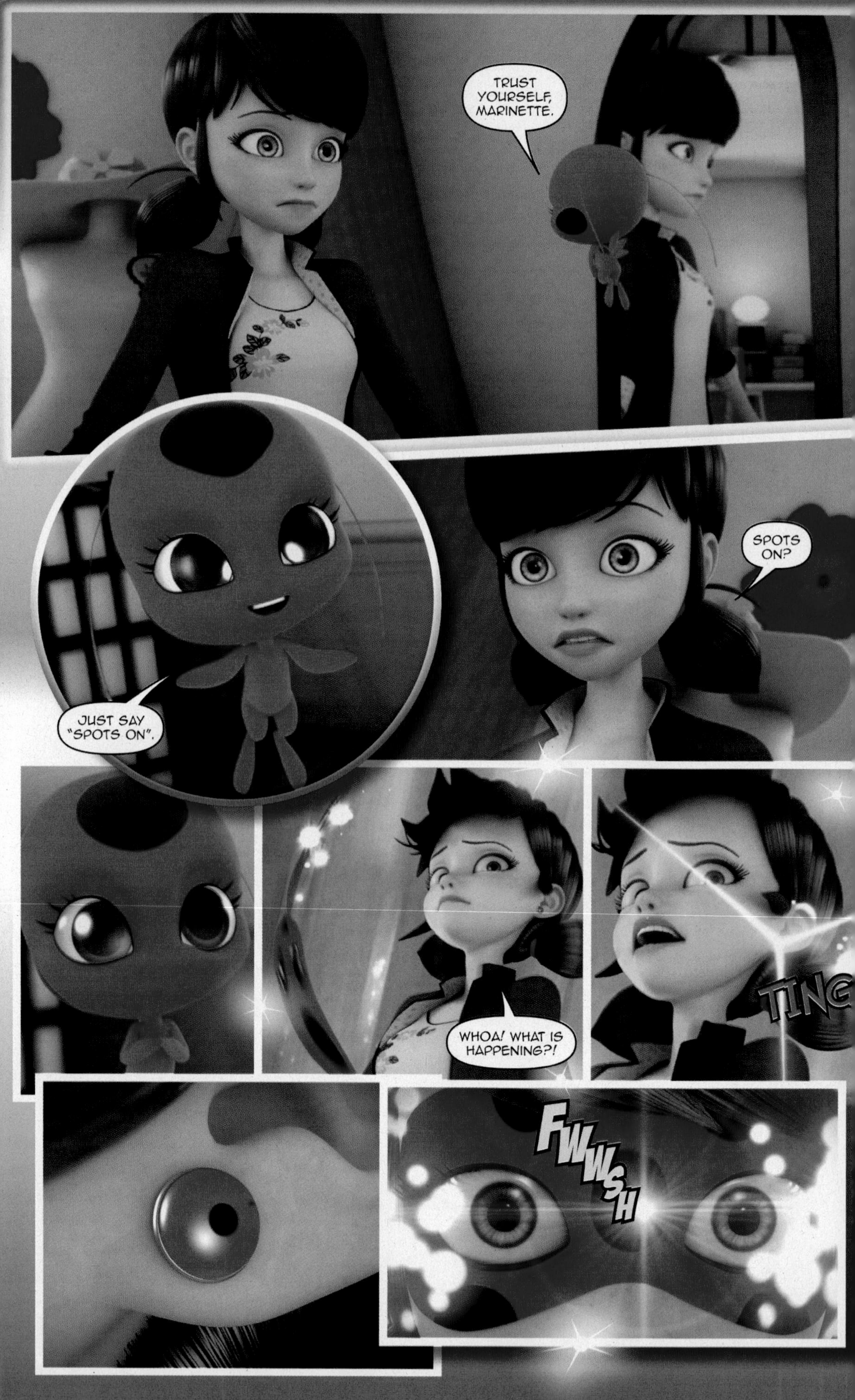
TRUST YOURSELF, MARINETTE.
JUST SAY "SPOTS ON".
SPOTS ON?
WHOA! WHAT IS HAPPENING?!
TING
FWWSH

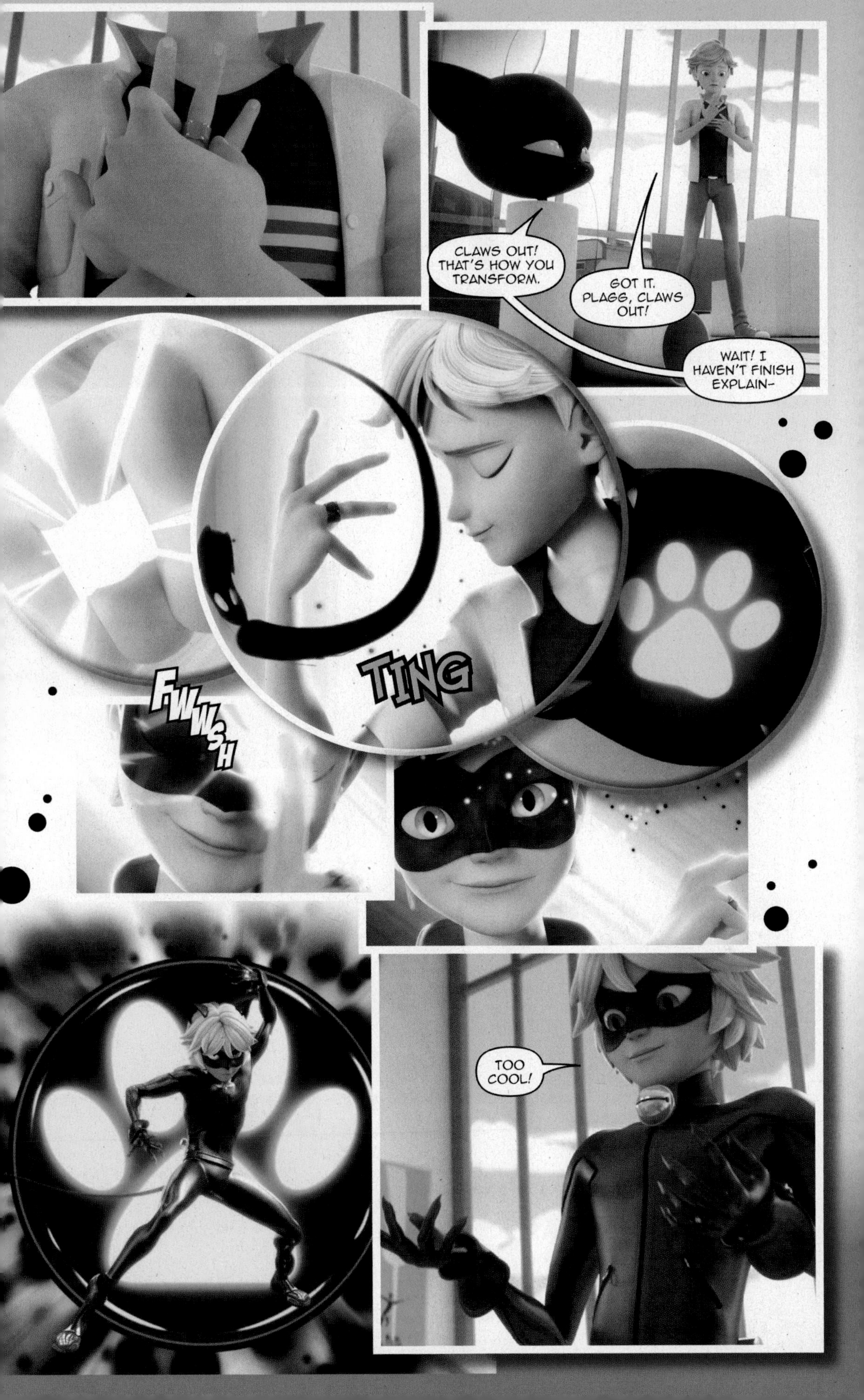
CLAWS OUT! THAT'S HOW YOU TRANSFORM.
GOT IT. PLAGG, CLAWS OUT!
WAIT! I HAVEN'T FINISH EXPLAIN-
TING
FWWSH
TOO COOL!

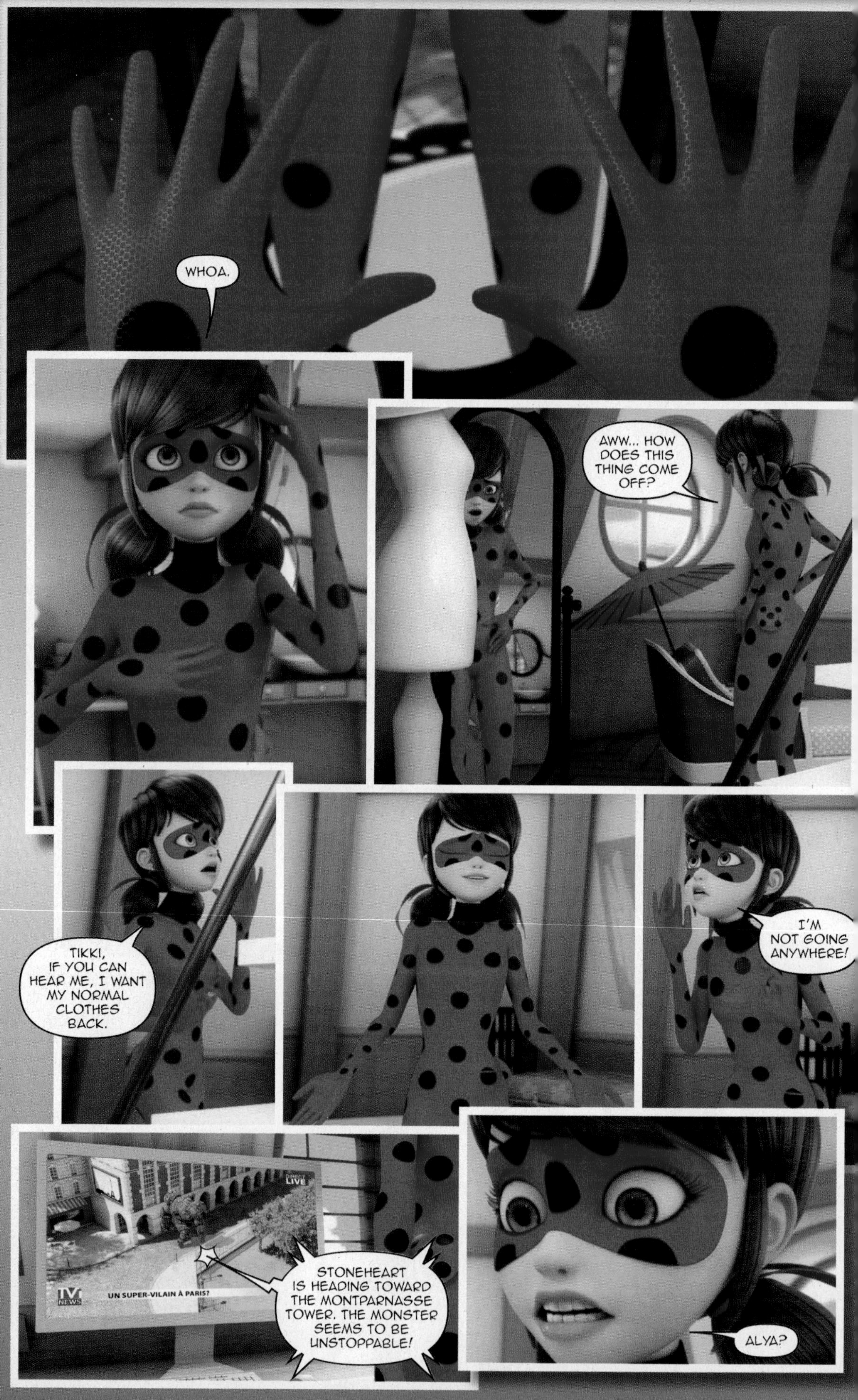
WHOA.
AWW... HOW DOES THIS THING COME OFF?
TIKKI, IF YOU CAN HEAR ME, I WANT MY NORMAL CLOTHES BACK.
I'M NOT GOING ANYWHERE!
DIRECT LIVE
TV NEWS
UN SUPER-VILAIN À PARIS?
STONEHEART IS HEADING TOWARD THE MONTPARNASSE TOWER. THE MONSTER SEEMS TO BE UNSTOPPABLE!
ALYA?

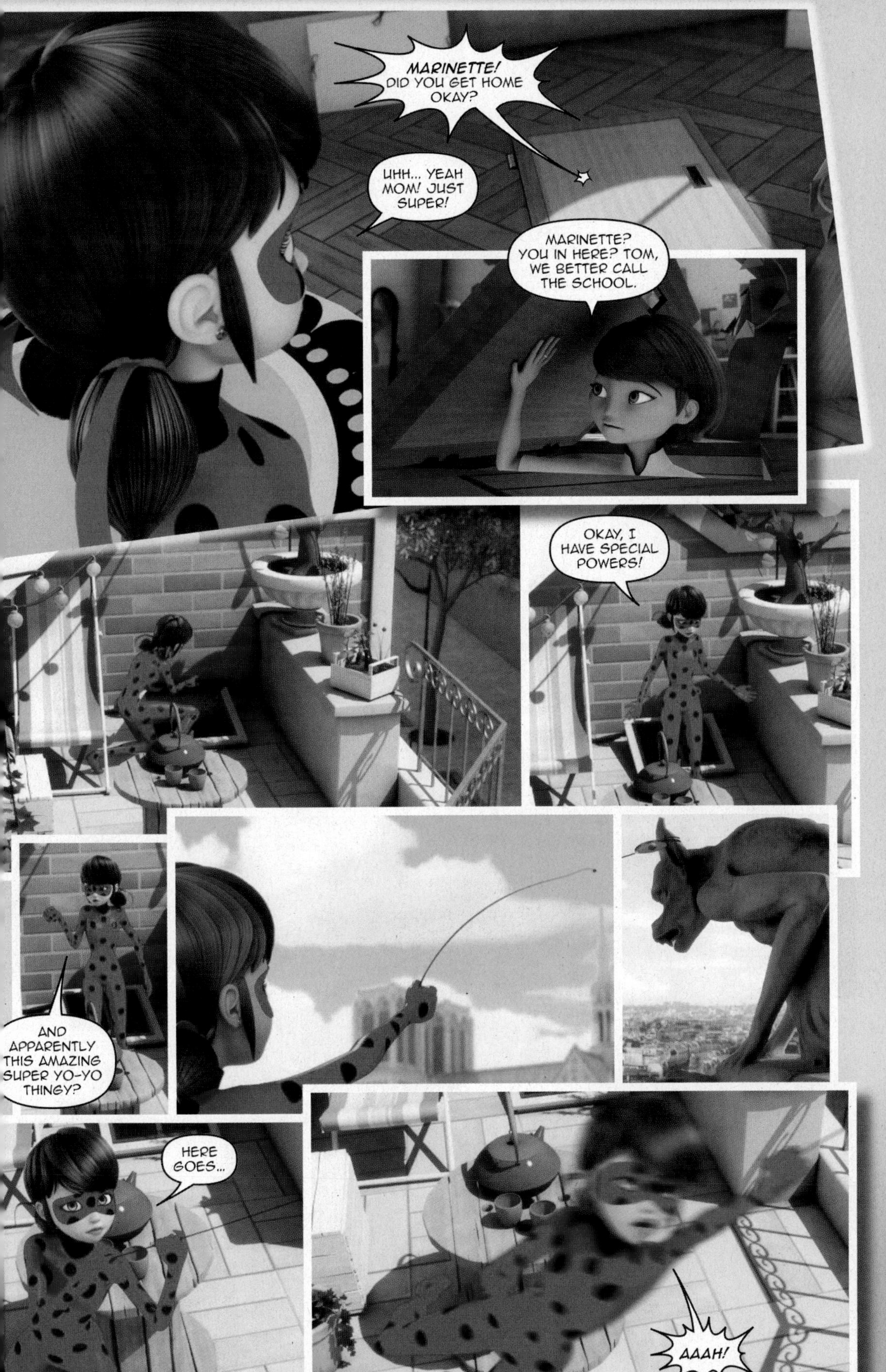
MARINETTE! DID YOU GET HOME OKAY?
UHH... YEAH MOM! JUST SUPER!
MARINETTE? YOU IN HERE? TOM, WE BETTER CALL THE SCHOOL.
OKAY, I HAVE SPECIAL POWERS!
AND APPARENTLY THIS AMAZING SUPER YO-YO THINGY?
HERE GOES...
AAAH!

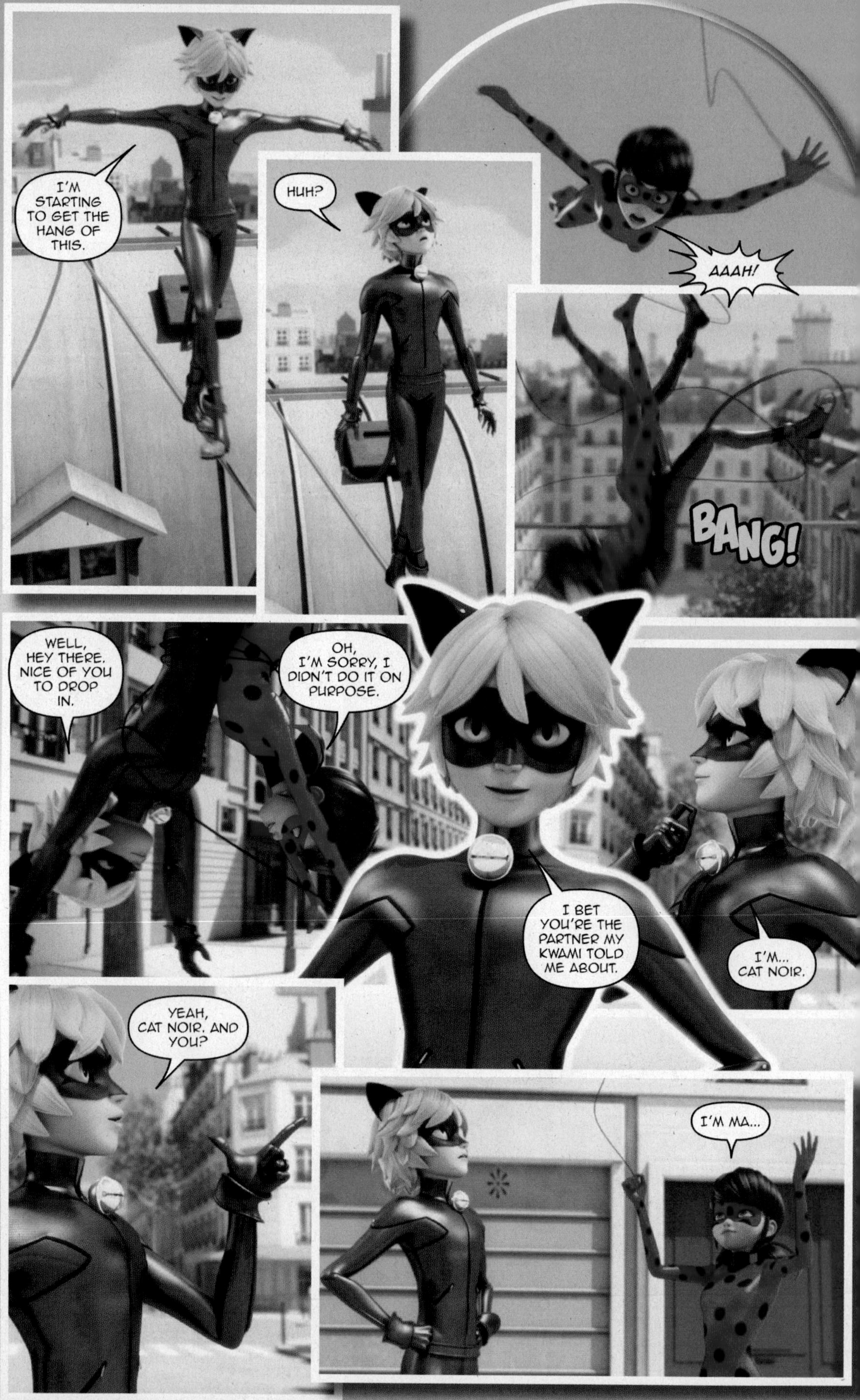
I'M STARTING TO GET THE HANG OF THIS.
HUH?
AAAH!
BANG!
WELL, HEY THERE. NICE OF YOU TO DROP IN.
OH, I'M SORRY, I DIDN'T DO IT ON PURPOSE.
I BET YOU'RE THE PARTNER MY KWAMI TOLD ME ABOUT.
I'M... CAT NOIR.
YEAH, CAT NOIR. AND YOU?
I'M MA...

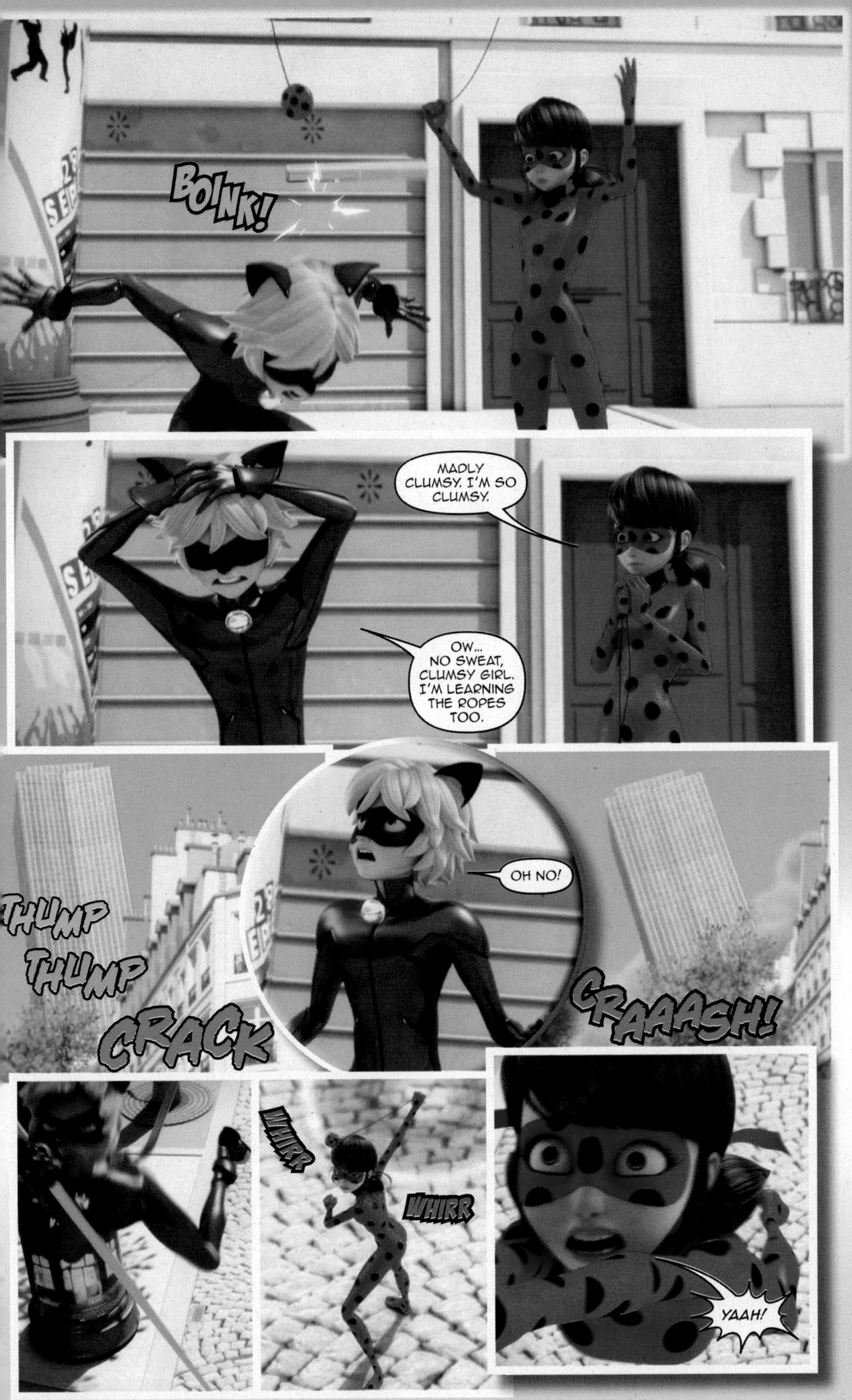
BOINK!
MADLY CLUMSY. I'M SO CLUMSY.
OW... NO SWEAT, CLUMSY GIRL. I'M LEARNING THE ROPES TOO.
THUMP
THUMP
CRACK
OH NO!
CRAAASH!
WHIRR
WHIRR
YAAH!

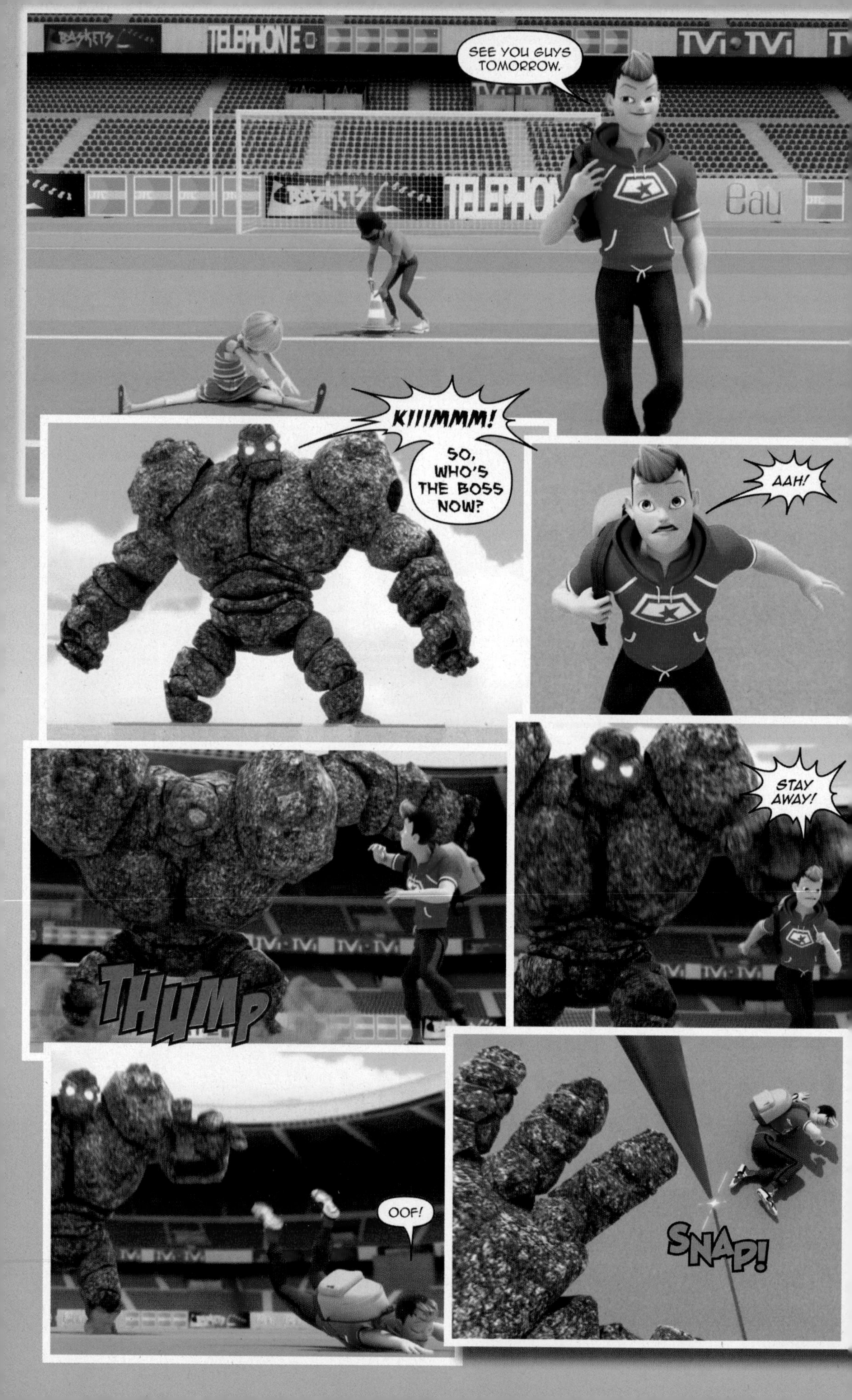

SEE YOU GUYS TOMORROW.
KIIIMMM!
SO, WHO'S THE BOSS NOW?
AAH!
THUMP
STAY AWAY!
OOF!
SNAP!

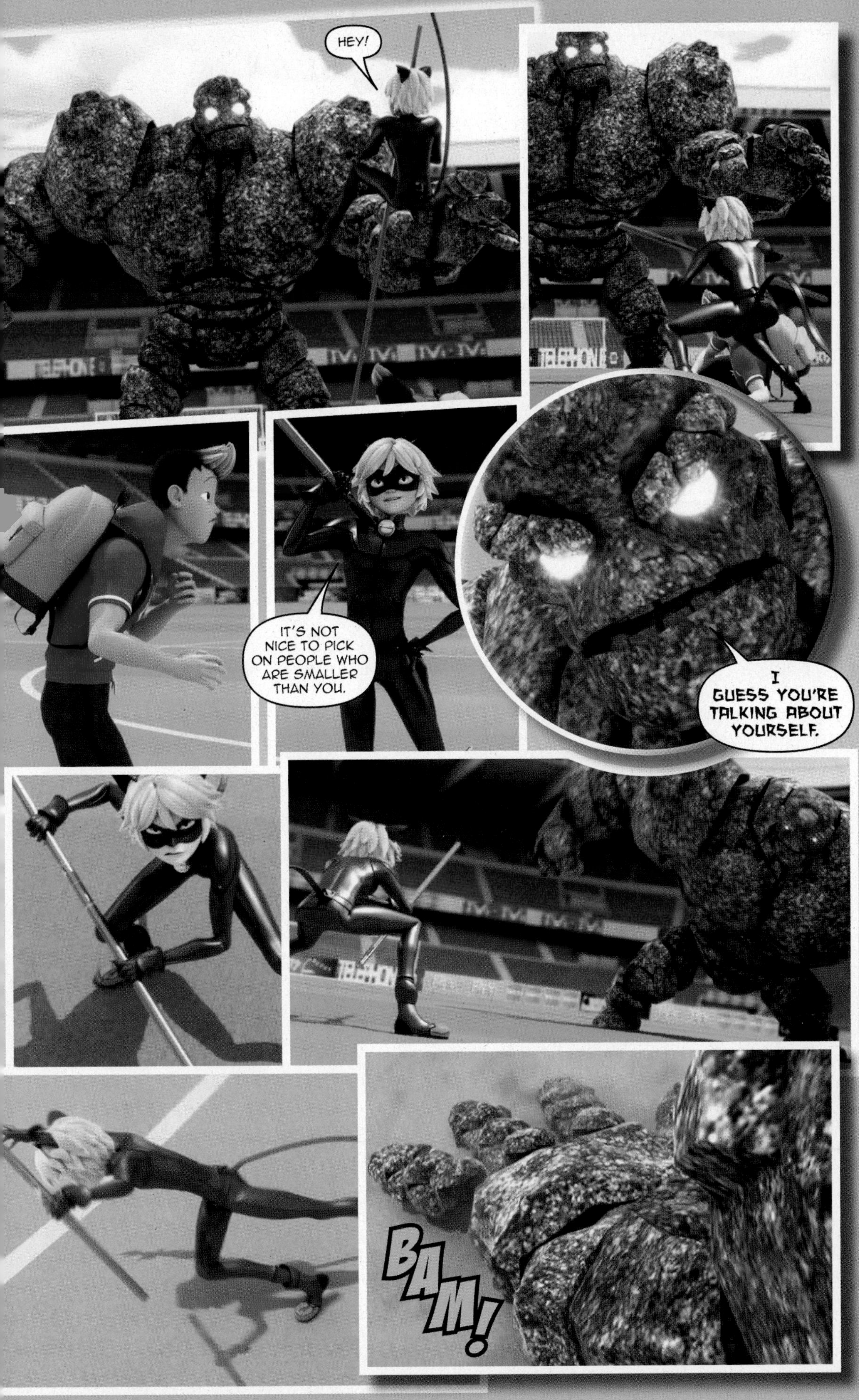
HEY!
IT'S NOT NICE TO PICK ON PEOPLE WHO ARE SMALLER THAN YOU.
I GUESS YOU'RE TALKING ABOUT YOURSELF.
BAM!

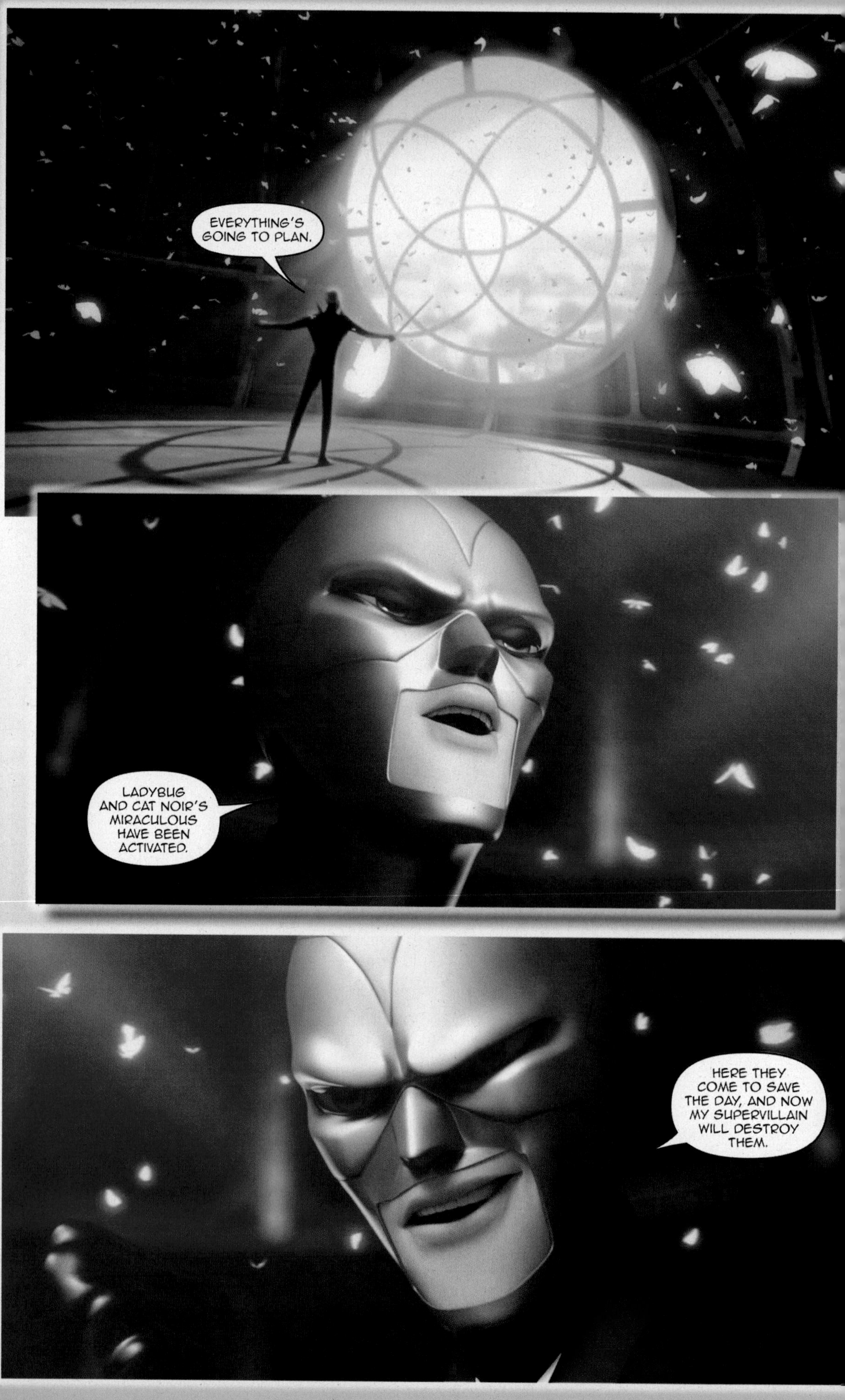
EVERYTHING'S GOING TO PLAN.
LADYBUG AND CAT NOIR'S MIRACULOUS HAVE BEEN ACTIVATED.
HERE THEY COME TO SAVE THE DAY, AND NOW MY SUPERVILLAIN WILL DESTROY THEM.

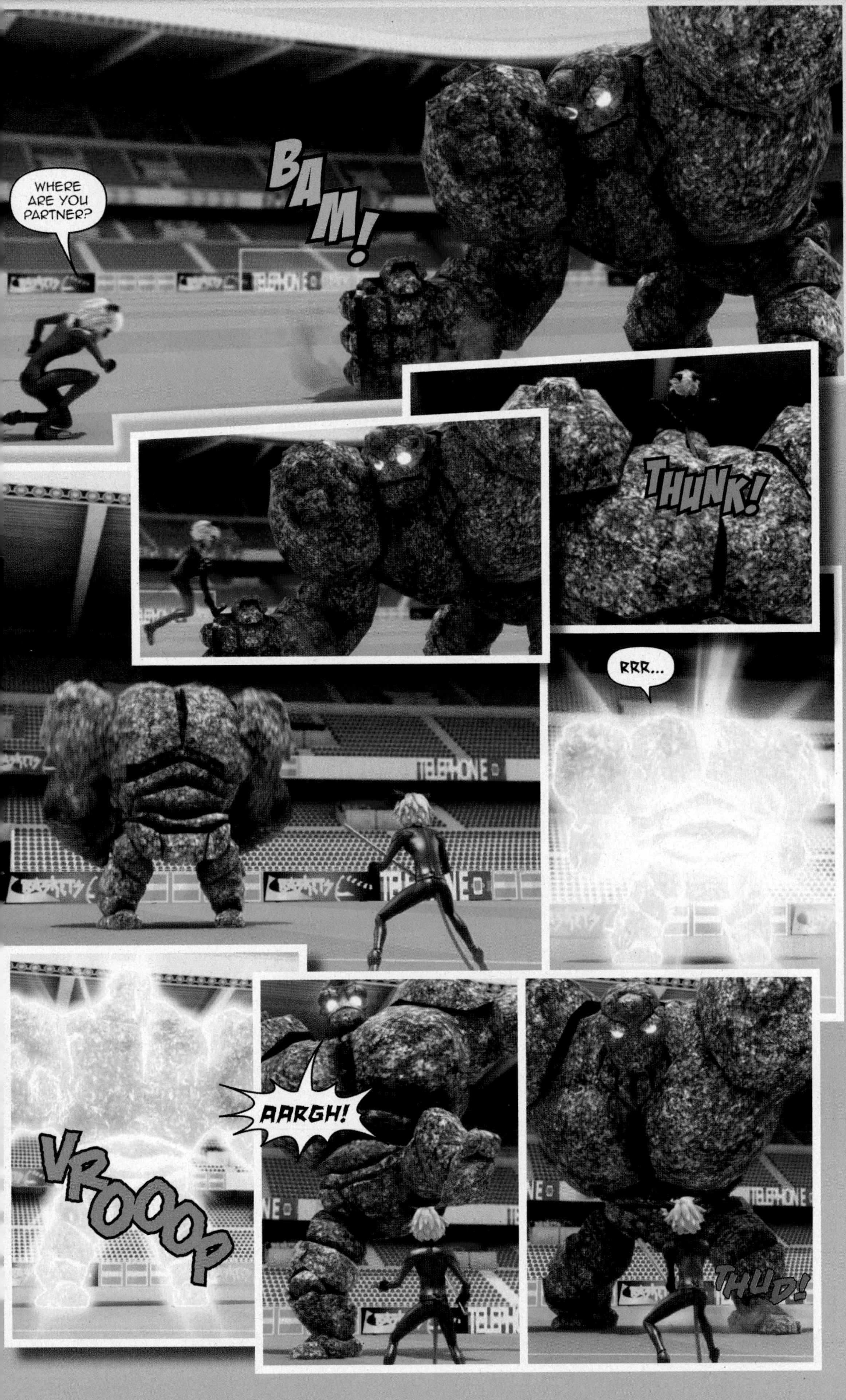
WHERE ARE YOU PARTNER?
BAM!
THUNK!
RRR...
VROOOP
AARGH!
THUD!

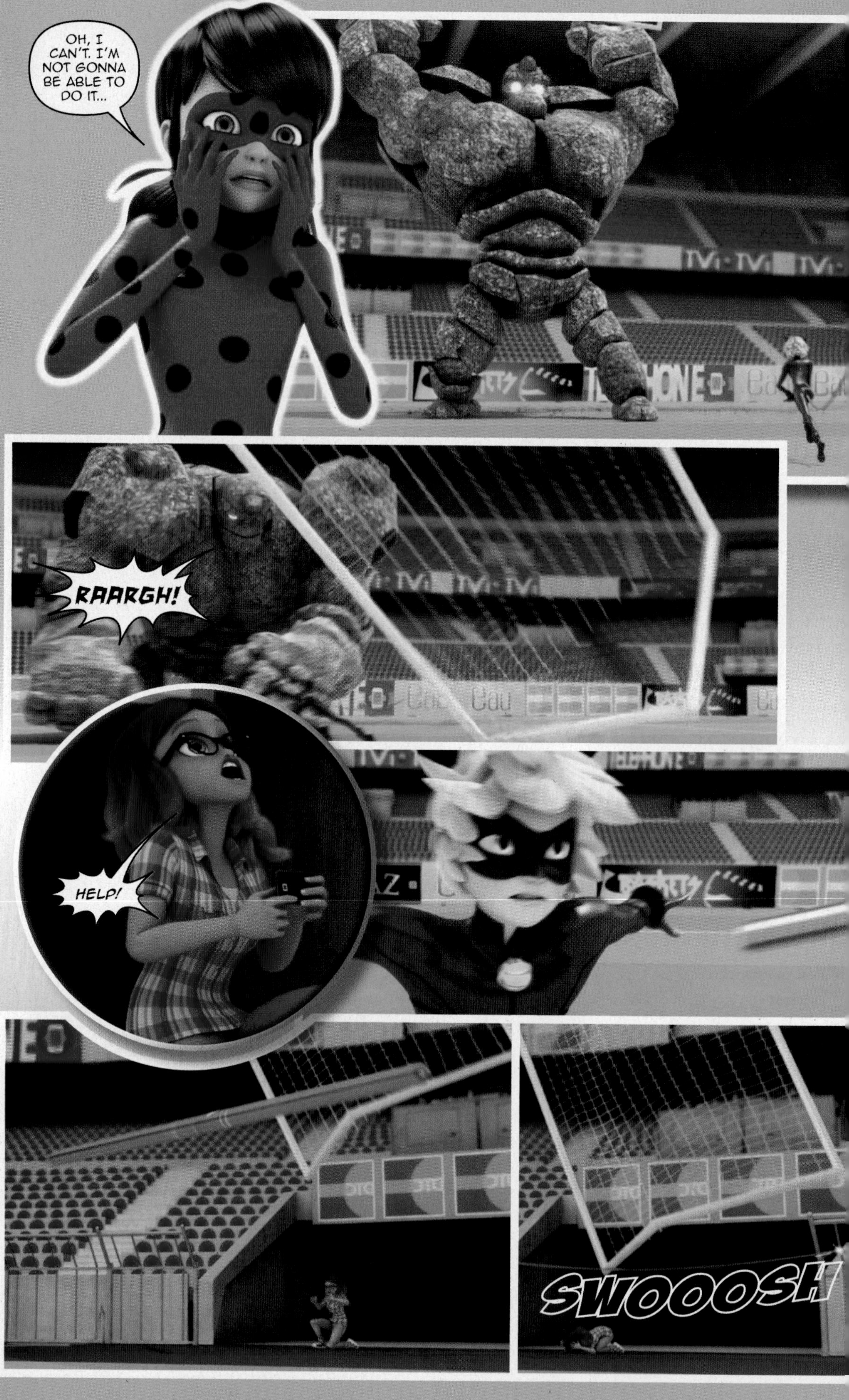
OH, I CAN'T. I'M NOT GONNA BE ABLE TO DO IT...
RAARGH!
HELP!
SWOOOSH

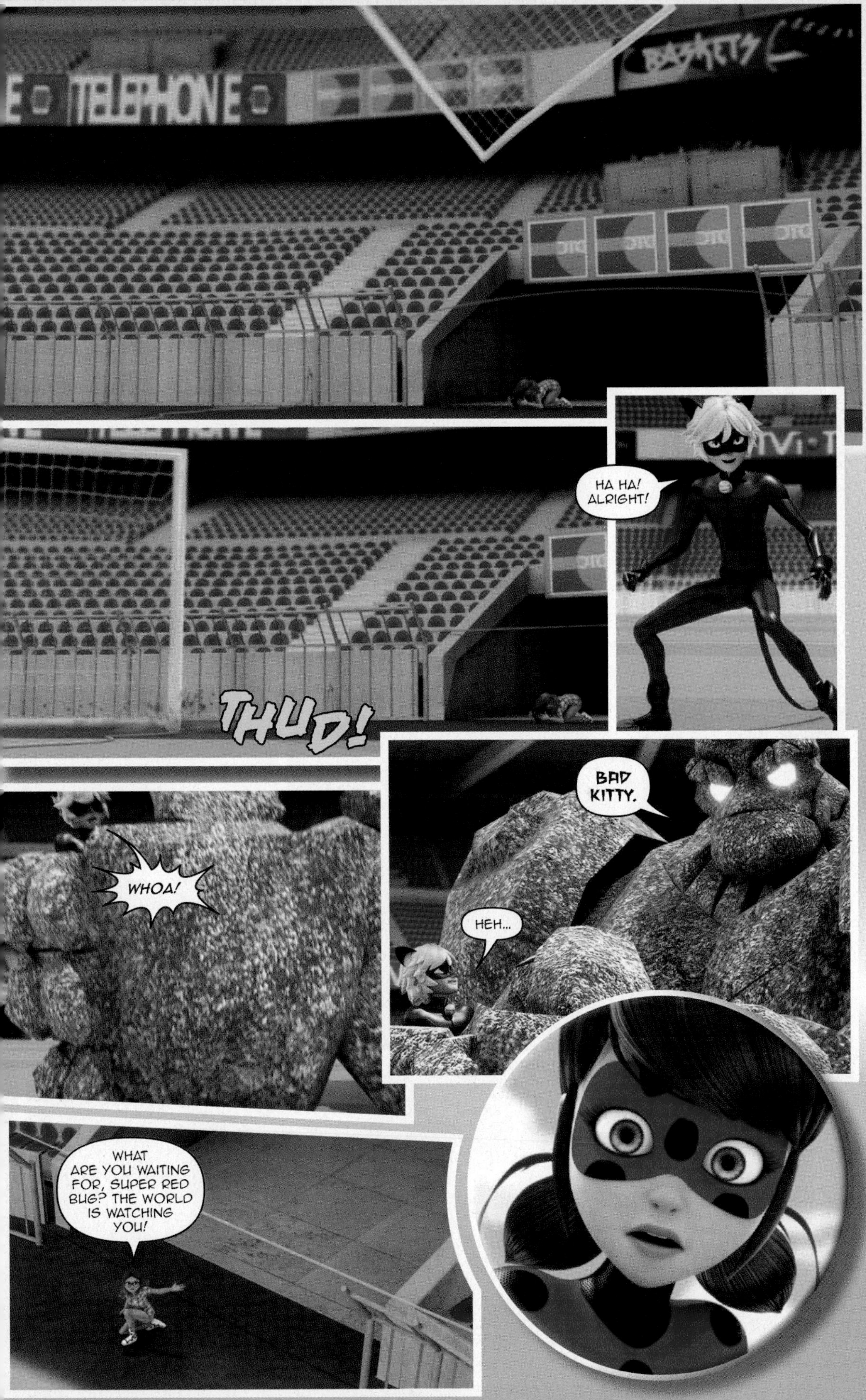
TELEPHONE
BASKETS
THUD!
HA HA! ALRIGHT!
WHOA!
BAD KITTY.
HEH...
WHAT ARE YOU WAITING FOR, SUPER RED BUG? THE WORLD IS WATCHING YOU!

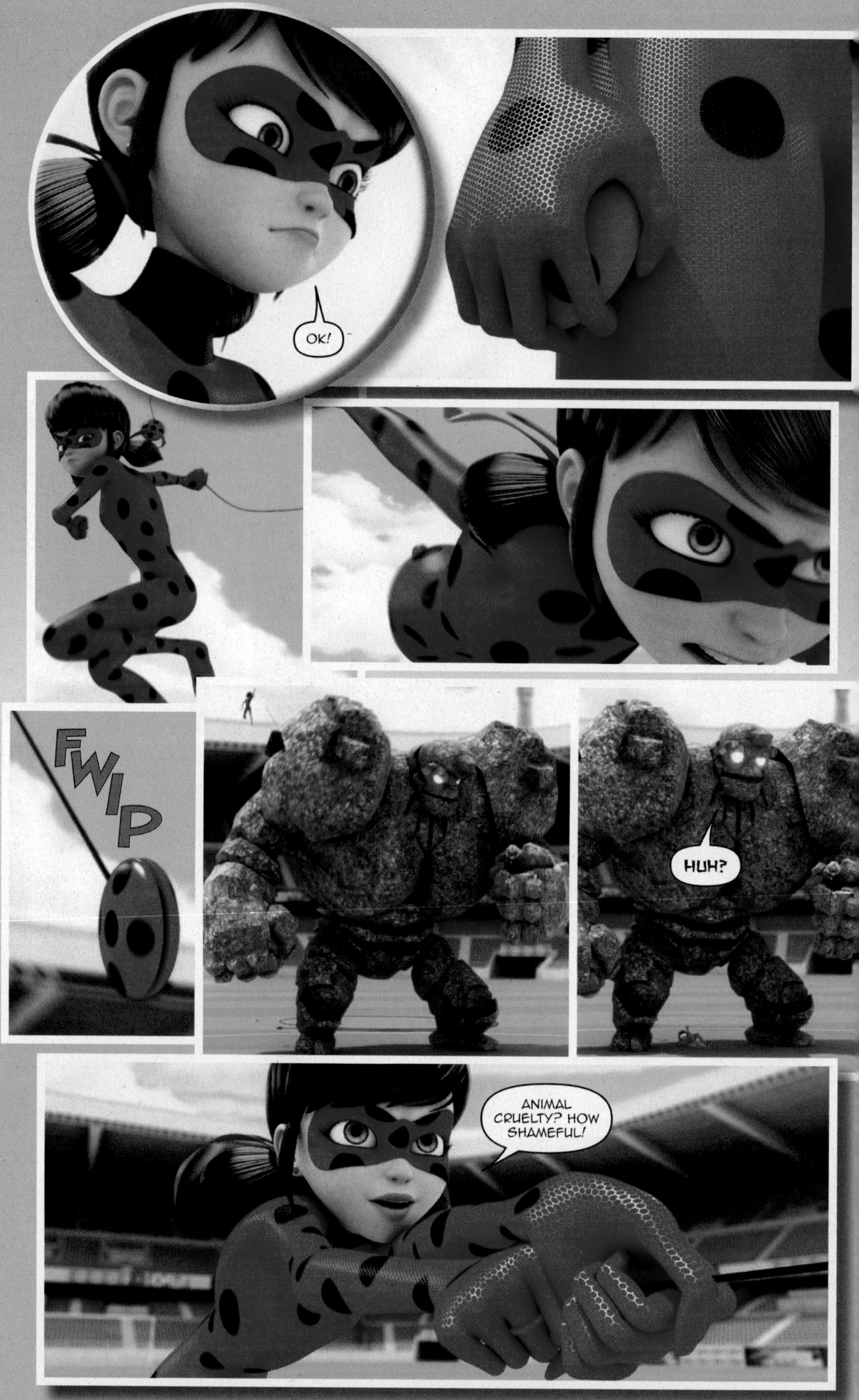
OK!
FWIP
HUH?
ANIMAL CRUELTY? HOW SHAMEFUL!

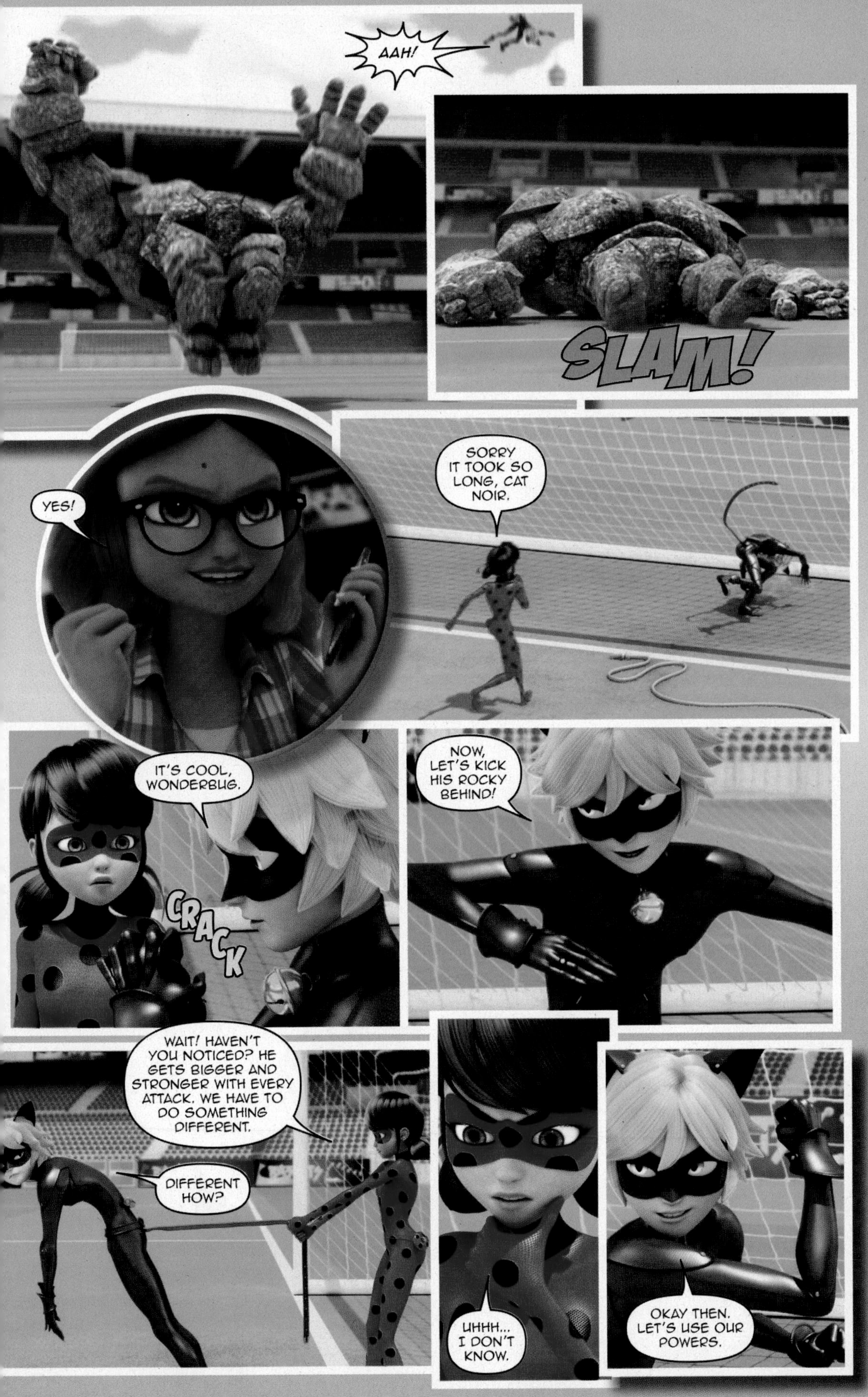
AAH!
SLAM!
YES!
SORRY IT TOOK SO LONG, CAT NOIR.
IT'S COOL, WONDERBUG.
CRACK
NOW, LET'S KICK HIS ROCKY BEHIND!
WAIT! HAVEN'T YOU NOTICED? HE GETS BIGGER AND STRONGER WITH EVERY ATTACK. WE HAVE TO DO SOMETHING DIFFERENT.
DIFFERENT HOW?
UHHH... I DON'T KNOW.
OKAY THEN. LET'S USE OUR POWERS.

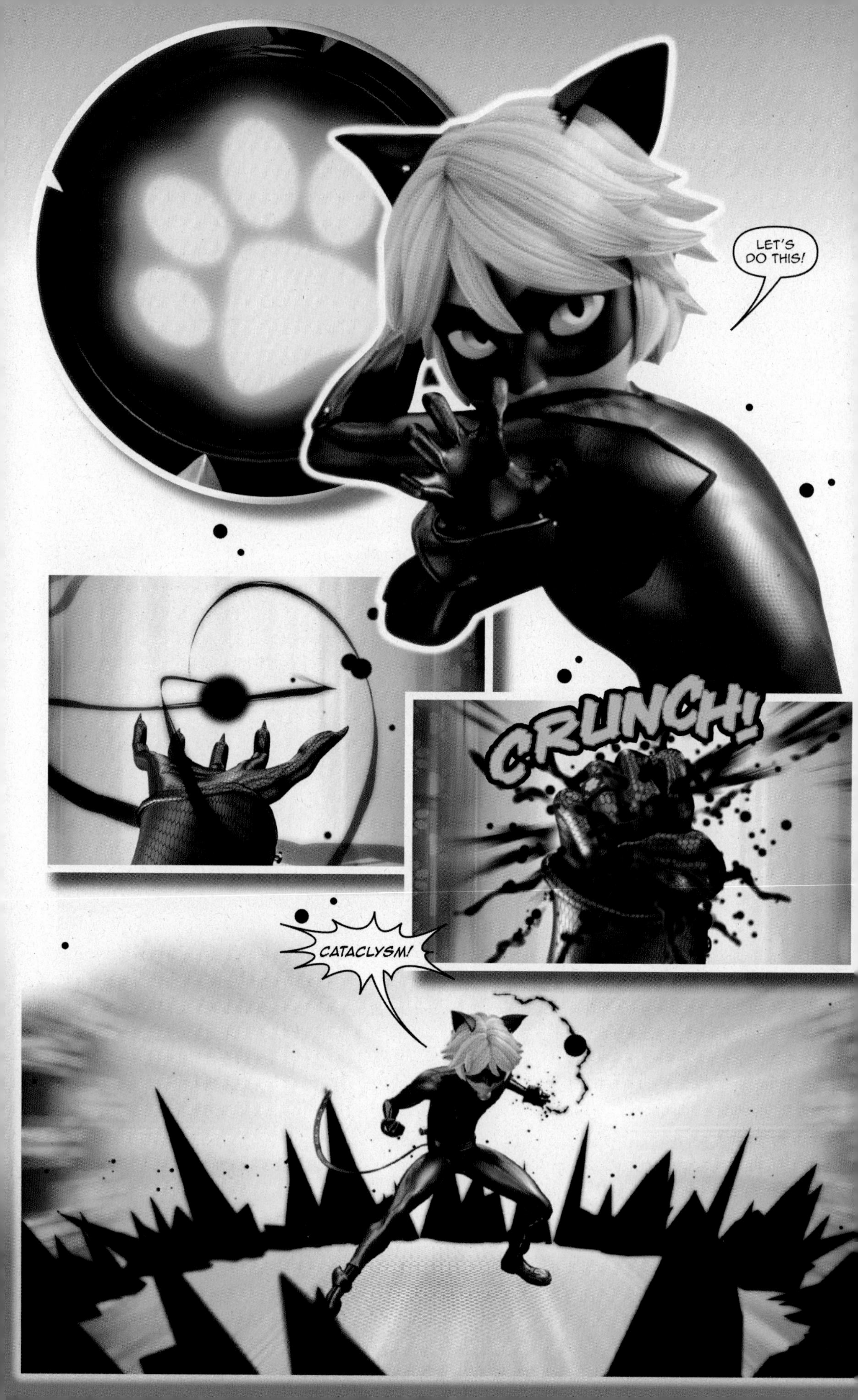
LET'S DO THIS!
CRUNCH!
CATACLYSM!

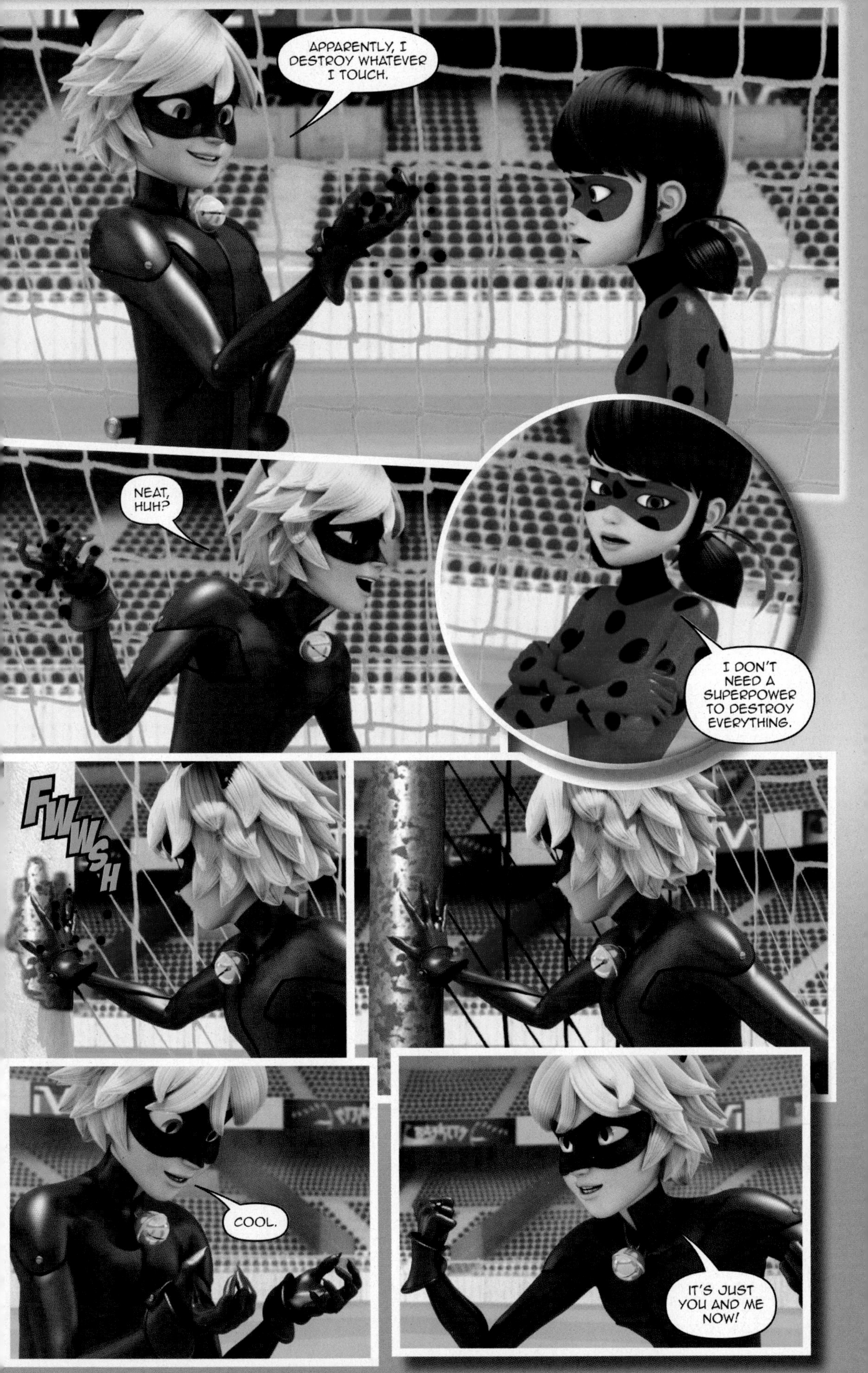
APPARENTLY, I DESTROY WHATEVER I TOUCH.
NEAT, HUH?
I DON'T NEED A SUPERPOWER TO DESTROY EVERYTHING.
FWWSH
COOL.
IT'S JUST YOU AND ME NOW!

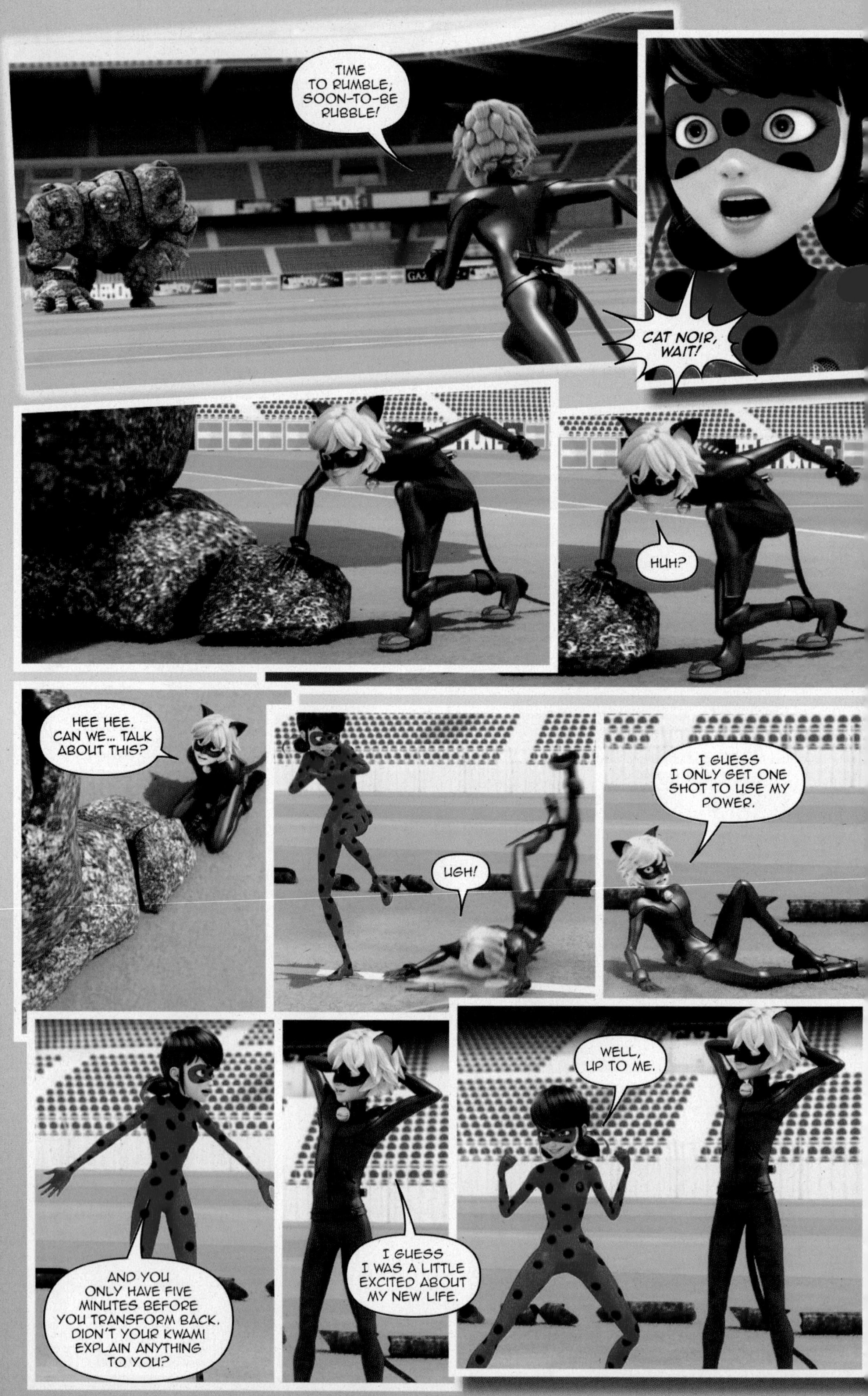
TIME TO RUMBLE; SOON-TO-BE RUBBLE!
CAT NOIR, WAIT!
HUH?
HEE HEE. CAN WE... TALK ABOUT THIS?
UGH!
I GUESS I ONLY GET ONE SHOT TO USE MY POWER.
AND YOU ONLY HAVE FIVE MINUTES BEFORE YOU TRANSFORM BACK. DIDN'T YOUR KWAMI EXPLAIN ANYTHING TO YOU?
I GUESS I WAS A LITTLE EXCITED ABOUT MY NEW LIFE.
WELL, UP TO ME.

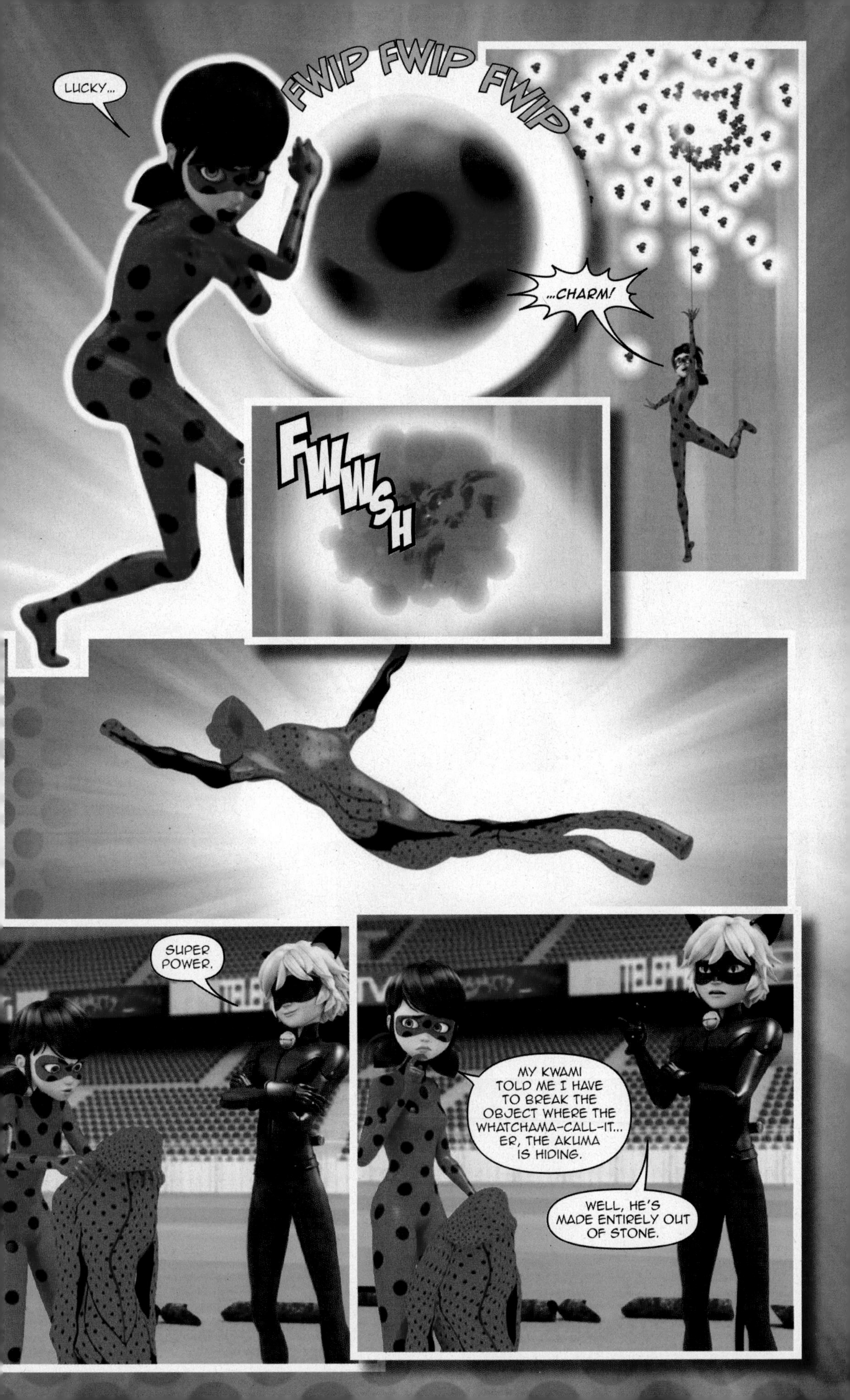
LUCKY...
FWIP FWIP FWIP
...CHARM!
FWIWSH
SUPER POWER.
MY KWAMI TOLD ME I HAVE TO BREAK THE OBJECT WHERE THE WHATCHAMA-CALL-IT... ER, THE AKUMA IS HIDING.
WELL, HE'S MADE ENTIRELY OUT OF STONE.

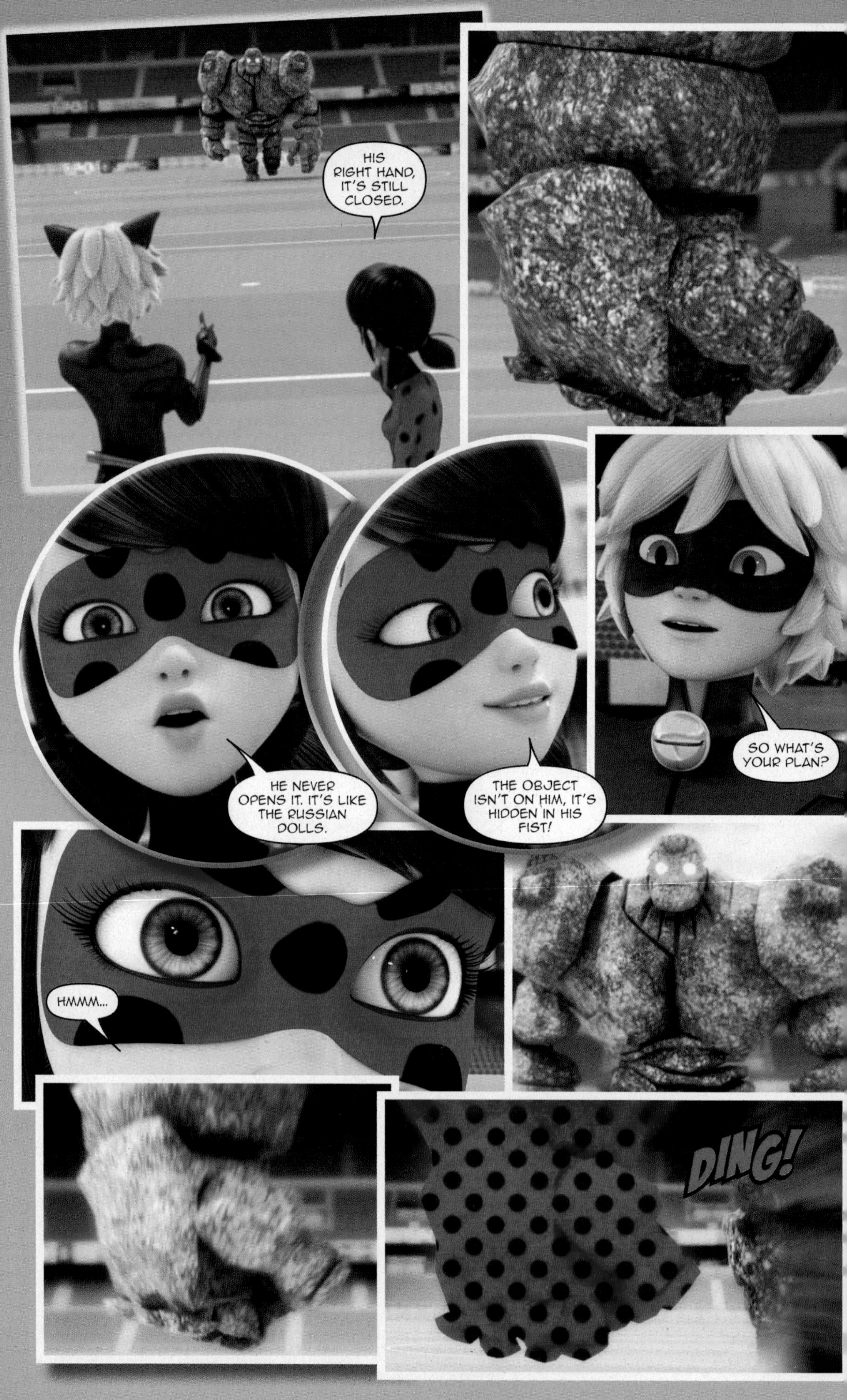
HIS RIGHT HAND, IT'S STILL CLOSED.
HE NEVER OPENS IT. IT'S LIKE THE RUSSIAN DOLLS.
THE OBJECT ISN'T ON HIM, IT'S HIDDEN IN HIS FIST!
SO WHAT'S YOUR PLAN?
HMMM...
DING!

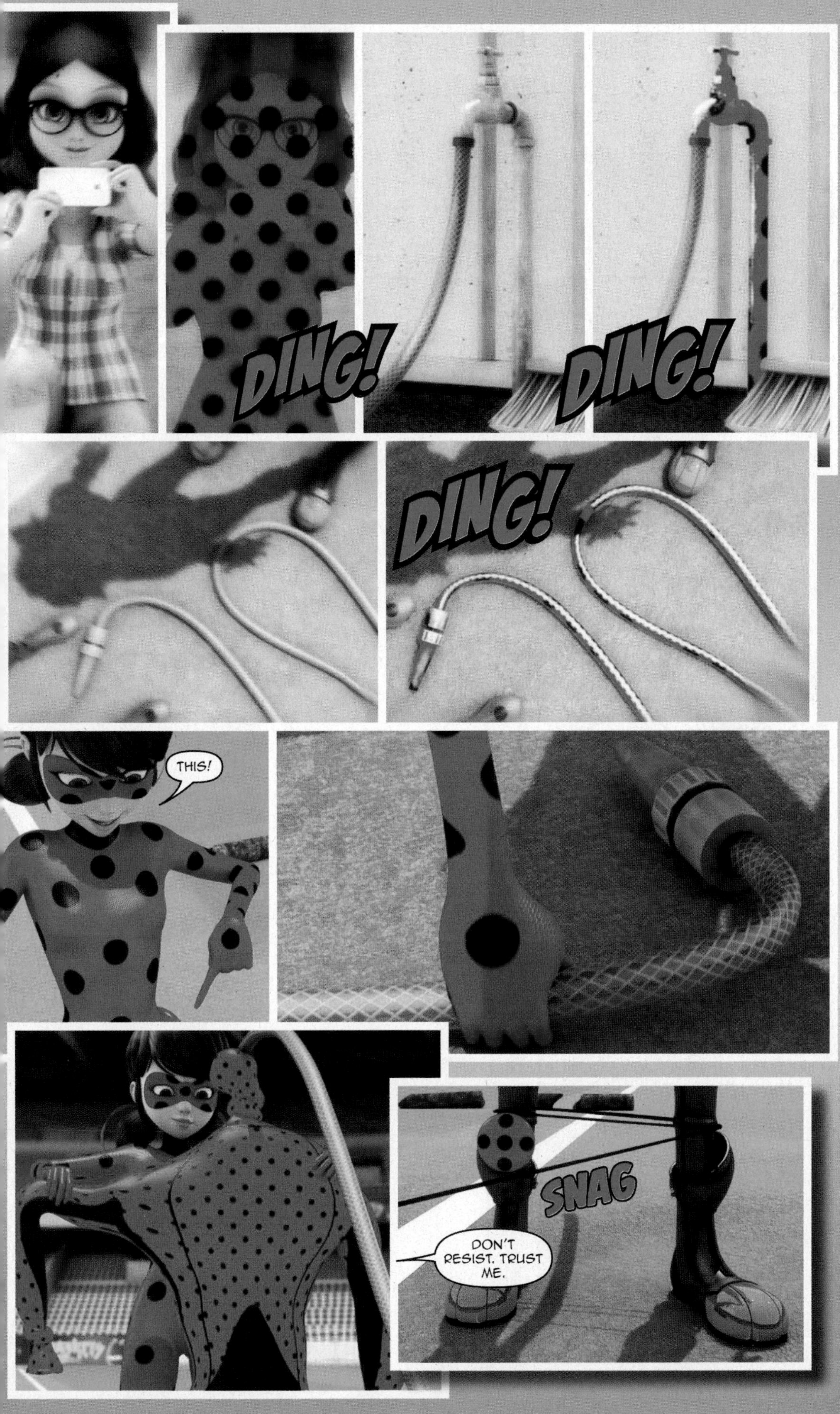
DING!
DING!
DING!
THIS!
SNAG
DON'T RESIST. TRUST ME.

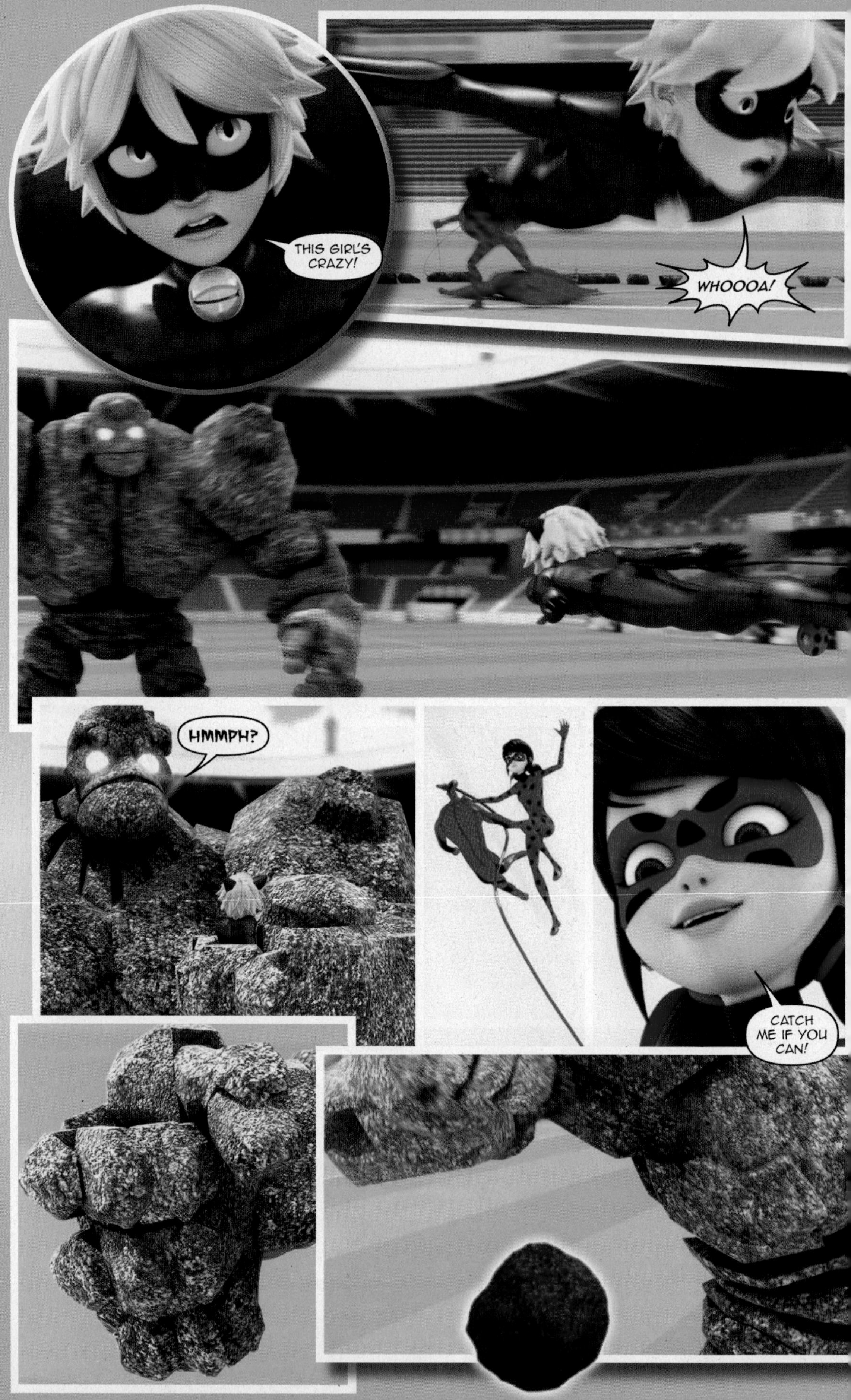
THIS GIRL'S CRAZY!
WHOOOA!
HMMPH?
CATCH ME IF YOU CAN!

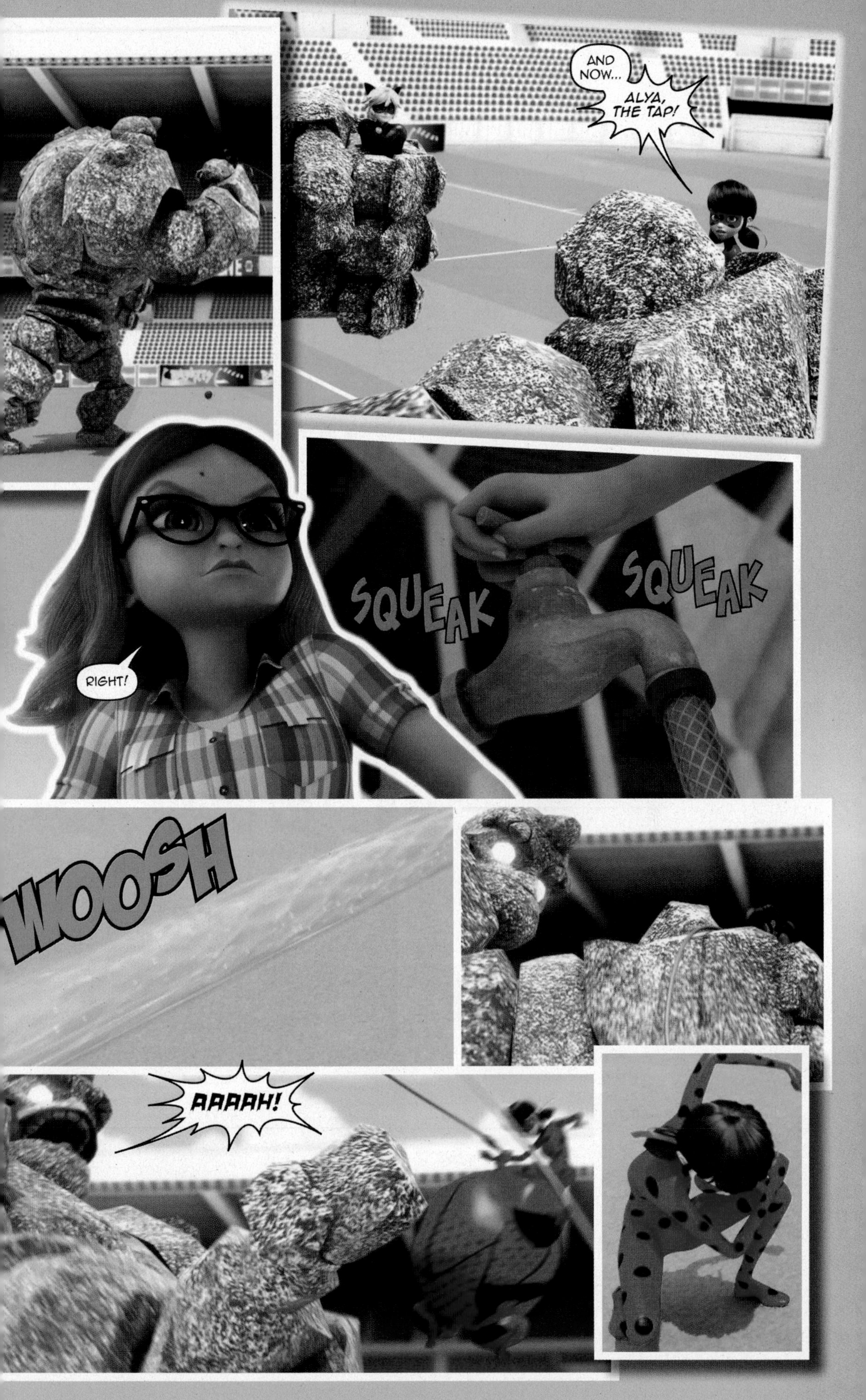
AND NOW...
ALYA, THE TAP!
RIGHT!
SQUEAK
SQUEAK
WOOSH
AAAAH!

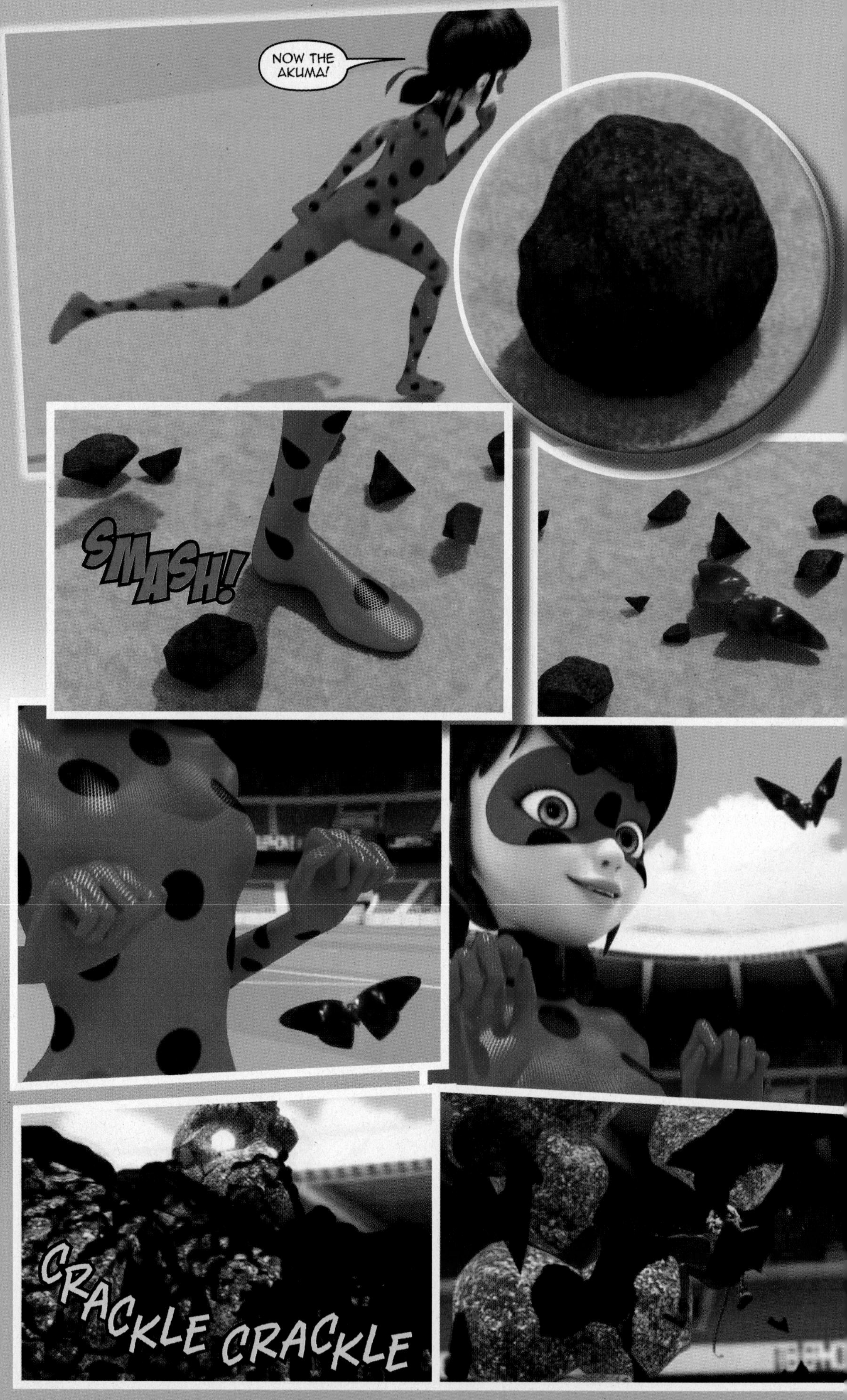
NOW THE AKUMA!
SMASH!
CRACKLE CRACKLE

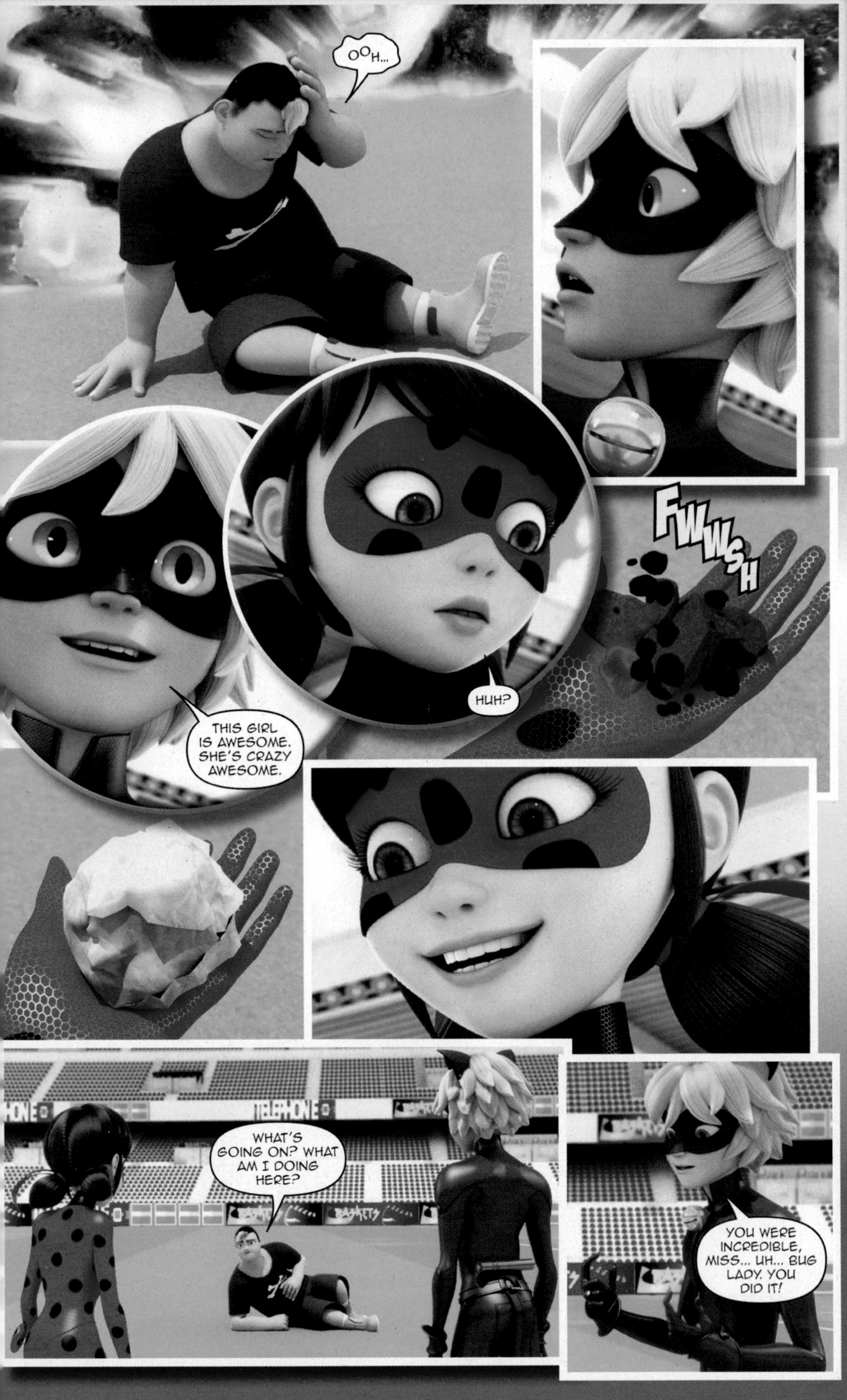
OOH...
THIS GIRL IS AWESOME. SHE'S CRAZY AWESOME.
HUH?
FWWSH
WHAT'S GOING ON? WHAT AM I DOING HERE?
YOU WERE INCREDIBLE, MISS... UH... BUG LADY. YOU DID IT!

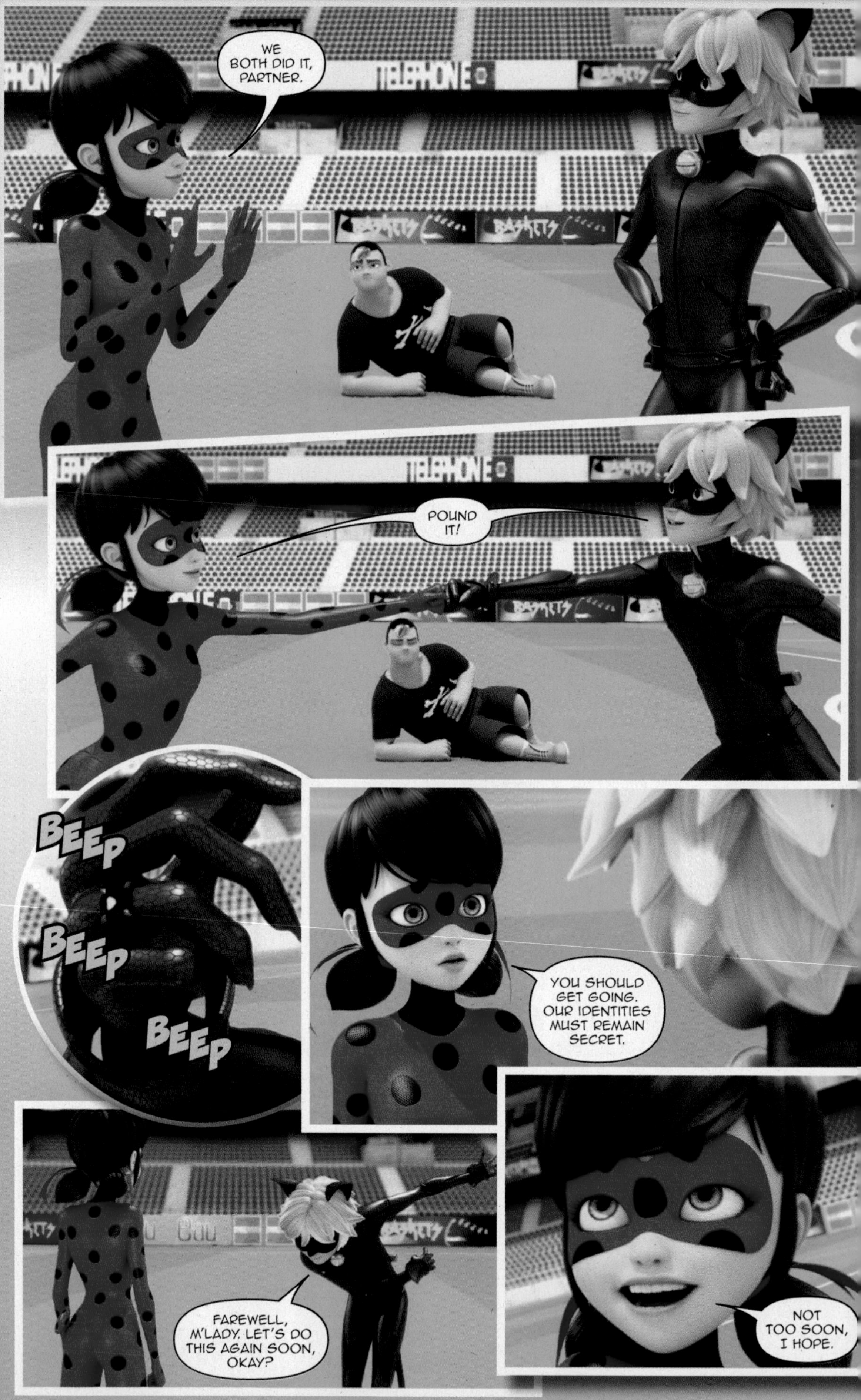
WE BOTH DID IT, PARTNER.
POUND IT!
BEEP
BEEP
BEEP
YOU SHOULD GET GOING. OUR IDENTITIES MUST REMAIN SECRET.
FAREWELL, M'LADY. LET'S DO THIS AGAIN SOON, OKAY?
NOT TOO SOON, I HOPE.

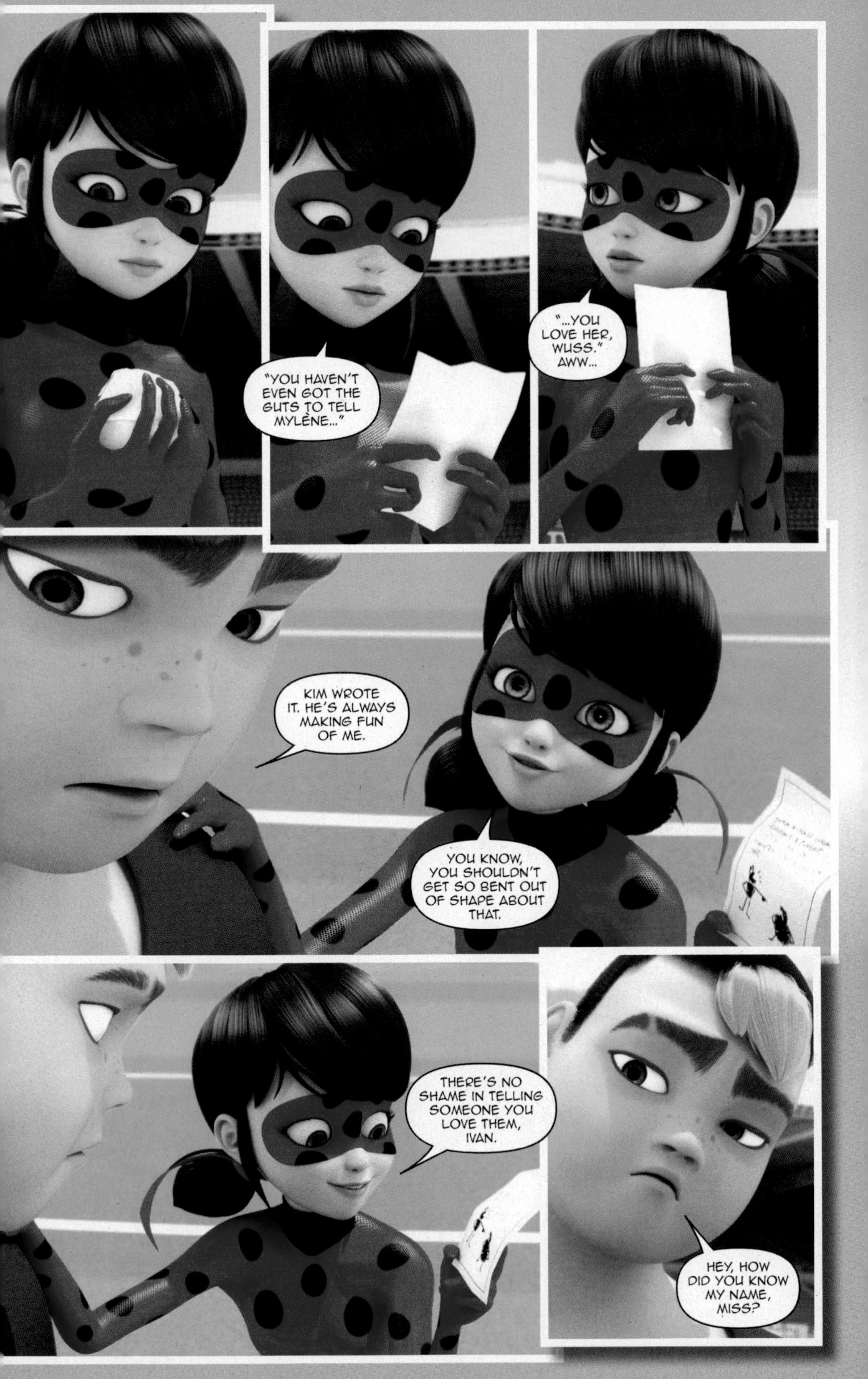
"YOU HAVEN'T EVEN GOT THE GUTS TO TELL MYLÈNE..."
"...YOU LOVE HER, WUSS." AWW...
KIM WROTE IT. HE'S ALWAYS MAKING FUN OF ME.
YOU KNOW, YOU SHOULDN'T GET SO BENT OUT OF SHAPE ABOUT THAT.
THERE'S NO SHAME IN TELLING SOMEONE YOU LOVE THEM, IVAN.
HEY, HOW DID YOU KNOW MY NAME, MISS?

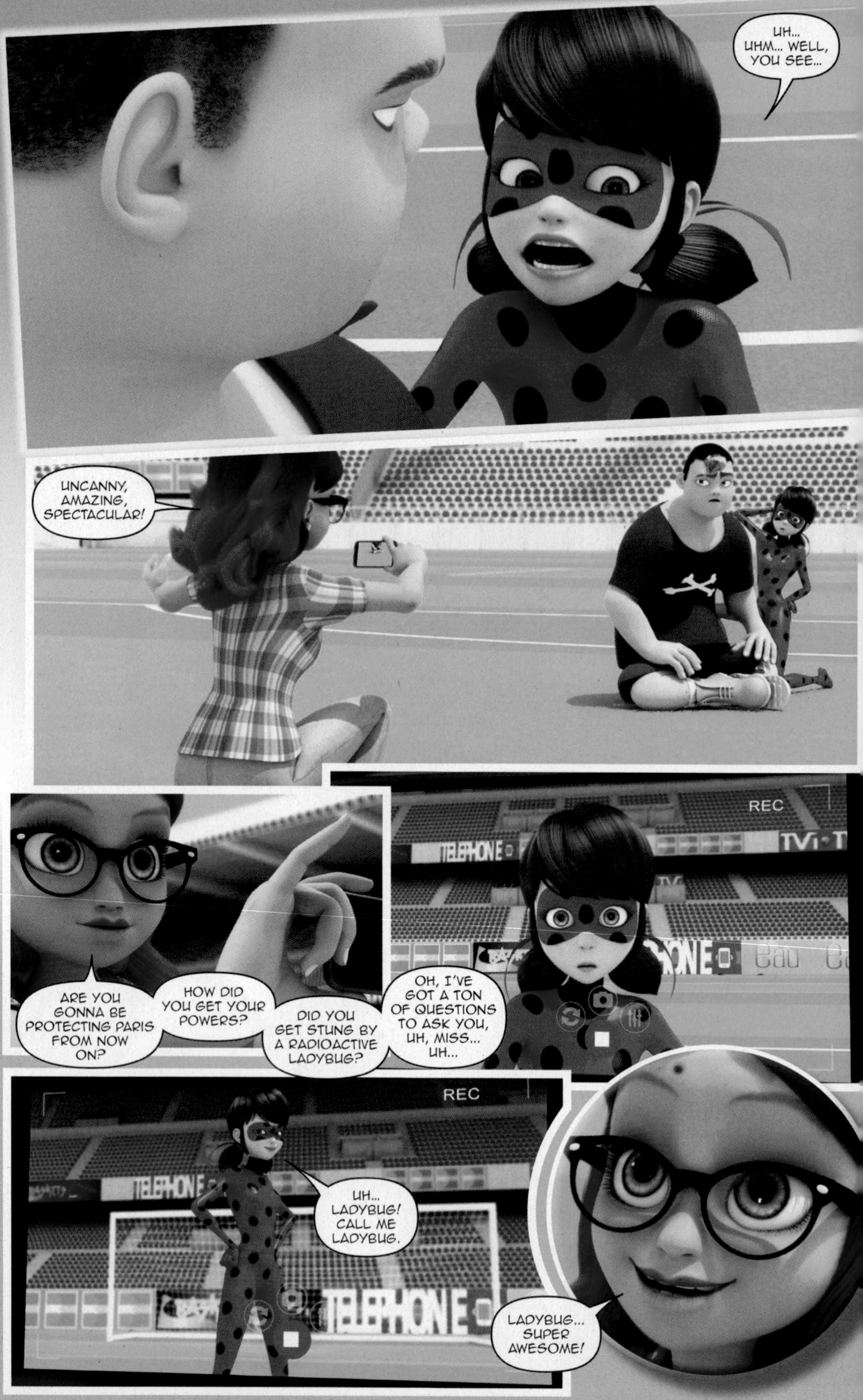
UH... UHM... WELL, YOU SEE...
UNCANNY, AMAZING, SPECTACULAR!
ARE YOU GONNA BE PROTECTING PARIS FROM NOW ON?
HOW DID YOU GET YOUR POWERS?
DID YOU GET STUNG BY A RADIOACTIVE LADYBUG?
OH, I'VE GOT A TON OF QUESTIONS TO ASK YOU, UH, MISS... UH...
REC
UH... LADYBUG! CALL ME LADYBUG.
LADYBUG... SUPER AWESOME!

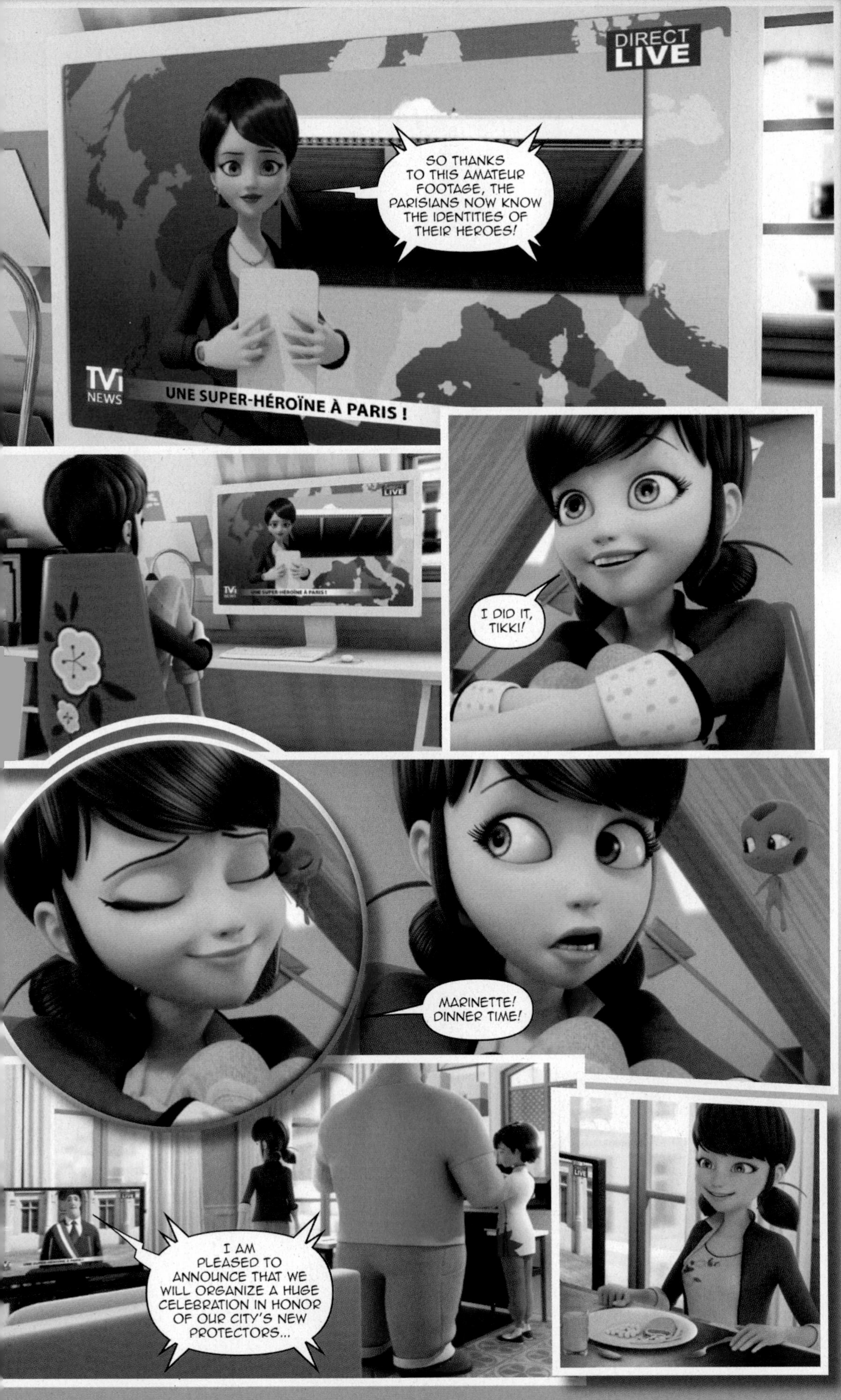
DIRECT
LIVE
SO THANKS TO THIS AMATEUR FOOTAGE, THE PARISIANS NOW KNOW THE IDENTITIES OF THEIR HEROES!
TVi NEWS
UNE SUPER-HÉROÏNE À PARIS !
I DID IT, TIKKI!
MARINETTE! DINNER TIME!
I AM PLEASED TO ANNOUNCE THAT WE WILL ORGANIZE A HUGE CELEBRATION IN HONOR OF OUR CITY'S NEW PROTECTORS...

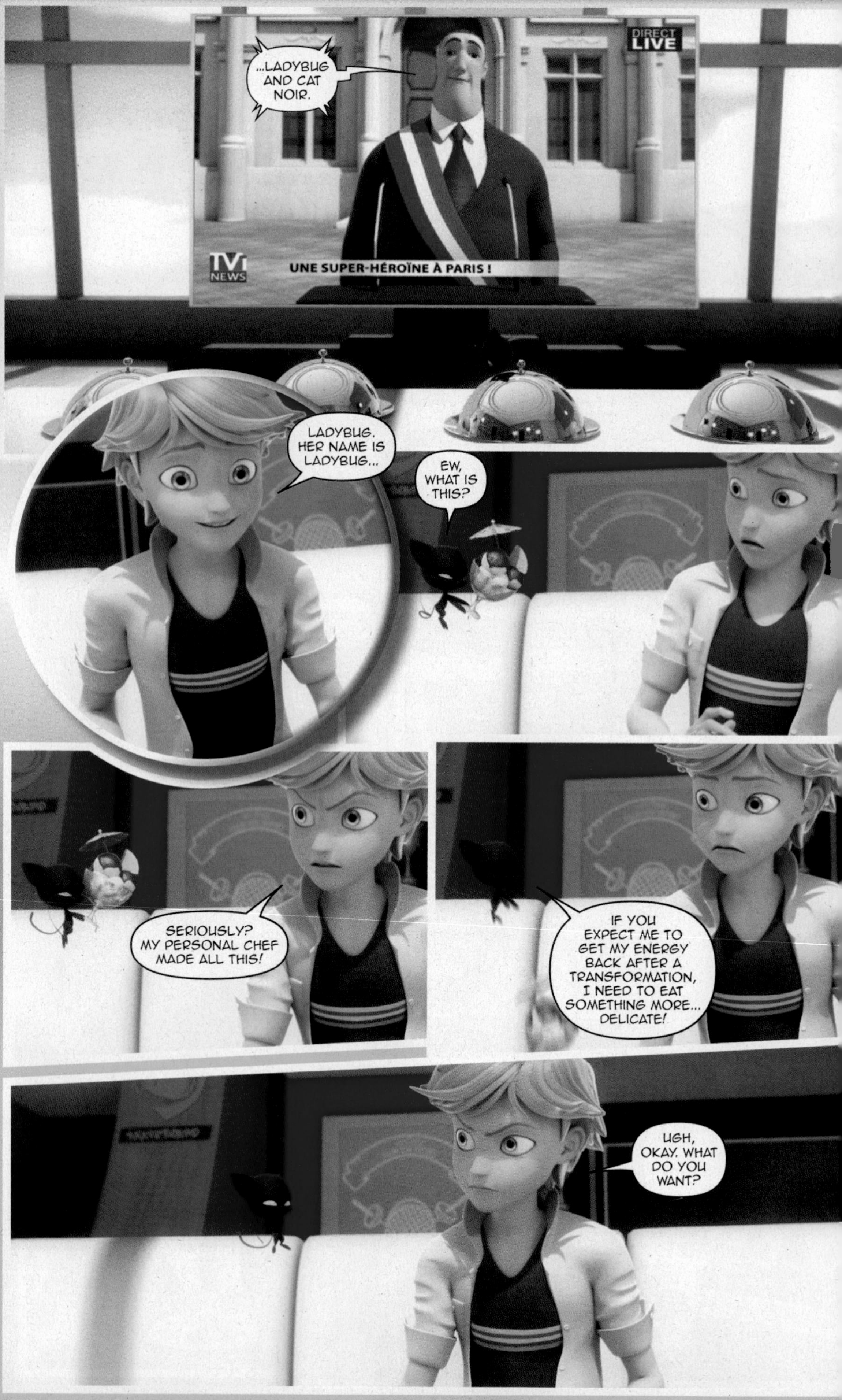
DIRECT
LIVE
...LADYBUG AND CAT NOIR.
TVi NEWS
UNE SUPER-HÉROÏNE À PARIS !
LADYBUG. HER NAME IS LADYBUG...
EW, WHAT IS THIS?
SERIOUSLY? MY PERSONAL CHEF MADE ALL THIS!
IF YOU EXPECT ME TO GET MY ENERGY BACK AFTER A TRANSFORMATION, I NEED TO EAT SOMETHING MORE... DELICATE!
UGH, OKAY. WHAT DO YOU WANT?

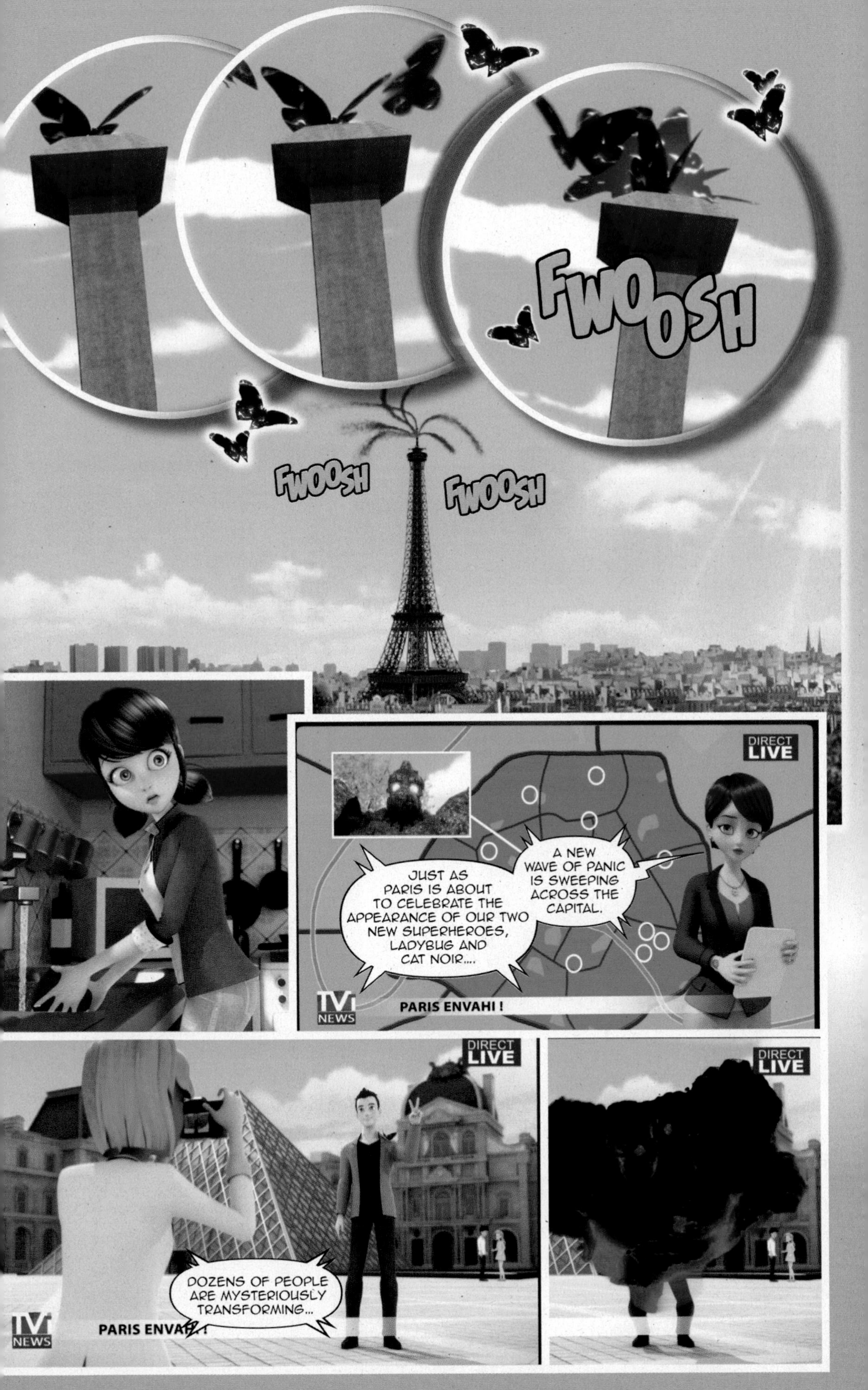
FWOOSH
FWOOSH
FWOOSH
DIRECT LIVE
JUST AS PARIS IS ABOUT TO CELEBRATE THE APPEARANCE OF OUR TWO NEW SUPERHEROES, LADYBUG AND CAT NOIR....
A NEW WAVE OF PANIC IS SWEEPING ACROSS THE CAPITAL.
TVi NEWS
PARIS ENVAHI !
DIRECT LIVE
DOZENS OF PEOPLE ARE MYSTERIOUSLY TRANSFORMING...
TVi NEWS
PARIS ENVAHI !
DIRECT LIVE

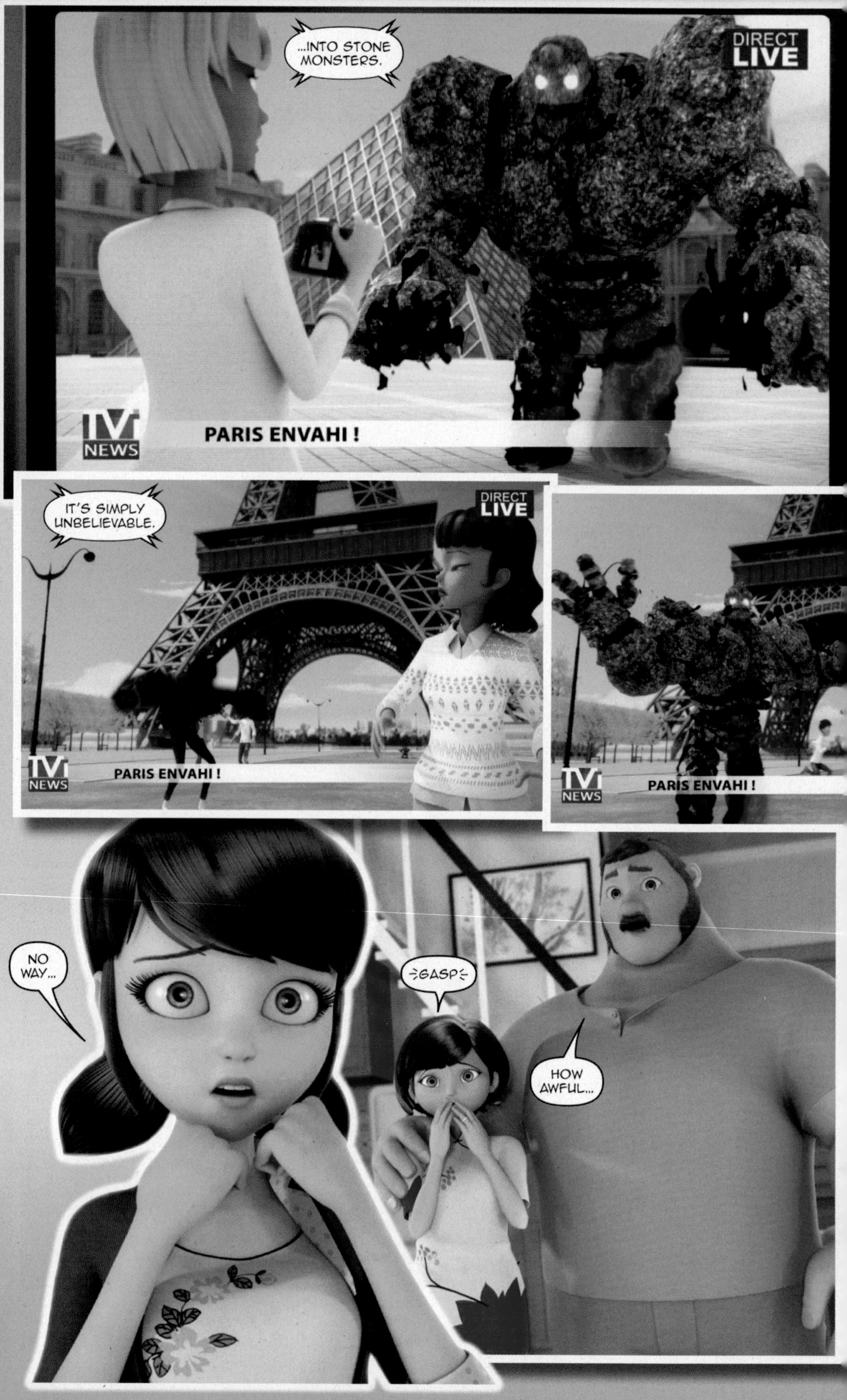
...INTO STONE MONSTERS.
DIRECT LIVE
TVi NEWS
PARIS ENVAHI !
IT'S SIMPLY UNBELIEVABLE.
DIRECT LIVE
TVi NEWS
PARIS ENVAHI !
TVi NEWS
PARIS ENVAHI !
NO WAY...
GASP
HOW AWFUL...

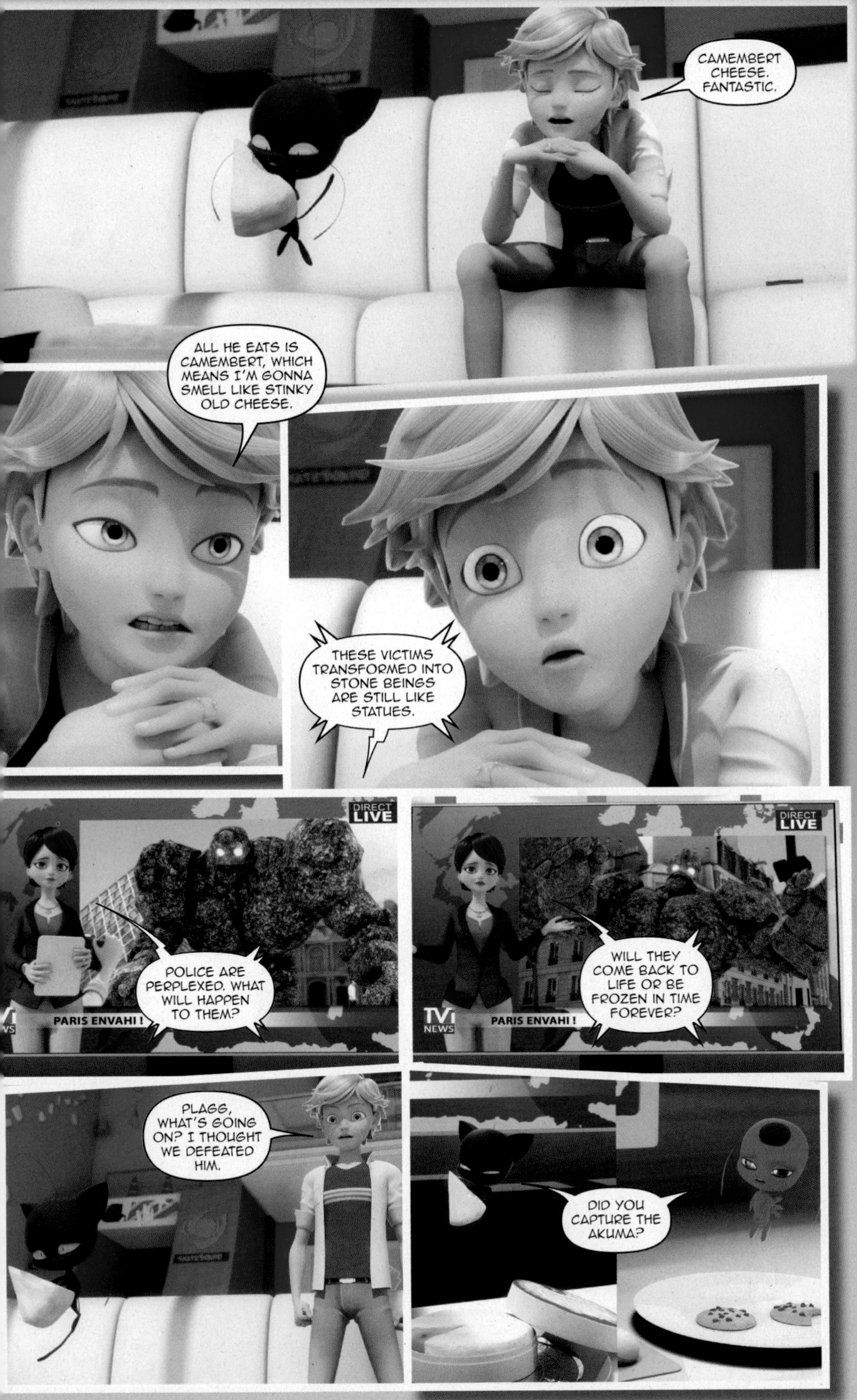
CAMEMBERT CHEESE. FANTASTIC.
ALL HE EATS IS CAMEMBERT, WHICH MEANS I'M GONNA SMELL LIKE STINKY OLD CHEESE.
THESE VICTIMS TRANSFORMED INTO STONE BEINGS ARE STILL LIKE STATUES.
DIRECT LIVE
PARIS ENVAHI !
POLICE ARE PERPLEXED. WHAT WILL HAPPEN TO THEM?
DIRECT LIVE
TVi NEWS
PARIS ENVAHI !
WILL THEY COME BACK TO LIFE OR BE FROZEN IN TIME FOREVER?
PLAGG, WHAT'S GOING ON? I THOUGHT WE DEFEATED HIM.
DID YOU CAPTURE THE AKUMA?

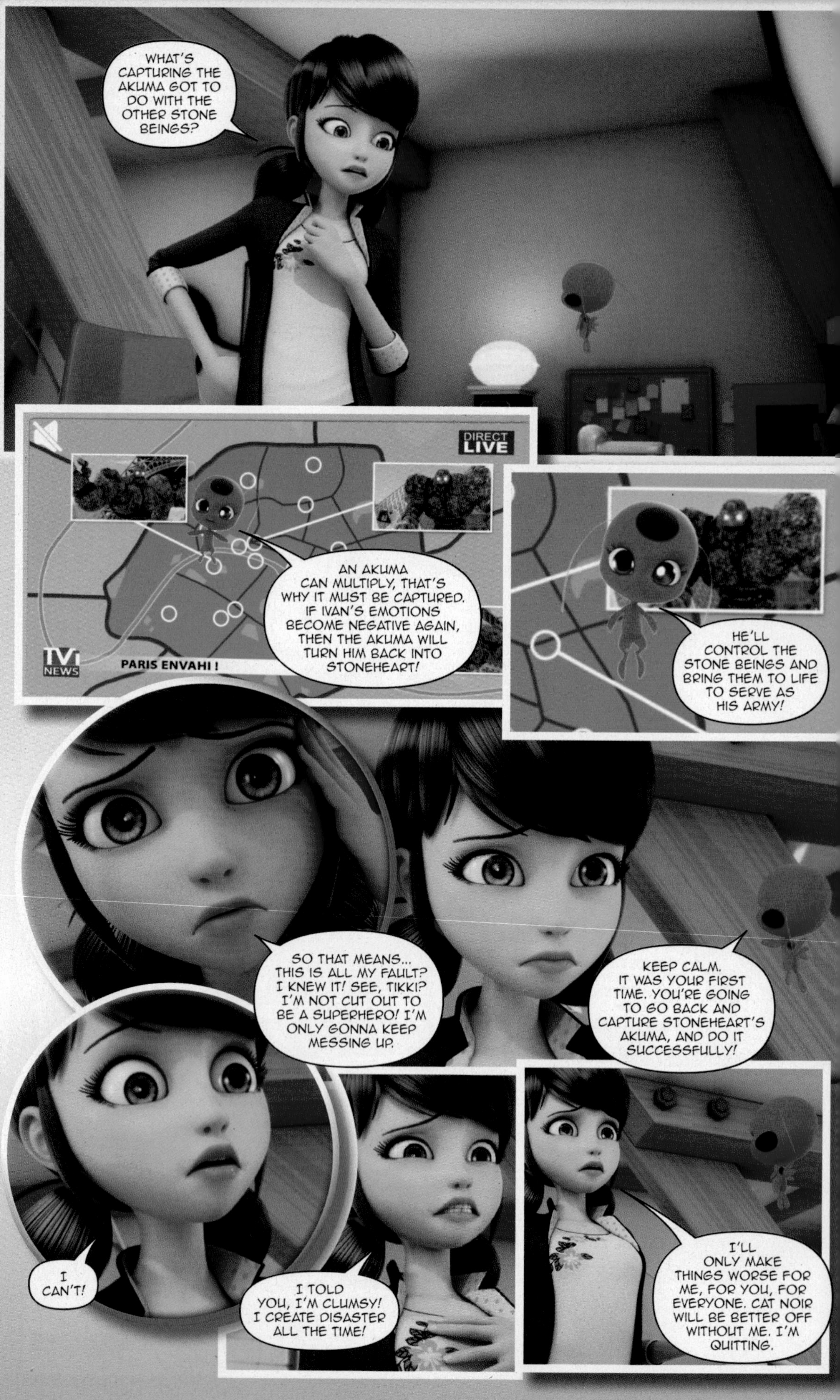
WHAT'S CAPTURING THE AKUMA GOT TO DO WITH THE OTHER STONE BEINGS?
DIRECT LIVE
TVi NEWS
PARIS ENVAHI !
AN AKUMA CAN MULTIPLY, THAT'S WHY IT MUST BE CAPTURED. IF IVAN'S EMOTIONS BECOME NEGATIVE AGAIN, THEN THE AKUMA WILL TURN HIM BACK INTO STONEHEART!
HE'LL CONTROL THE STONE BEINGS AND BRING THEM TO LIFE TO SERVE AS HIS ARMY!
SO THAT MEANS... THIS IS ALL MY FAULT? I KNEW IT! SEE, TIKKI? I'M NOT CUT OUT TO BE A SUPERHERO! I'M ONLY GONNA KEEP MESSING UP.
KEEP CALM. IT WAS YOUR FIRST TIME. YOU'RE GOING TO GO BACK AND CAPTURE STONEHEART'S AKUMA, AND DO IT SUCCESSFULLY!
I CAN'T!
I TOLD YOU, I'M CLUMSY! I CREATE DISASTER ALL THE TIME!
I'LL ONLY MAKE THINGS WORSE FOR ME, FOR YOU, FOR EVERYONE. CAT NOIR WILL BE BETTER OFF WITHOUT ME. I'M QUITTING.

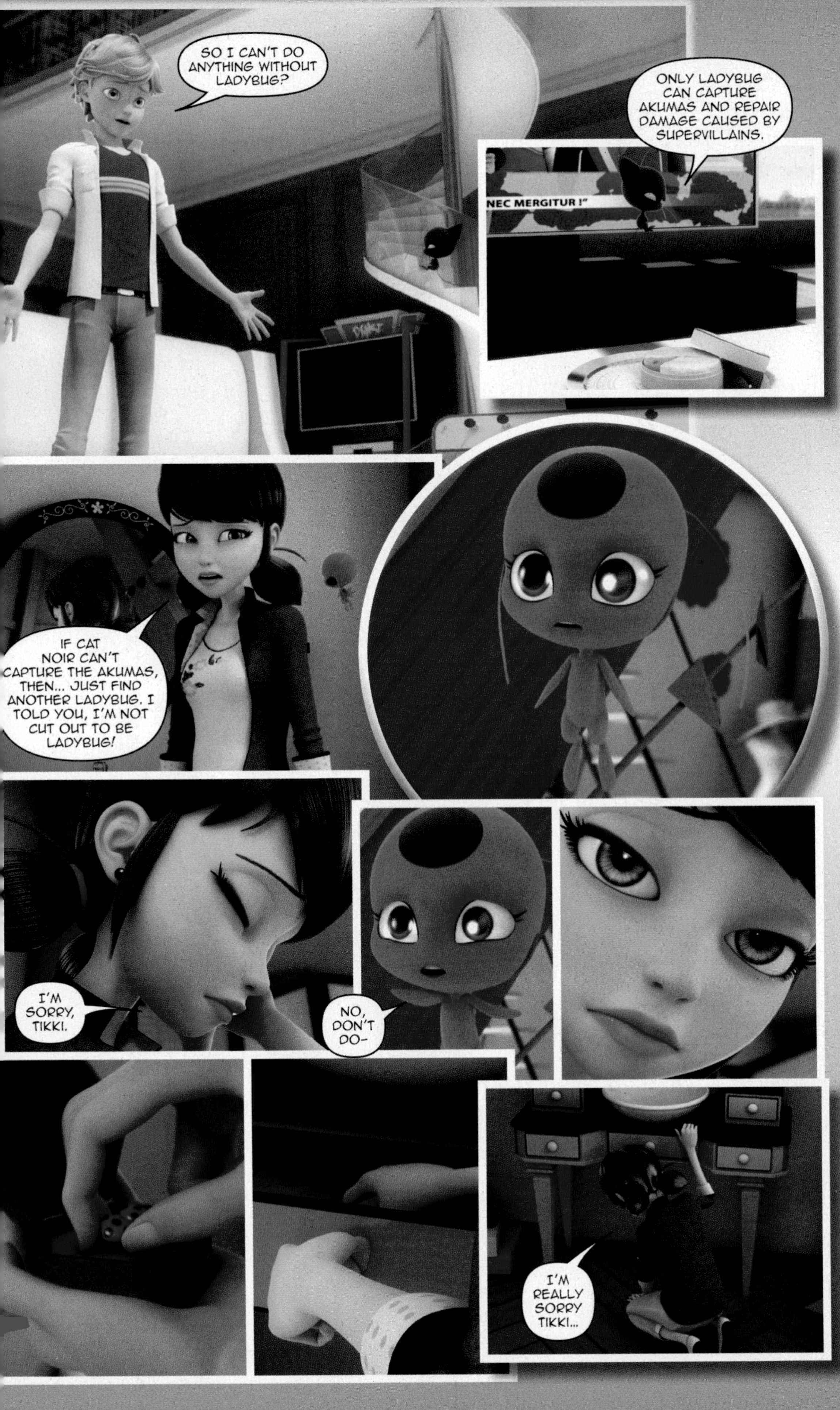
SO I CAN'T DO ANYTHING WITHOUT LADYBUG?
ONLY LADYBUG CAN CAPTURE AKUMAS AND REPAIR DAMAGE CAUSED BY SUPERVILLAINS.
NEC MERGITUR !"
IF CAT NOIR CAN'T CAPTURE THE AKUMAS, THEN... JUST FIND ANOTHER LADYBUG. I TOLD YOU, I'M NOT CUT OUT TO BE LADYBUG!
I'M SORRY, TIKKI.
NO, DON'T DO–
I'M REALLY SORRY TIKKI...

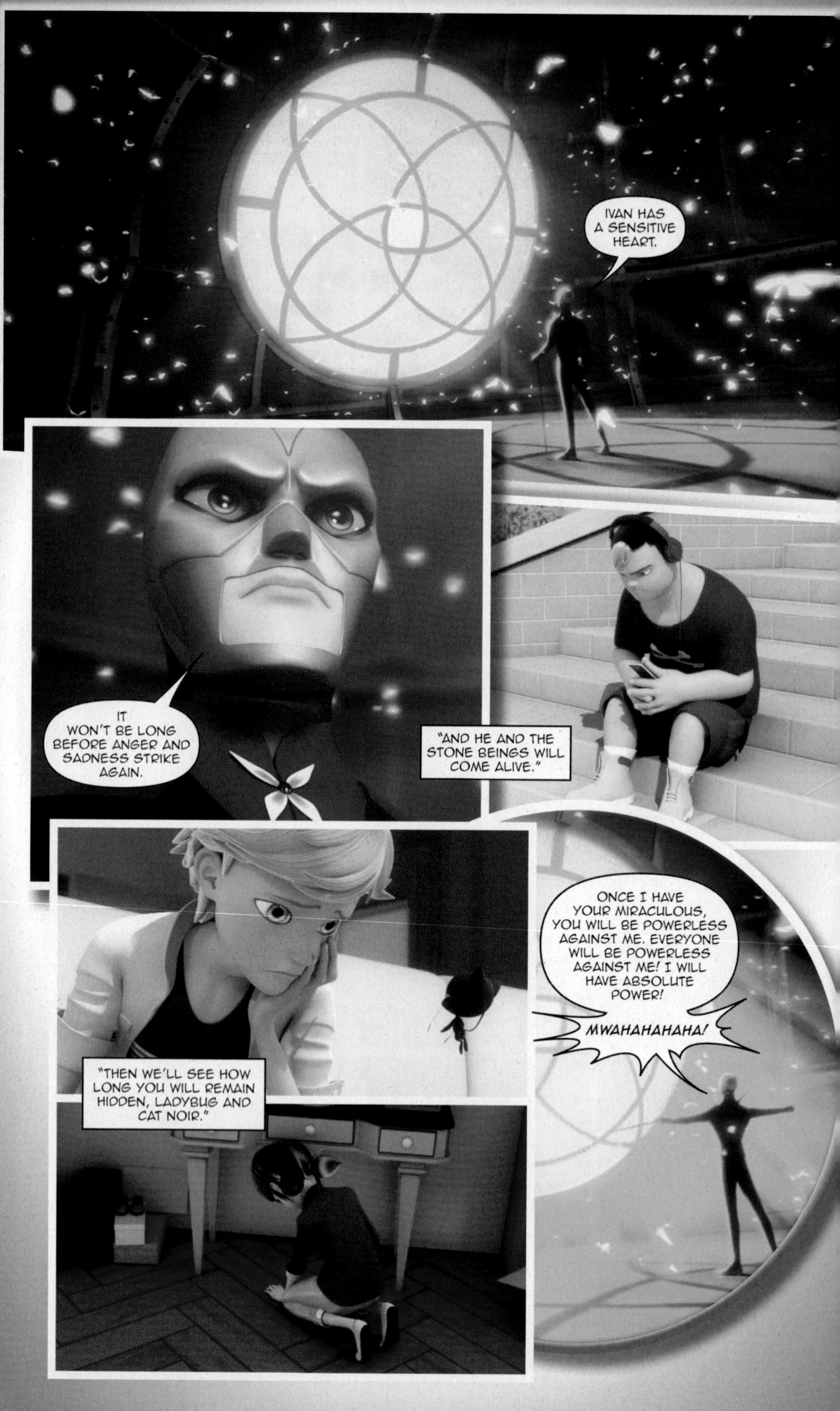
IVAN HAS A SENSITIVE HEART.
IT WON'T BE LONG BEFORE ANGER AND SADNESS STRIKE AGAIN.
"AND HE AND THE STONE BEINGS WILL COME ALIVE."
ONCE I HAVE YOUR MIRACULOUS, YOU WILL BE POWERLESS AGAINST ME. EVERYONE WILL BE POWERLESS AGAINST ME! I WILL HAVE ABSOLUTE POWER!
MWAHAHAHAHA!
"THEN WE'LL SEE HOW LONG YOU WILL REMAIN HIDDEN, LADYBUG AND CAT NOIR."

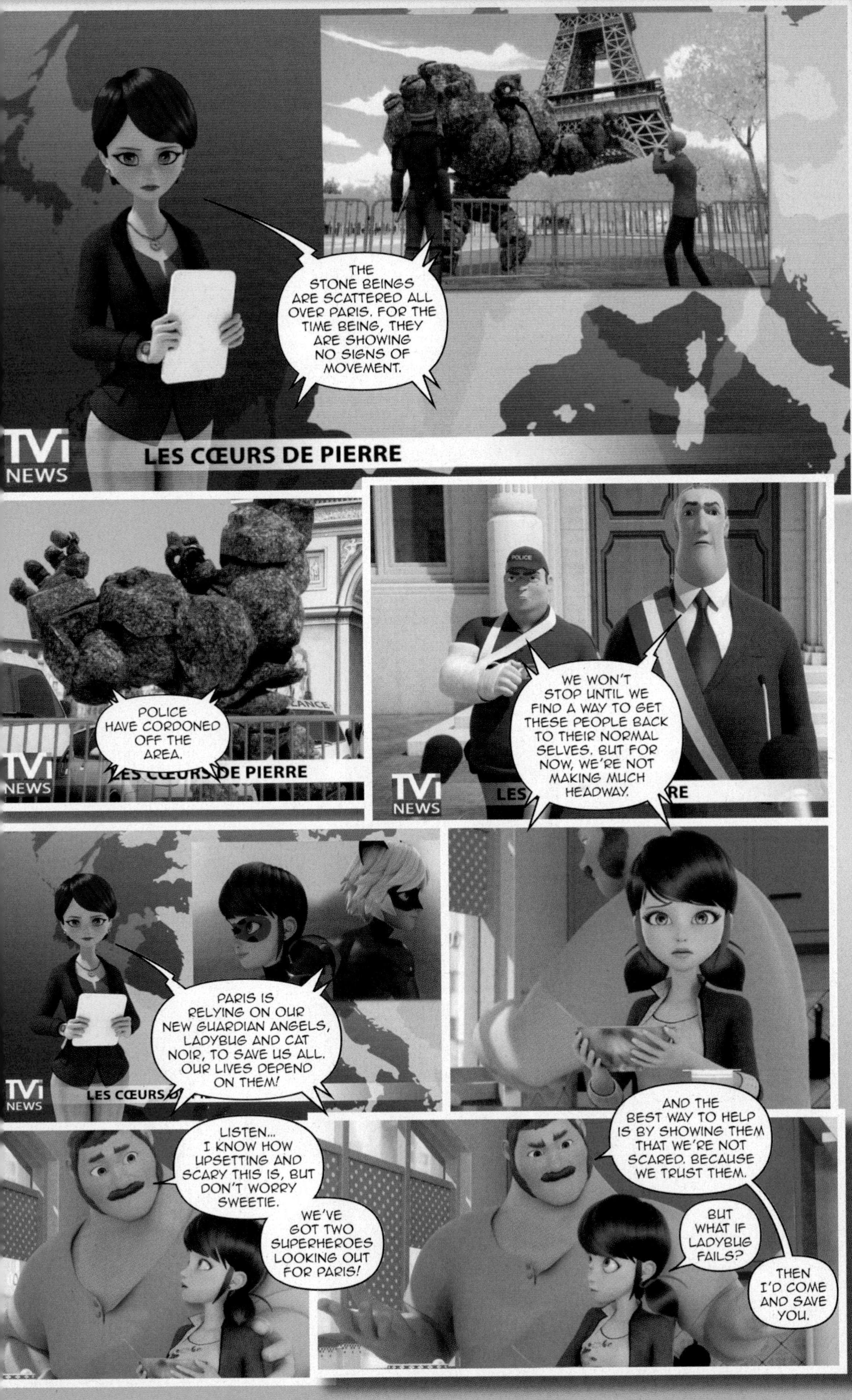
THE STONE BEINGS ARE SCATTERED ALL OVER PARIS. FOR THE TIME BEING, THEY ARE SHOWING NO SIGNS OF MOVEMENT.
TVi NEWS
LES CŒURS DE PIERRE
POLICE HAVE CORDONED OFF THE AREA.
TVi NEWS
LES CŒURS DE PIERRE
POLICE
WE WON'T STOP UNTIL WE FIND A WAY TO GET THESE PEOPLE BACK TO THEIR NORMAL SELVES. BUT FOR NOW, WE'RE NOT MAKING MUCH HEADWAY.
TVi NEWS
PARIS IS RELYING ON OUR NEW GUARDIAN ANGELS, LADYBUG AND CAT NOIR, TO SAVE US ALL. OUR LIVES DEPEND ON THEM!
TVi NEWS
LISTEN... I KNOW HOW UPSETTING AND SCARY THIS IS, BUT DON'T WORRY SWEETIE.
WE'VE GOT TWO SUPERHEROES LOOKING OUT FOR PARIS!
AND THE BEST WAY TO HELP IS BY SHOWING THEM THAT WE'RE NOT SCARED. BECAUSE WE TRUST THEM.
BUT WHAT IF LADYBUG FAILS?
THEN I'D COME AND SAVE YOU.

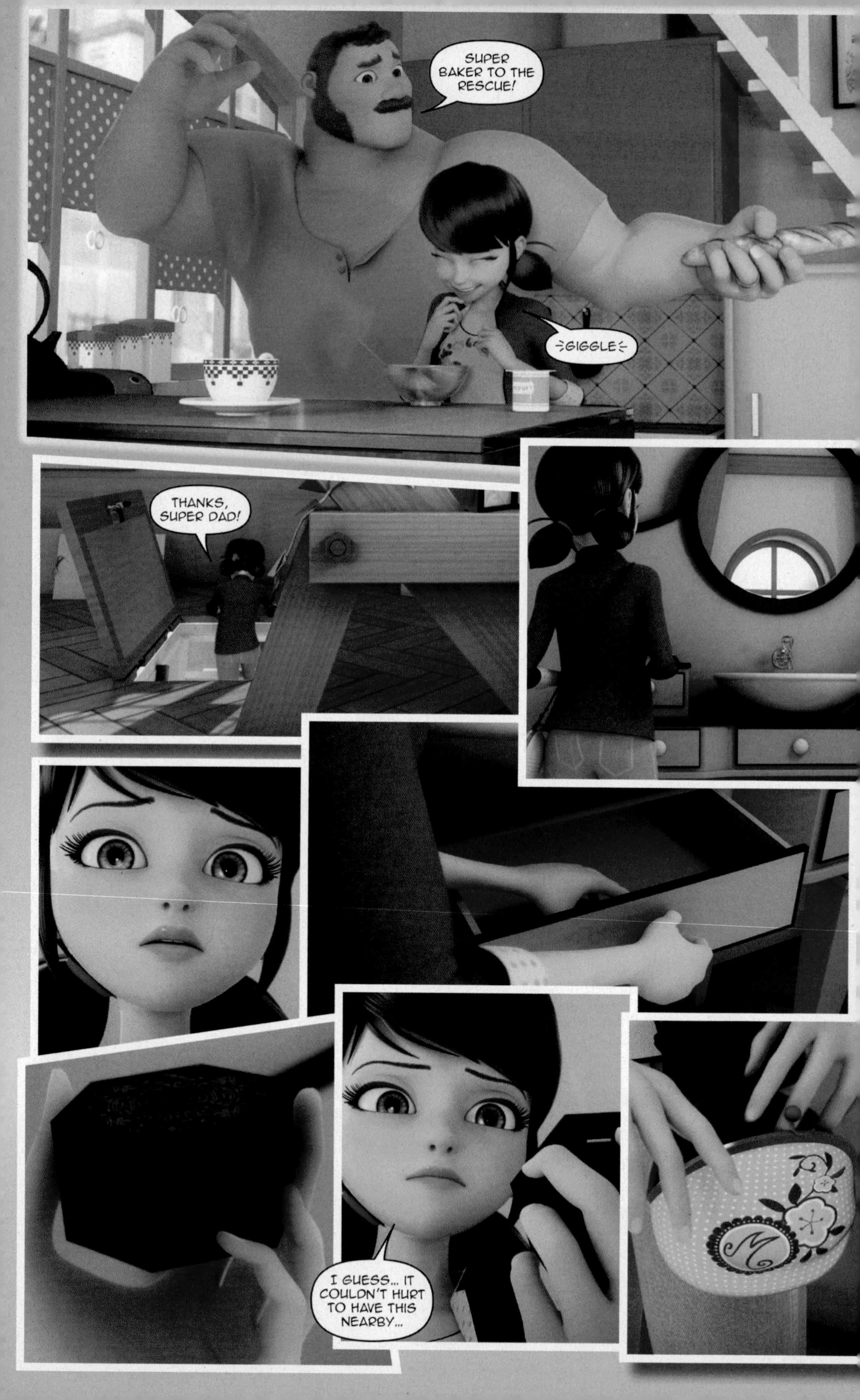
SUPER BAKER TO THE RESCUE!
GIGGLE
THANKS, SUPER DAD!
I GUESS... IT COULDN'T HURT TO HAVE THIS NEARBY...

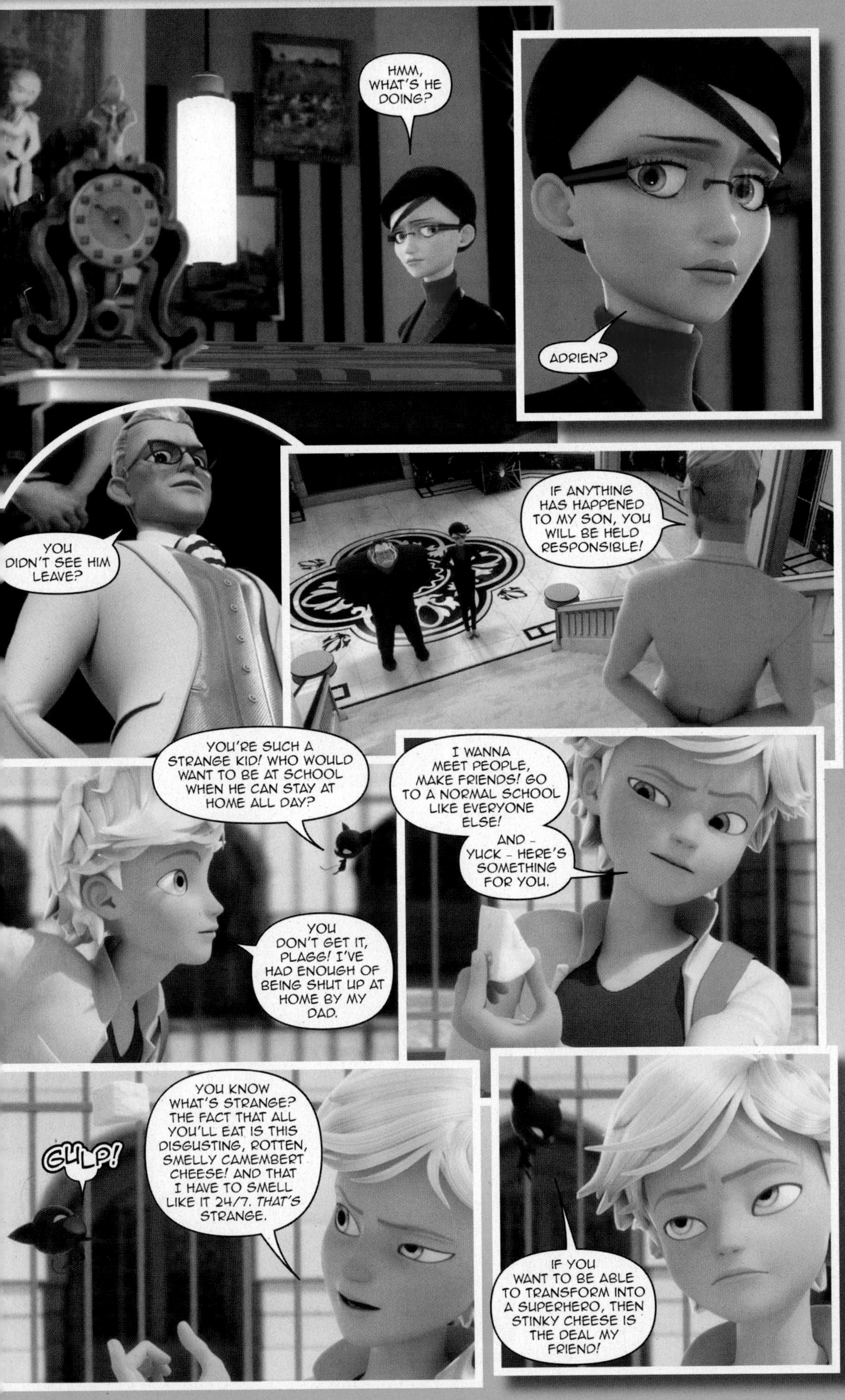
HMM, WHAT'S HE DOING?
ADRIEN?
YOU DIDN'T SEE HIM LEAVE?
IF ANYTHING HAS HAPPENED TO MY SON, YOU WILL BE HELD RESPONSIBLE!
YOU'RE SUCH A STRANGE KID! WHO WOULD WANT TO BE AT SCHOOL WHEN HE CAN STAY AT HOME ALL DAY?
YOU DON'T GET IT, PLAGG! I'VE HAD ENOUGH OF BEING SHUT UP AT HOME BY MY DAD.
I WANNA MEET PEOPLE, MAKE FRIENDS! GO TO A NORMAL SCHOOL LIKE EVERYONE ELSE!
AND - YUCK - HERE'S SOMETHING FOR YOU.
GULP!
YOU KNOW WHAT'S STRANGE? THE FACT THAT ALL YOU'LL EAT IS THIS DISGUSTING, ROTTEN, SMELLY CAMEMBERT CHEESE! AND THAT I HAVE TO SMELL LIKE IT 24/7. *THAT'S* STRANGE.
IF YOU WANT TO BE ABLE TO TRANSFORM INTO A SUPERHERO, THEN STINKY CHEESE IS THE DEAL MY FRIEND!

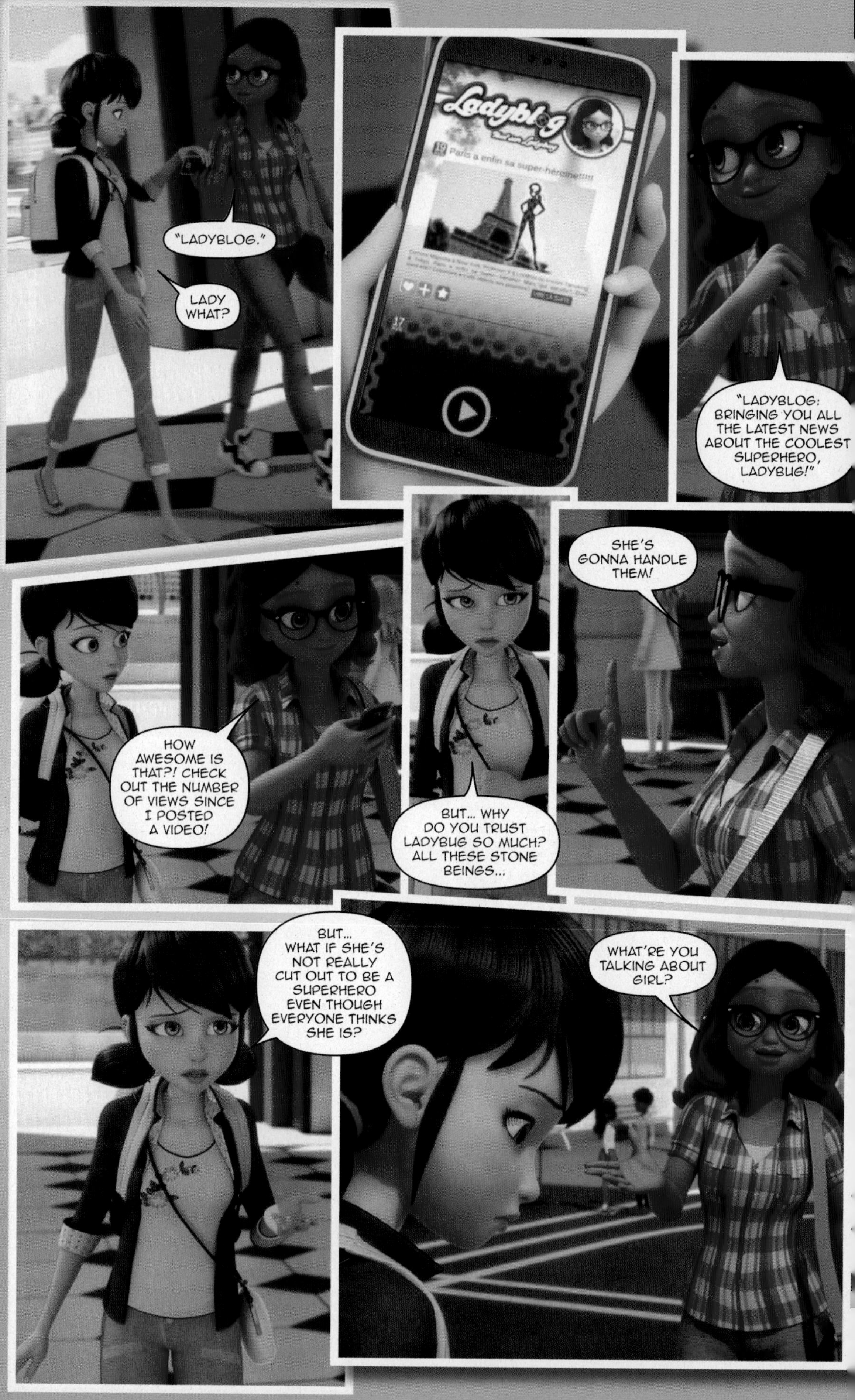
"LADYBLOG."
LADY WHAT?
Ladyblog
Paris a enfin sa super-héroïne!!!!!
"LADYBLOG: BRINGING YOU ALL THE LATEST NEWS ABOUT THE COOLEST SUPERHERO, LADYBUG!"
HOW AWESOME IS THAT?! CHECK OUT THE NUMBER OF VIEWS SINCE I POSTED A VIDEO!
BUT... WHY DO YOU TRUST LADYBUG SO MUCH? ALL THESE STONE BEINGS...
SHE'S GONNA HANDLE THEM!
BUT... WHAT IF SHE'S NOT REALLY CUT OUT TO BE A SUPERHERO EVEN THOUGH EVERYONE THINKS SHE IS?
WHAT'RE YOU TALKING ABOUT GIRL?

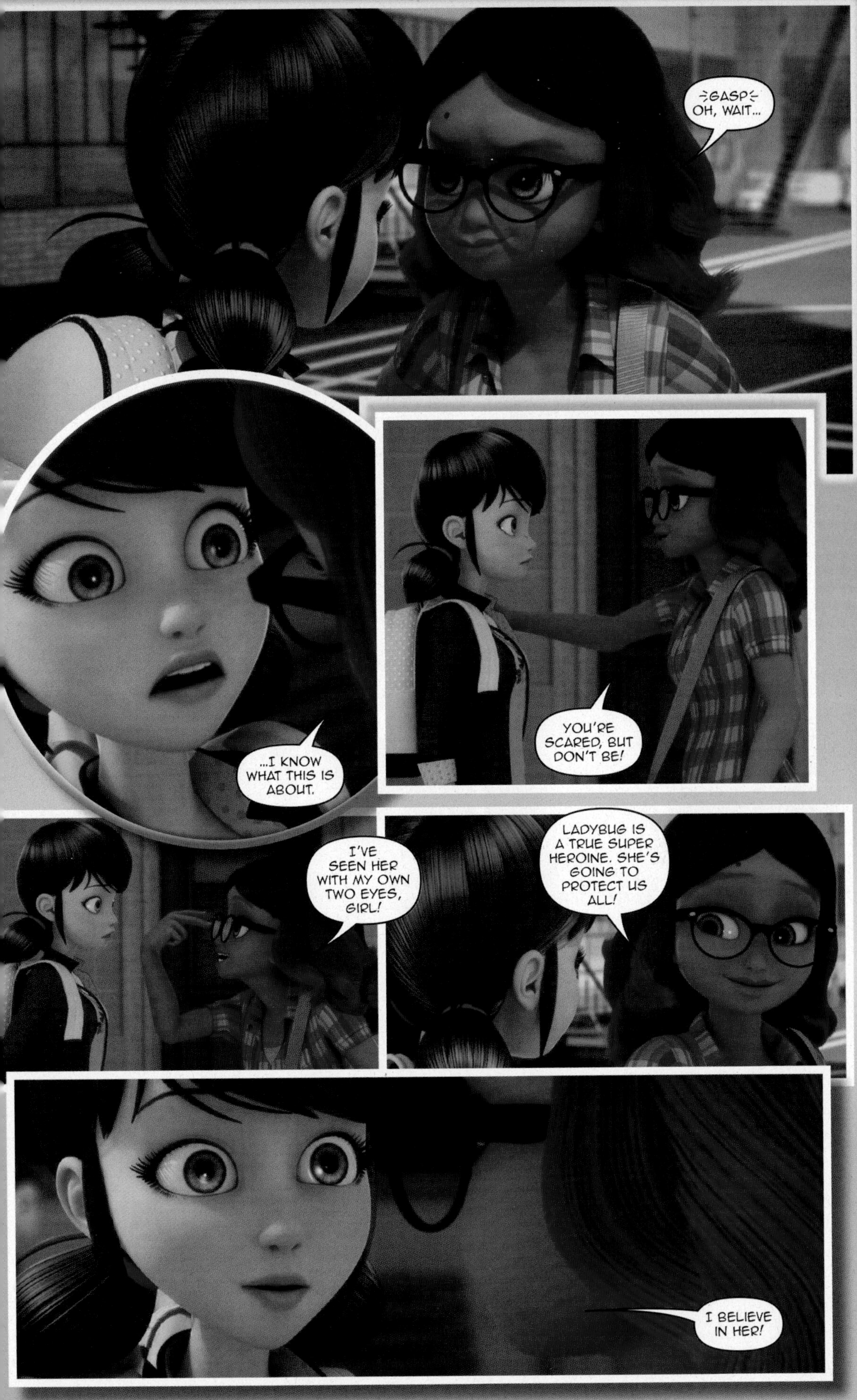
GASP
OH, WAIT...
...I KNOW WHAT THIS IS ABOUT.
YOU'RE SCARED, BUT DON'T BE!
I'VE SEEN HER WITH MY OWN TWO EYES, GIRL!
LADYBUG IS A TRUE SUPER HEROINE. SHE'S GOING TO PROTECT US ALL!
I BELIEVE IN HER!

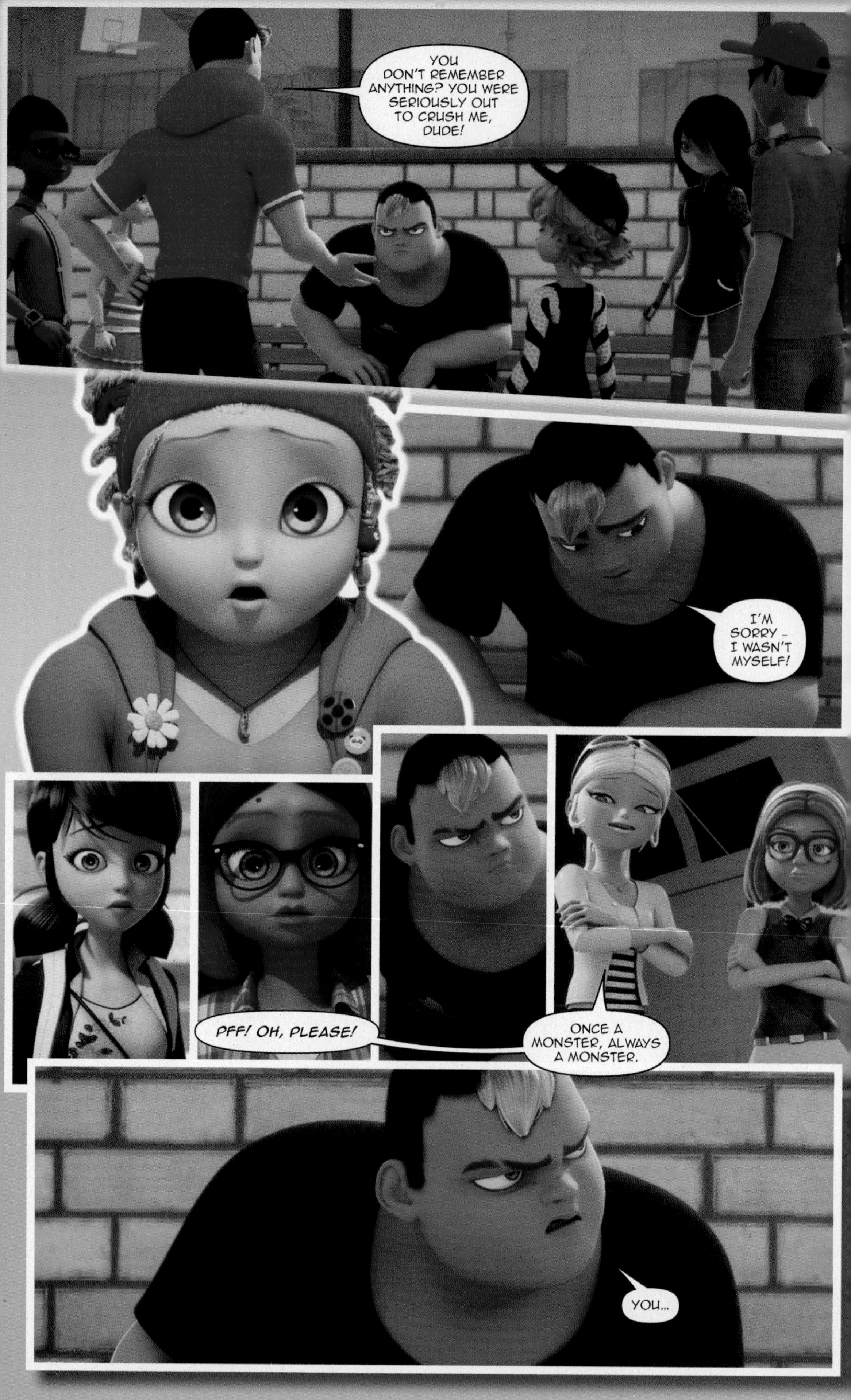
YOU DON'T REMEMBER ANYTHING? YOU WERE SERIOUSLY OUT TO CRUSH ME, DUDE!
I'M SORRY – I WASN'T MYSELF!
PFF! OH, PLEASE!
ONCE A MONSTER, ALWAYS A MONSTER.
YOU...

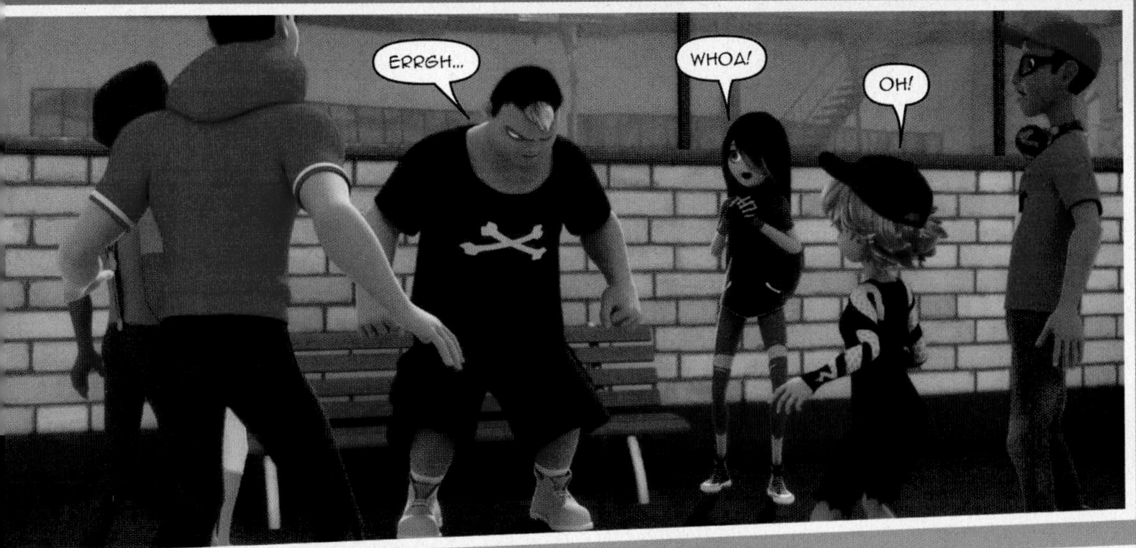
ERRGH...
WHOA!
OH!

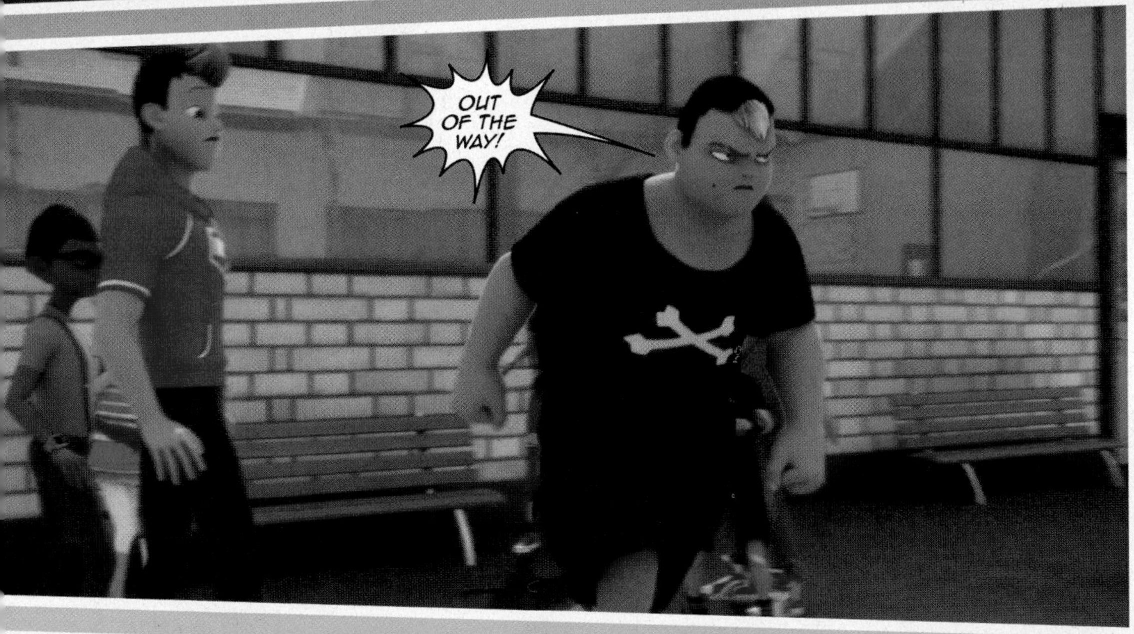
OUT OF THE WAY!

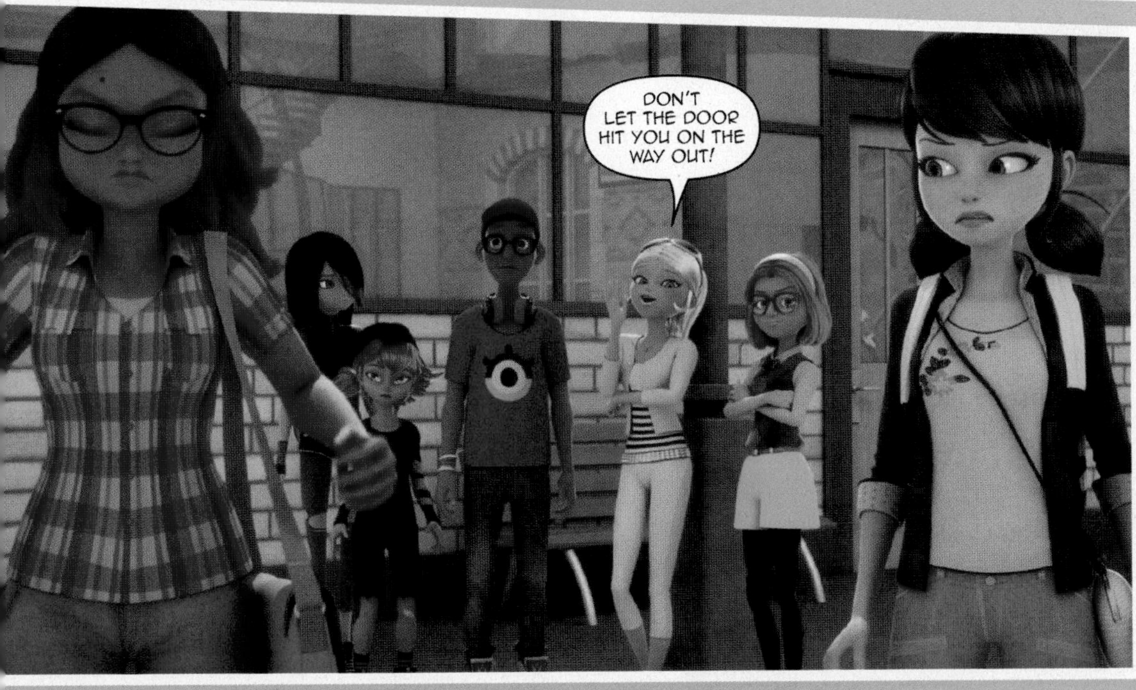
DON'T LET THE DOOR HIT YOU ON THE WAY OUT!

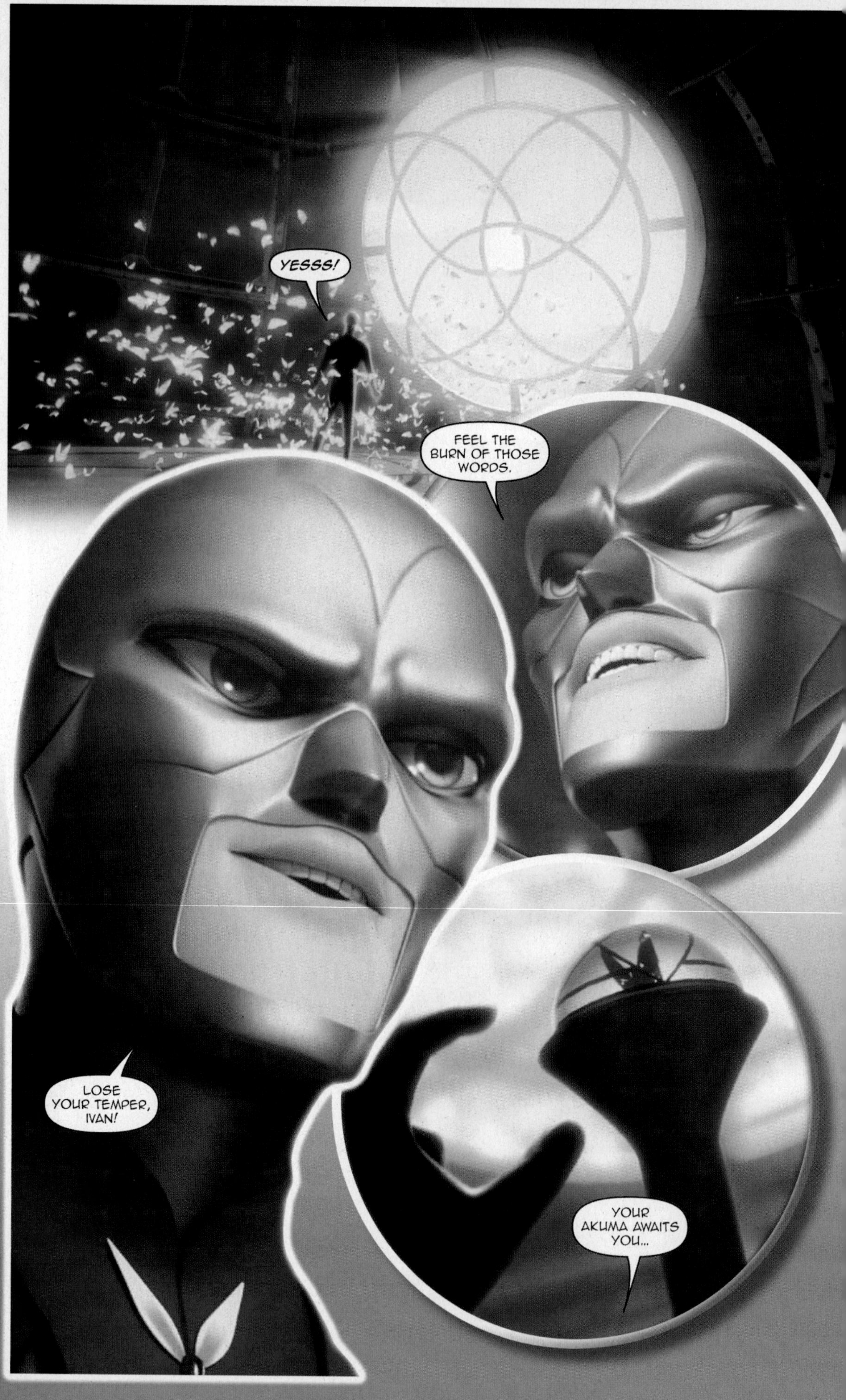
YESSS!
FEEL THE BURN OF THOSE WORDS.
LOSE YOUR TEMPER, IVAN!
YOUR AKUMA AWAITS YOU...

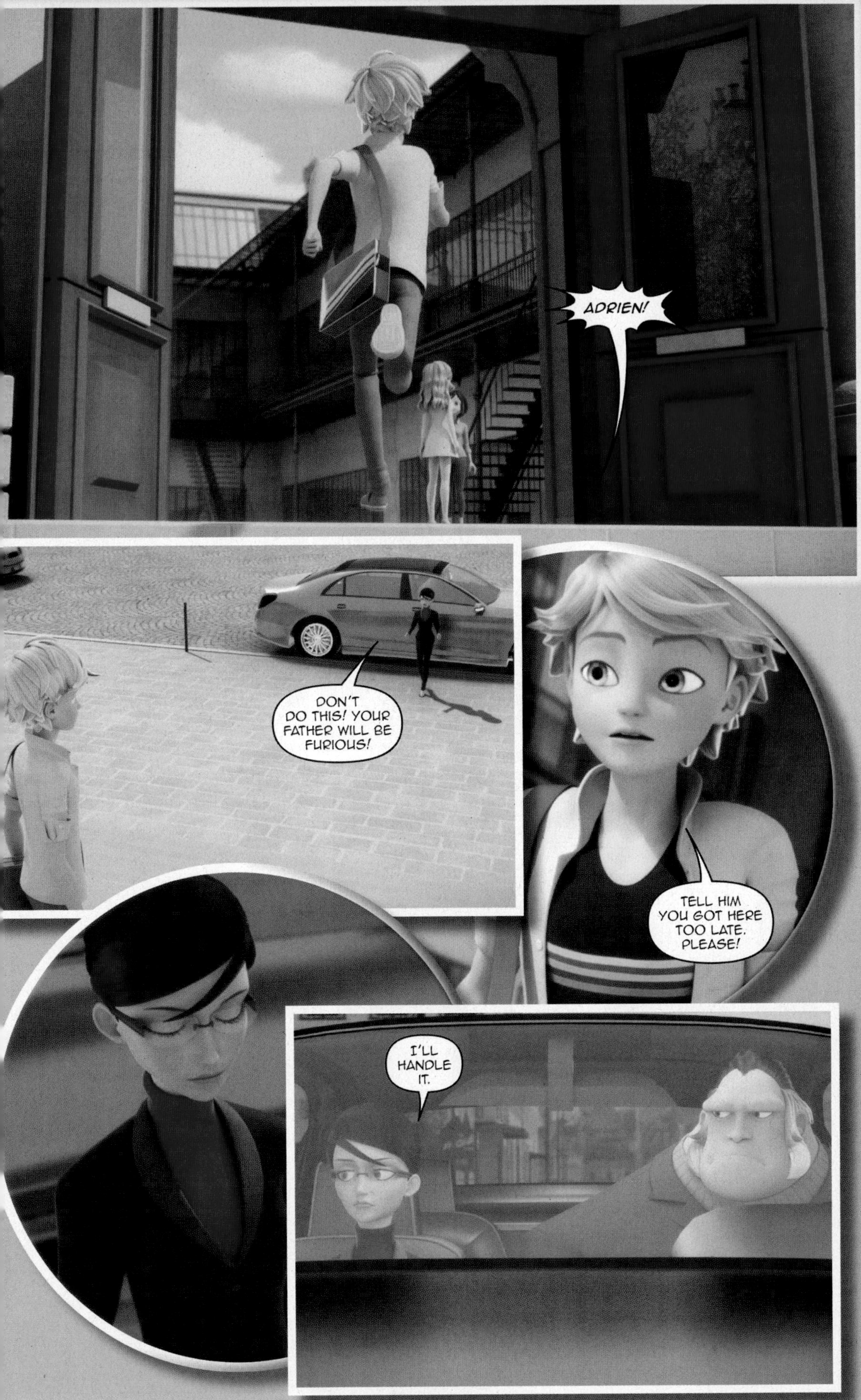
ADRIEN!
DON'T DO THIS! YOUR FATHER WILL BE FURIOUS!
TELL HIM YOU GOT HERE TOO LATE. PLEASE!
I'LL HANDLE IT.

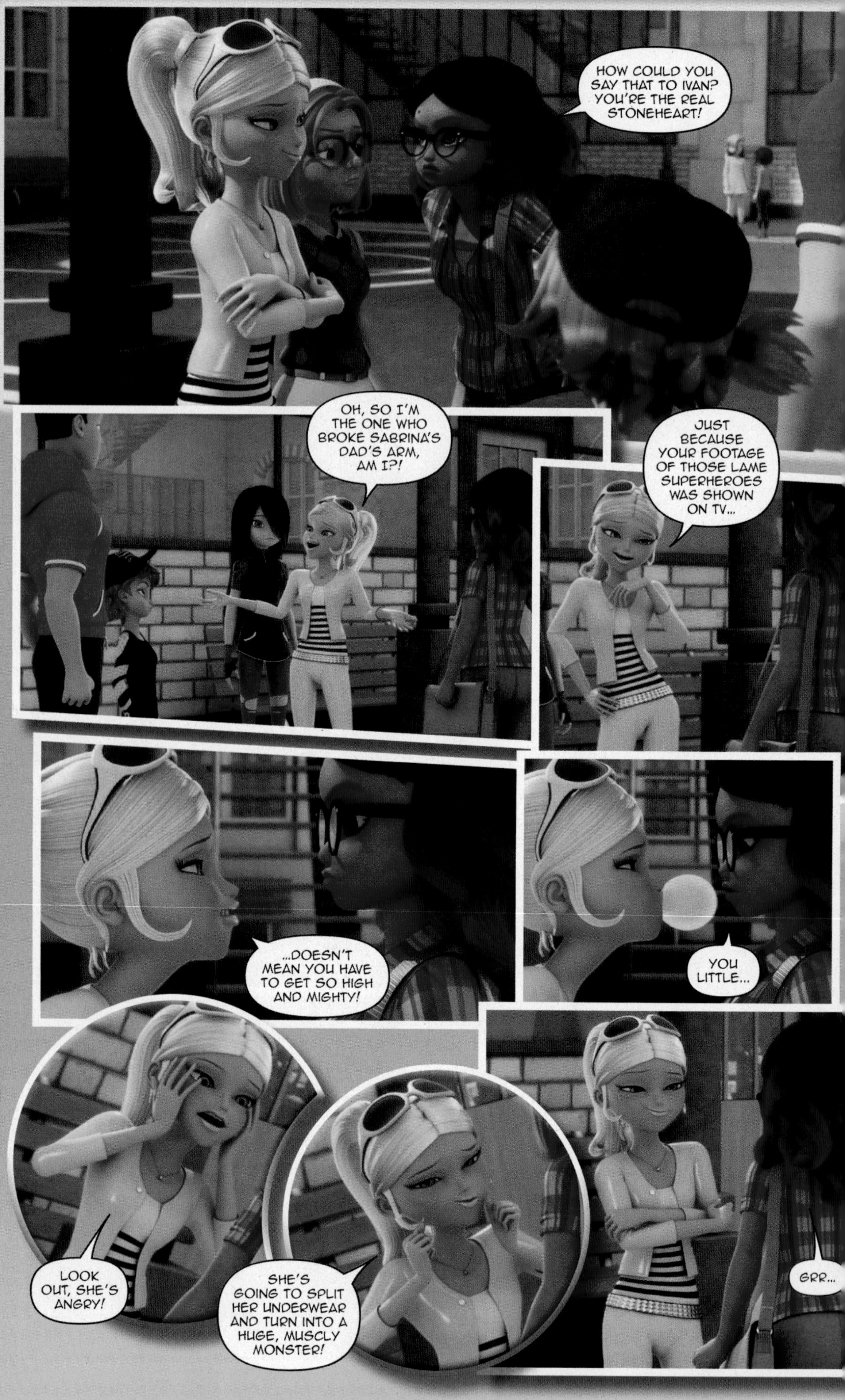
HOW COULD YOU SAY THAT TO IVAN? YOU'RE THE REAL STONEHEART!
OH, SO I'M THE ONE WHO BROKE SABRINA'S DAD'S ARM, AM I?!
JUST BECAUSE YOUR FOOTAGE OF THOSE LAME SUPERHEROES WAS SHOWN ON TV...
...DOESN'T MEAN YOU HAVE TO GET SO HIGH AND MIGHTY!
YOU LITTLE...
LOOK OUT, SHE'S ANGRY!
SHE'S GOING TO SPLIT HER UNDERWEAR AND TURN INTO A HUGE, MUSCLY MONSTER!
GRR...

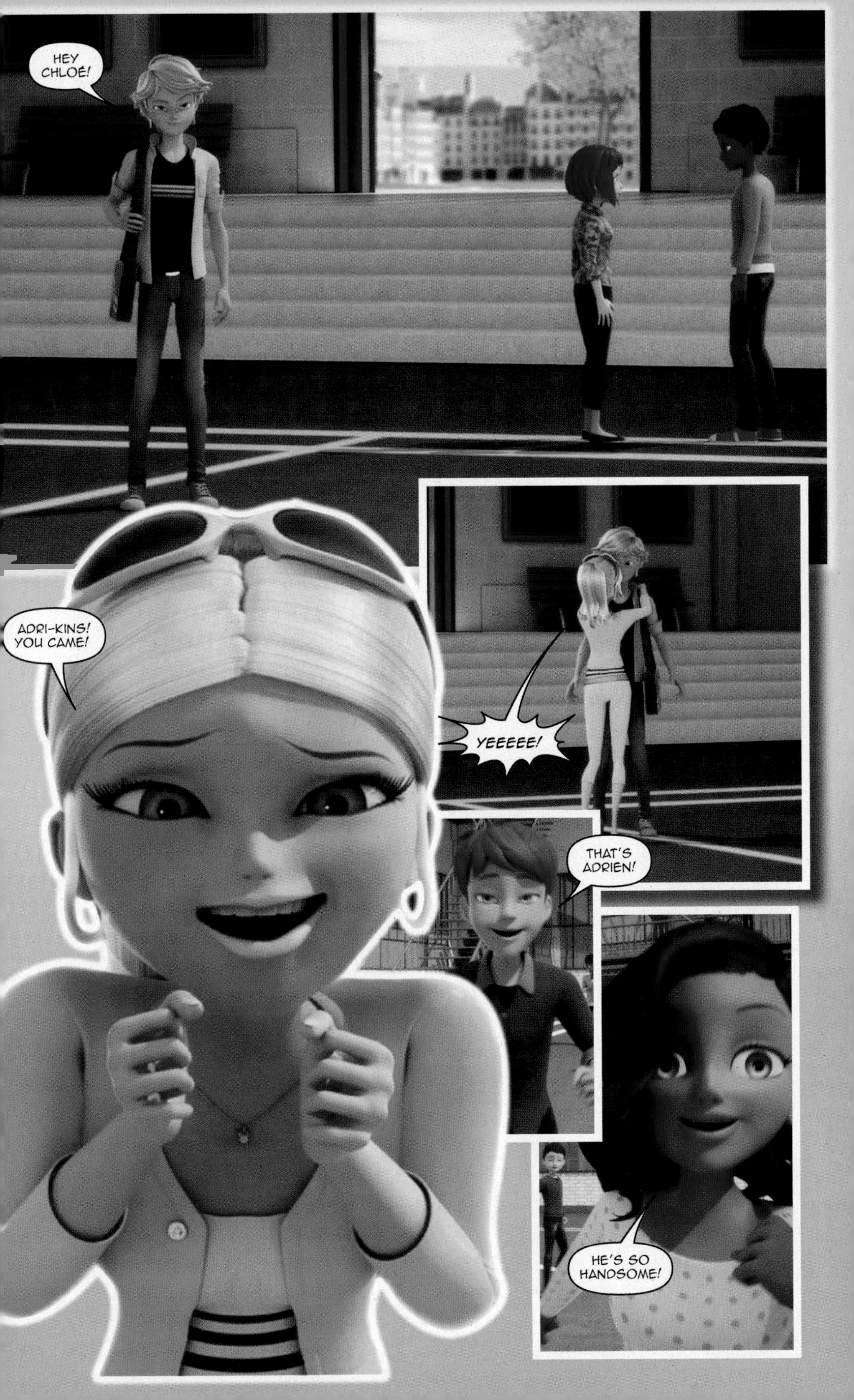
HEY CHLOÉ!
ADRI-KINS! YOU CAME!
YEEEEE!
THAT'S ADRIEN!
HE'S SO HANDSOME!

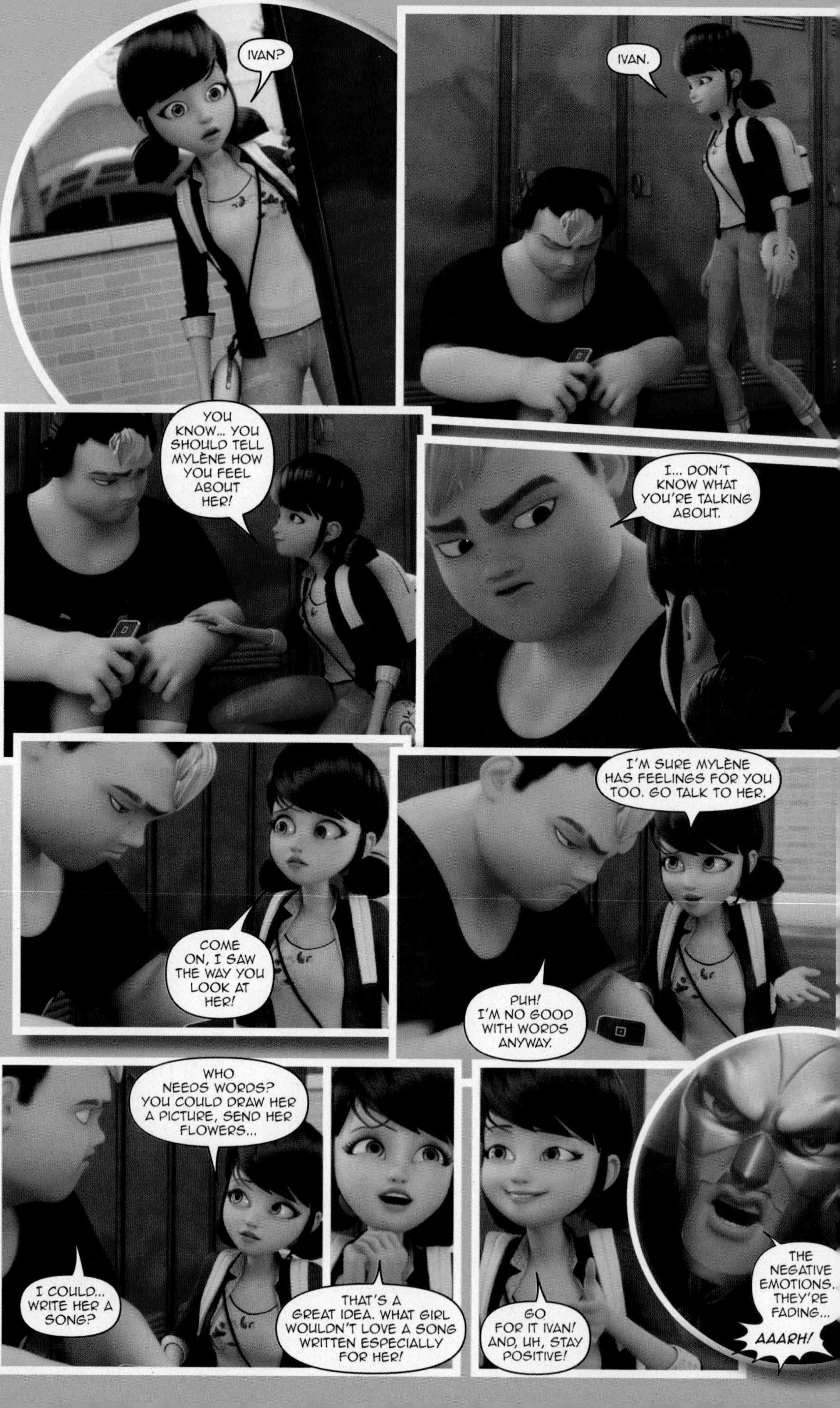
IVAN?
IVAN.
YOU KNOW... YOU SHOULD TELL MYLÈNE HOW YOU FEEL ABOUT HER!
I... DON'T KNOW WHAT YOU'RE TALKING ABOUT.
COME ON, I SAW THE WAY YOU LOOK AT HER!
I'M SURE MYLÈNE HAS FEELINGS FOR YOU TOO. GO TALK TO HER.
PUH! I'M NO GOOD WITH WORDS ANYWAY.
WHO NEEDS WORDS? YOU COULD DRAW HER A PICTURE, SEND HER FLOWERS...
I COULD... WRITE HER A SONG?
THAT'S A GREAT IDEA. WHAT GIRL WOULDN'T LOVE A SONG WRITTEN ESPECIALLY FOR HER!
GO FOR IT IVAN! AND, UH, STAY POSITIVE!
THE NEGATIVE EMOTIONS. THEY'RE FADING...
AAARH!

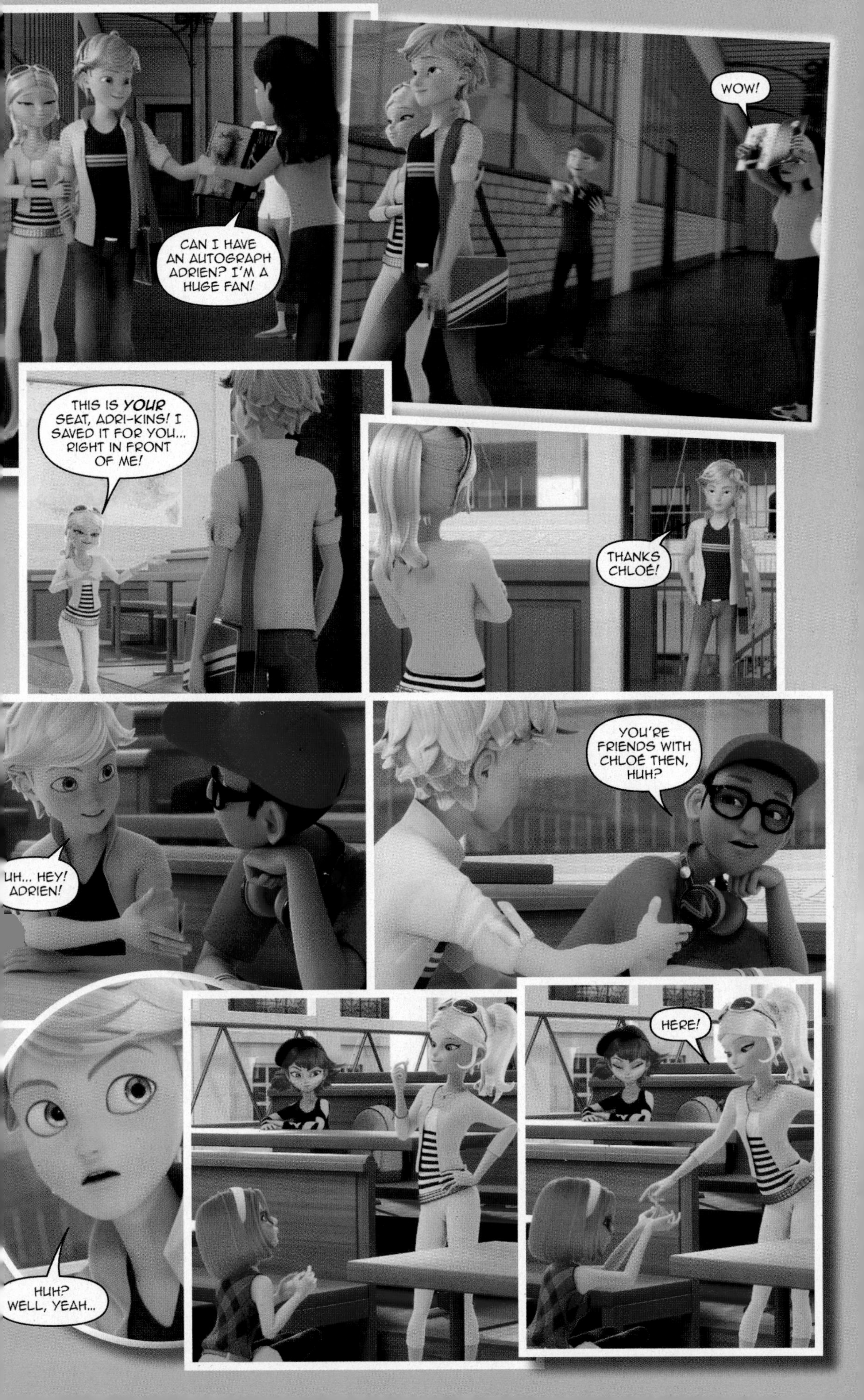
CAN I HAVE AN AUTOGRAPH ADRIEN? I'M A HUGE FAN!
WOW!
THIS IS YOUR SEAT, ADRI-KINS! I SAVED IT FOR YOU... RIGHT IN FRONT OF ME!
THANKS CHLOÉ!
UH... HEY! ADRIEN!
YOU'RE FRIENDS WITH CHLOÉ THEN, HUH?
HUH? WELL, YEAH...
HERE!

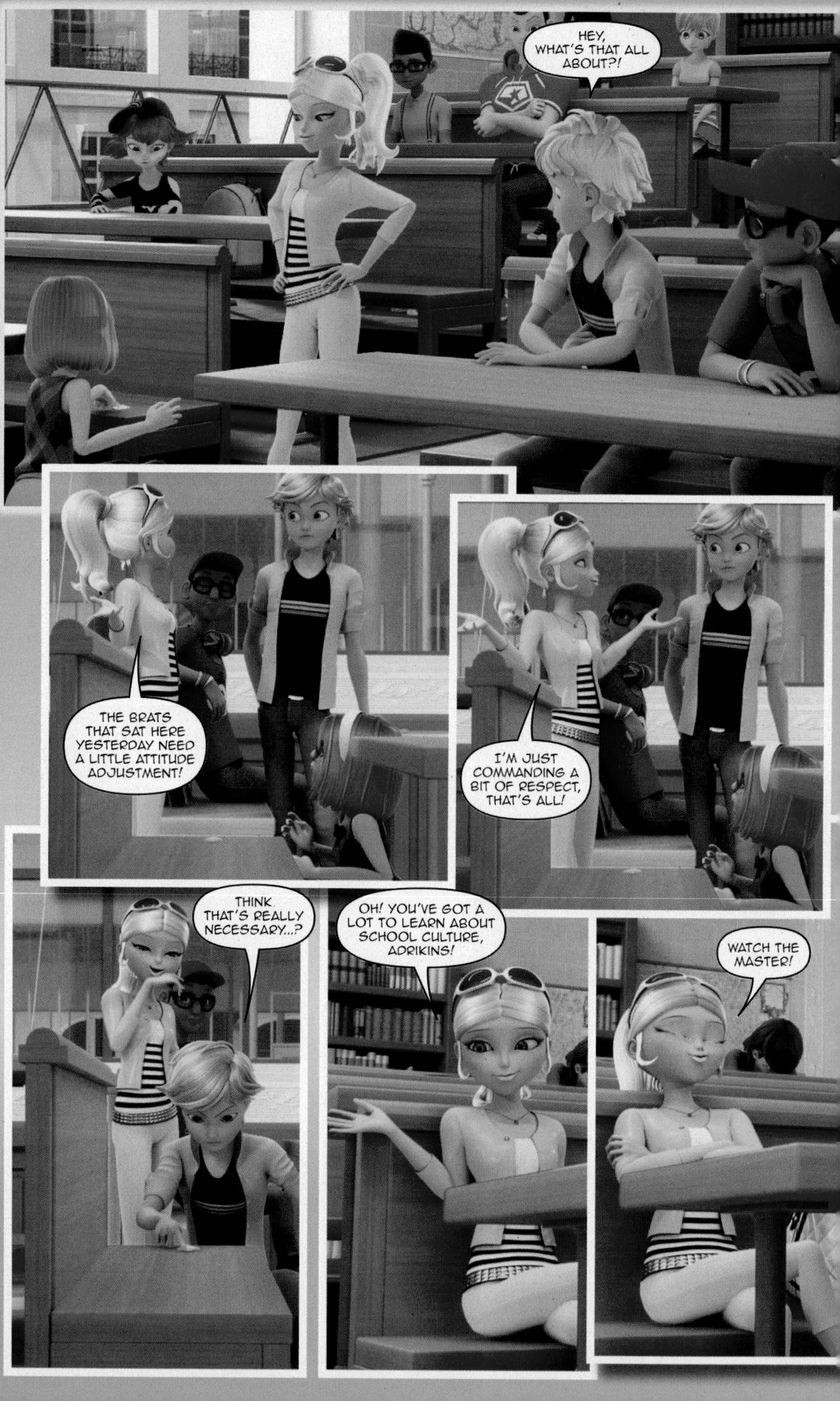
HEY, WHAT'S THAT ALL ABOUT?!
THE BRATS THAT SAT HERE YESTERDAY NEED A LITTLE ATTITUDE ADJUSTMENT!
I'M JUST COMMANDING A BIT OF RESPECT, THAT'S ALL!
THINK. THAT'S REALLY NECESSARY...?
OH! YOU'VE GOT A LOT TO LEARN ABOUT SCHOOL CULTURE, ADRIKINS!
WATCH THE MASTER!

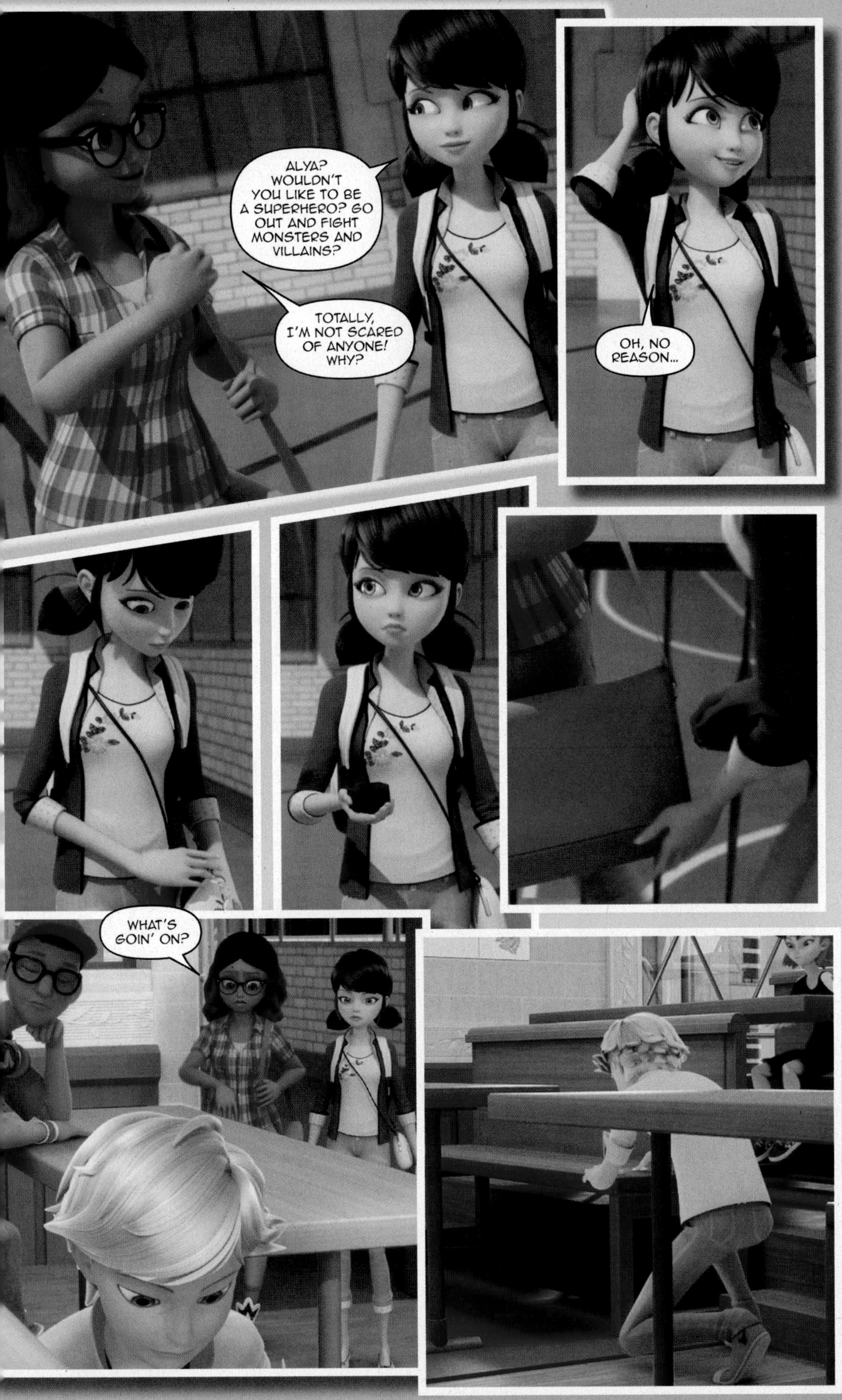
ALYA? WOULDN'T YOU LIKE TO BE A SUPERHERO? GO OUT AND FIGHT MONSTERS AND VILLAINS?
TOTALLY, I'M NOT SCARED OF ANYONE! WHY?
OH, NO REASON...
WHAT'S GOIN' ON?

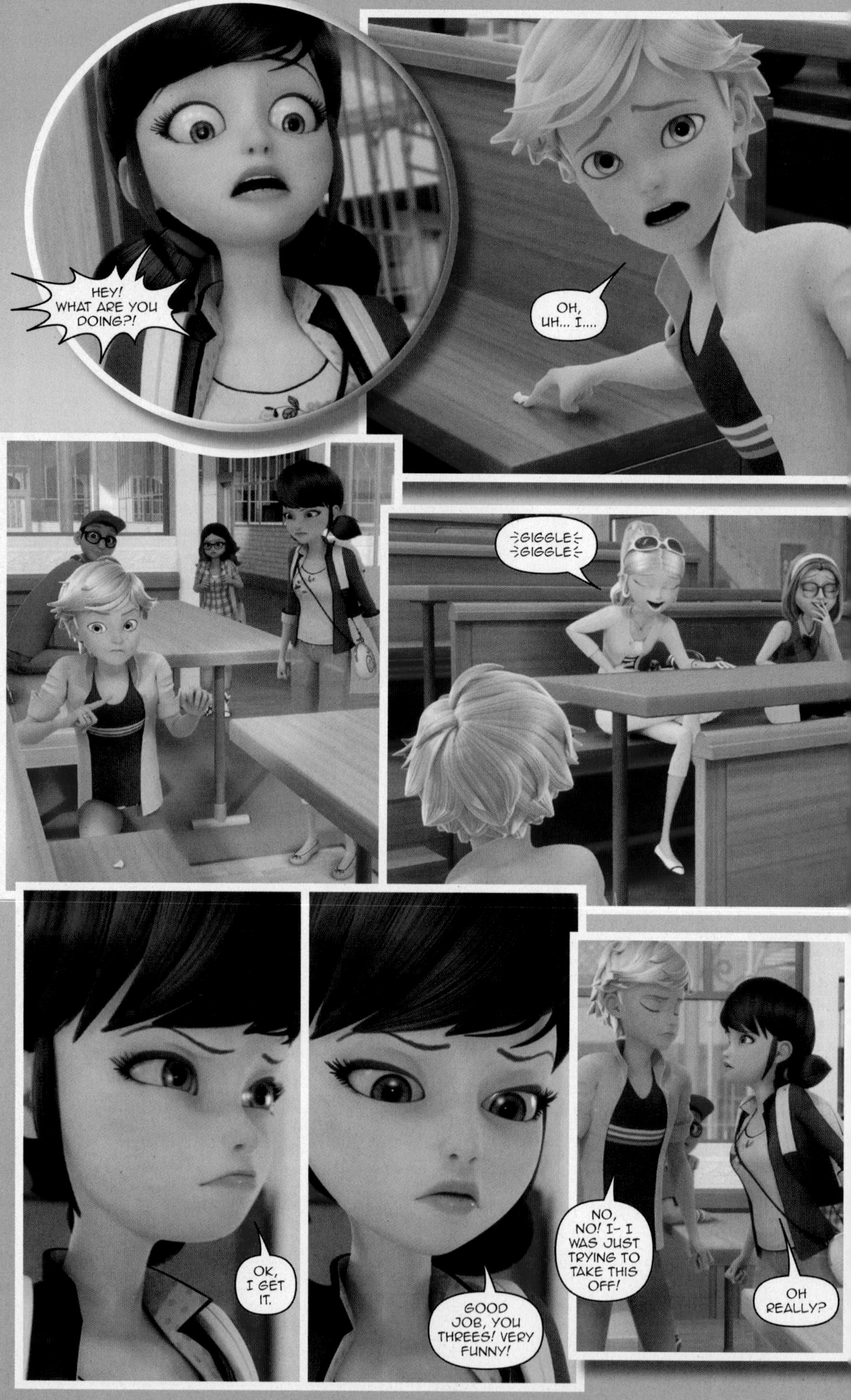
HEY! WHAT ARE YOU DOING?!
OH, UH... I....
GIGGLE GIGGLE
OK, I GET IT.
GOOD JOB, YOU THREES! VERY FUNNY!
NO, NO! I- I WAS JUST TRYING TO TAKE THIS OFF!
OH REALLY?

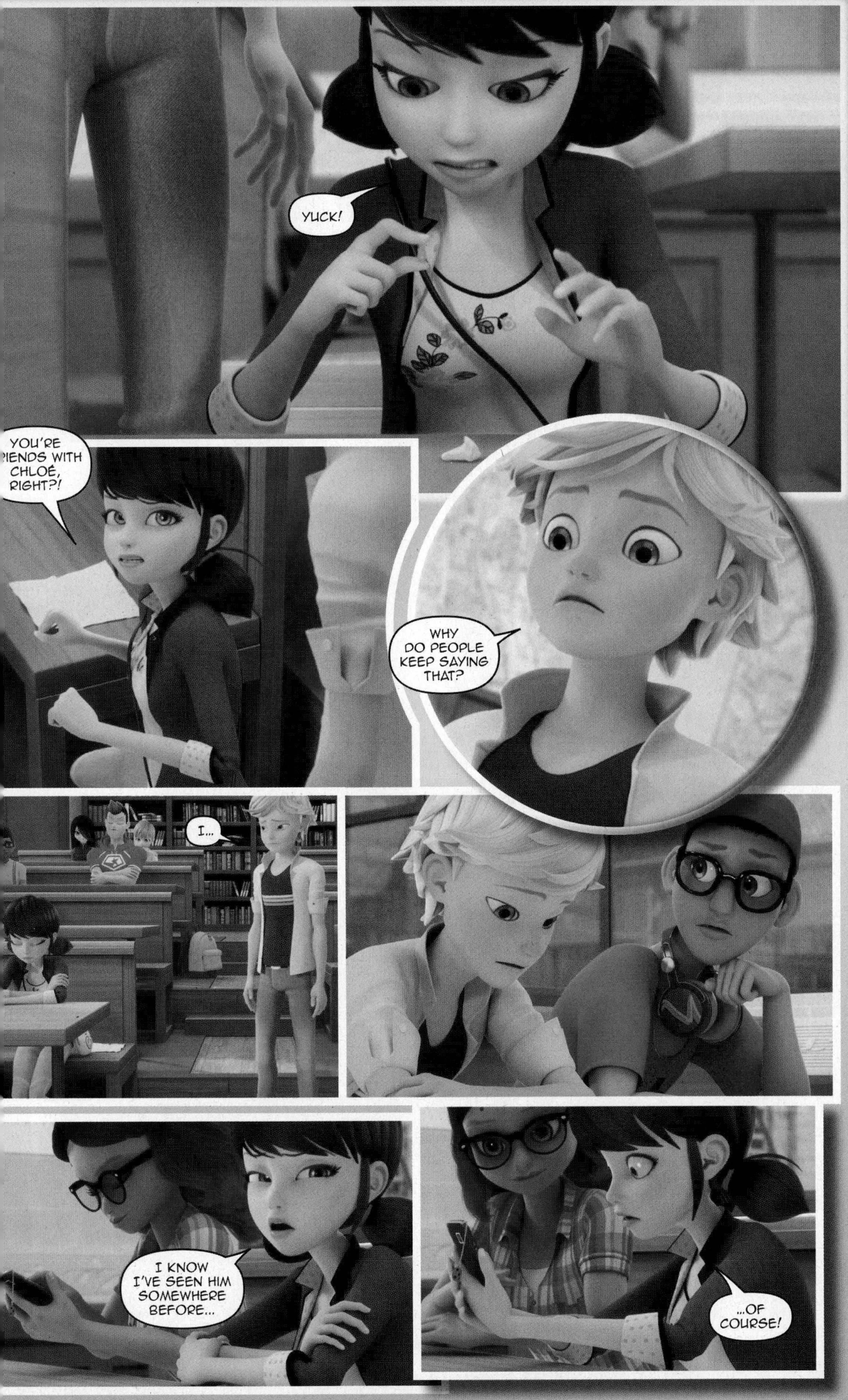
YUCK!
YOU'RE FRIENDS WITH CHLOÉ, RIGHT?!
WHY DO PEOPLE KEEP SAYING THAT?
I...
I KNOW I'VE SEEN HIM SOMEWHERE BEFORE...
...OF COURSE!

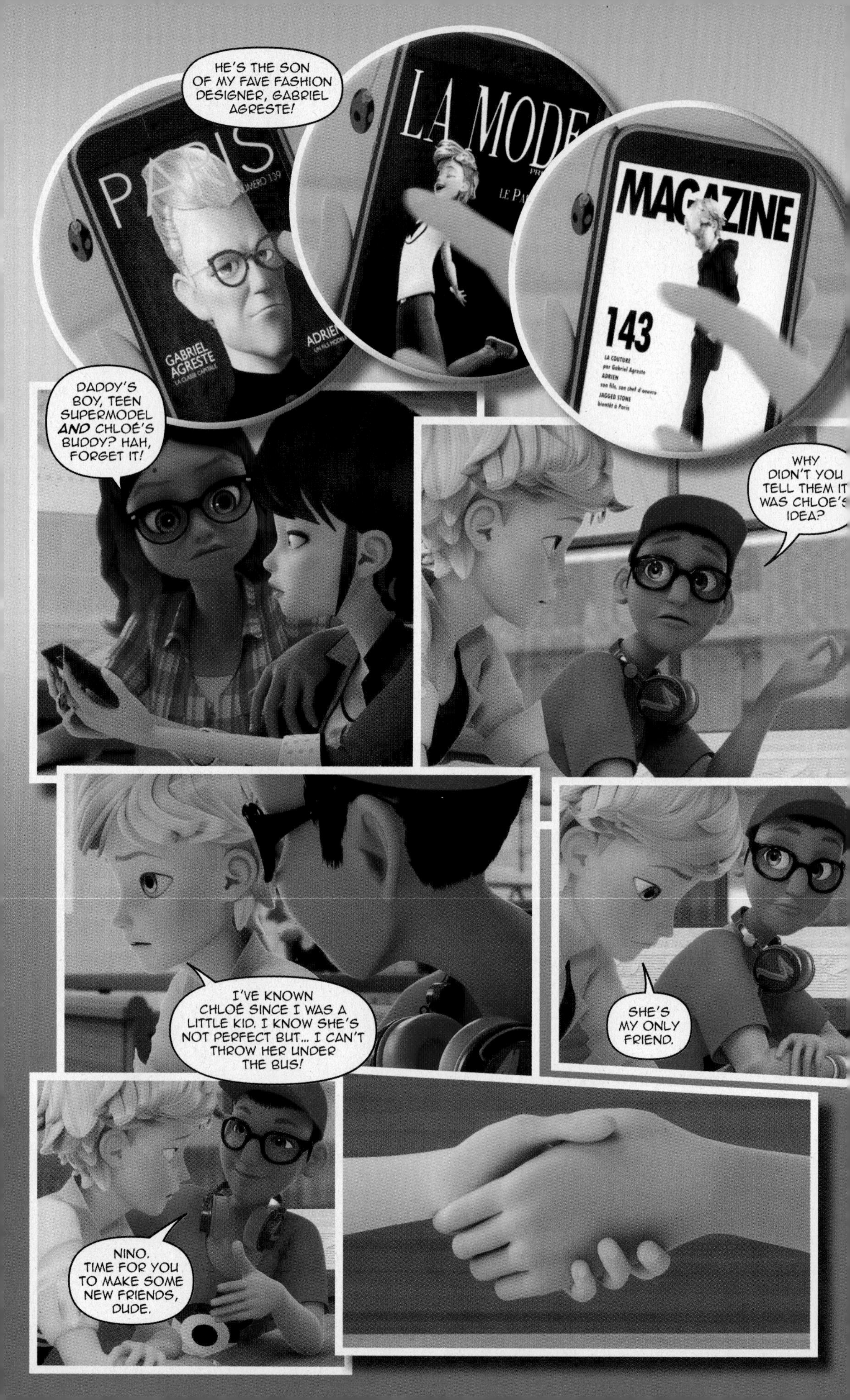
HE'S THE SON OF MY FAVE FASHION DESIGNER, GABRIEL AGRESTE!
PARIS
GABRIEL AGRESTE
LA CLASSE CAPITALE
LA MODE
MAGAZINE
143
LA COUTURE
par Gabriel Agreste
ADRIEN
son fils, son chef d'oeuvre
JAGGED STONE
bientôt à Paris
DADDY'S BOY, TEEN SUPERMODEL **AND** CHLOÉ'S BUDDY? HAH, FORGET IT!
WHY DIDN'T YOU TELL THEM IT WAS CHLOE'S IDEA?
I'VE KNOWN CHLOÉ SINCE I WAS A LITTLE KID. I KNOW SHE'S NOT PERFECT BUT... I CAN'T THROW HER UNDER THE BUS!
SHE'S MY ONLY FRIEND.
NINO. TIME FOR YOU TO MAKE SOME NEW FRIENDS, DUDE.

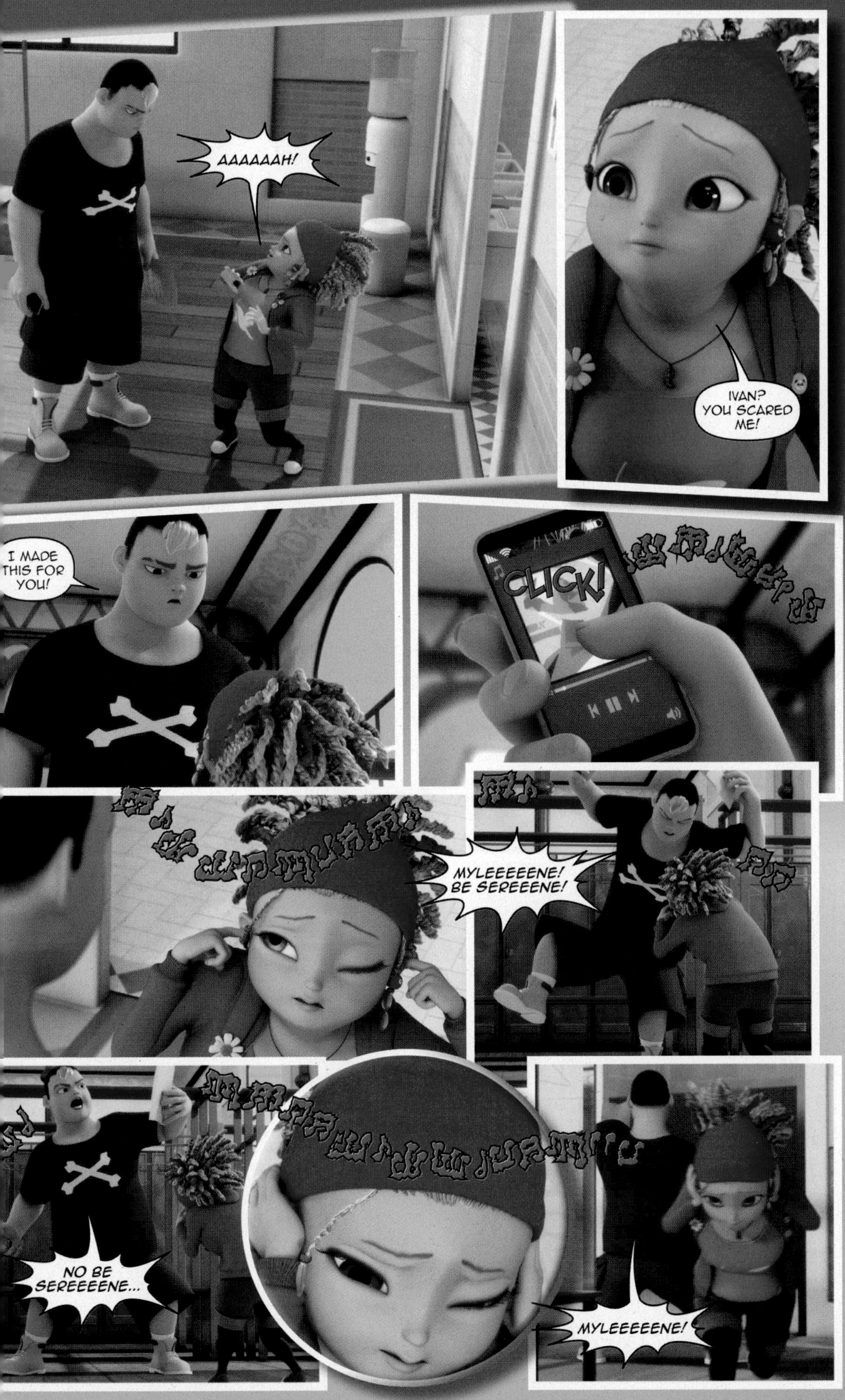
AAAAAAH!
IVAN? YOU SCARED ME!
I MADE THIS FOR YOU!
CLICK!
MYLEEEEENE! BE SEREEENE!
NO BE SEREEEENE...
MYLEEEEENE!

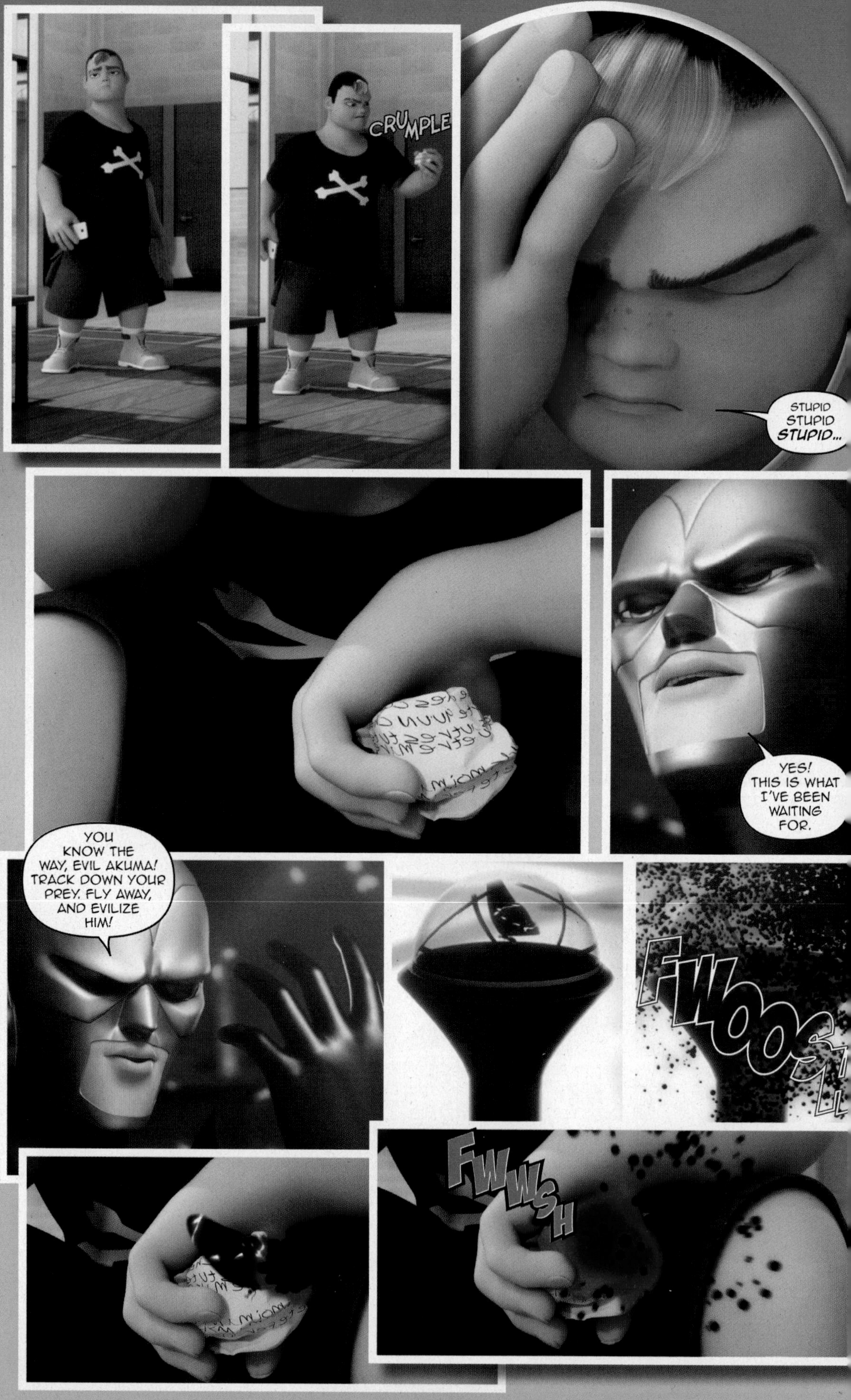
CRUMPLE
STUPID STUPID STUPID...
YES! THIS IS WHAT I'VE BEEN WAITING FOR.
YOU KNOW THE WAY, EVIL AKUMA! TRACK DOWN YOUR PREY. FLY AWAY, AND EVILIZE HIM!
FWOOSH
FWWSH

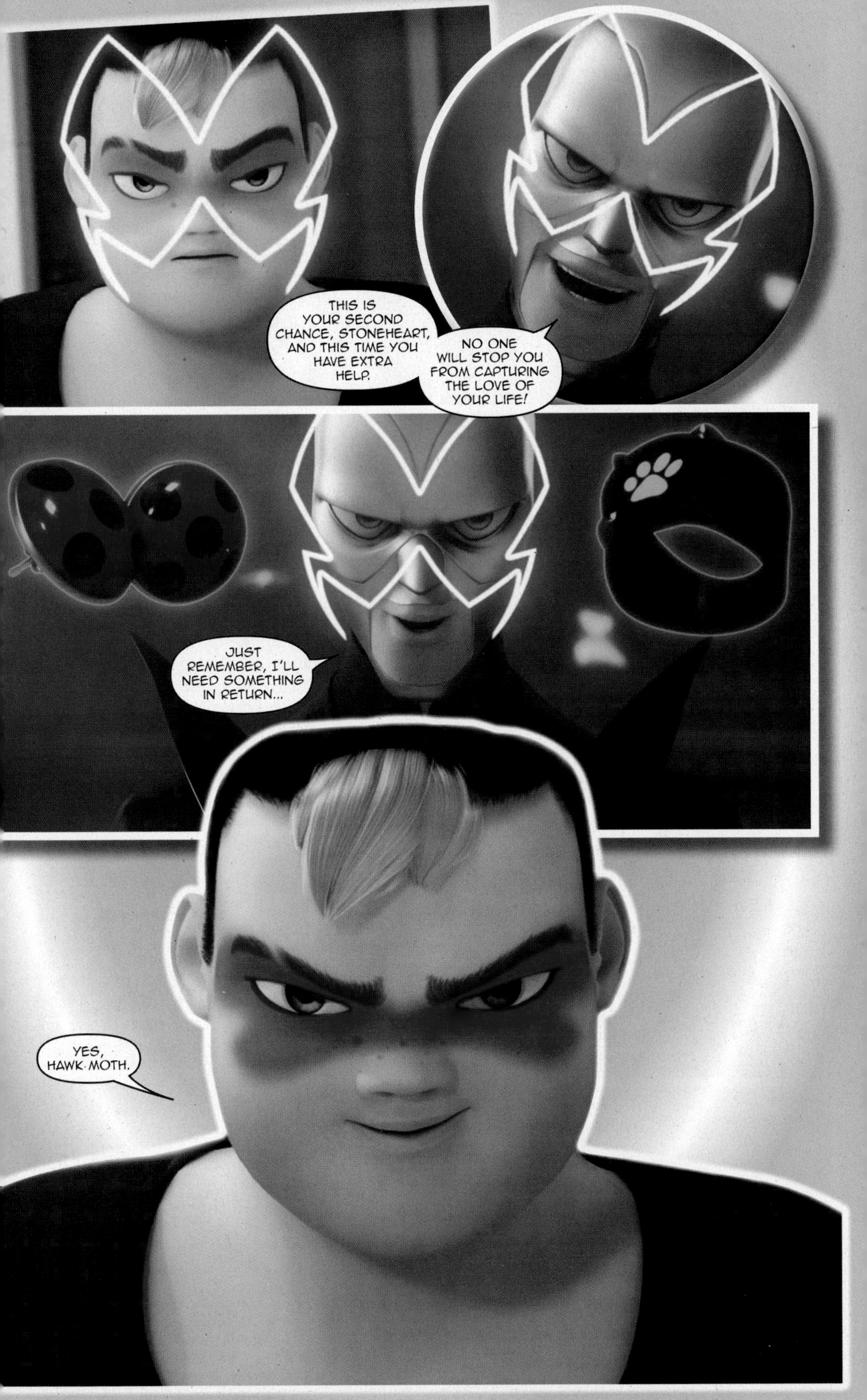
THIS IS YOUR SECOND CHANCE, STONEHEART, AND THIS TIME YOU HAVE EXTRA HELP.
NO ONE WILL STOP YOU FROM CAPTURING THE LOVE OF YOUR LIFE!
JUST REMEMBER, I'LL NEED SOMETHING IN RETURN...
YES, HAWK MOTH.

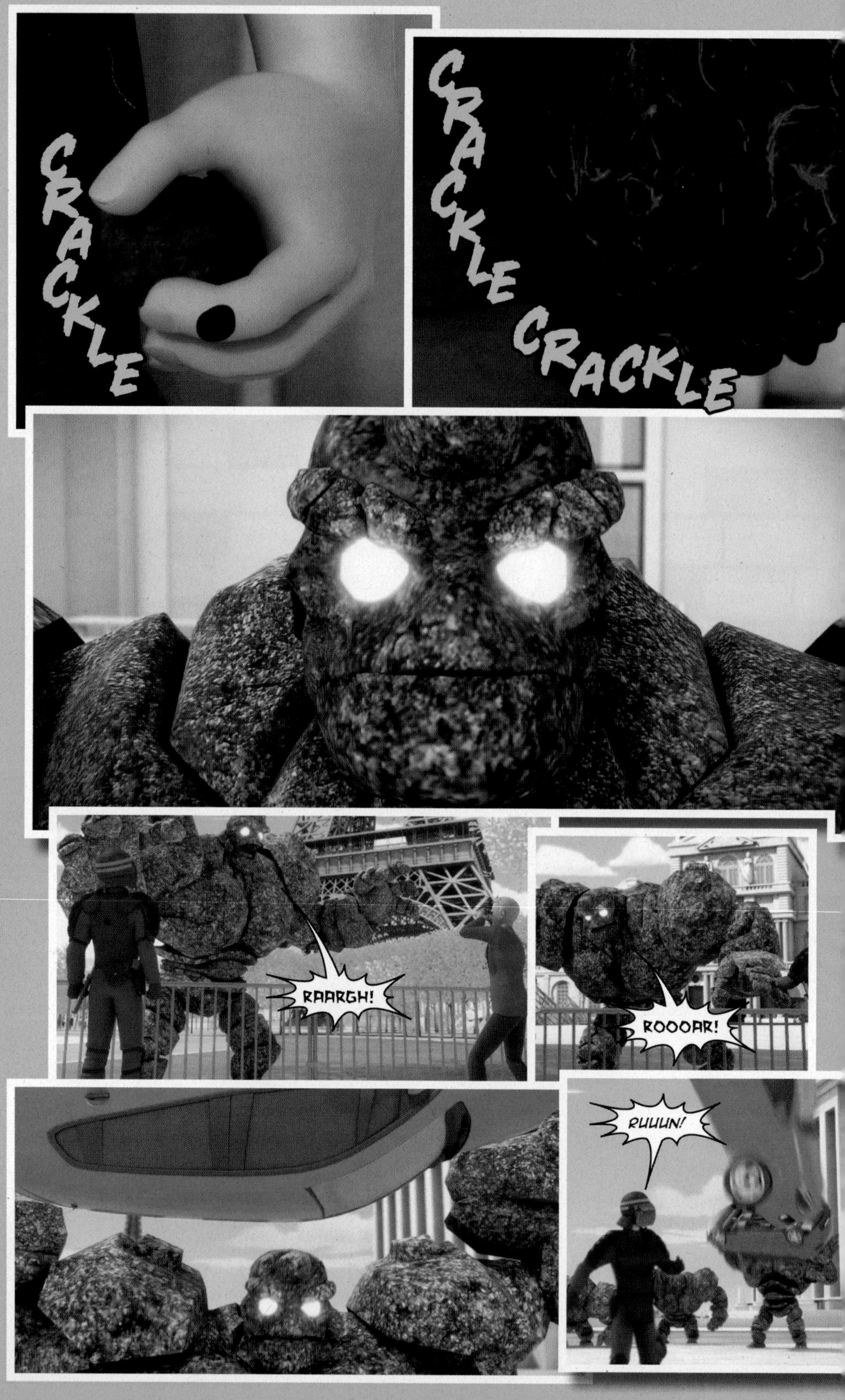
CRACKLE
CRACKLE CRACKLE
RAARGH!
ROOOAR!
RUUUN!

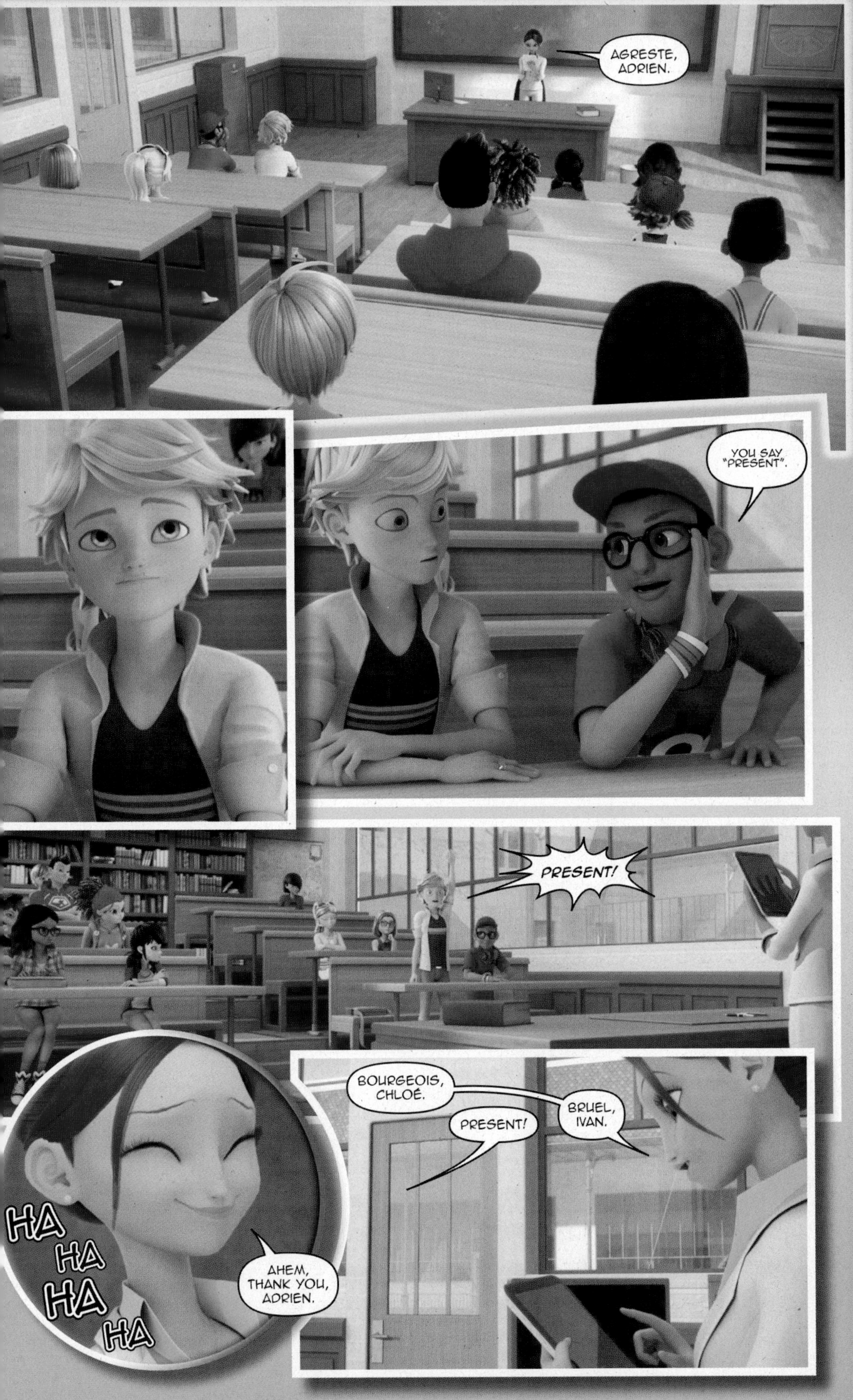
AGRESTE, ADRIEN.
YOU SAY "PRESENT".
PRESENT!
HA HA HA HA
AHEM, THANK YOU, ADRIEN.
BOURGEOIS, CHLOÉ.
PRESENT!
BRUEL, IVAN.

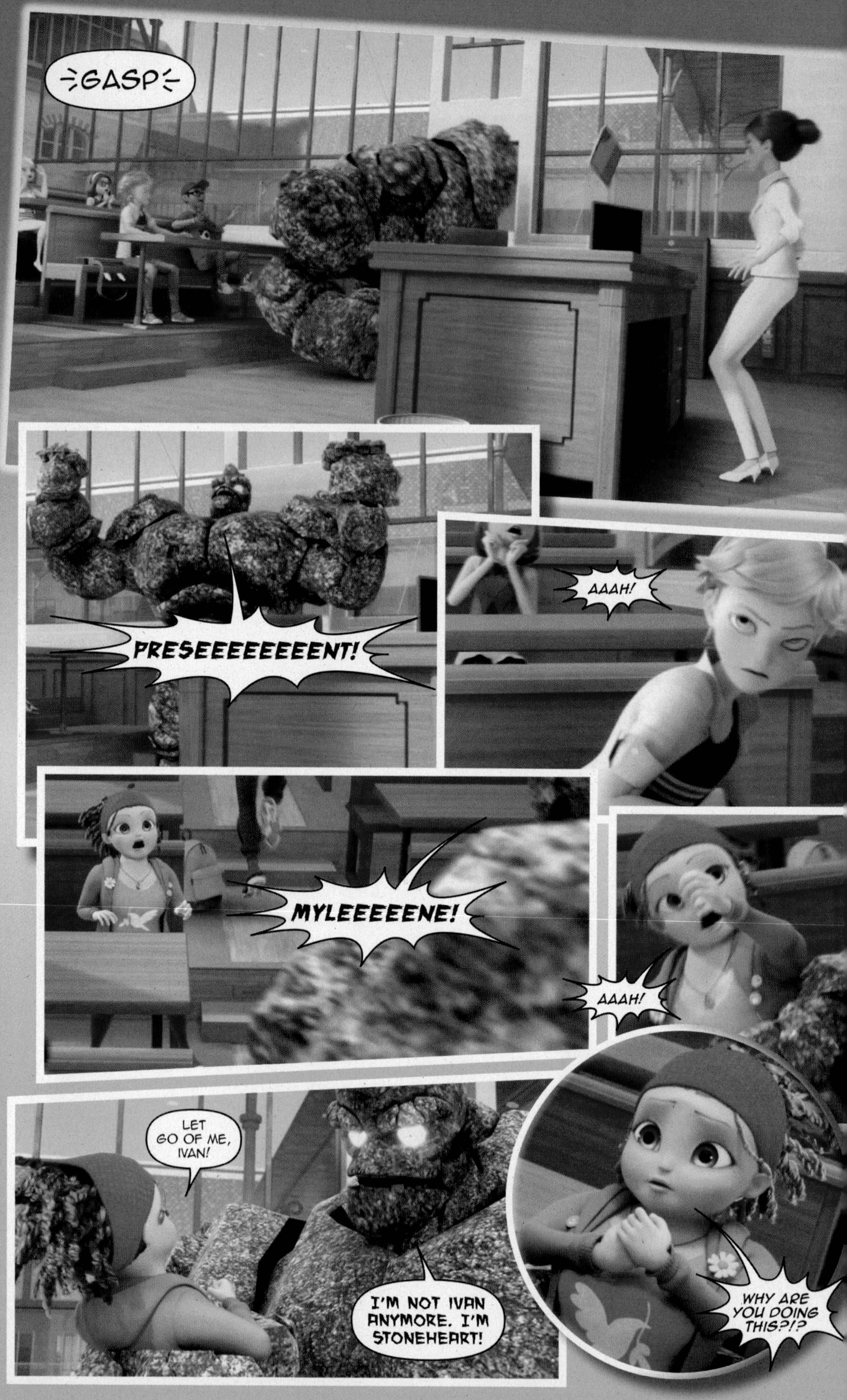
GASP
PRESEEEEEEEENT!
AAAH!
MYLEEEEENE!
AAAH!
LET GO OF ME, IVAN!
I'M NOT IVAN ANYMORE. I'M STONEHEART!
WHY ARE YOU DOING THIS?!?

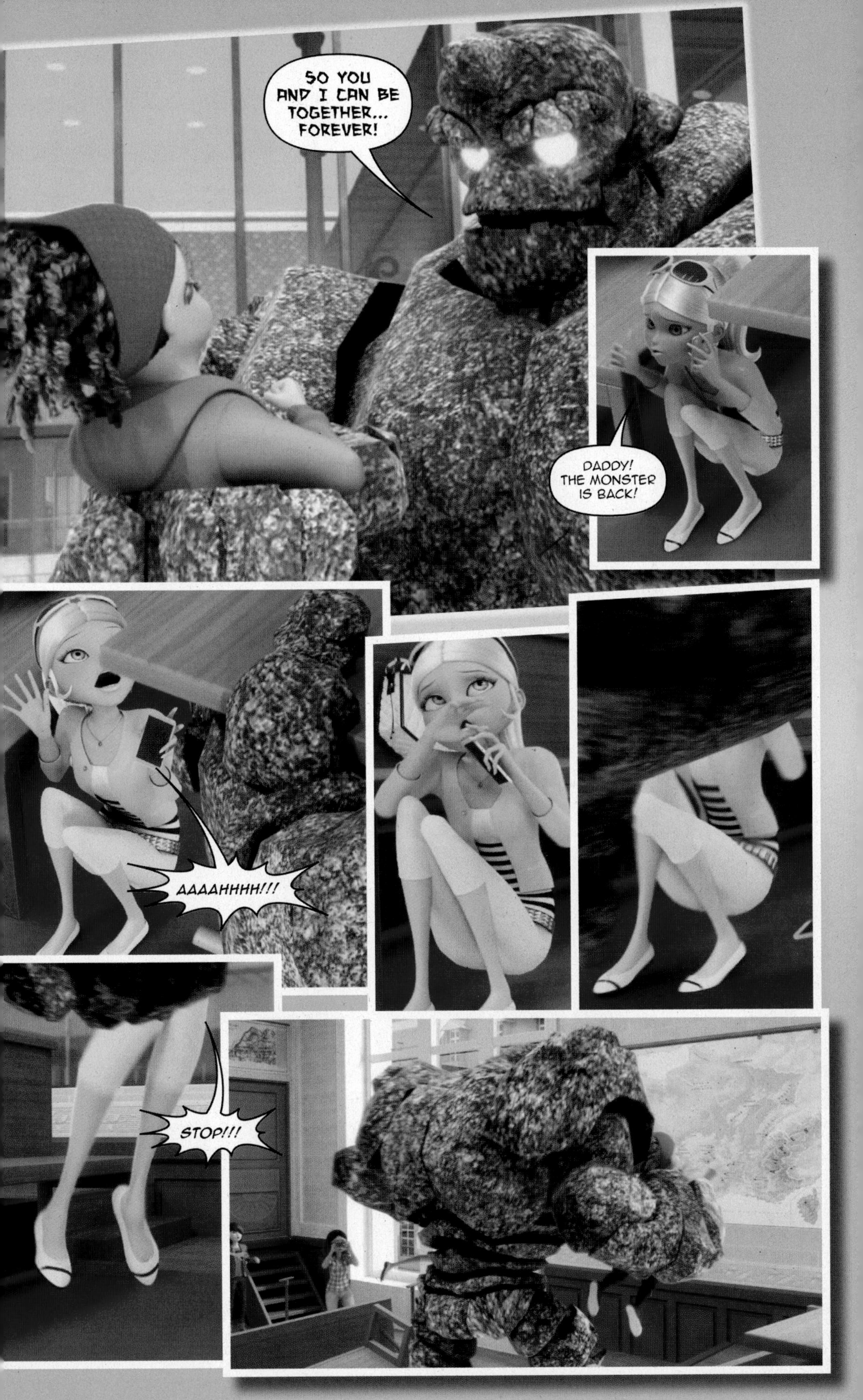
SO YOU AND I CAN BE TOGETHER... FOREVER!
DADDY! THE MONSTER IS BACK!
AAAAHHHH!!!
STOP!!!

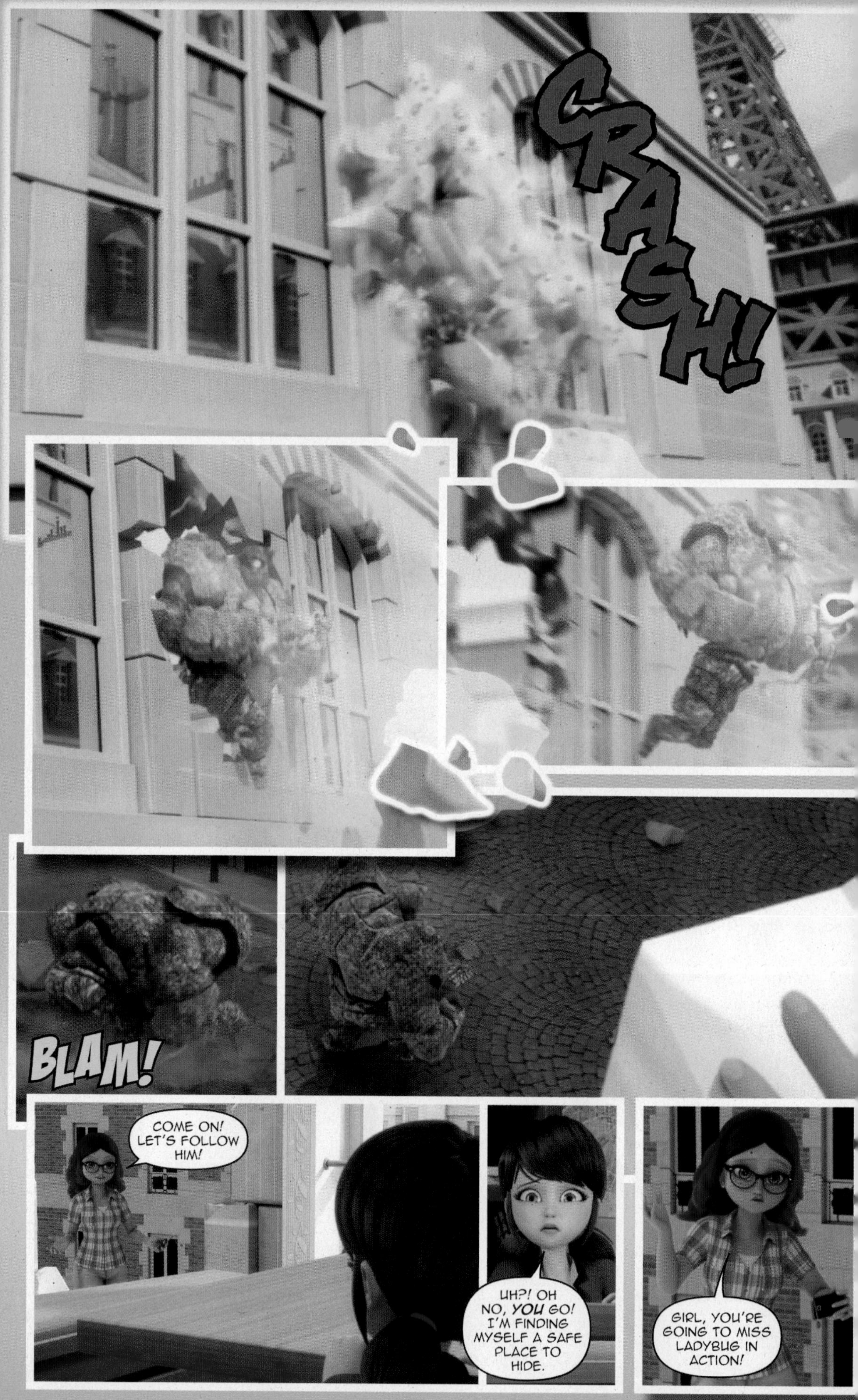
CRASH!
BLAM!
COME ON! LET'S FOLLOW HIM!
UH?! OH NO, YOU GO! I'M FINDING MYSELF A SAFE PLACE TO HIDE.
GIRL, YOU'RE GOING TO MISS LADYBUG IN ACTION!

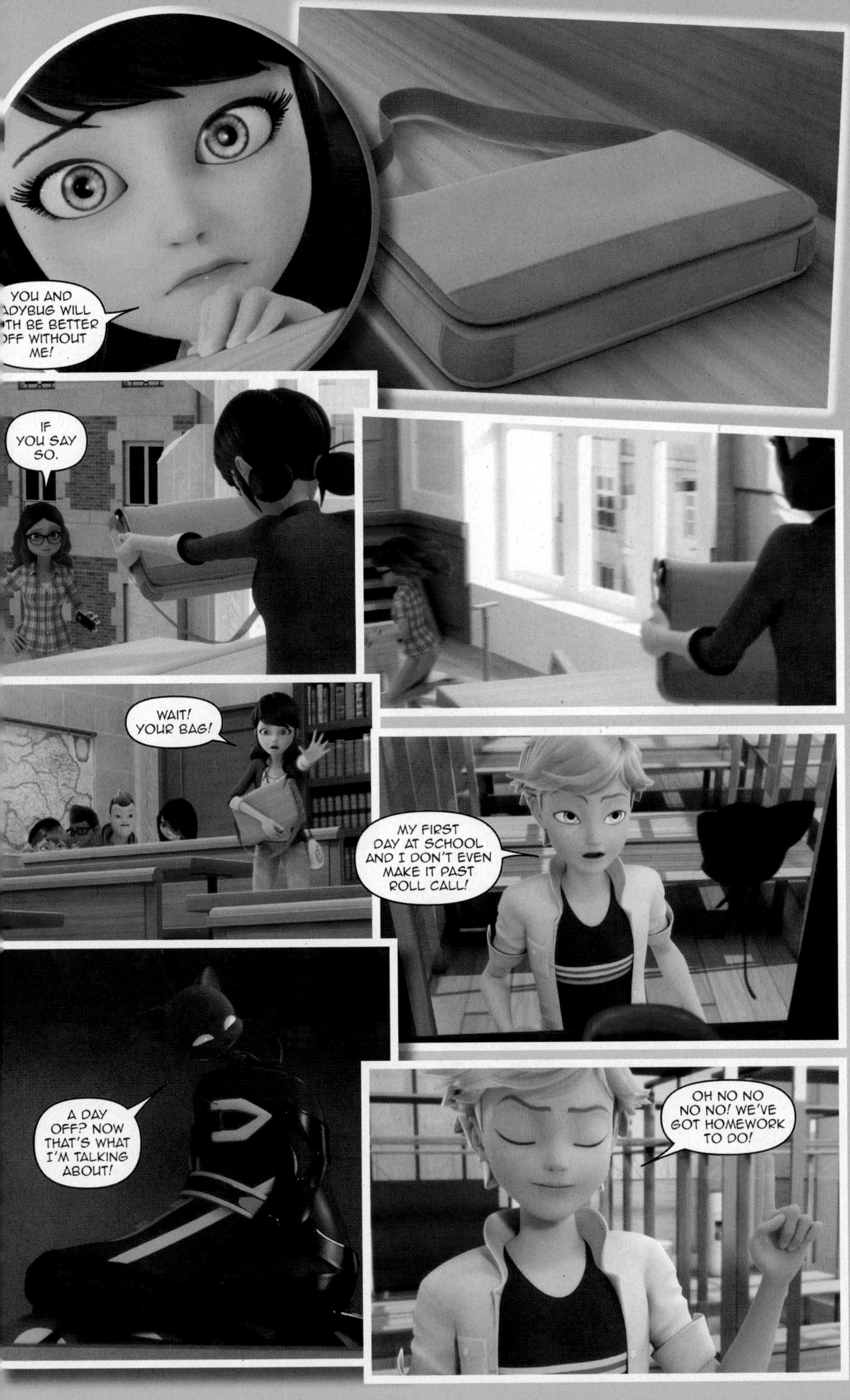
YOU AND
ADYBUG WILL
TH BE BETTER
OFF WITHOUT
ME!
IF YOU SAY SO.
WAIT! YOUR BAG!
MY FIRST DAY AT SCHOOL AND I DON'T EVEN MAKE IT PAST ROLL CALL!
A DAY OFF? NOW THAT'S WHAT I'M TALKING ABOUT!
OH NO NO NO NO! WE'VE GOT HOMEWORK TO DO!

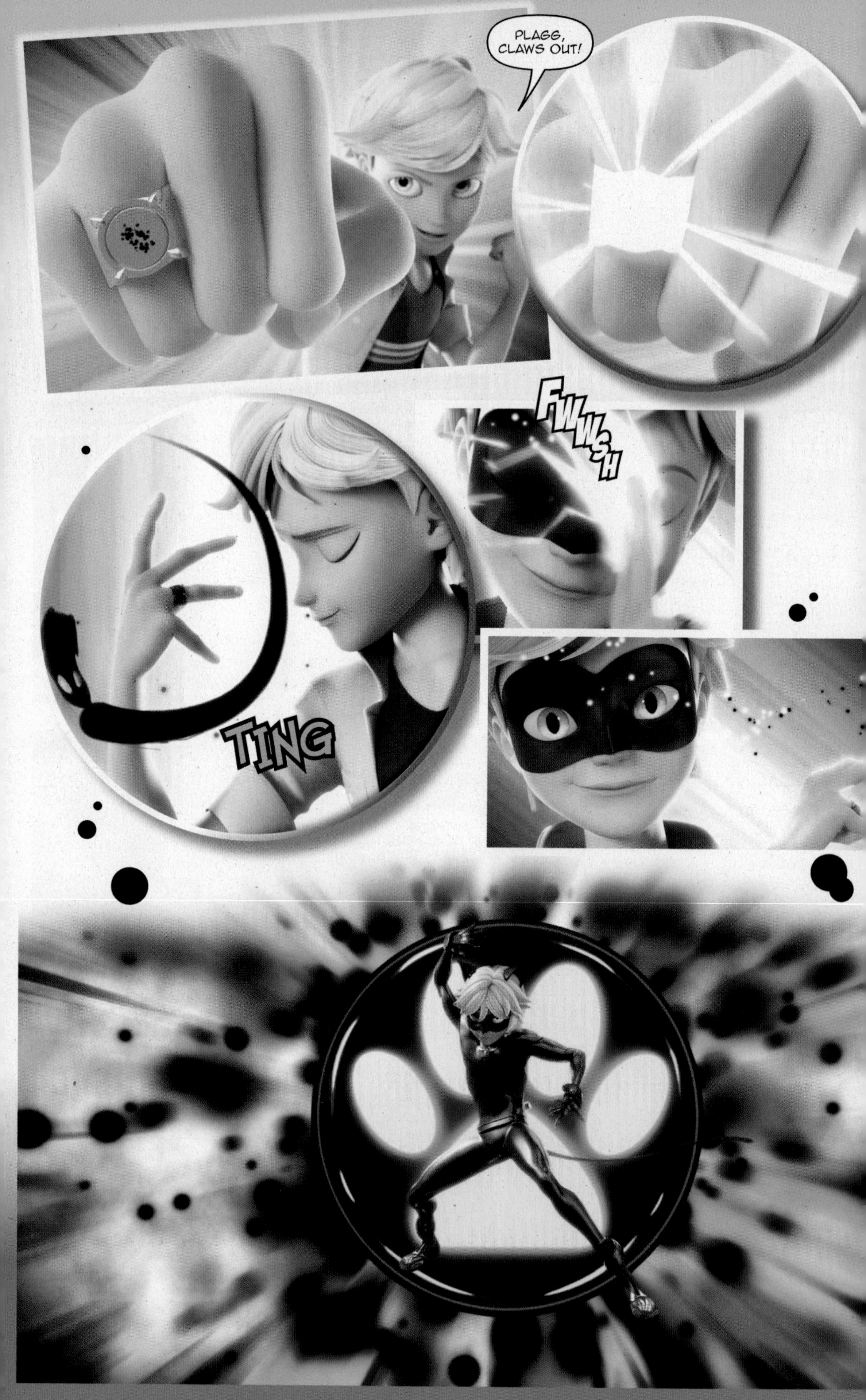
PLAGG, CLAWS OUT!
FWWSH
TING

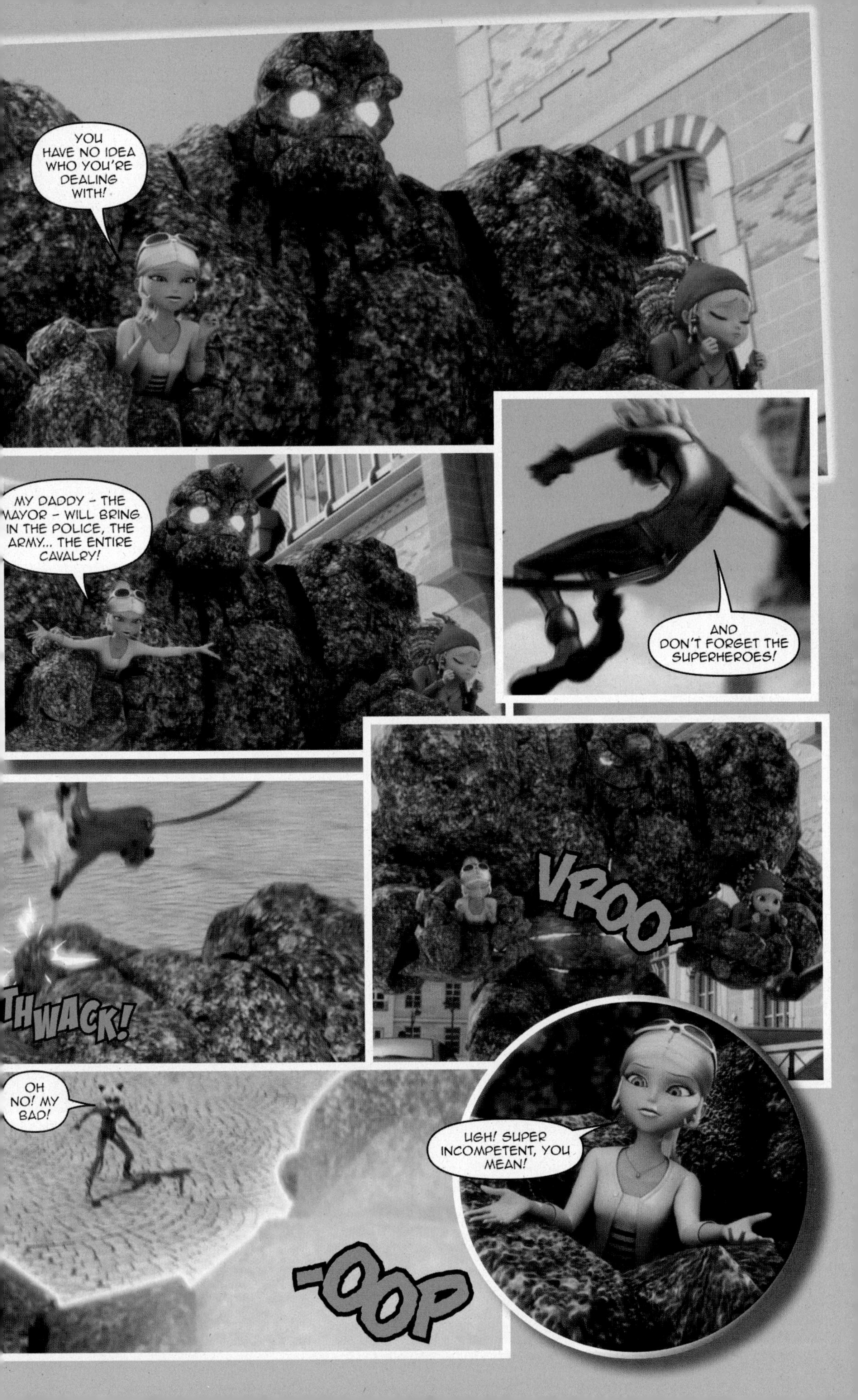
YOU HAVE NO IDEA WHO YOU'RE DEALING WITH!
MY DADDY – THE MAYOR – WILL BRING IN THE POLICE, THE ARMY... THE ENTIRE CAVALRY!
AND DON'T FORGET THE SUPERHEROES!
THWACK!
VROO-
OH NO! MY BAD!
-OOP
UGH! SUPER INCOMPETENT, YOU MEAN!

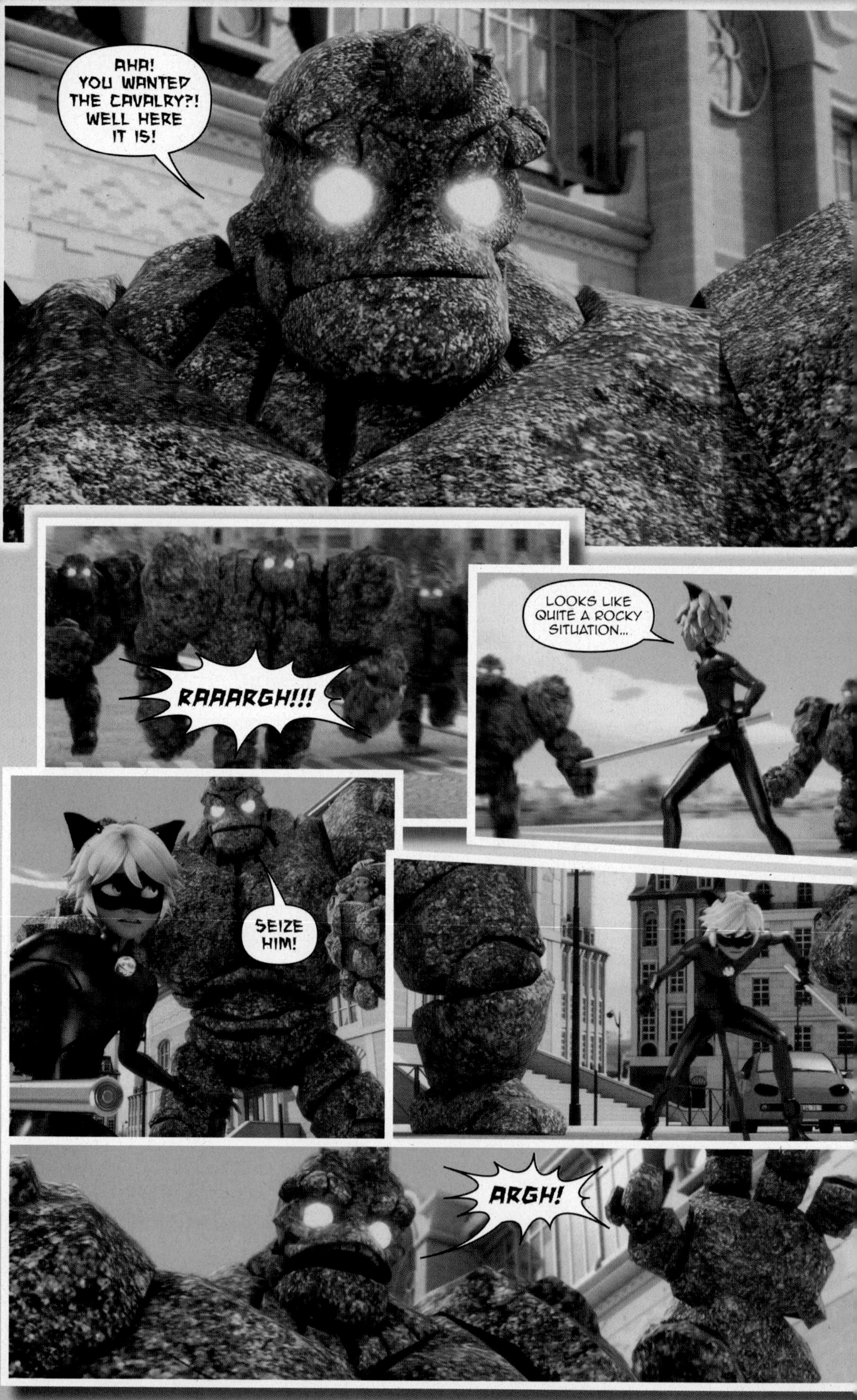
AHA! YOU WANTED THE CAVALRY?! WELL HERE IT IS!
RAAARGH!!!
LOOKS LIKE QUITE A ROCKY SITUATION...
SEIZE HIM!
ARGH!

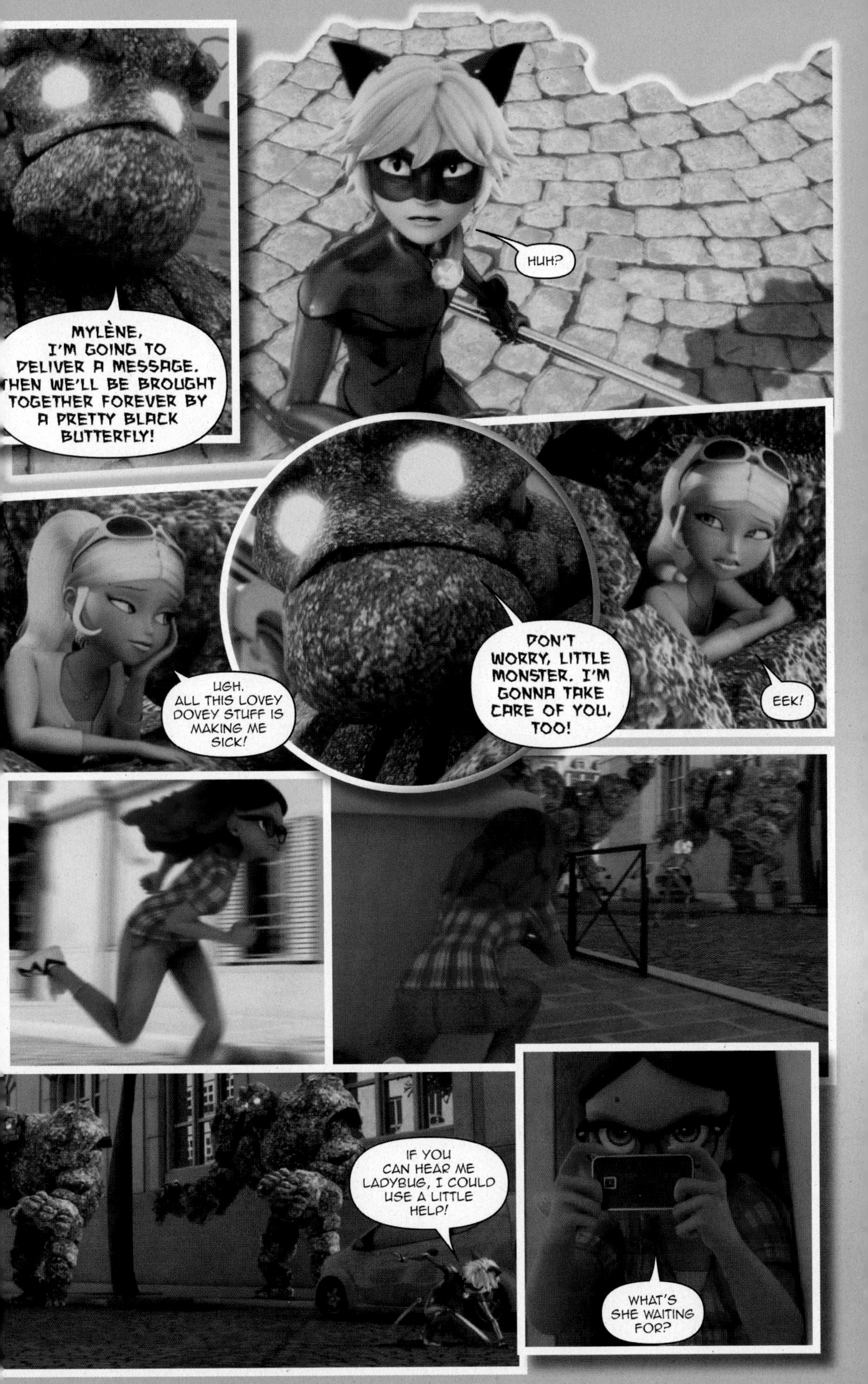
MYLÈNE, I'M GOING TO DELIVER A MESSAGE. THEN WE'LL BE BROUGHT TOGETHER FOREVER BY A PRETTY BLACK BUTTERFLY!
HUH?
UGH. ALL THIS LOVEY DOVEY STUFF IS MAKING ME SICK!
DON'T WORRY, LITTLE MONSTER. I'M GONNA TAKE CARE OF YOU, TOO!
EEK!
IF YOU CAN HEAR ME LADYBUG, I COULD USE A LITTLE HELP!
WHAT'S SHE WAITING FOR?

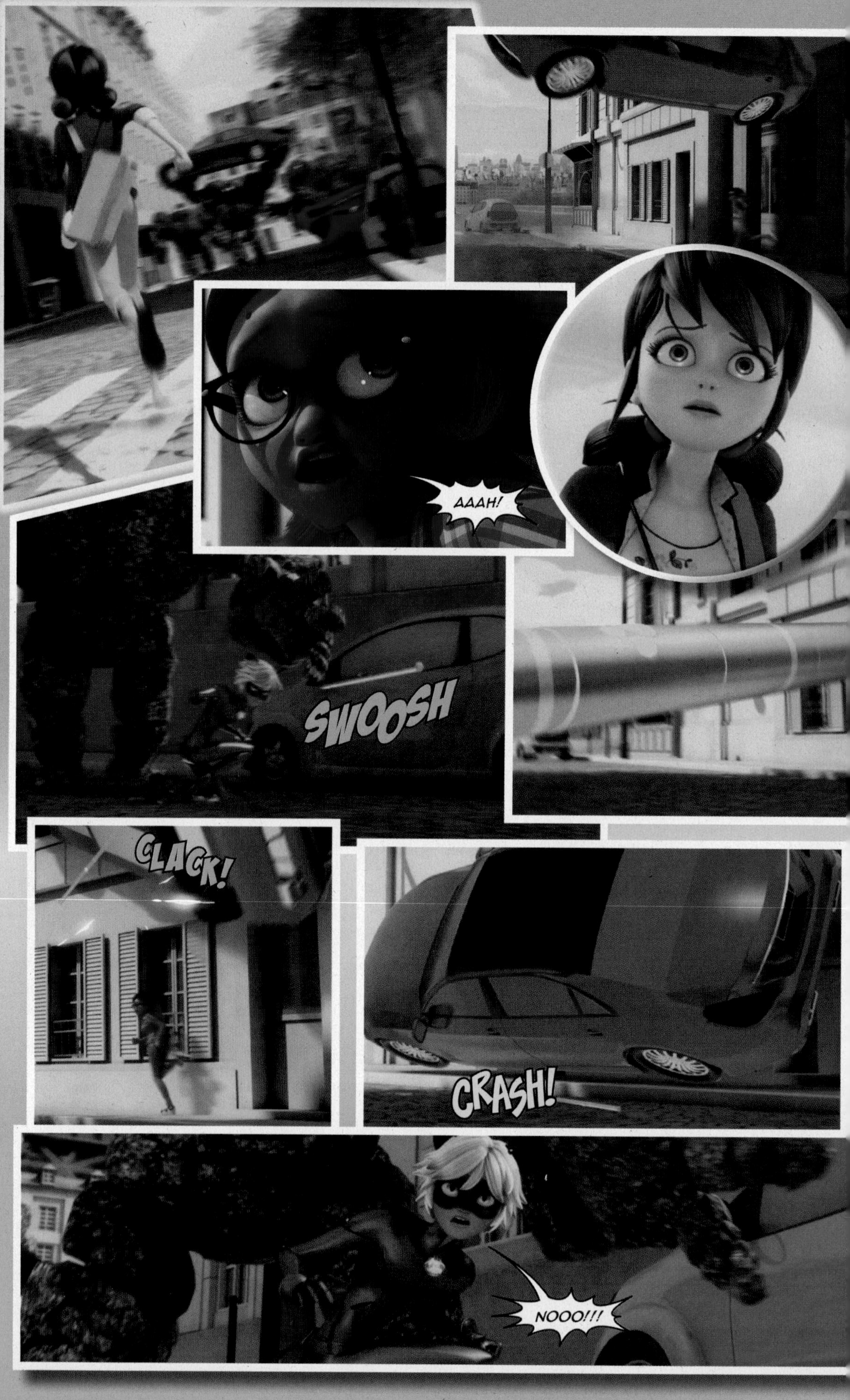
AAAH!
SWOOSH
CLACK!
CRASH!
NOOO!!!

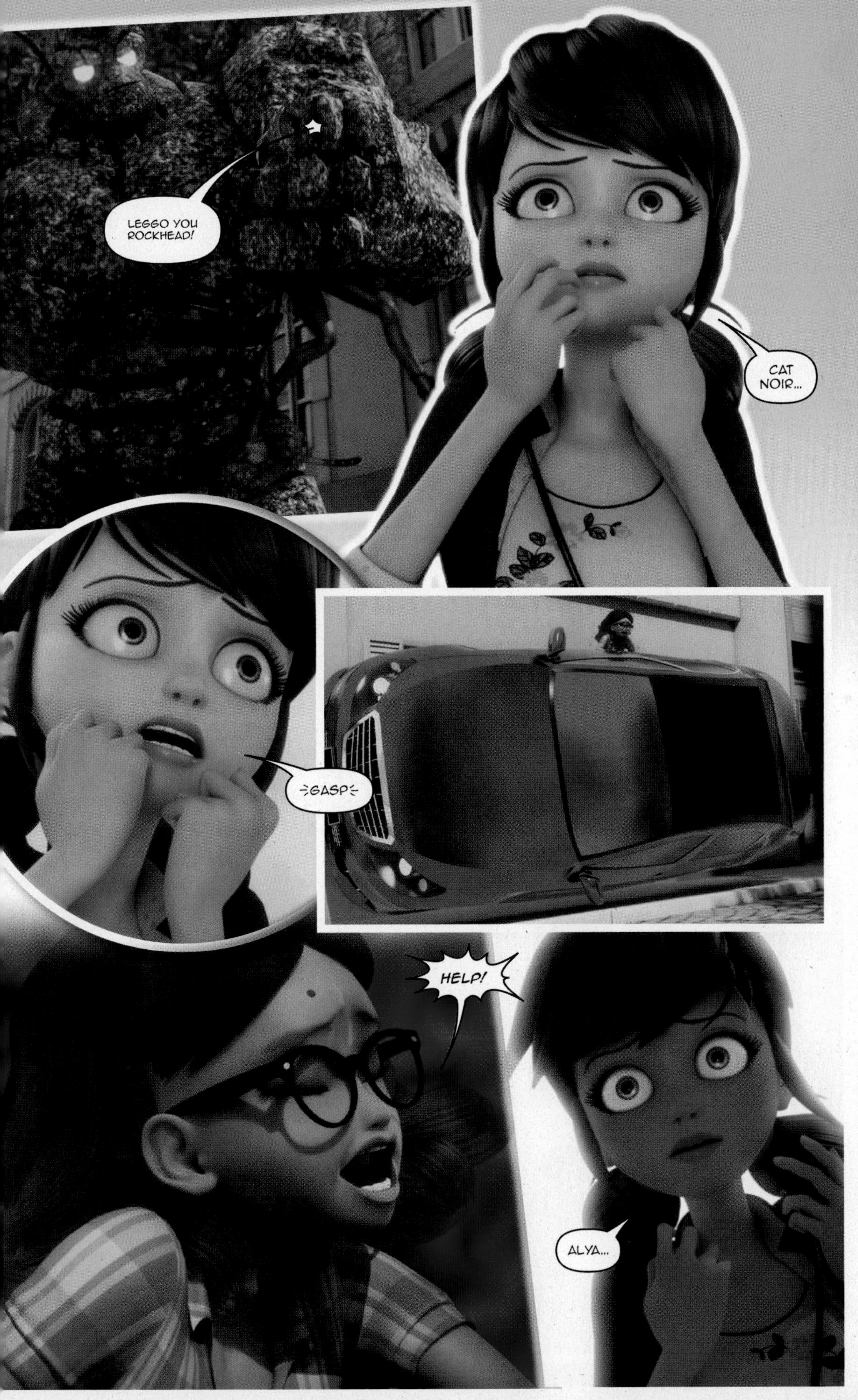
LEGGO YOU ROCKHEAD!
CAT NOIR...
=GASP=
HELP!
ALYA...

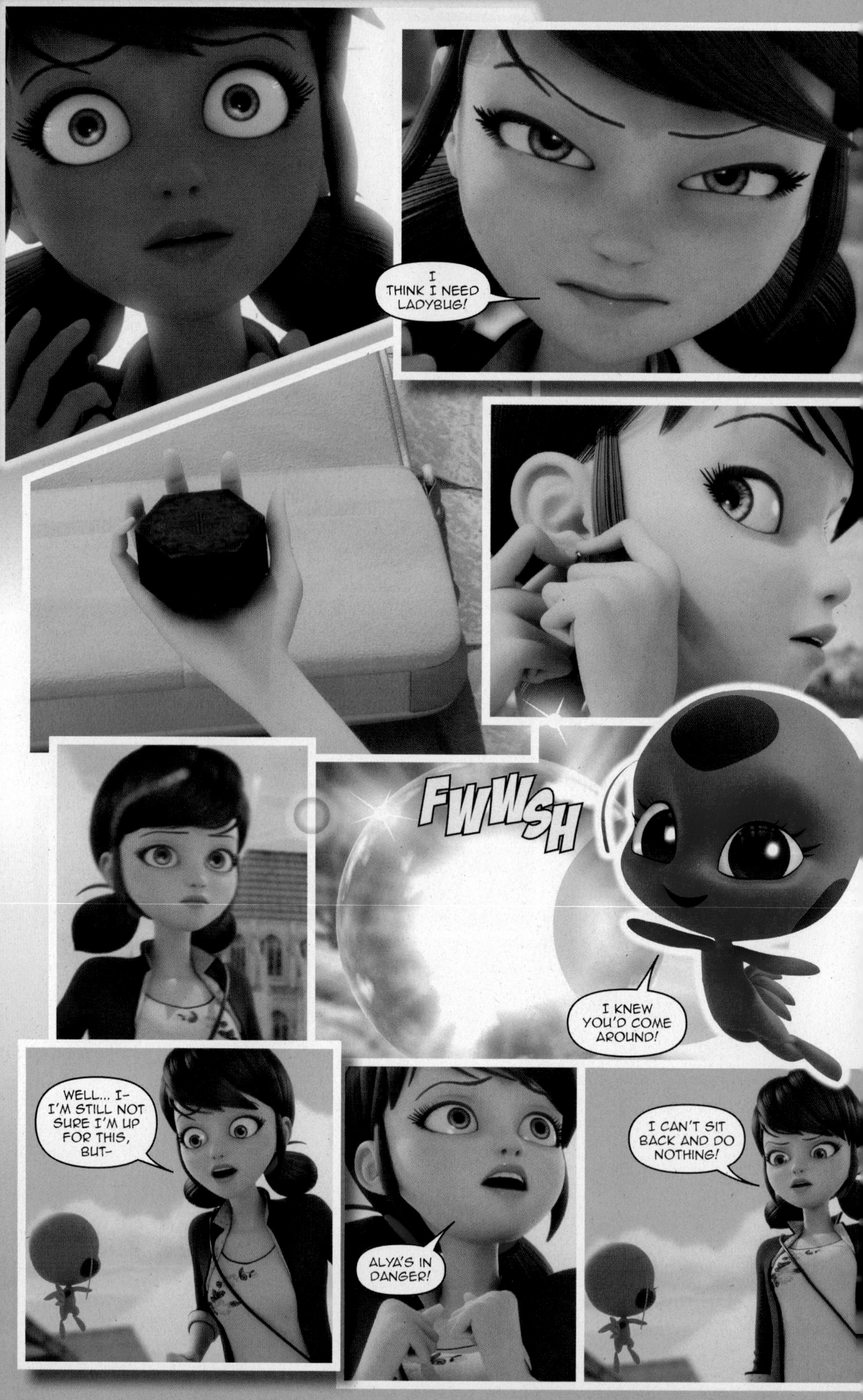
I THINK I NEED LADYBUG!
FWWSH
I KNEW YOU'D COME AROUND!
WELL... I- I'M STILL NOT SURE I'M UP FOR THIS, BUT-
ALYA'S IN DANGER!
I CAN'T SIT BACK AND DO NOTHING!

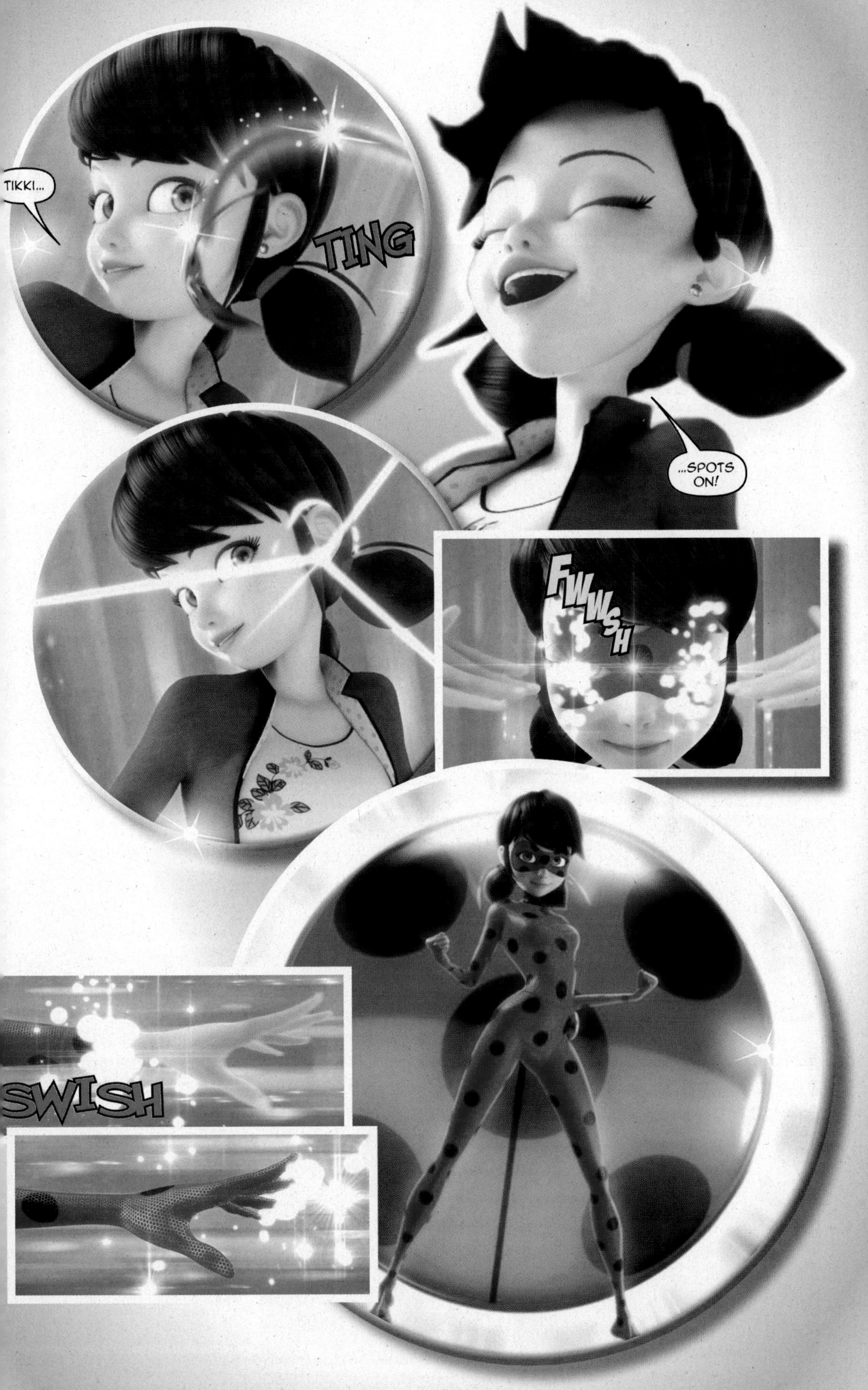
TIKKI...
TING
...SPOTS ON!
FWWSH
SWISH

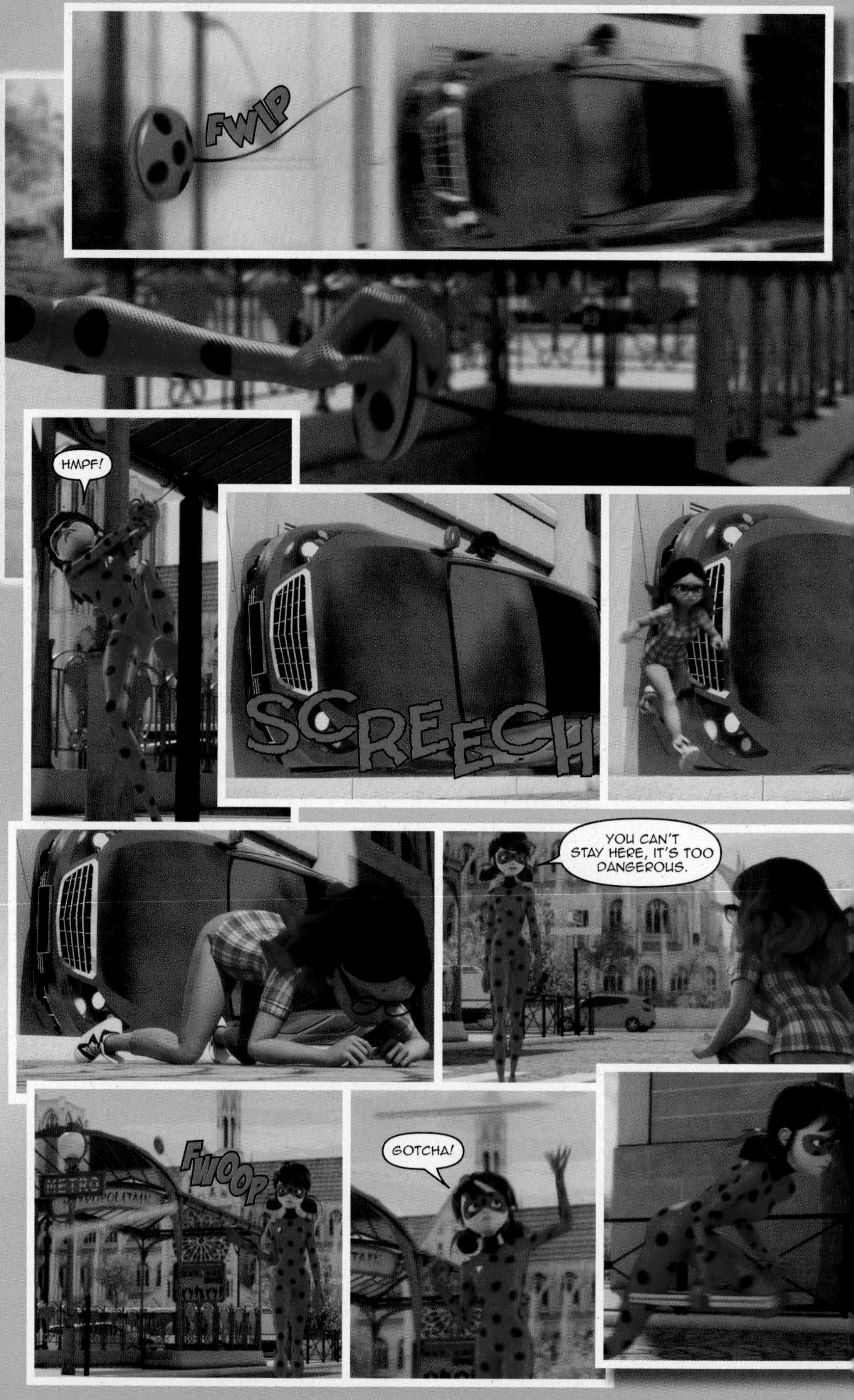
FWIP
HMPF!
SCREECH
YOU CAN'T STAY HERE, IT'S TOO DANGEROUS.
METRO
FWOOP
GOTCHA!

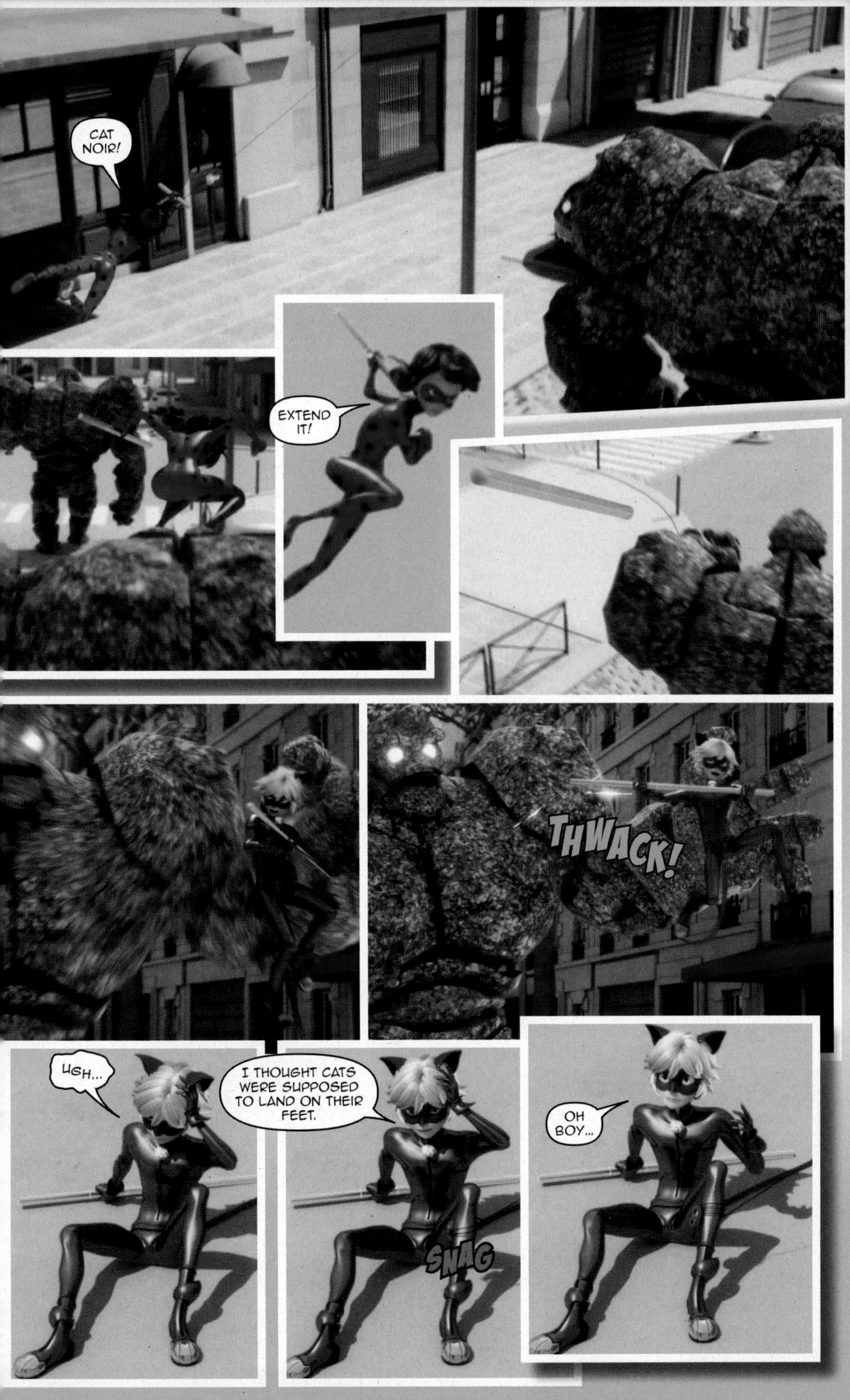
CAT NOIR!
EXTEND IT!
THWACK!
UGH...
I THOUGHT CATS WERE SUPPOSED TO LAND ON THEIR FEET.
SNAG
OH BOY...

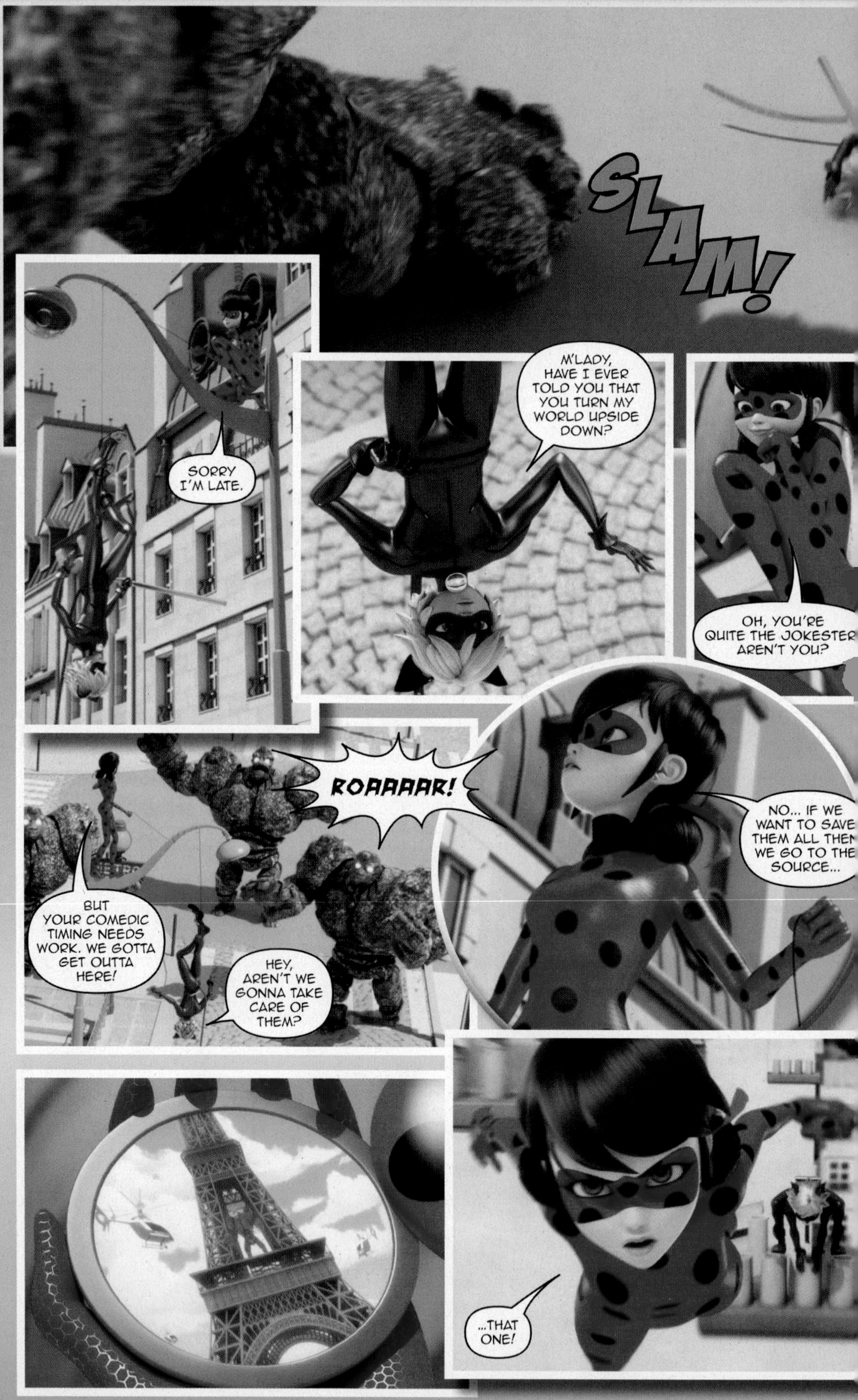
SLAM!
SORRY I'M LATE.
M'LADY, HAVE I EVER TOLD YOU THAT YOU TURN MY WORLD UPSIDE DOWN?
OH, YOU'RE QUITE THE JOKESTER AREN'T YOU?
ROAAAAR!
BUT YOUR COMEDIC TIMING NEEDS WORK. WE GOTTA GET OUTTA HERE!
HEY, AREN'T WE GONNA TAKE CARE OF THEM?
NO... IF WE WANT TO SAVE THEM ALL THEN WE GO TO THE SOURCE...
...THAT ONE!

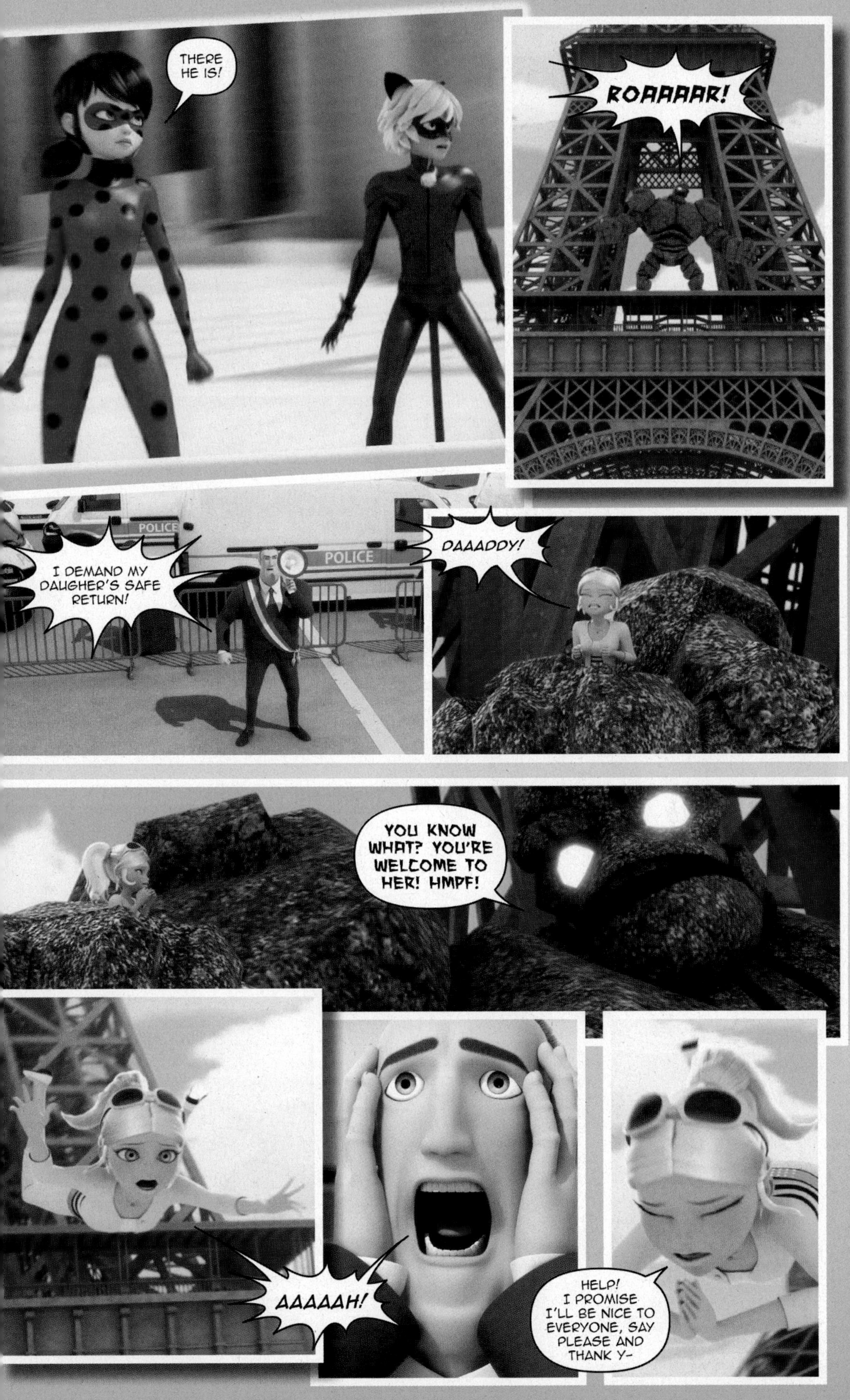
THERE HE IS!
ROAAAAR!
I DEMAND MY DAUGHER'S SAFE RETURN!
DAAADDY!
YOU KNOW WHAT? YOU'RE WELCOME TO HER! HMPF!
AAAAAH!
HELP! I PROMISE I'LL BE NICE TO EVERYONE, SAY PLEASE AND THANK Y-

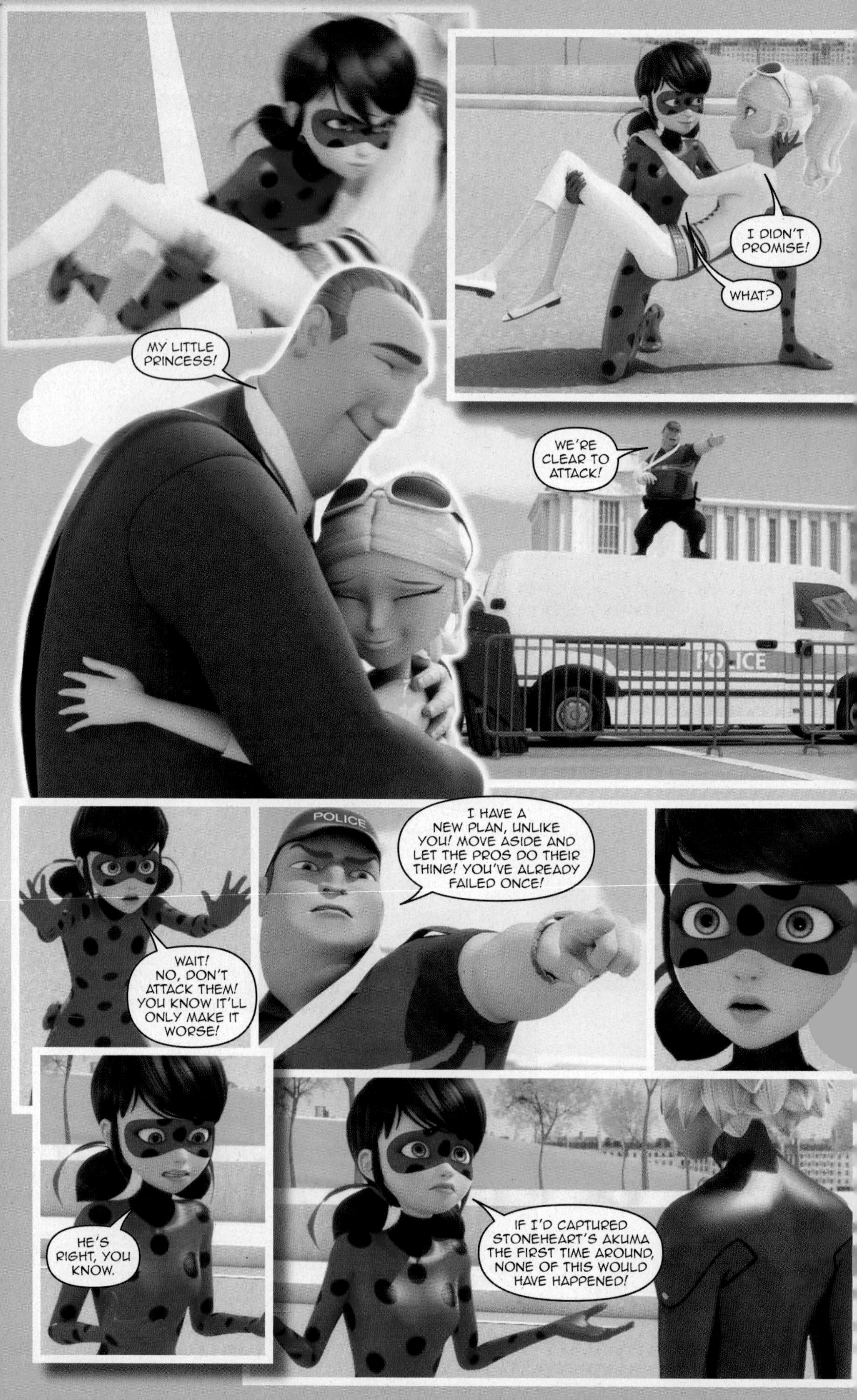
I DIDN'T PROMISE!
WHAT?
MY LITTLE PRINCESS!
WE'RE CLEAR TO ATTACK!
WAIT! NO, DON'T ATTACK THEM! YOU KNOW IT'LL ONLY MAKE IT WORSE!
I HAVE A NEW PLAN, UNLIKE YOU! MOVE ASIDE AND LET THE PROS DO THEIR THING! YOU'VE ALREADY FAILED ONCE!
HE'S RIGHT, YOU KNOW.
IF I'D CAPTURED STONEHEART'S AKUMA THE FIRST TIME AROUND, NONE OF THIS WOULD HAVE HAPPENED!
POLICE

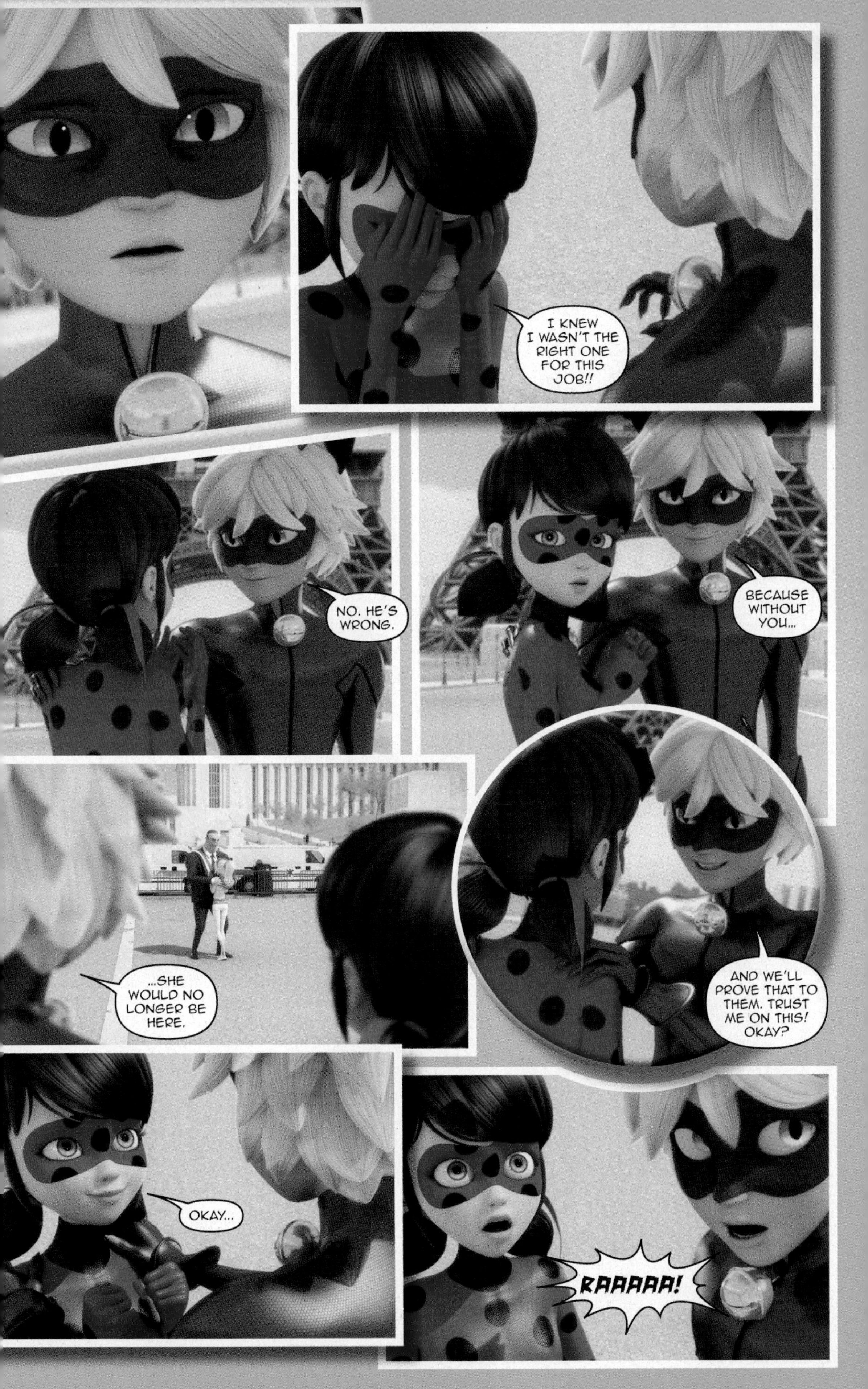
I KNEW I WASN'T THE RIGHT ONE FOR THIS JOB!!
NO. HE'S WRONG.
BECAUSE WITHOUT YOU...
...SHE WOULD NO LONGER BE HERE.
AND WE'LL PROVE THAT TO THEM. TRUST ME ON THIS! OKAY?
OKAY...
RAAAAA!

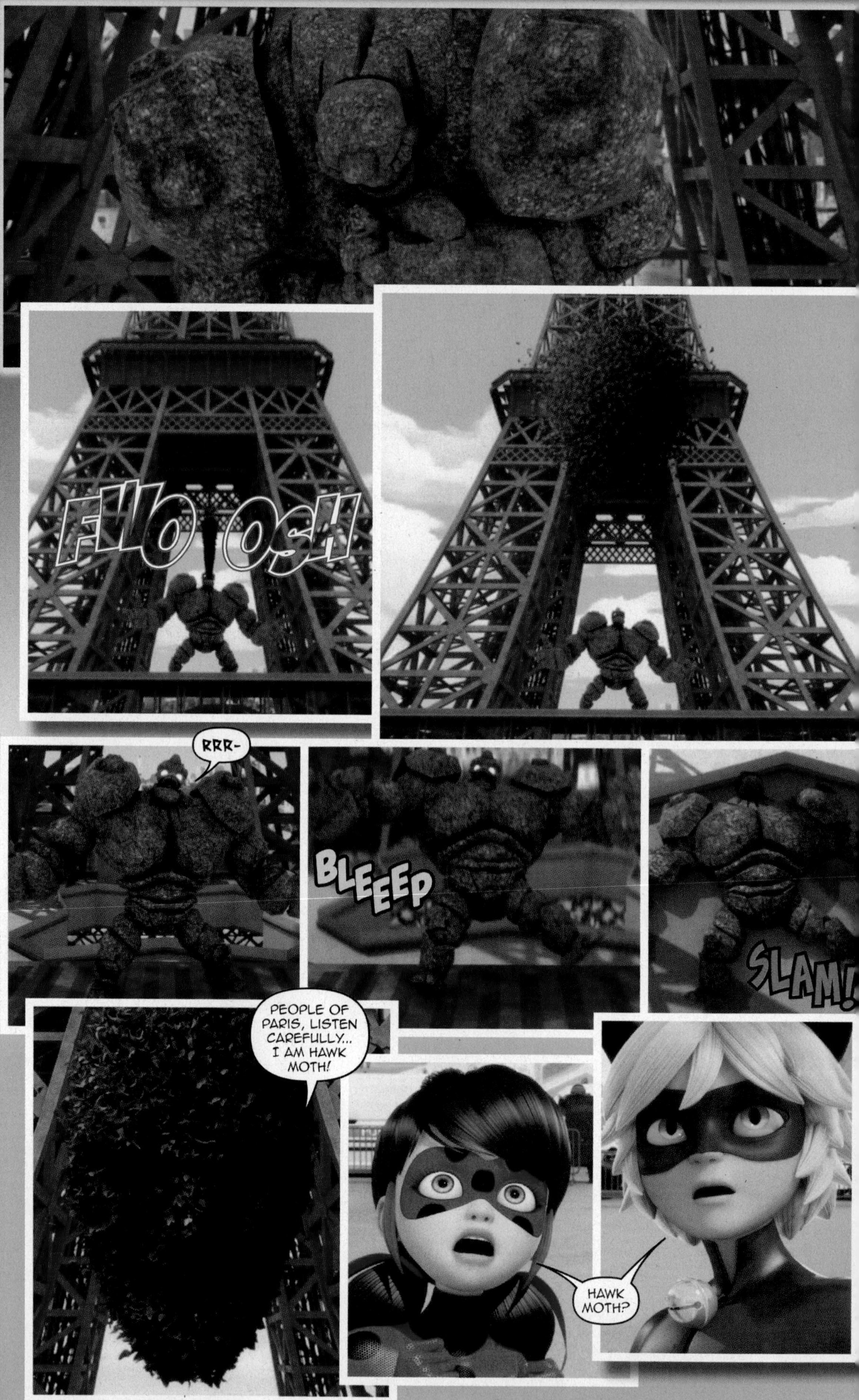
FWOOSH
RRR-
BLEEEP
SLAM!
PEOPLE OF PARIS, LISTEN CAREFULLY... I AM HAWK MOTH!
HAWK MOTH?

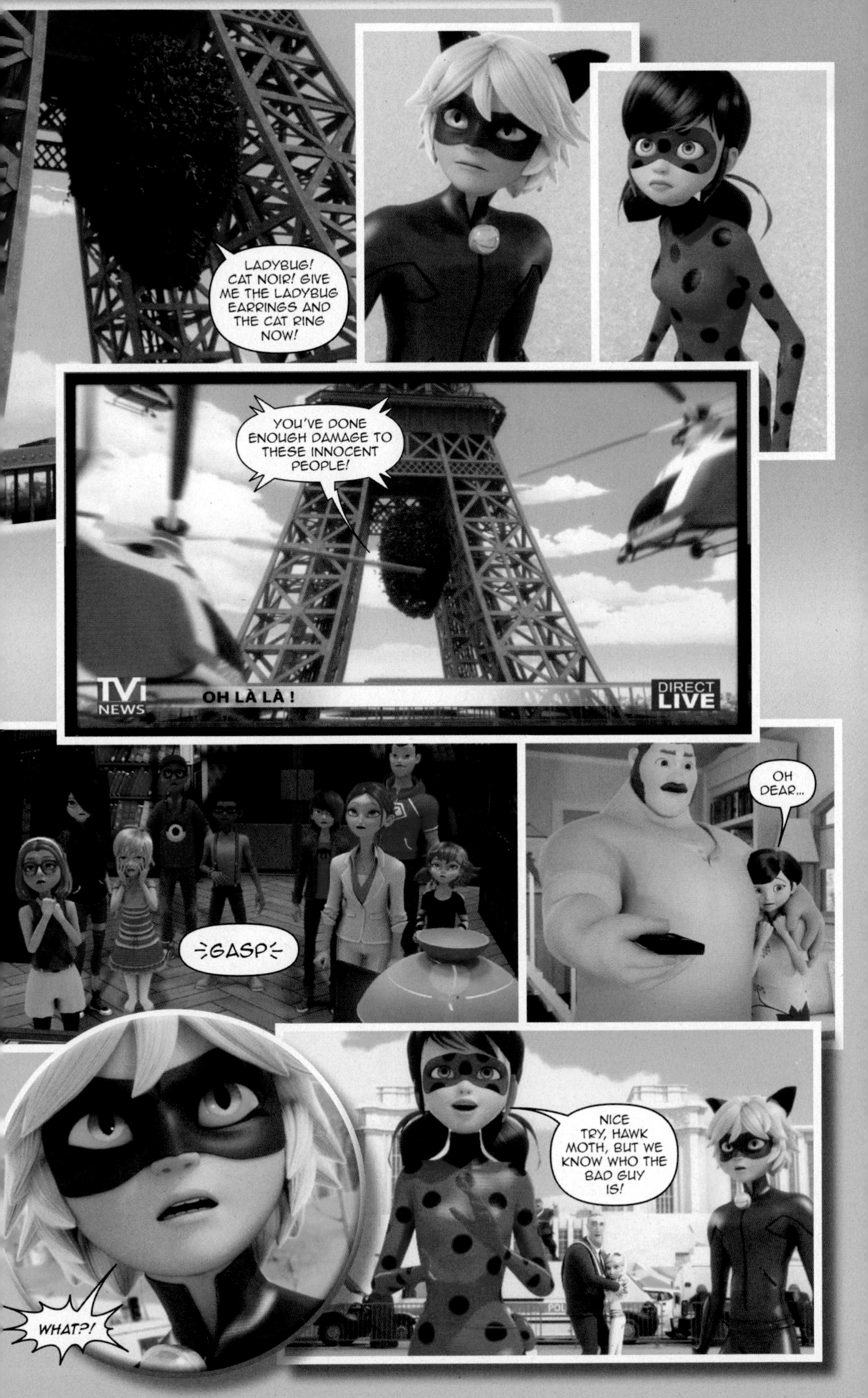
LADYBUG! CAT NOIR! GIVE ME THE LADYBUG EARRINGS AND THE CAT RING NOW!
YOU'VE DONE ENOUGH DAMAGE TO THESE INNOCENT PEOPLE!
TVi NEWS
OH LÀ LÀ !
DIRECT LIVE
GASP
OH DEAR...
NICE TRY, HAWK MOTH, BUT WE KNOW WHO THE BAD GUY IS!
WHAT?!

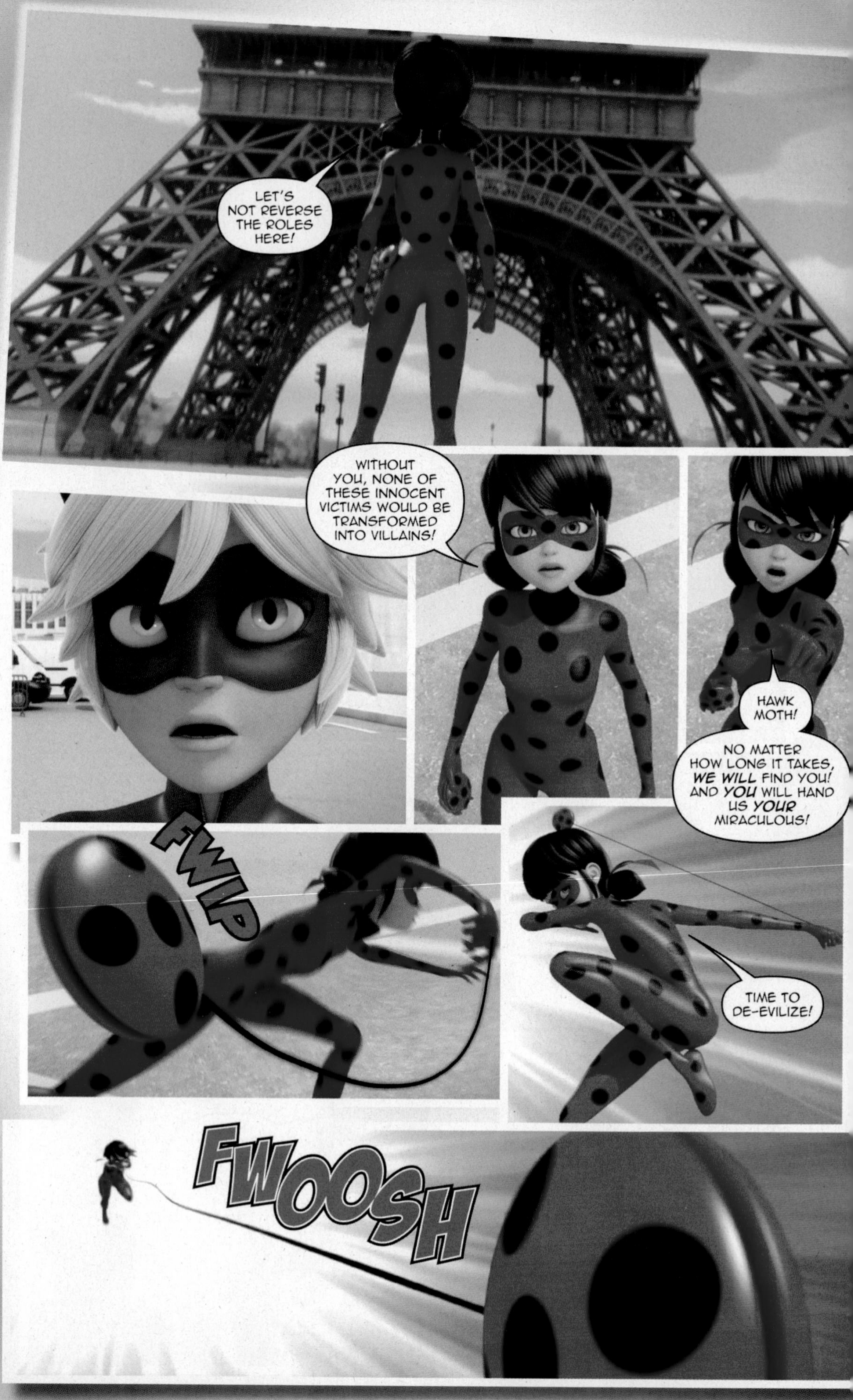

LET'S NOT REVERSE THE ROLES HERE!
WITHOUT YOU, NONE OF THESE INNOCENT VICTIMS WOULD BE TRANSFORMED INTO VILLAINS!
HAWK MOTH!
NO MATTER HOW LONG IT TAKES, WE WILL FIND YOU! AND YOU WILL HAND US YOUR MIRACULOUS!
FWIP
TIME TO DE-EVILIZE!
FWOOSH

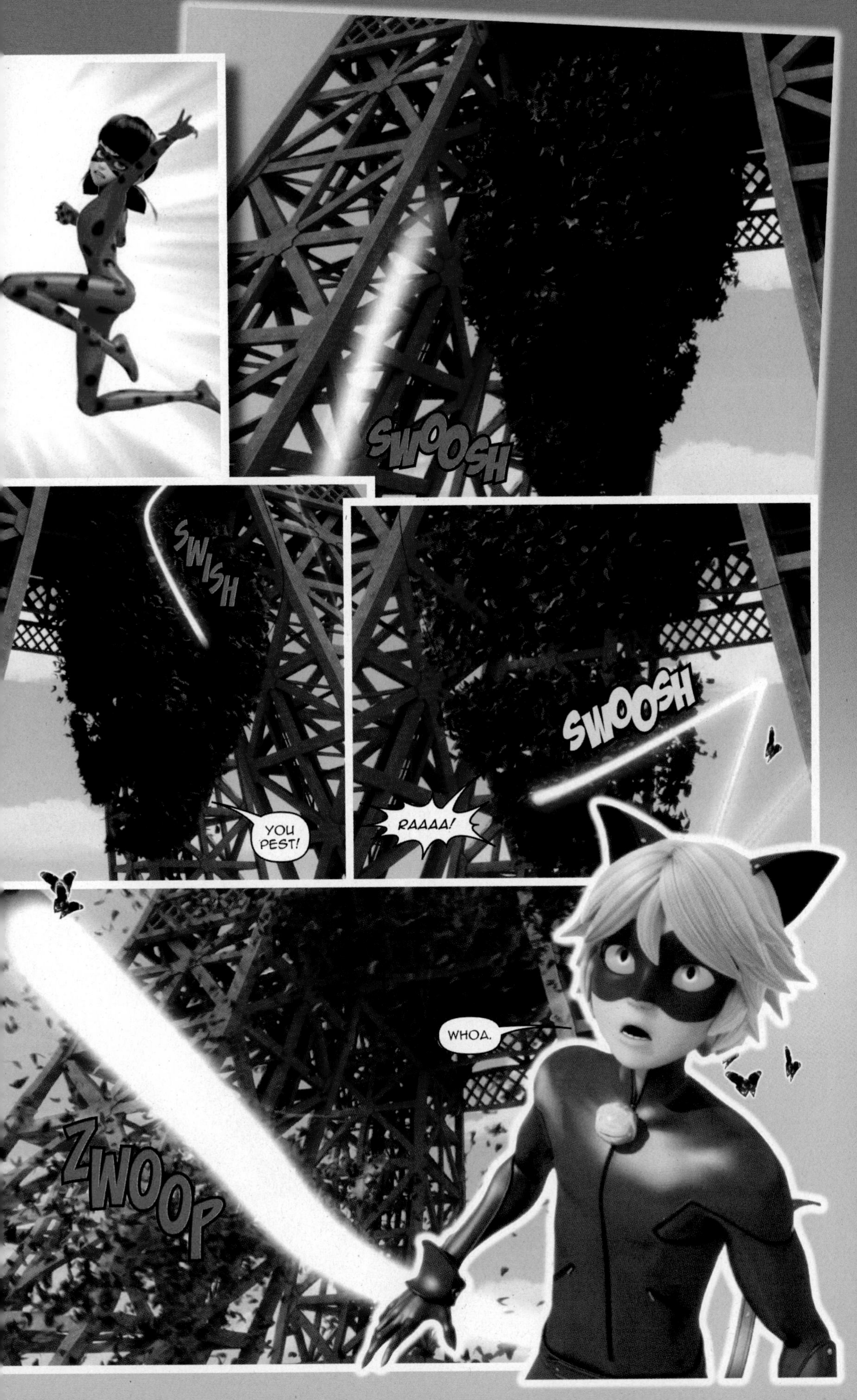
SWOOSH
SWISH
YOU PEST!
RAAAA!
SWOOSH
WHOA.
ZWOOP

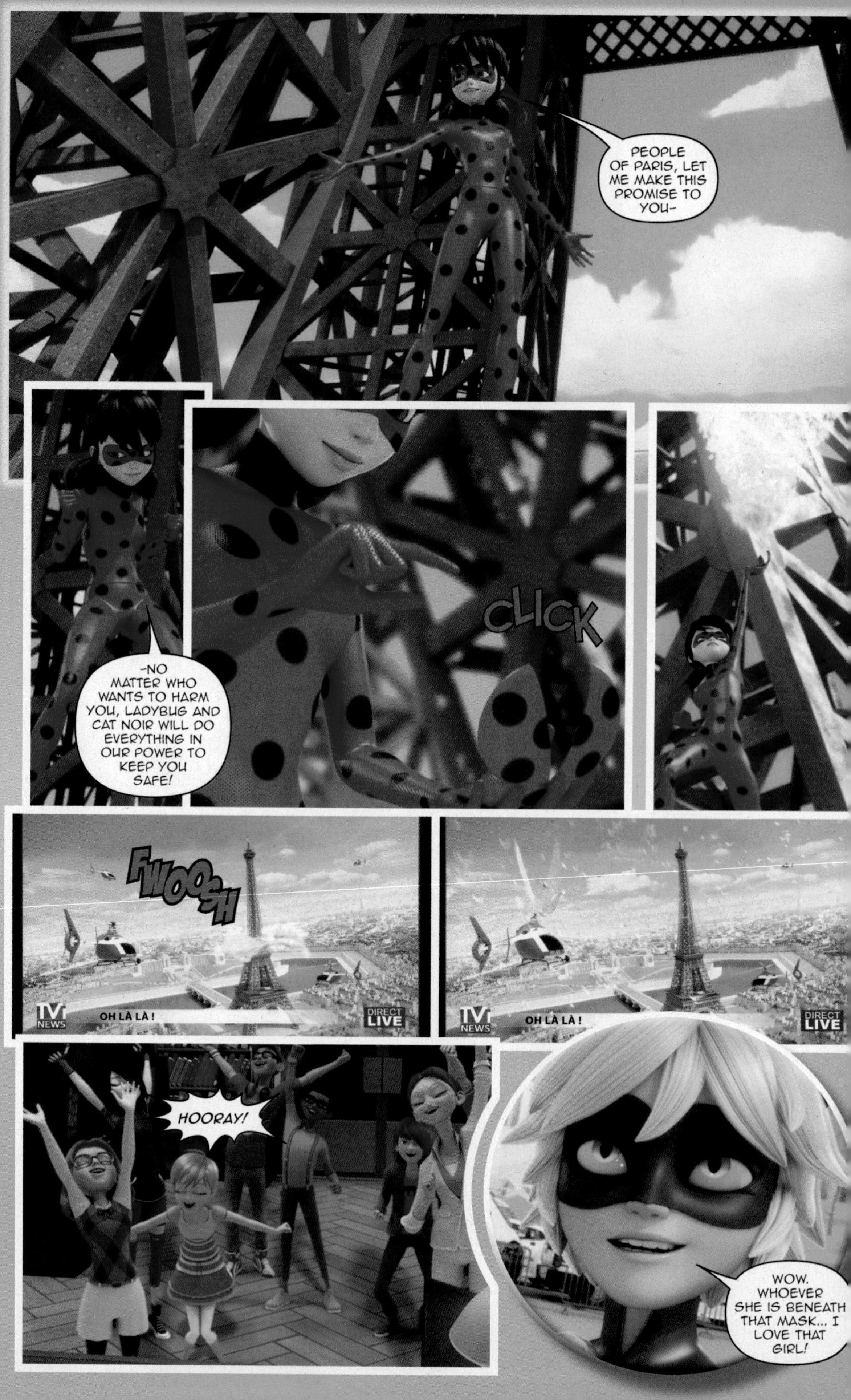
PEOPLE OF PARIS, LET ME MAKE THIS PROMISE TO YOU-
-NO MATTER WHO WANTS TO HARM YOU, LADYBUG AND CAT NOIR WILL DO EVERYTHING IN OUR POWER TO KEEP YOU SAFE!
CLICK
FWOOSH
TV NEWS
OH LÀ LÀ !
DIRECT LIVE
TV NEWS
OH LÀ LÀ !
DIRECT LIVE
HOORAY!
WOW. WHOEVER SHE IS BENEATH THAT MASK... I LOVE THAT GIRL!

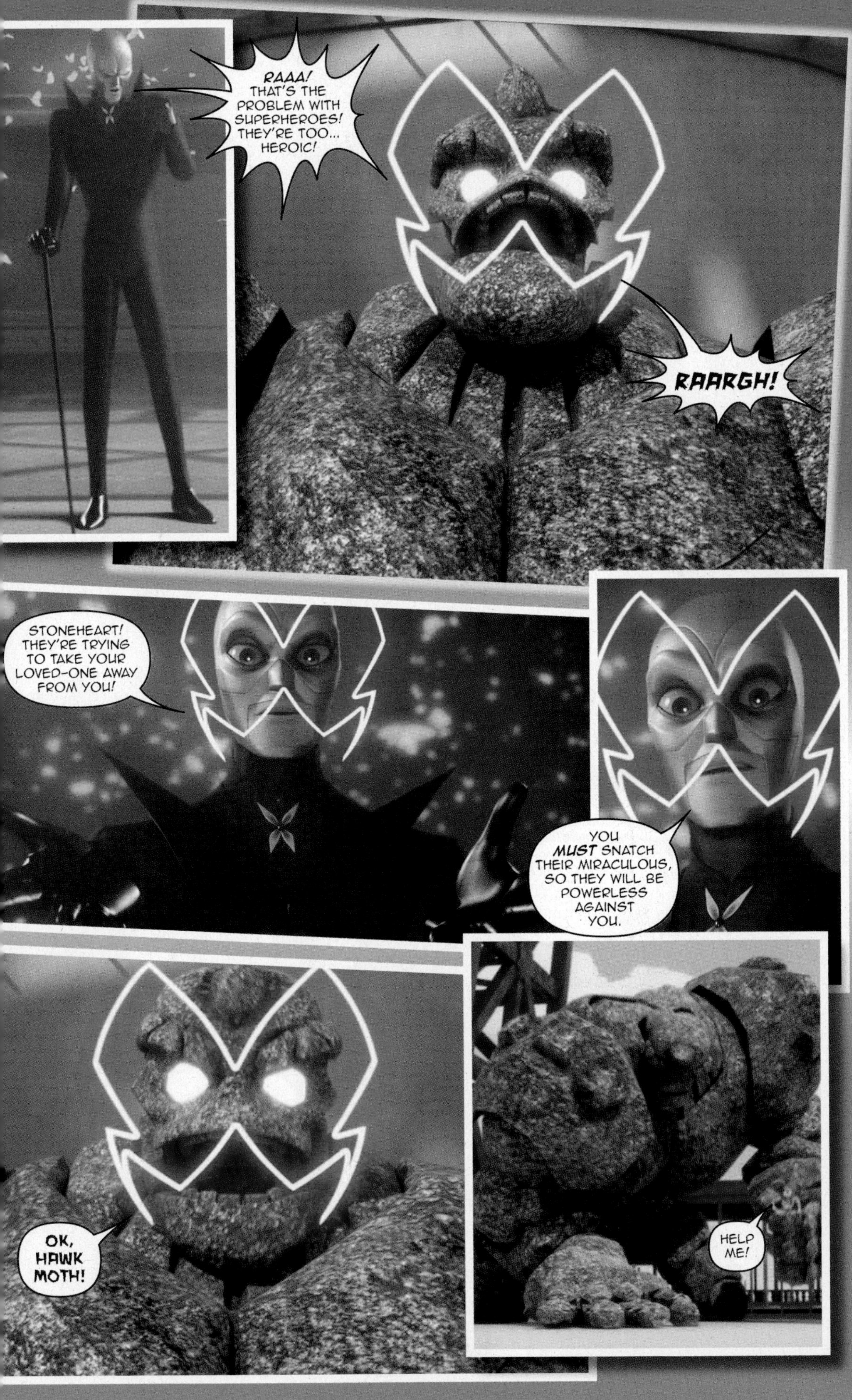
RAAA! THAT'S THE PROBLEM WITH SUPERHEROES! THEY'RE TOO... HEROIC!
RAARGH!
STONEHEART! THEY'RE TRYING TO TAKE YOUR LOVED-ONE AWAY FROM YOU!
YOU MUST SNATCH THEIR MIRACULOUS, SO THEY WILL BE POWERLESS AGAINST YOU.
OK, HAWK MOTH!
HELP ME!

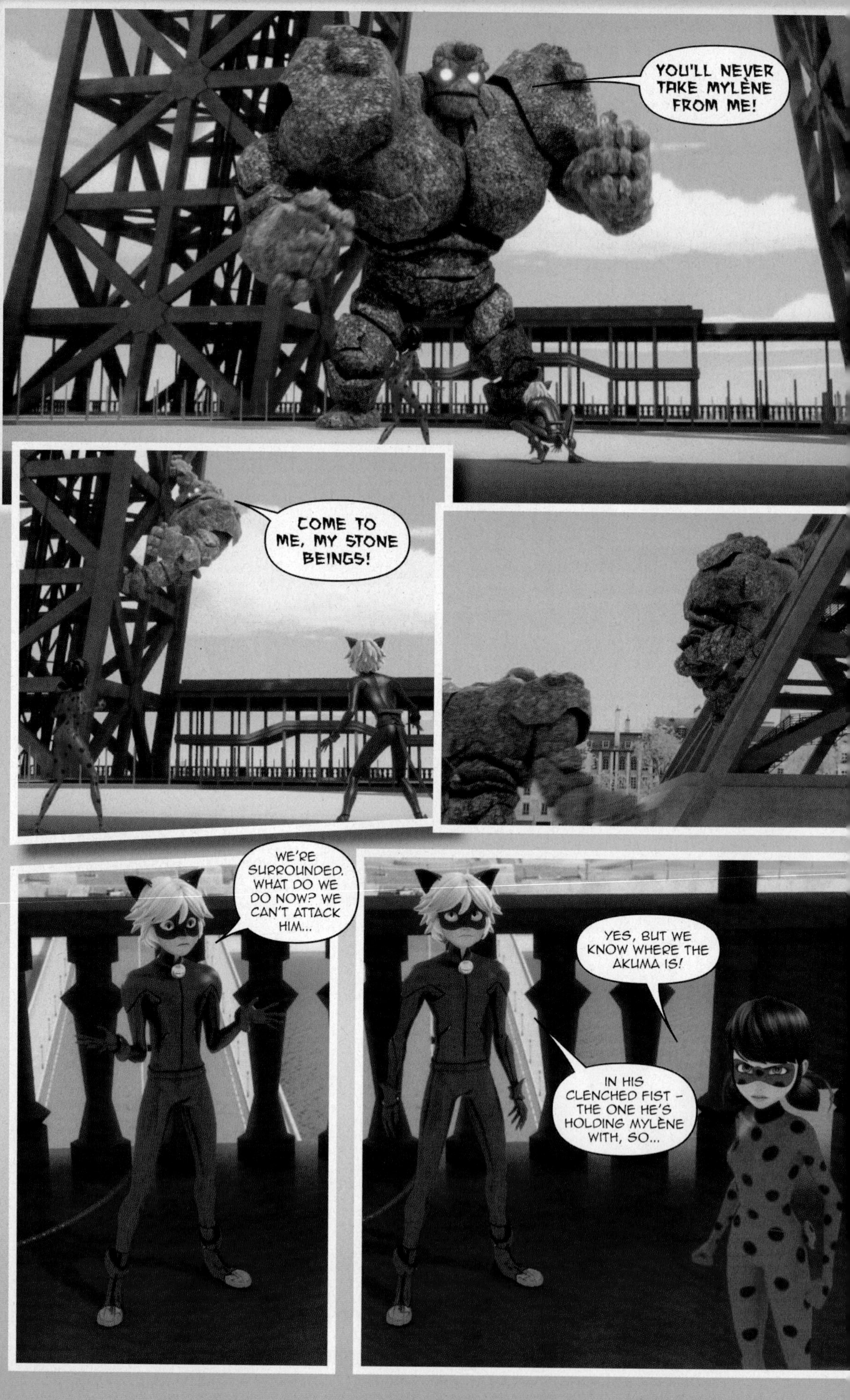
YOU'LL NEVER TAKE MYLÈNE FROM ME!
COME TO ME, MY STONE BEINGS!
WE'RE SURROUNDED. WHAT DO WE DO NOW? WE CAN'T ATTACK HIM...
YES, BUT WE KNOW WHERE THE AKUMA IS!
IN HIS CLENCHED FIST – THE ONE HE'S HOLDING MYLÈNE WITH, SO...

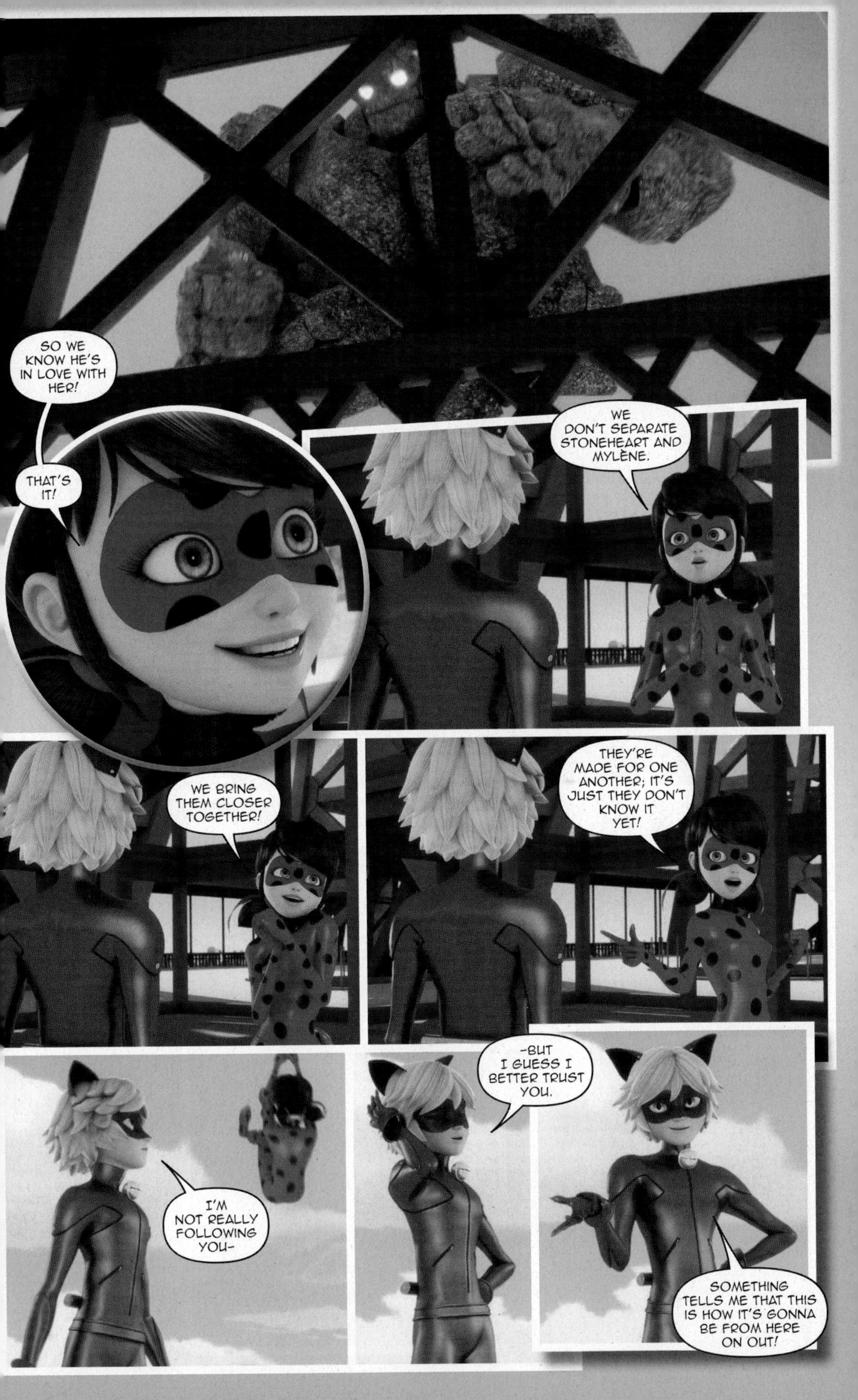
SO WE KNOW HE'S IN LOVE WITH HER!
THAT'S IT!
WE DON'T SEPARATE STONEHEART AND MYLÈNE.
WE BRING THEM CLOSER TOGETHER!
THEY'RE MADE FOR ONE ANOTHER; IT'S JUST THEY DON'T KNOW IT YET!
I'M NOT REALLY FOLLOWING YOU-
-BUT I GUESS I BETTER TRUST YOU.
SOMETHING TELLS ME THAT THIS IS HOW IT'S GONNA BE FROM HERE ON OUT!

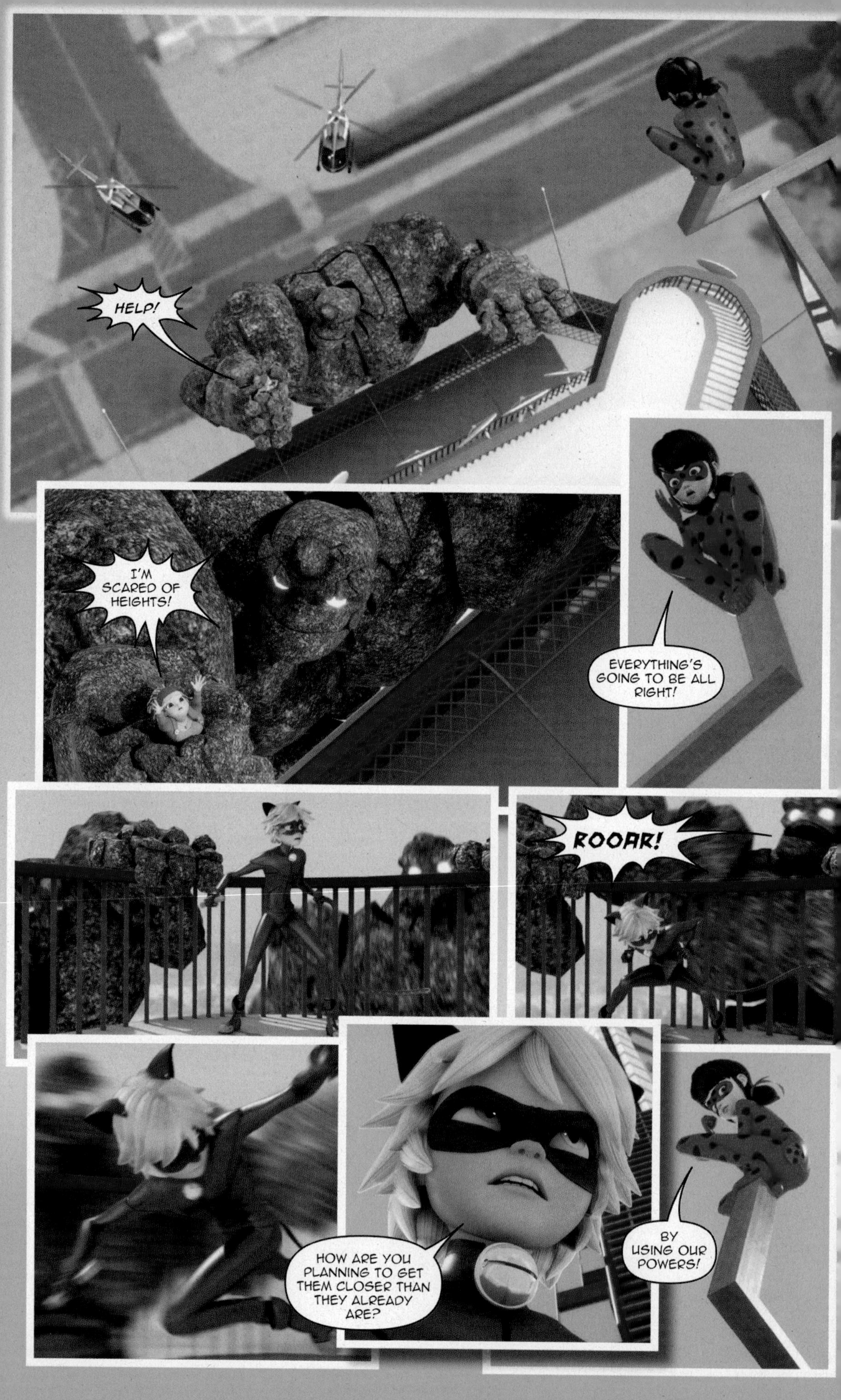
HELP!
I'M SCARED OF HEIGHTS!
EVERYTHING'S GOING TO BE ALL RIGHT!
ROOAR!
HOW ARE YOU PLANNING TO GET THEM CLOSER THAN THEY ALREADY ARE?
BY USING OUR POWERS!

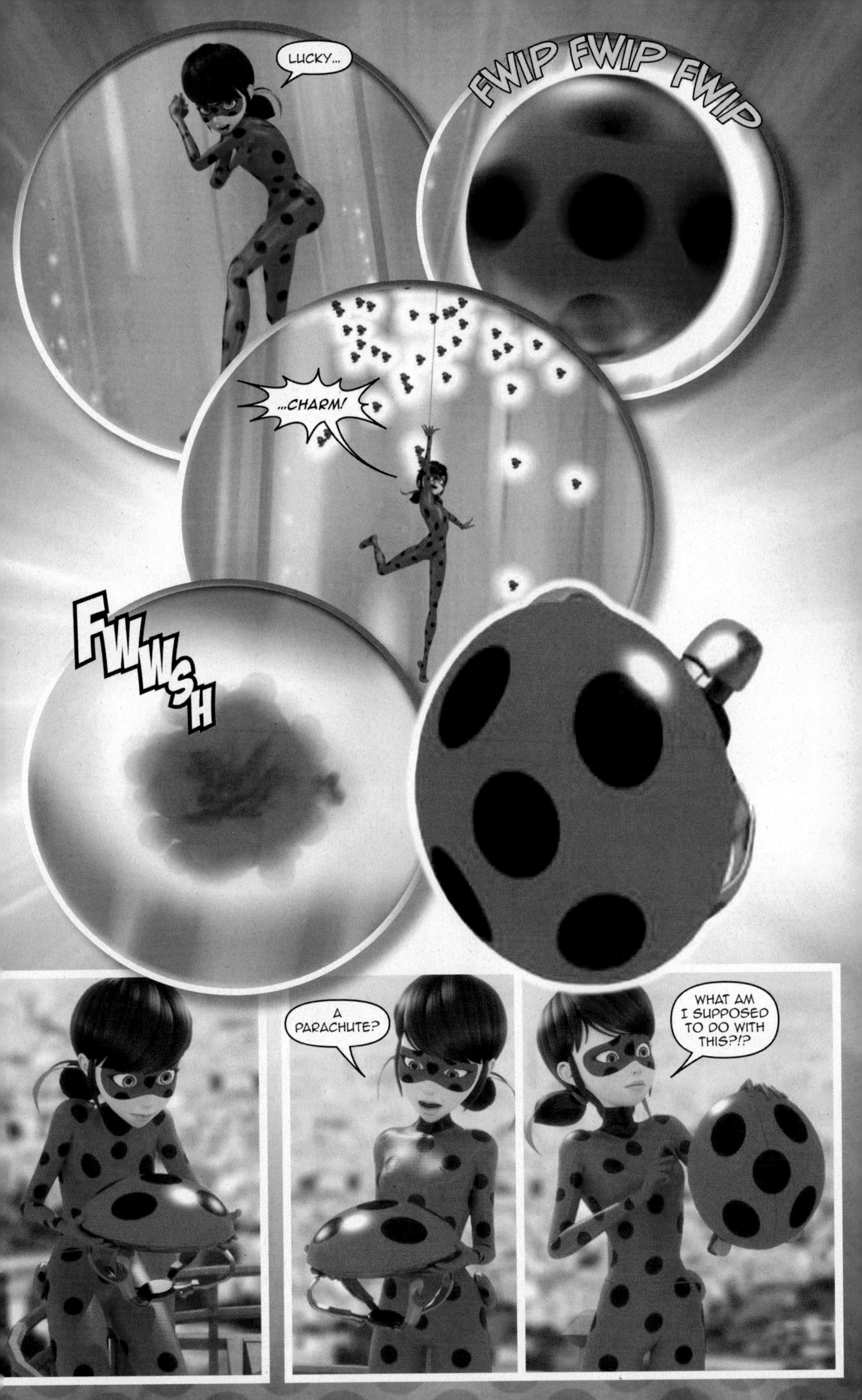
LUCKY...
FWIP FWIP FWIP
...CHARM!
FWWSH
A PARACHUTE?
WHAT AM I SUPPOSED TO DO WITH THIS?!?

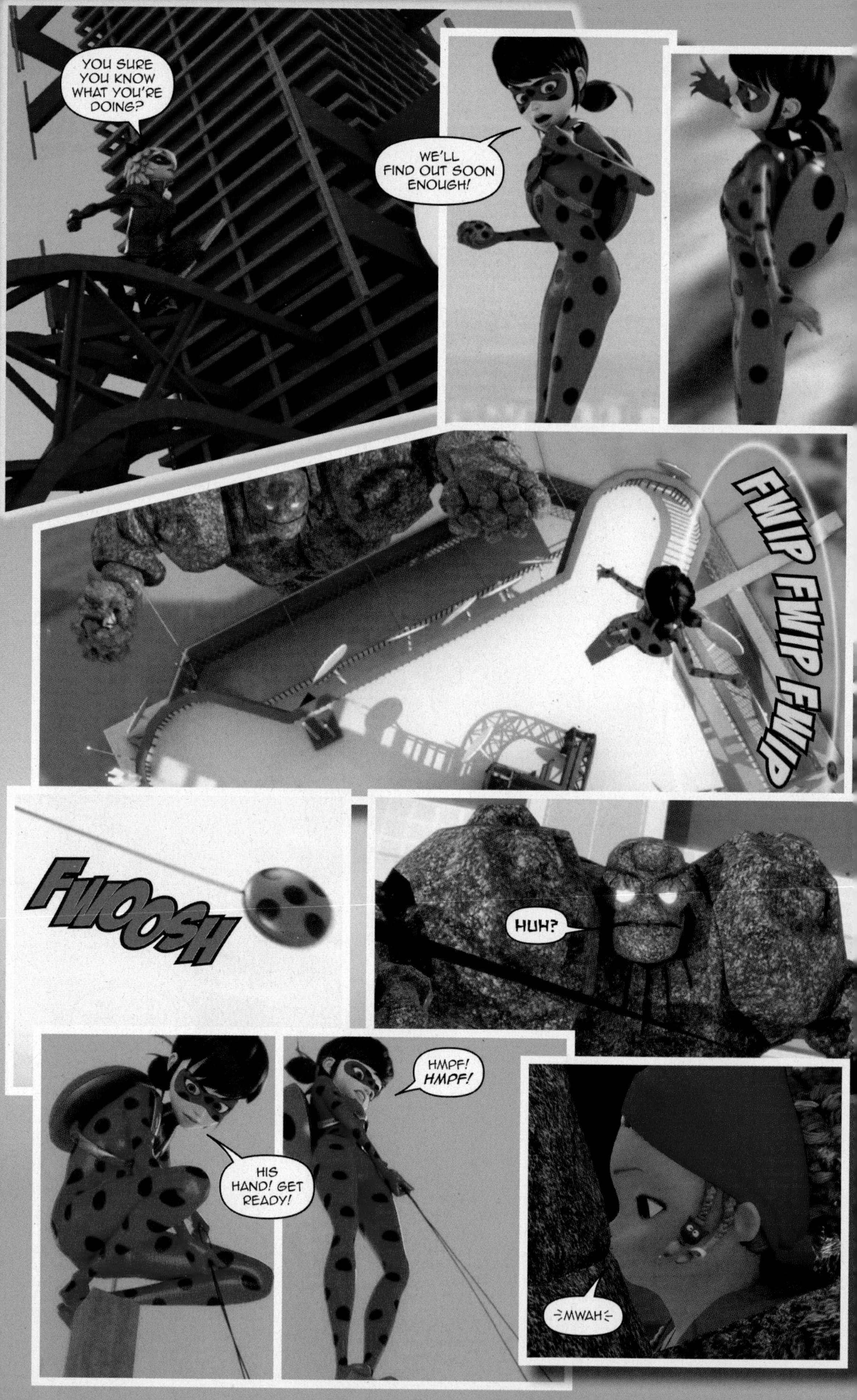
YOU SURE YOU KNOW WHAT YOU'RE DOING?
WE'LL FIND OUT SOON ENOUGH!
FWIP FWIP FWIP
FWOOSH
HUH?
HIS HAND! GET READY!
HMPF! HMPF!
MWAH

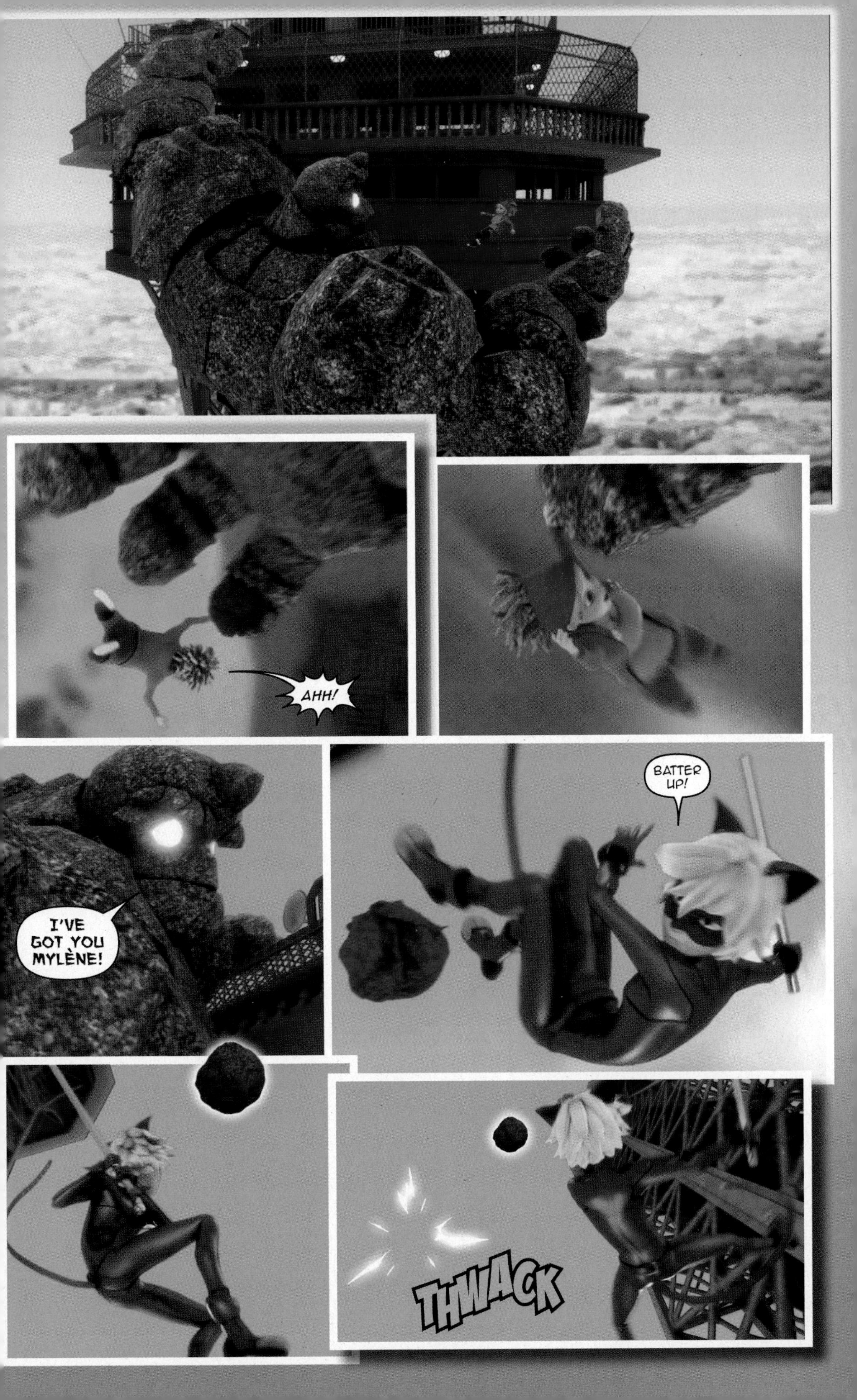
AHH!
I'VE GOT YOU MYLÈNE!
BATTER UP!
THWACK

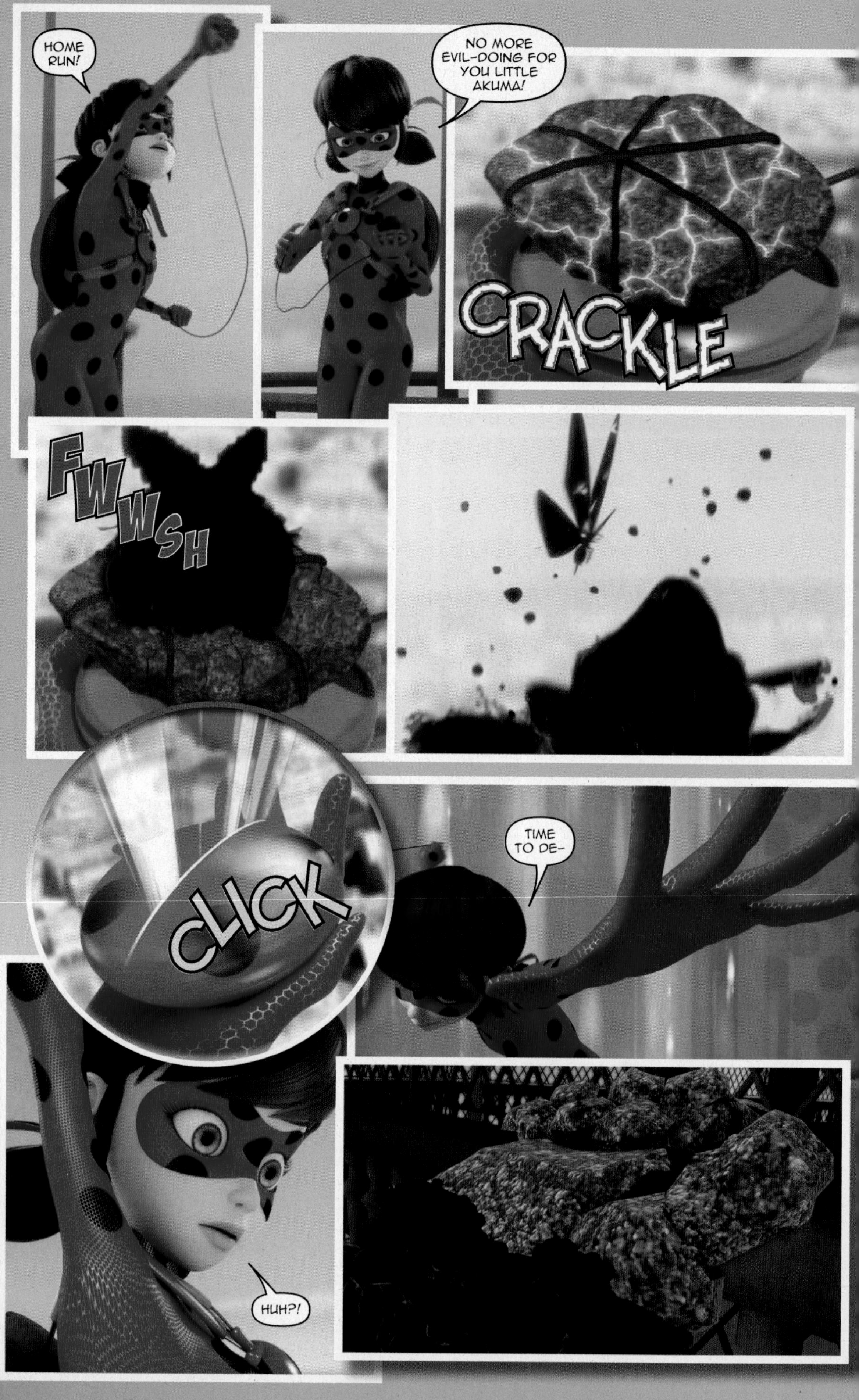
HOME RUN!
NO MORE EVIL-DOING FOR YOU LITTLE AKUMA!
CRACKLE
FWWSH
CLICK
TIME TO DE-
HUH?!

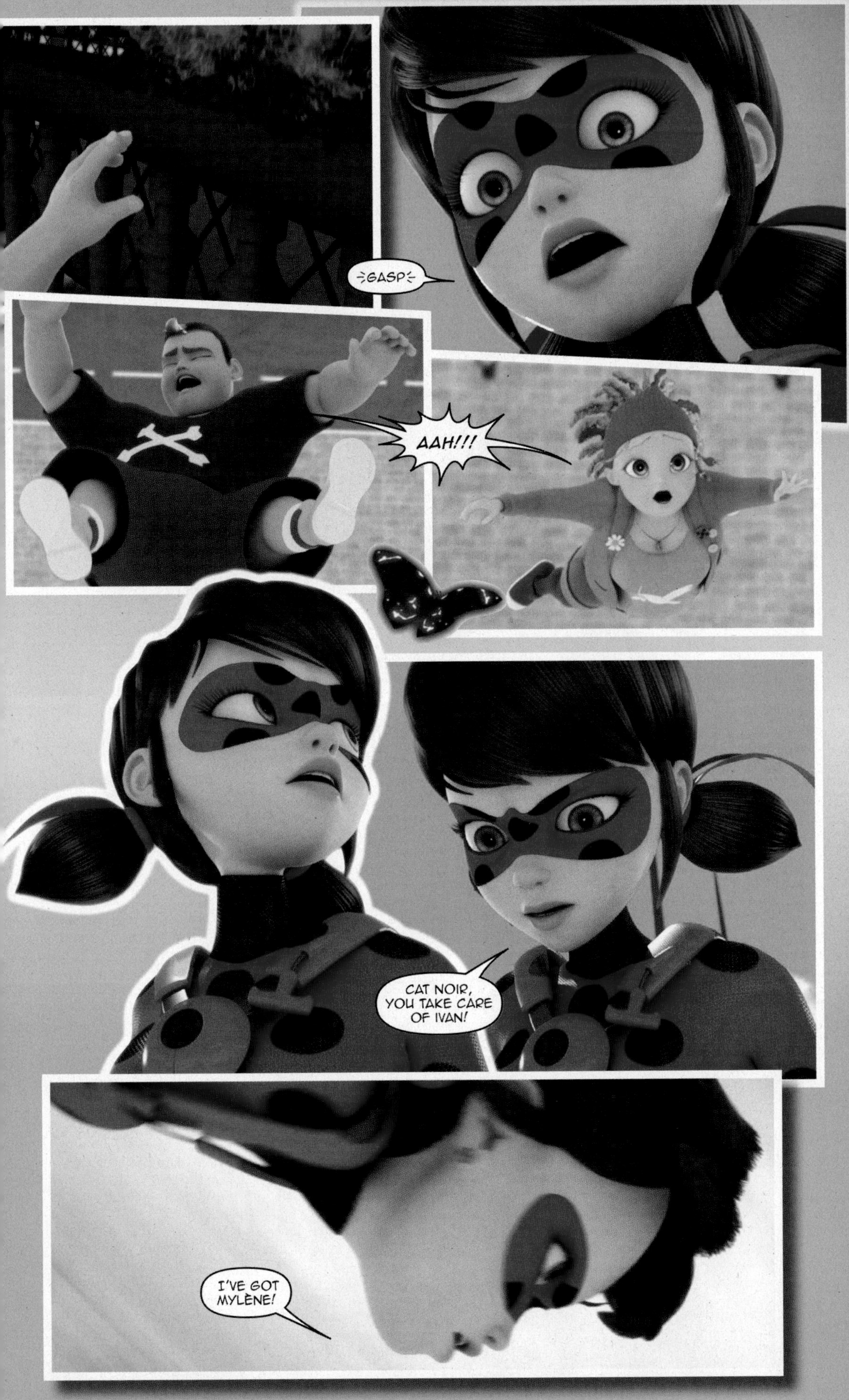
GASP
AAH!!!
CAT NOIR, YOU TAKE CARE OF IVAN!
I'VE GOT MYLÈNE!

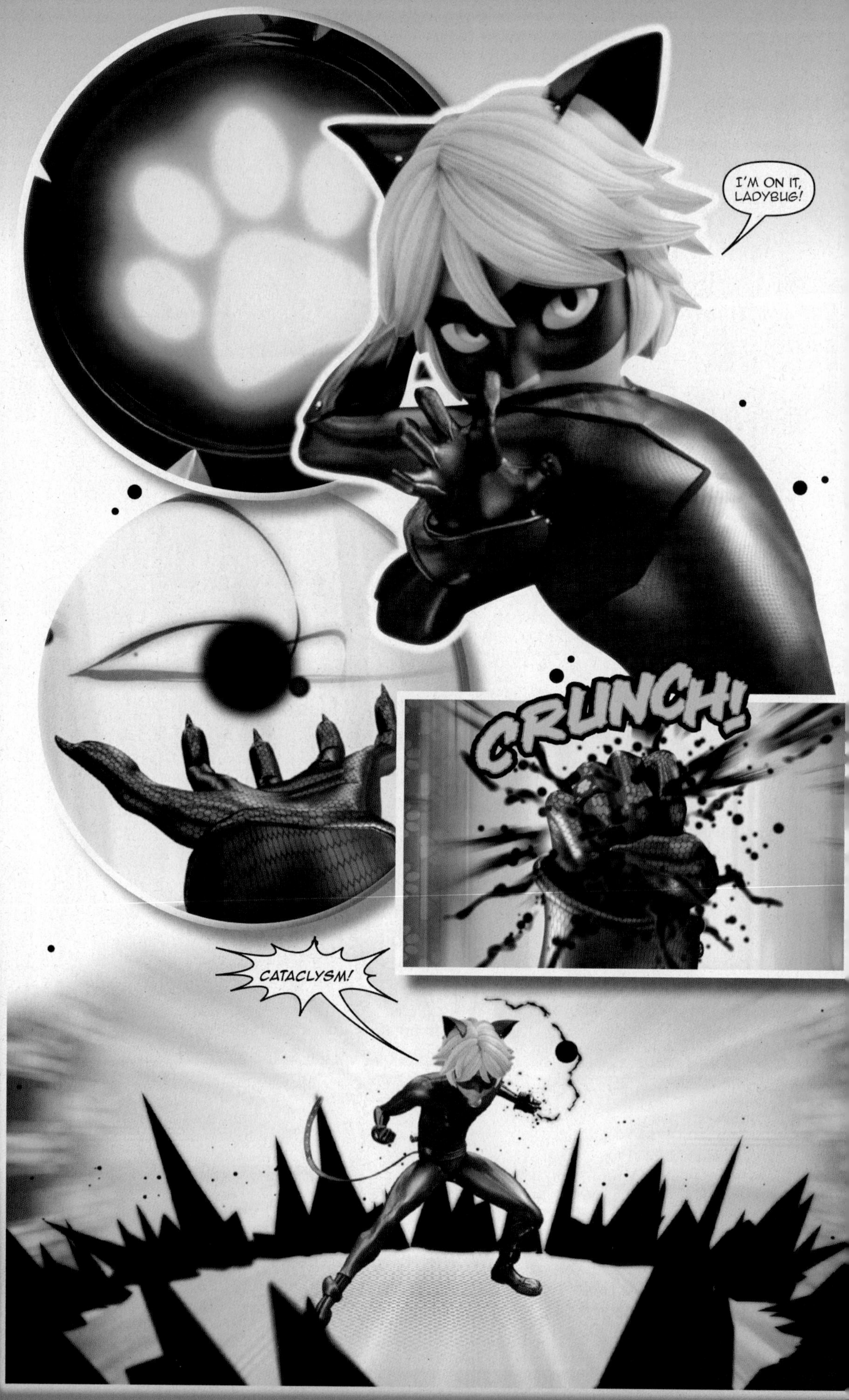
I'M ON IT, LADYBUG!
CRUNCH!
CATACLYSM!

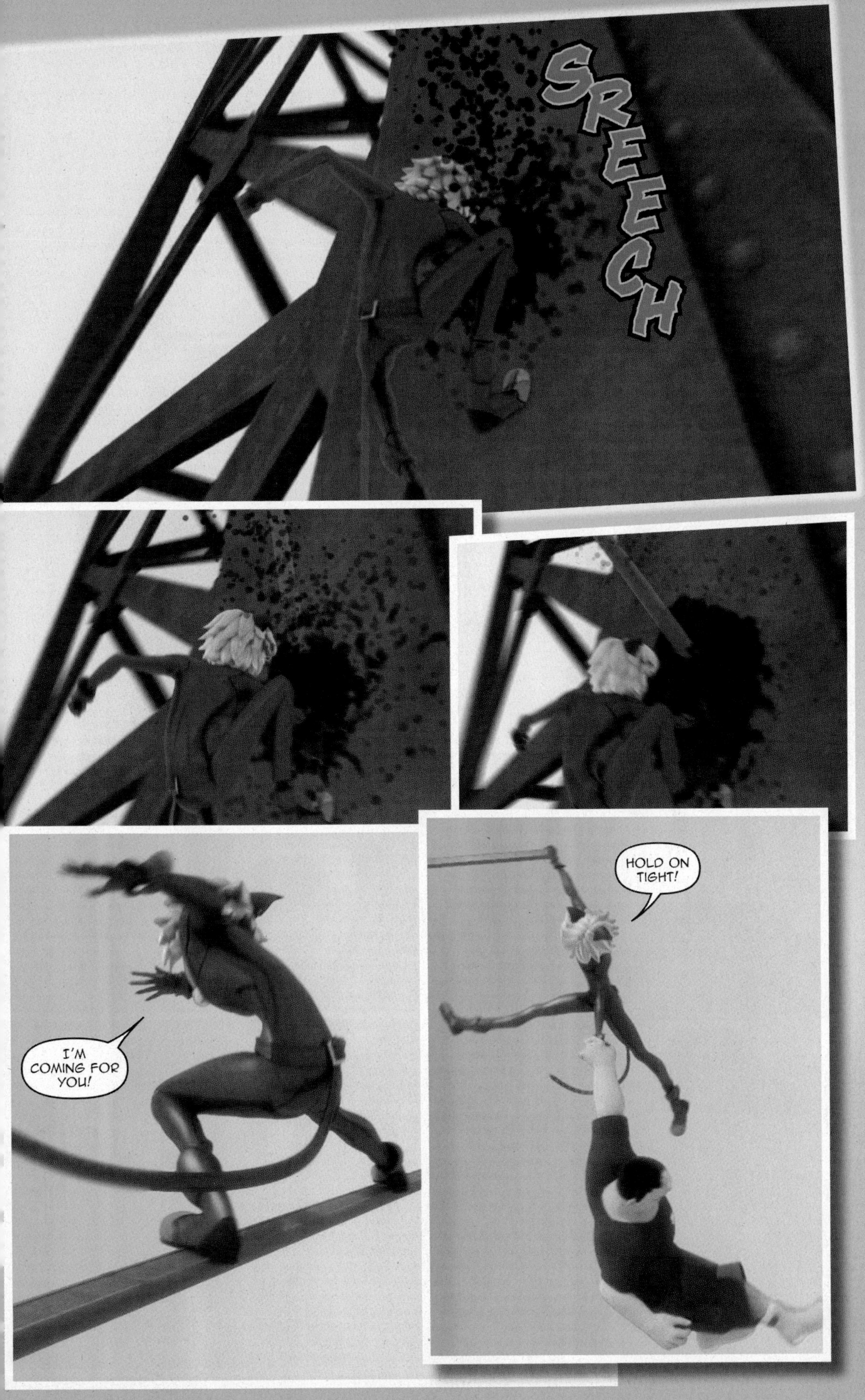
SREECH
I'M COMING FOR YOU!
HOLD ON TIGHT!

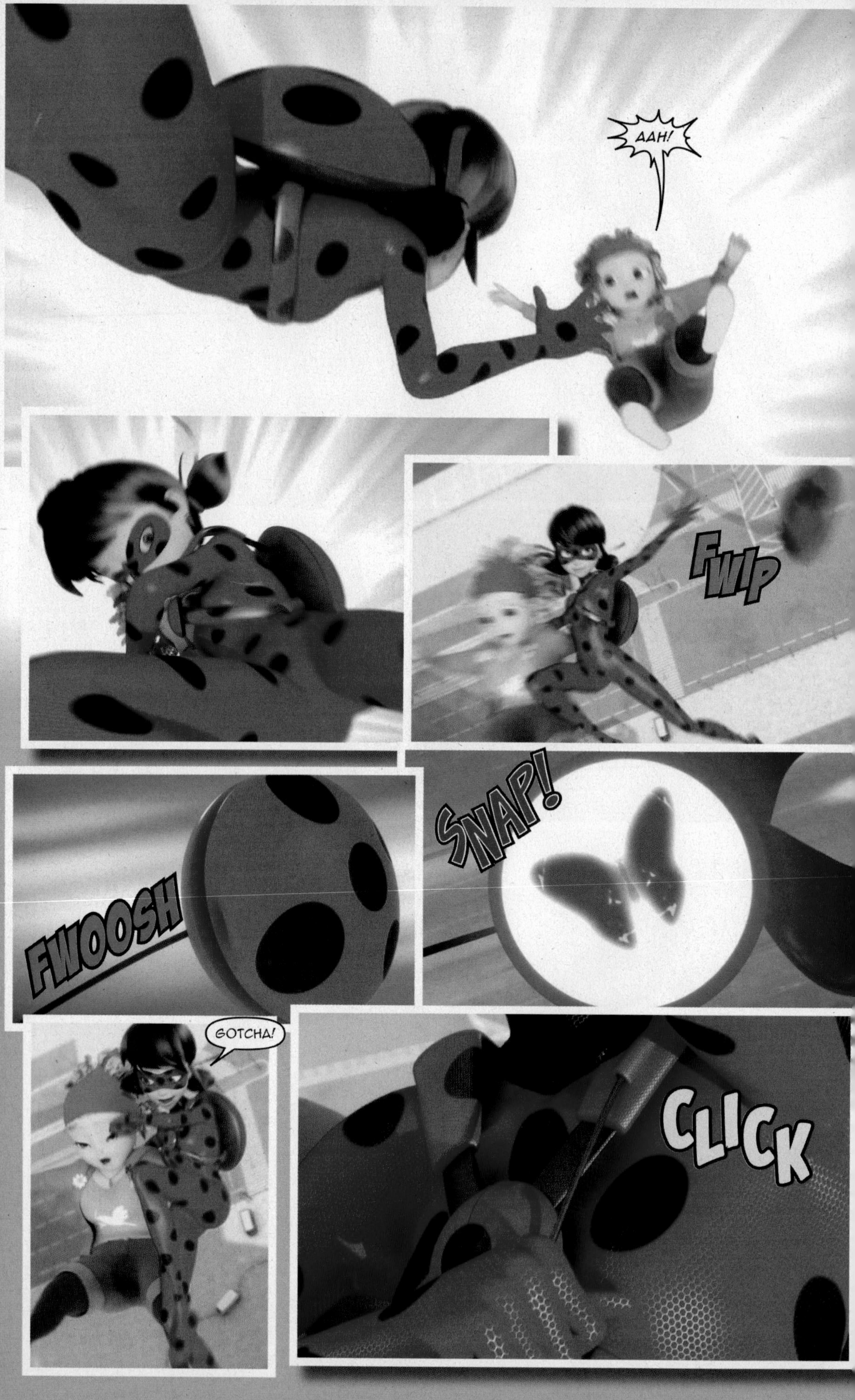
AAH!
FWIP
FWOOSH
SNAP!
GOTCHA!
CLICK

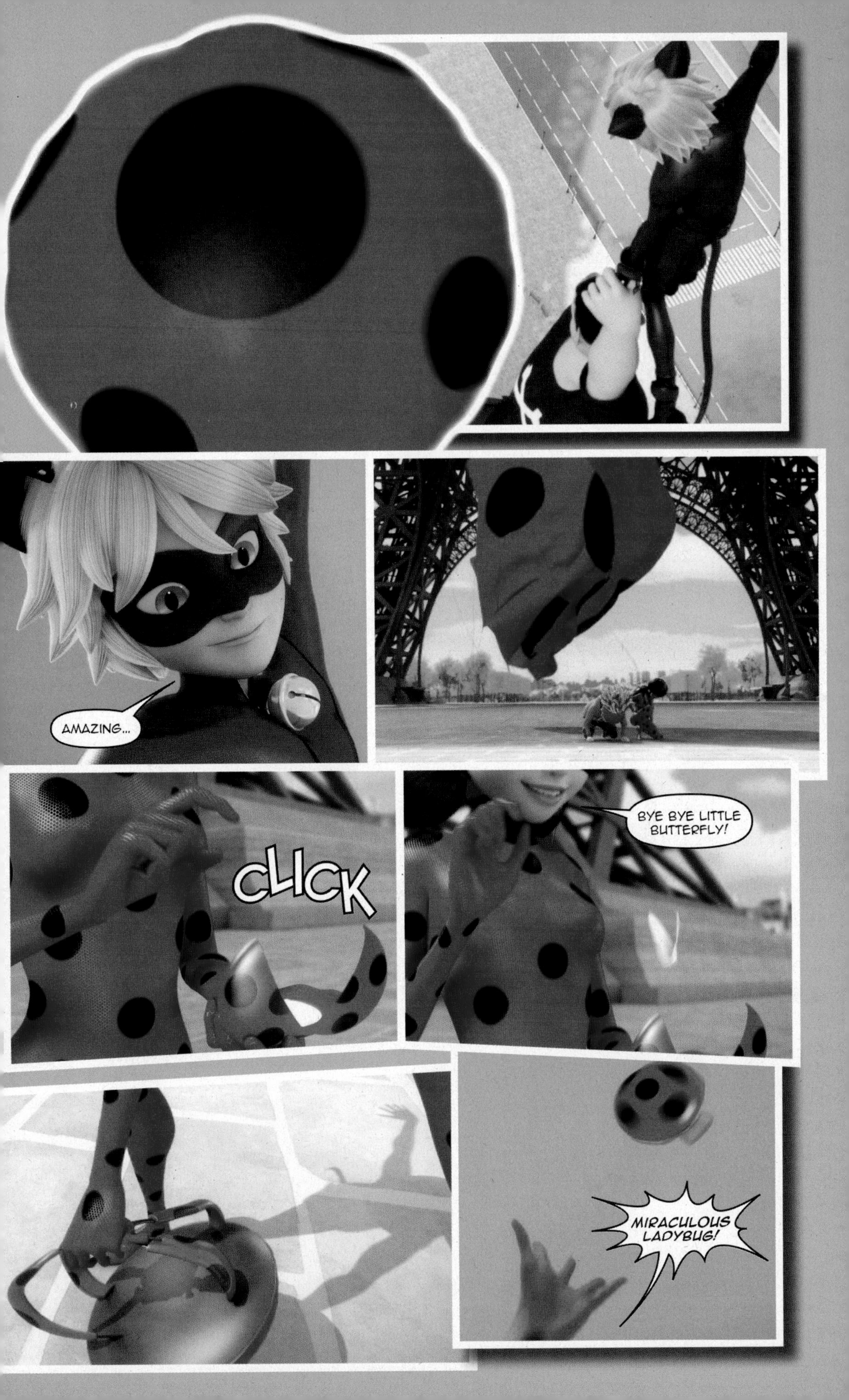
AMAZING...
CLICK
BYE BYE LITTLE BUTTERFLY!
MIRACULOUS LADYBUG!

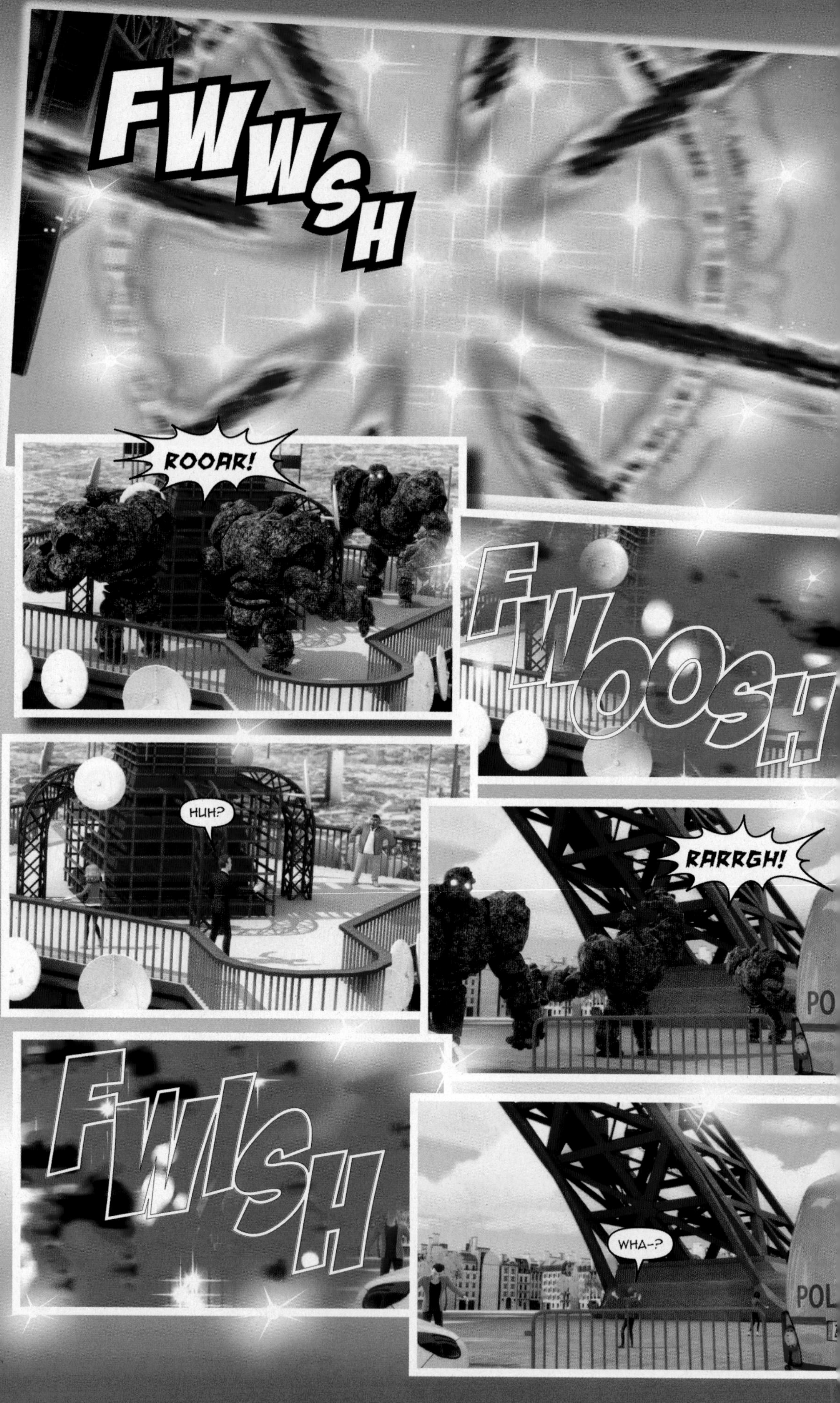
FWWSH
ROOAR!
FWOOSH
HUH?
RARRGH!
FWISH
WHA-?

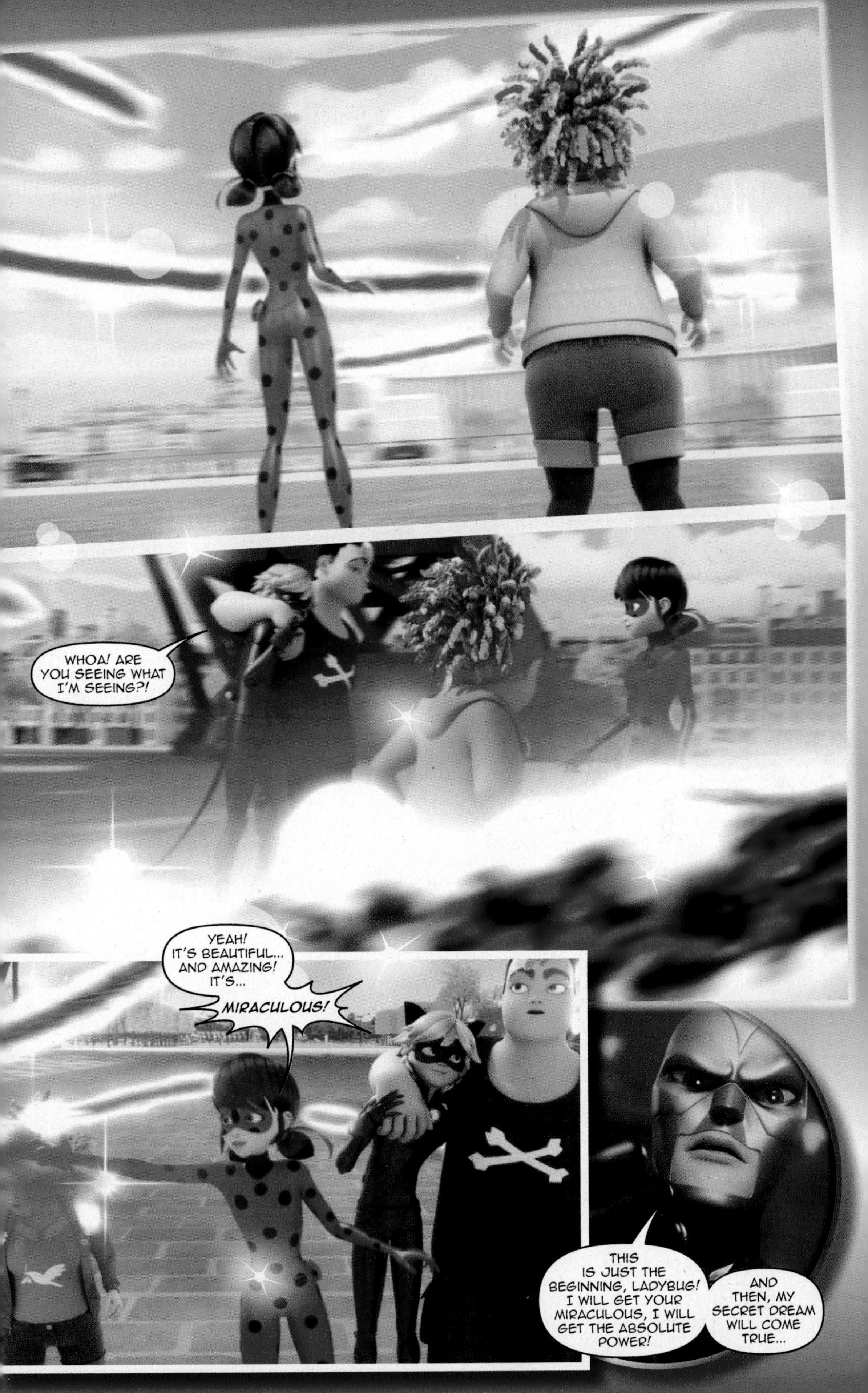
WHOA! ARE YOU SEEING WHAT I'M SEEING?!
YEAH! IT'S BEAUTIFUL... AND AMAZING! IT'S...
MIRACULOUS!
THIS IS JUST THE BEGINNING, LADYBUG! I WILL GET YOUR MIRACULOUS, I WILL GET THE ABSOLUTE POWER!
AND THEN, MY SECRET DREAM WILL COME TRUE...

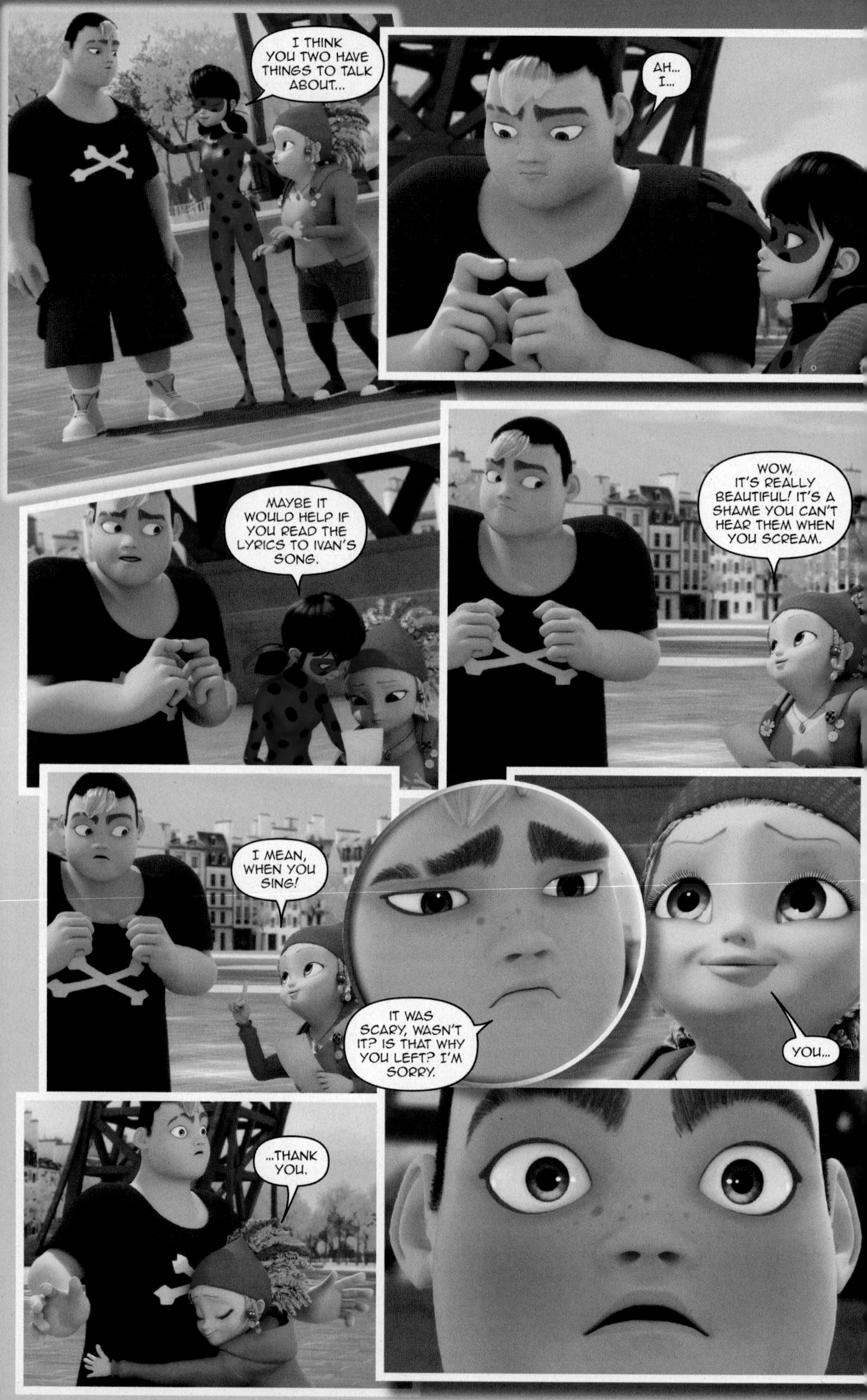
I THINK YOU TWO HAVE THINGS TO TALK ABOUT...
AH... I...
MAYBE IT WOULD HELP IF YOU READ THE LYRICS TO IVAN'S SONG.
WOW, IT'S REALLY BEAUTIFUL! IT'S A SHAME YOU CAN'T HEAR THEM WHEN YOU SCREAM.
I MEAN, WHEN YOU SING!
YOU...
IT WAS SCARY, WASN'T IT? IS THAT WHY YOU LEFT? I'M SORRY.
...THANK YOU.

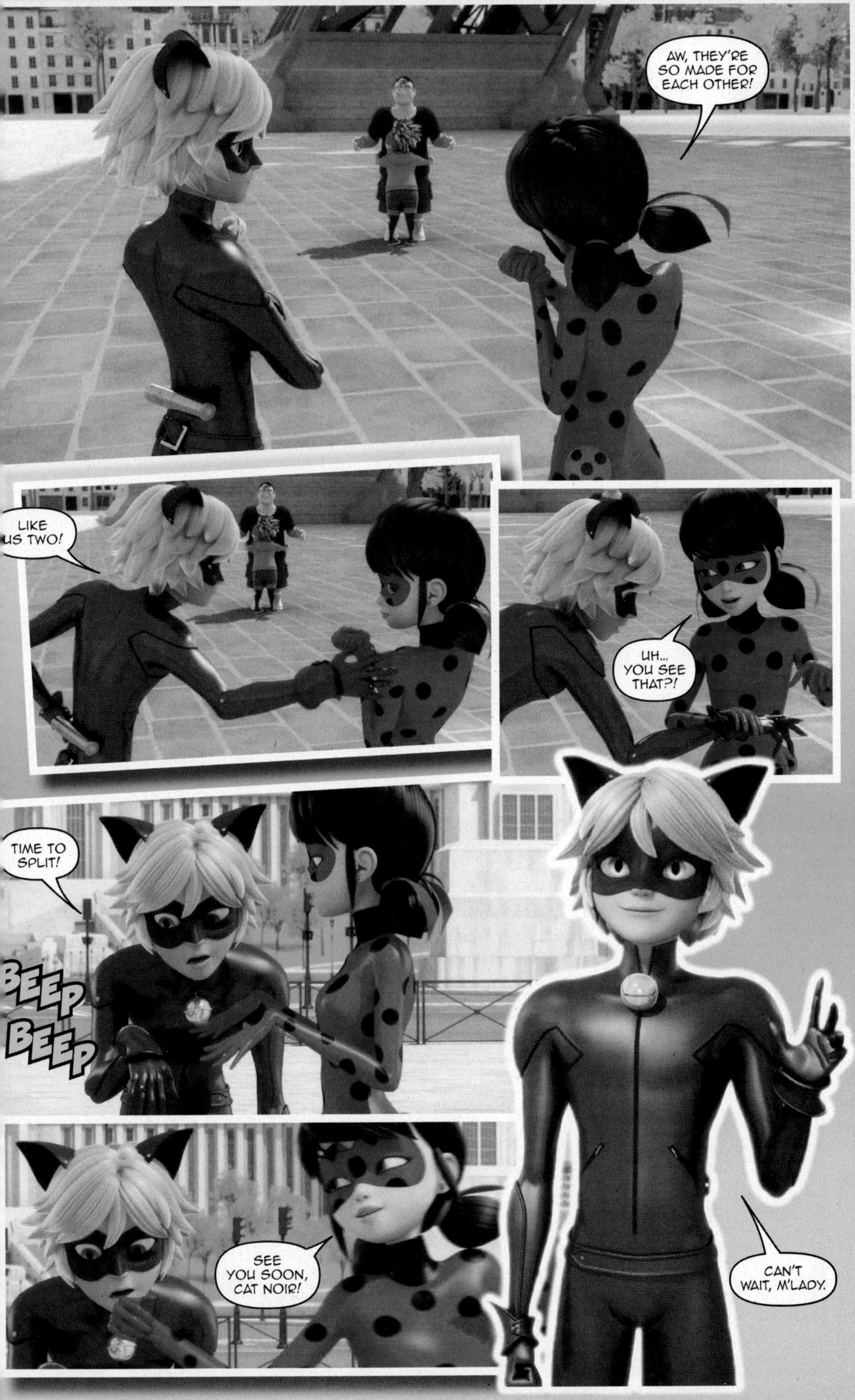
AW, THEY'RE SO MADE FOR EACH OTHER!
LIKE US TWO!
UH... YOU SEE THAT?!
TIME TO SPLIT!
BEEP BEEP
SEE YOU SOON, CAT NOIR!
CAN'T WAIT, M'LADY.

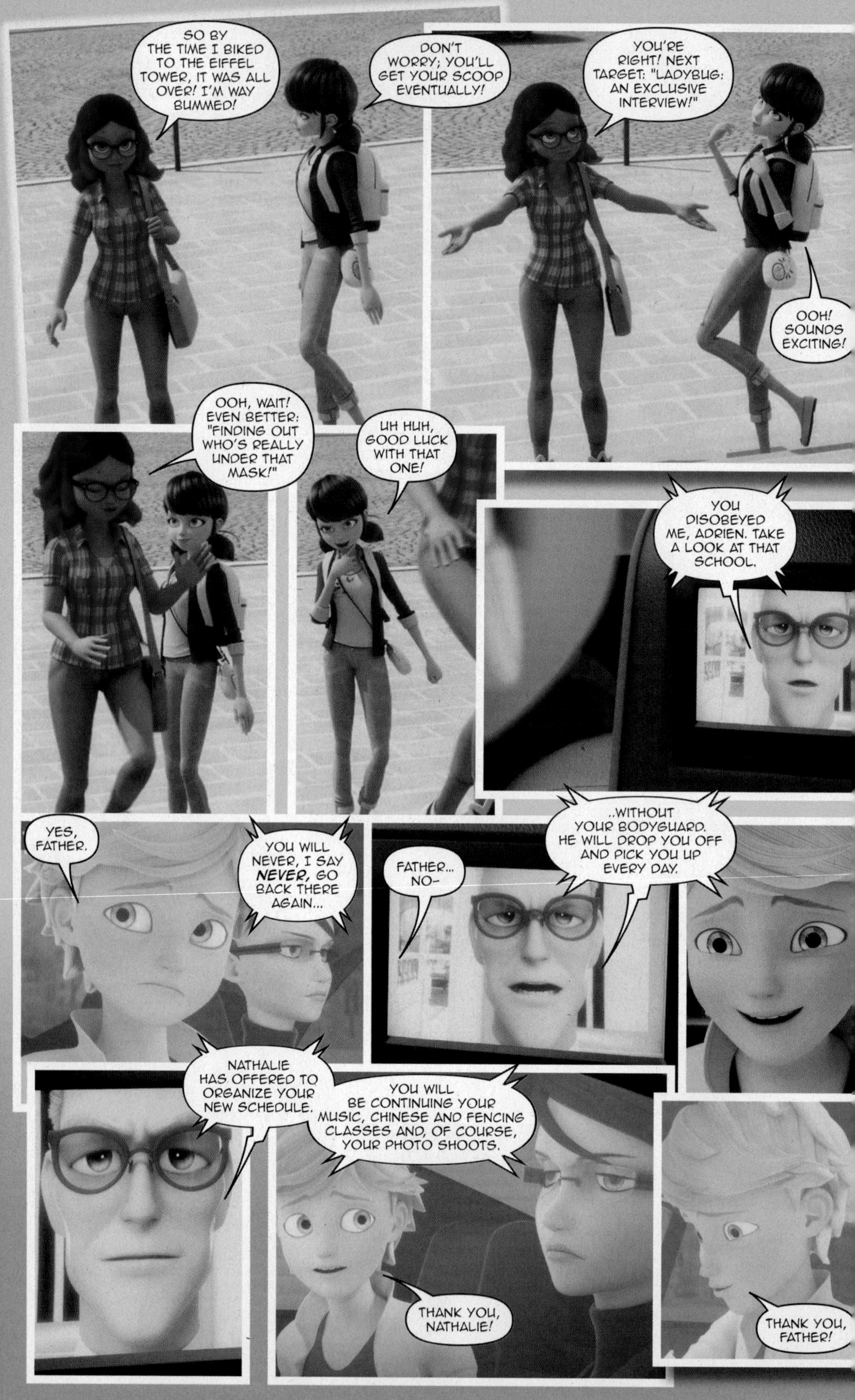
SO BY THE TIME I BIKED TO THE EIFFEL TOWER, IT WAS ALL OVER! I'M WAY BUMMED!
DON'T WORRY; YOU'LL GET YOUR SCOOP EVENTUALLY!
YOU'RE RIGHT! NEXT TARGET: "LADYBUG: AN EXCLUSIVE INTERVIEW!"
OOH! SOUNDS EXCITING!
OOH, WAIT! EVEN BETTER: "FINDING OUT WHO'S REALLY UNDER THAT MASK!"
UH HUH, GOOD LUCK WITH THAT ONE!
YOU DISOBEYED ME, ADRIEN. TAKE A LOOK AT THAT SCHOOL.
YES, FATHER.
YOU WILL NEVER, I SAY NEVER, GO BACK THERE AGAIN...
FATHER... NO-
..WITHOUT YOUR BODYGUARD. HE WILL DROP YOU OFF AND PICK YOU UP EVERY DAY.
NATHALIE HAS OFFERED TO ORGANIZE YOUR NEW SCHEDULE.
YOU WILL BE CONTINUING YOUR MUSIC, CHINESE AND FENCING CLASSES AND, OF COURSE, YOUR PHOTO SHOOTS.
THANK YOU, NATHALIE!
THANK YOU, FATHER!

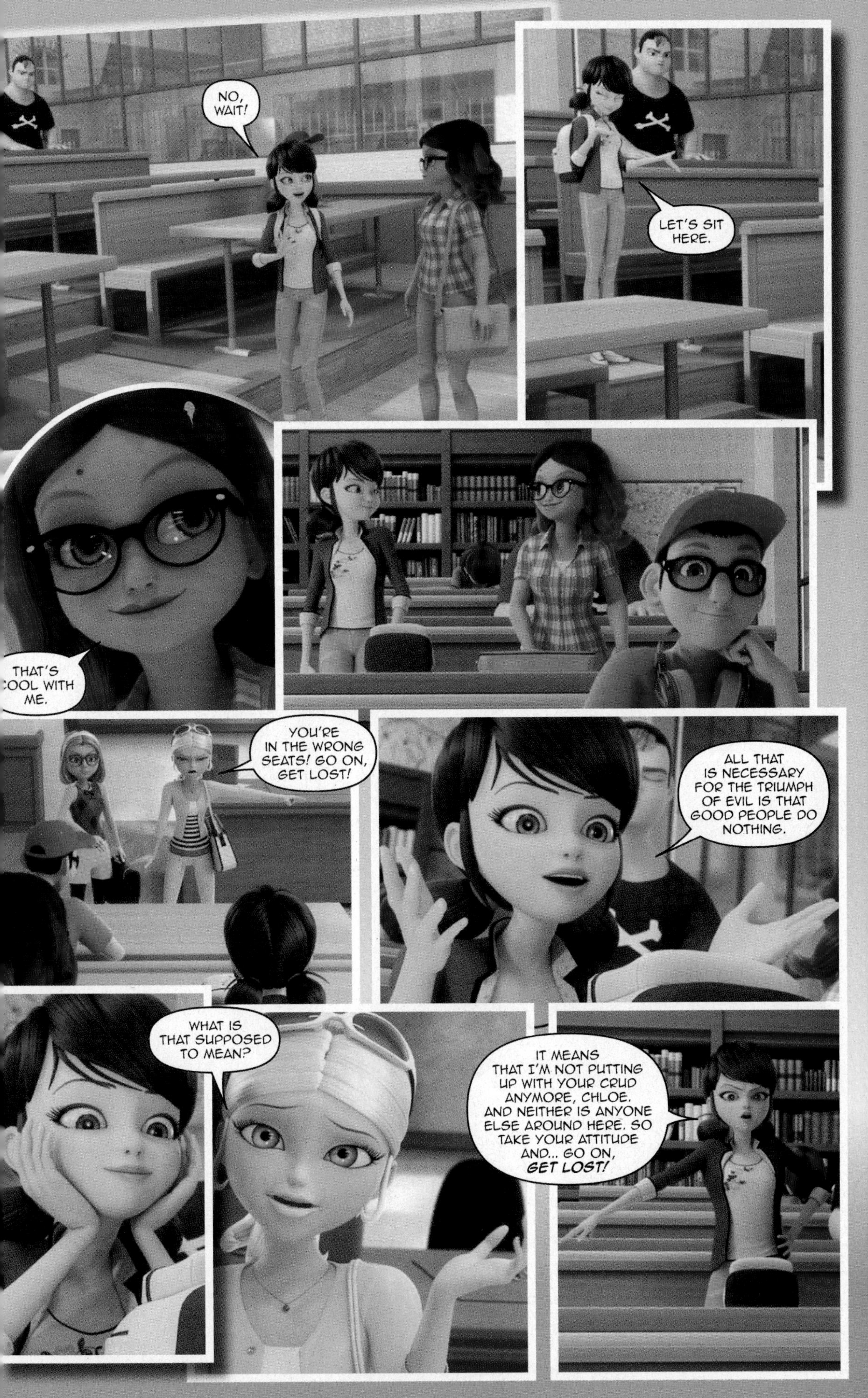
NO, WAIT!
LET'S SIT HERE.
THAT'S COOL WITH ME.
YOU'RE IN THE WRONG SEATS! GO ON, GET LOST!
ALL THAT IS NECESSARY FOR THE TRIUMPH OF EVIL IS THAT GOOD PEOPLE DO NOTHING.
WHAT IS THAT SUPPOSED TO MEAN?
IT MEANS THAT I'M NOT PUTTING UP WITH YOUR CRUD ANYMORE, CHLOE. AND NEITHER IS ANYONE ELSE AROUND HERE. SO TAKE YOUR ATTITUDE AND... GO ON, GET LOST!

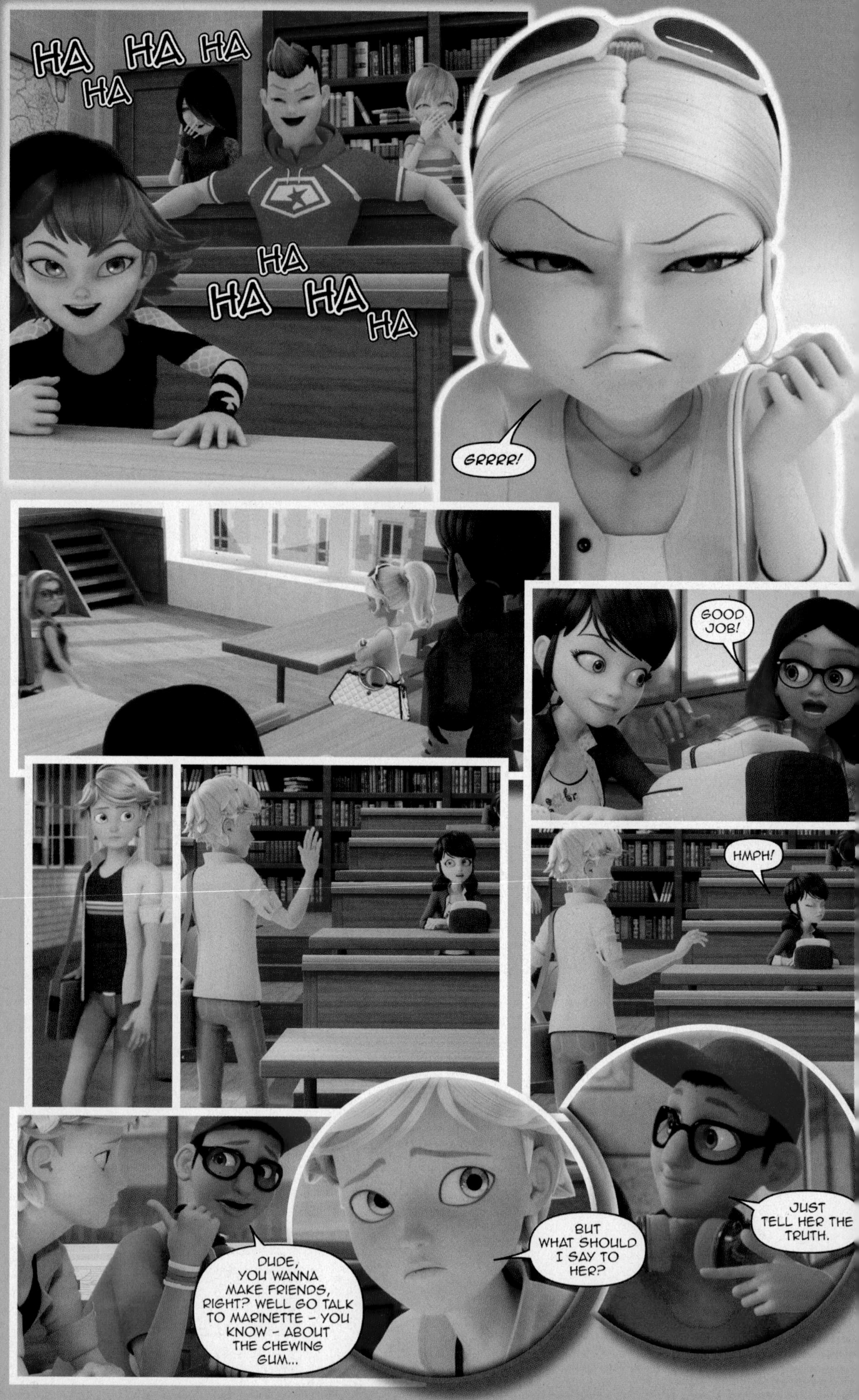
HA HA HA
HA
HA
HA HA
HA
GRRRR!
GOOD JOB!
HMPH!
DUDE, YOU WANNA MAKE FRIENDS, RIGHT? WELL GO TALK TO MARINETTE - YOU KNOW - ABOUT THE CHEWING GUM...
BUT WHAT SHOULD I SAY TO HER?
JUST TELL HER THE TRUTH.

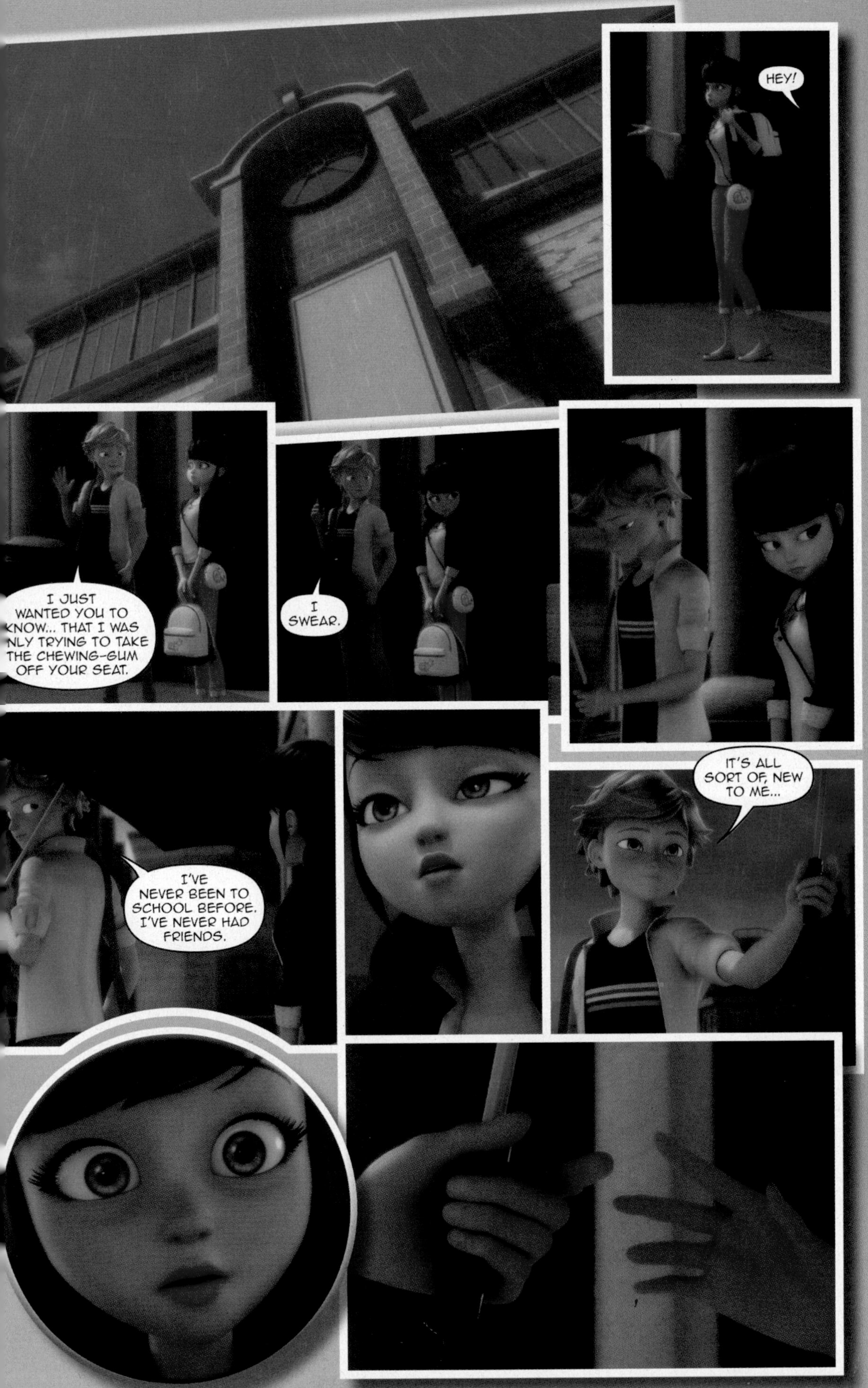
HEY!
I JUST WANTED YOU TO KNOW... THAT I WAS NLY TRYING TO TAKE THE CHEWING-GUM OFF YOUR SEAT.
I SWEAR.
I'VE NEVER BEEN TO SCHOOL BEFORE. I'VE NEVER HAD FRIENDS.
IT'S ALL SORT OF, NEW TO ME...

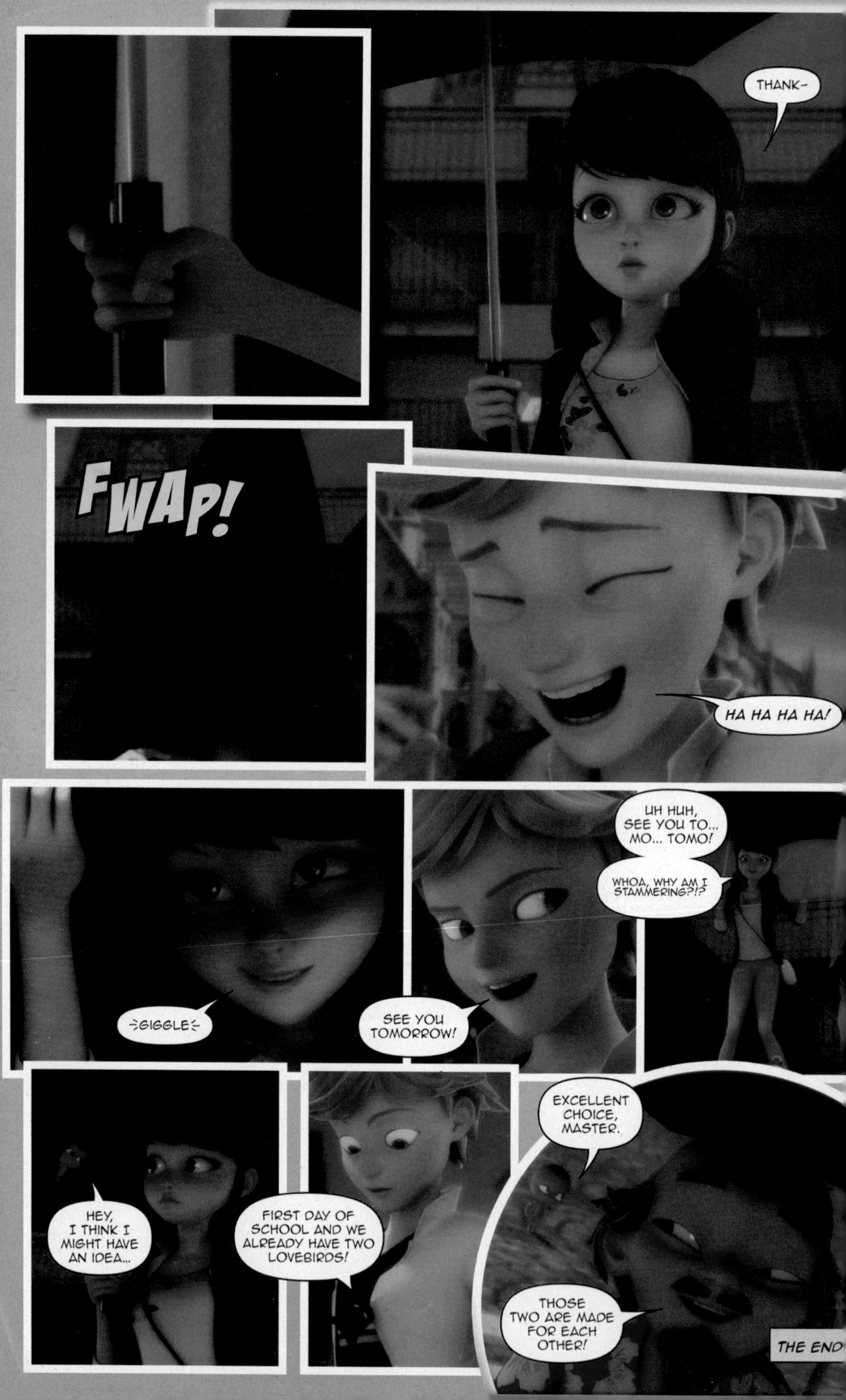
THANK-
FWAP!
HA HA HA HA!
~GIGGLE~
SEE YOU TOMORROW!
UH HUH, SEE YOU TO... MO... TOMO!
WHOA, WHY AM I STAMMERING?!?
HEY, I THINK I MIGHT HAVE AN IDEA...
FIRST DAY OF SCHOOL AND WE ALREADY HAVE TWO LOVEBIRDS!
EXCELLENT CHOICE, MASTER.
THOSE TWO ARE MADE FOR EACH OTHER!
THE END